MW01064305

searching
for
grace

searching
for
grace

cynthia kear

First published in Great Britain 1997 by
HMR, an imprint of Harold Martin & Redman Ltd.
The Wells House, Holywell Road, Malvern Wells,
Worcestershire WR14 4LH

British Library Cataloguing in Publication Data

A catalogue record for this book is available
from the British Library

ISBN 1 901730 02 6

Typeset and Designed by Harold Martin & Redman Ltd
Printed and Bound in Great Britain

For Kathleen

From the Golden Gate
To the Pont Du Carrousel.
And all points in between.

Acknowledgements

The encouragement of several early readers, Nancy Drooker, Aileen Friedman, Alix Sabin and, most especially, my mother, Joan Lyons Kear, spurred me on.

Michael Mannion not only took the cover photo, but generously shared his professional experience and advice. This book came to life on our walks in his New York City. RAO – now·and always.

My sister, Pegie Connaughton, supplied an endless stream of loving support.

Karin Evans (who also lent her photographic talents), Susan Hogeland, Michael R. Murphy and Kathleen Taggart saw me through – word by word. The gift, individual and collective, of their intelligence, insight and friendship is enormous.

The editorial contribution of Catherine Whiting and Tony Harold at Harold, Martin & Redman has been invaluable. For that, as well as Tony's faith and enthusiasm, I am fortunate.

To you all, many thanks.

Pale sunlight,
pale the wall.

Love moves away,
The light changes.

I need more grace
than I thought.

from *Dissolver of the Sugar*
by Rumi

PART ONE

The Land Rover bumped along the worn and dusty road, moving across the great expanse of open, golden countryside. A continuous sandy cloud followed in its wake. Inside, the three women jounced in their seats as the vehicle followed the uneven road. They were traveling south from Nairobi and had just crossed the border into Tanzania. They had left at dawn; the noon sun was now directly overhead.

"So why on earth did you invite him?" Roz shot Mead what was intended to be a scorching glance.

Mead, not turning her head from the window replied, "I didn't invite him. He invited himself."

Roz, hands firmly on the wheel which twisted forcefully with the rugged road, responded dubiously. "Uh-uh."

"Believe me, Roz, I didn't invite him."

From the back seat Linda yelled, "What are you guys talking about?"

Roz shouted over her shoulder. "We're talking about Lover Boy who's about to butt in on our Kilimanjaro hike which, need I remind you, we agreed was supposed to be all women."

"What?" Linda yelled again.

Roz shook her head and shouted, "The landscape."

"Yeah," Linda said. "Ever since we turned off that tarmac road back at Makuyuni, it's been another world. Fabulous, isn't it?"

Mead turned her head toward Roz, who cracked a droll smile. "Fabulous," Roz dryly agreed. She continued. "Well, if he invited himself, why didn't you un-invite him, for God sakes?"

"It's not so easy to turn Peter down."

"Oh, are we defenseless against his animal magnetism?" Roz mocked.

Linda, her loose hair flapping about her face shouted again. "How much farther to the park entrance?"

Annoyed at another interruption, Roz looked at the odometer, "Twenty kilometers," she shouted curtly. In the mirror on the back of the visor Mead saw Linda visibly wilt. Mead gave Roz a reprimanding look that Roz completely ignored.

"So?" Roz persisted. "Are we? Defenseless?"

"Look, I am sorry. You're annoyed. I would be too."

"That's a pretty blasé apology."

"I know we said it would be all women. But I couldn't. It's complicated. One of those horribly long boring stories. Besides, when you meet him you'll see for yourself."

"Should we have added chastity belts to our respective packs?"

Mead exhaled deeply and turned her back to Roz's disappointment and sarcasm. Through the open window she expectantly surveyed the Tanzanian countryside and muttered. "You'll just have to see for yourself."

* * *

Elizabeth looked up from her computer screen and out the window into the steely blue-gray dusk of the winter afternoon. The streets below were edged with the gray-white remnants of last week's snowfall. Central Park was covered with a hard, thin coat of white, excepting the rock outcroppings and where the children had turned the hill to mud with their sledding. Gazing down Fifth Avenue, beyond the Plaza, Elizabeth could see the Christmas decorations of the various stores and hotels. She shivered, feeling the day infiltrate the double-paned glass window, steaming at the edges as the stealthy cold met the hissing warmth of her study. From her vista the evening, despite its deep chill, looked so inviting: the press of crowds hurrying in the night; the cabs bumper to bumper forming yellow blocks in the black streets; people jamming the sidewalks, hurrying in all directions. She could almost hear their laughter expelled in clouds of happy exhalation.

A longing suddenly tugged at Elizabeth's usually resistant, stoic heart. She wished she could have all her children assembled for a few days, wished that they could be a tightly knit group cheerfully heading toward some cozy restaurant or to the Lincoln Center. But Avery was dogsledding in Canada, Rand and Tricia had agreed to visit her parents this year, Luce was in San Francisco and Mead was in Africa. Half sighing, to the point where she could feel the ache but not release it (for she was wholly unwilling to do that) she returned her attention to the computer screen.

She should pay more attention to her wanderings; these little mental diversions of hers got quite costly when she was on-line, as she was now. Yes, she thought, I'm on-line, surfing the Net, cruising the information highway, collecting e-mail from Mead, my youngest daughter on fellowship in Africa. No, no, she wasn't collecting e-mail. She was downloading. She, Mrs. Walter William Bennett, wife of the distinguished Doctor Walter William Bennett, a retired surgeon of some modest professional reputation, was sitting in the study of her Manhattan co-op downloading Mead's latest e-mail entry from Nairobi. Seventy years old, and she was wending her way through the World

Wide Web! In the blue-gray of the computer screen, in the blue-gray of the wintry dusk, an indisputable spark filled her periwinkle eyes as she smiled with a degree of satisfaction.

She was not a beautiful woman; no one looking at her would say she was. Many said that she looked wonderful, but Elizabeth simply chalked that up to either stilted manners or their surprise that she was still alive. But everyone would concur that she was animated by a lively intelligence, and most found her engaging and always current. She had a small reputation for occasional blasts of honesty that were quite disarming, generally blunt and frequently amusing. I can get away with a lot more at my age, she thought. So I do.

A certain subdued Puritanism was revealed in her angular face, despite her midwestern upbringing, despite her avowed atheism. Perhaps this was due to her sallow complexion, her sparse lips, her straight nose and flat forehead, all of which bespoke practicality, hard work, thrift and discipline. Even with the fine net of wrinkles, her face was not slack. There was a tautness that presided and suggested a well-controlled, well-tempered life, not anxiety or nervousness. Elizabeth had left those traits behind decades ago, finding them, at last, completely useless. Drag on my engines, she had lightheartedly said at the time, a tone she always struck when announcing serious personal decisions to her family.

Onscreen another installment of Mead's *Kenyan Letters* flickered. "Mother," Mead had clicked into the keyboard, and thousands of miles away Elizabeth could hear her exasperation, "Mother, these are simply short notes, letters I send electronically versus snail mail. Don't make more out of them than they are." That had been her sole entry that day, not wanting to dilute her message or give her mother any opportunity to overlook it among several thoughts.

Elizabeth got it, of course, just as she would have if Mead had buried the line in copious paragraphs. She chose to ignore it, knowing full well her daughter's tendency to diminish her achievements, to be self-deprecating. Anyone could see the significance of the events Mead was now recording. A promising young doctor of infectious diseases at a major research hospital in Chicago, on a fellowship exchange at a hospital in Nairobi, fully funded at that. Just thirty-five years old. And, besides her important work, she and several other health professionals had decided to climb Mount Kilimanjaro. Important work combined with adventure from a fast-tracking young medico. Well, you didn't have to be her mother, Elizabeth thought, to see the need to record and preserve this time, this experience. And, if she could help organize and edit in the process she was only too happy.

"The African sun is quite deceiving," Mead wrote. "It feels warm but if you're not used to it, it'll burn you to a crisp. If it weren't for all the pollution from cars and trucks and buses, the air would be quite temperate. But the traffic chokes everything up. All the people from the countryside truck their wares and vegetables into the city during the night making a hell of a clatter. Just like ancient Rome. I'll be glad to get a dose of alpine air. Some quiet. And just to get away.

"The suffering here is so direct. The devastation undeniable. Refugees stream into the city by the hundreds each day – from Uganda, Rwanda, Burundi, the Sudan. Non-stop. Their lives, especially in pain, are so raw. Makes me realize how buffered I am in my work at the hospital and lab.

"Even though I knew the numbers before arriving, seeing the faces, the endless faces, of those statistics almost overwhelms me. The projections are that by 2000 sub-Saharan Africa will have 31% of the HIV/AIDS population. And they only have 10% of the world population. The rate of male-to-female infection is 1:1 and 90% of all infected children live here. Already a million and a half children have been orphaned by this pandemic.

"The population in Nairobi is well over a million, though no one really has a good handle on it. The last census was done in the late 1980s. But with the annual growth rate of over 4% and with all the people flooding in, who knows? Even if there are only one million, I feel I've seen almost half of them by now. And the other half million have either tried to sell me something or wanted me to buy them something. It's an utterly surreal environment – where beauty, innocence, ignorance and plague all come together. Probably compounded by lack of sleep."

Elizabeth paused her reading to imagine Mead, clad all in khaki except for her white lab coat, looking utterly exhausted, surrounded by silently imploring fly-covered faces, and Mead, as always, calmly, steadily trudging on.

The front door opened and closed. Walter hung his coat, picked up the daily mail and evening paper that she had neatly arranged on the hallway table and called, "Lizbeth?" In the blue light of the computer screen she gently shook herself out of her reverie and pulled the throat of her turtleneck closer to her chin.

* * *

The halogen lamp on the credenza behind Jacob Malowitz shimmered like a full-bodied halo. Luce, sitting in a sleek black leather chair across the desk from him, thought she should paint his portrait. *"Gallery Owner with Halo?"* she thought. *"Good Fairy Illuminated?"* She chuckled to herself as she listened to Jacob.

"Really, Luce, the last batch of paintings that you shipped are unbelievable. The article in *Art World* helped, mind you, but as soon as I hang one, it sells."

"So I'm now also a critical success?" Luce asked facetiously but with a hint of judgment.

"The critics love your new work." He smiled complicitously. "AND they sell. Best of both worlds."

"My new spiritual direction is quite a hit," Luce laughed mockingly.

"Those art critics – as perceptive and astute as ever. Excuse me." Jacob took a phone call that came in on his direct line, then another, all the while giving Luce looks of happy reassurance.

Luce didn't mind. She rather enjoyed the interruptions, the electric buzz of business, especially when it was her business. The constant phone calls, the stir of activity were a marked contrast to the solitude and quiet of her studio, wonderful in its infrequency. And she loved to watch Jacob at work, master art critic, master curator, master promoter, master salesman. Over the years that they had worked together, since he had first stumbled upon her work in her Greenpoint studio almost ten years ago, Luce had observed that mastery develop.

Now as she sat in a room she knew by heart, every detail etched in her mind, listening to Jacob seamlessly move from genuine passion to the ruthlessly flawless close, Luce filled with pleasure and admiration. Jacob was pitching her *Neighborhood* series, a collection of paintings she had done on California highway landscapes, to a Parisian gallery owner. Jacob, Luce thought, returning to her mental painting, a sleek panther dressed in the requisite black of the art world, a study in black with his expensive double-breasted suit, black tee shirt (should something that probably cost a hundred dollars be called a tee shirt? Luce wondered), fine, Italian black leather loafers, designer black wire-rim glasses, salt-and-pepper hair cut with a simplicity and style that said expensive. Apart from his personality, which she found truly endearing, she thought him a beautiful specimen, all agility and fluidity, line and proportion. His whole demeanor spoke of sensitivity, success and assurance. Not a hint remained of the arrogance, poverty or desperation she had vaguely whiffed when they first met. In the windowless office, austere and clean, Luce mentally painted his deep brown eyes, his sharp, slightly

13

beaked nose, his small full mouth. *"Jewish Saint,"* she toyed. And as she continued to assemble him in sharp planes scraped with her mental putty knife, she painted with an insightful palette acquired over the years of their association, an association both professional and personal. Luce indulgently let herself drift back to that Sunday afternoon when they had met, the only bright spot in the entire weekend of open studios. It was her studio at Greenpoint. Her first studio. A small bleak space that she would always recall with fondness, not the spacious studio that she now had in what had become the trendy multimedia gulch section of San Francisco.

Jacob, in full curator mode, had pensively eyed Luce's canvases. After an excruciatingly long silence he quietly said, "I like it. I like what you've done here." That weekend she had vowed never to participate in open studios again and thought for the hundredth time that day that she'd go home and study the classifieds. She was raw from the inane comments people stupidly, brusquely made. She felt exposed, abraded. Luce had held her breath and waited for the proverbial "but" to follow. It didn't.

Luce, then much younger, had resigned herself to the fact that her representational style was looked down upon and considered decidedly unfashionable among the contemporary art elite. Since leaving art school she had made a few faint attempts at abstraction and expressionism, to fuse media, to be contemporary. But it all rang false to her and offended her eye. The work was forced. It didn't flow from her heart down her arm, didn't tingle her hands, didn't fuse the brush with her finger tips. She burned those feeble attempts at acceptability and went back to her representational style with a surety and resignation previously unfelt. She returned to both the style and the subject matter that resonated for her. In fact, it was a painting of her father that Jacob had studied that weekend.

Jacob had shifted his studious, penetrating gaze from the canvas to Luce. "Tell me about this work." He stepped aside so that she could assume the central position in front of the canvas.

"It's my father sitting on the porch of our summer house at the shore." Her tongue went limp, as though her brain had suddenly disengaged. She had never before talked about her work to anyone but a few friends. Now she felt awkward, incapable of the task.

"It's amazing how you have combined the searing heat of the day with a distinctive plastic space around him that's so terribly cold. I love how the two co-exist."

"It's a more attractive dynamic on canvas than in real life."

Jacob had laughed. "Family, thank God they at least give us good material." His tone put her at ease. "The relative scale of the porch, the vast sea, it's all correct, and yet you still manage to have him dominate the center. Despite his position on the far edge of the canvas, looking at this I feel as if I'm drawn into his vortex. Unwillingly. The tension is palpable. You've got quite a talent." He faced her directly. "I'd like to hang this in my gallery."

That was when Jacob's gallery was three flights up a rundown building off Prince Street. Now he had an entire building, owned not rented, at Green and Broadway. Luce had a permanent wall reserved for whatever she shipped him. So many things, she mused, had changed.

"Luce, will you have dinner with me?" He replaced the receiver and gazed over the top of his glasses at her. "There's someone I'd like you to meet."

"Oh, I see. And just who is this someone?"

"A woman I met a few weeks ago. Her name's Jennifer. Jenny. She's wonderful. I think this could be it."

Luce smiled and bit her tongue, not wanting to remind Jacob of the many times she had heard those same words from him. After all these years, she had come to respect his deep-rooted optimism. And marvel at it, sometimes even with a hint of jealousy.

"Not tonight, Jacob. I'm meeting an old friend." Jacob knitted his brows in question. "Just a friend, Jacob."

"Look, I'm not going to let you slip through my net these next few days, coming here for business and only appearing at the opening of your show. How 'bout dinner tomorrow?" Luce shook her head. "The following night?"

"Sure. Give me a call at my hotel in the morning." She went around to his side of the desk. The phone rang again as he stood to meet her. She pushed him gently back into his chair, handed him the receiver and bent to kiss him on the top of his head.

"Might be an important sale," she whispered.

He smiled, caught her hand as it slipped off his shoulder and held it briefly. "Soon," he mouthed quietly, "We'll catch up."

Luce walked through the main gallery, which was humming with the activity of Jacob's staff putting the finishing touches to her show. Several assistants smiled obsequiously at her, which sent a deep chill of discomfort down her spine. Keeping her glance straight ahead, she hoped that her placid demeanor hid the total sense of dread she felt. Through the glass front door she saw the descending darkness full of city lights and nameless people. Shutting the door tightly behind her, she breathed deeply of crisp winter air and anonymity.

* * *

Linda leaned forward, pointed ahead and shouted over the air whipping through all four open windows of the Land Rover, "Let's stop up by that lake. We can look around and stretch a bit. I'm getting some serious tush fatigue back here."

The Rover hit a deep crater and all three women took a bounce up, with Linda hitting her head against the roof.

"Shit," Linda hissed, rubbing her head.

"Must be an omen that it's time for lunch." Roz smiled slyly and drew to a sudden stop. Linda was thrown forward, hitting her lower jaw against the back of Roz's seat. "Sorry," Roz said, nonchalantly getting out of the Land Rover.

"Ouch," Mead offered sympathetically. "Are you okay?"

"I guess," Linda muttered.

"Thank God you're traveling with trained physicians, huh?" Mead joked tepidly.

Linda was in no mood. "I'm beginning to see why the death rate goes down when doctors go on strike. You guys are health hazards."

Linda got out, restrained herself from slamming the door and stomped off in the opposite direction from Roz, who marched resolutely toward the lake's edge. Mead slumped in the seat, leaned her head back and sighed. She couldn't believe that she was actually looking forward to Peter's presence. At least he's a known entity, she thought. But surely that is a barometer of how awful things are. I must be crazy taking a week-long trip with two virtual strangers.

They had met at the cocktail party put on for the new rotation of visiting Western medical staff. Roz was a dermatologist serving her fellowship at Aga Khan Platinum Jubilee Hospital. She had a robust private practice in Laguna Beach, California. The bulk of her work was devoted to relieving the film community of liver spots, burst spider veins, stretch marks and restoring sun-damaged skin. Besides these lucrative superficial jobs that were the bread-and-butter of her practice, she had developed some innovative techniques for dealing with melanomas, specifically squamous cell cancer. Now she spent part of each year taking these procedures to remote, sun-drenched parts of the world and training the local doctors. Mead respected her craft, the serious part. Reports on her were mixed. The medical community in Nairobi was small and never suffered a shortage of opinions or gossip. Mead had noted that some found Roz's manner off-putting and thought that she was too brusque with the patients, patronizing to the nurses and occasionally arrogant with her colleagues. But others, especially the admin types, held her in high regard. She was hard, but so were the circumstances. Except for the gaudy display of gold and diamonds that Linda frequently advised against ("For God's sake, Roz, don't go walking around this town alone loaded like a damn Rodeo Drive jewelry store!"), Mead liked her, her intelligence, her commitment and her tough exterior. They were traits she recognized.

Linda, who was already a month into her rotation, was the Head Pediatric Nurse at New Jersey Children's Hospital. She was working at the Mater Misericordia, a maternity hospital in the south part of Nairobi. Of the three, only Linda was married. Professionally she was also considered top-notch, but Mead couldn't help secretly feeling some of the condescension that Roz frequently showed. "Don't get me wrong, Mead, I think Linda's great. But," she paused to sip her gin and tonic as they sat on the porch of the Norfolk Hotel in downtown Nairobi, "she's not a doctor. And, well, she is kind of soft. It's not just her field. Oh, never mind. The truth is that she's sweet. Really sweet." Mead could tell by her controlled benign expression that sweet was a trait Roz clearly considered despicable. "That's not really fair," Mead countered. "Extreme malnutrition. AIDS mothers, AIDS babies. Every virus we know of, and then some we don't. That hardly qualifies as soft."

"Mead, you're right," Roz conceded, with a tone that barely suggested concession. "Absolutely. Let's talk about something else."

But they had all hit it off at the cocktail party, well enough to grab an occasional dinner or round of drinks together when their respective crowded schedules allowed. Certainly the circumstances they found themselves in, three American women donating their professional time and training for a three-month hitch in Nairobi, thousands of miles from home, in unfamiliar territory, helped forge what otherwise would have been flimsy bonds. When, after Mead's first non-stop month, the opportunity presented itself for them to get away, get out of the city, see and taste some of the famed adventure of the land, they eagerly seized it and planned this trip.

Mead had definitely seen hints of how things might go. Linda had wanted to fly to Lamu on the coast, get rooms in a five-star Western hotel, lie on the beach and read. "Christ, I might as well book myself into the Hotel del Coronado in San Diego if we're going to do that!" Roz had protested. "Except for what I hear are very accommodating beach boys, who could tell the difference?"

"Hey," Linda had retorted, "There's some very interesting Arabian history in that town."

Roz smirked, and they continued to wrangle, emphatically on Roz's part, whiny on Linda's. At last Roz magnanimously agreed to consider, and very non-committally at that Mead noted, Lamu for their next R & R. Linda begrudgingly acquiesced.

In truth, Mead's preference was to visit a game park, then climb Kilimanjaro. Seeing that the winds favored Roz, she held her tongue and stayed out of their disagreement. Since she was going to get her way, she might as well appear objective. Nothing lost in that tactic.

Now Mead rubbed her face then straightened the maps and guide books which littered the space between her and Roz's seat, as if that might help straighten the present situation. Taking a deep breath, she got out of the Land Rover.

"Can't you be nice?" she whispered as she approached Roz who was crouched and peering intently through her binoculars, scanning the other side of the lake.

Without taking them down Roz asked, "Why?"

"Because we're going to be together for seven and a half more days, for one." Mead already resented finding herself in the middle.

"I've worked very hard to get to a point in my life where I don't have to be nice. Linda just needs to understand that it's not personal."

"That's a bit ludicrous, isn't it, especially since it's very personal. You may think she's a wimp, but she's not stupid."

"I'm having a fine time. Hey, look over on the other side and in that acacia tree to the west."

Mead did and her efforts were rewarded with the sight of a lioness, protruding stomach full of recent prey, legs dangling from both sides of a good sized bough, sleeping. Linda joined them, having seen the lioness from her vantage point farther down the lake. They stood, quietly exchanging looks of awe and good fortune at their first sighting. For a moment they forgot themselves and their differences, drawn together by the thrill of nature.

* * *

"Walter, we really should make some plans for our anniversary." They were sitting in their living room after a tasty, low-fat dinner. Walter, elbow resting on a pile of magazines by his side, nodded his head from behind a copy of *Artificial Intelligence Quarterly*. "Well, fifty years is quite a lot of time together," Elizabeth continued. "And the children are all expecting us to have some sort of celebration. Their schedules are all so impossibly full. We need to plan something well in advance if we want them all to be able to attend." Walter again murmured his accord.

Elizabeth suspected Walter's hesitancy to commit to a family gathering was because he was still smarting from their last assembly. They had gathered last August to spend the usual week together at the beach cottage. Some discussions had become rather heated. And the children, (children! why Luce, the oldest, was going to be forty-five!), sniffed Walter's vulnerability, which was growing Elizabeth acknowledged, in direct proportion to his years in retirement. She shook her head with disdain at the memory. They all had their turn with him that week, challenging him, his knowledge, his currency, making it painfully clear that they were the specialists in their respective fields, they were in the game and on top of it to boot. Except for Luce who sat in that quiet, intent way of hers, which both Elizabeth and Walter found so disconcerting. With Luce, the lack of discussion and argument only heightened the already sizable gulf they felt.

Elizabeth could easily understand the children's behavior. She had been there, at all the key moments over the years, at every step as Walter prodded and pushed them to work, to study, to achieve, to make the grade, to bring home the prizes, to be the best. It was their job, he had made it perfectly clear, to master all the subjects but to excel in science and math. Would he have been so harsh and unrelenting, Elizabeth now wondered, if he had realized then that it would inevitably culminate in his being toppled?

For her part, she had stayed out of the line of fire. Long ago she made the decision that that was simply the best course of action, both for the moment and for the long run. She had made her primary allegiance to Walter in the early years of their marriage. After much struggle she saw that she could not win their arguments about how the children would be raised. The level of vigor and righteousness he brought to the task always won out. Initially it had caused a rift between them and she left him for almost a year when Luce was just a baby. When finally she saw that he would not budge, and she knew someone had to if the marriage was going to survive, she relented.

Similarly, through the years, she never took sides with the children, never intervened. How could she ever know the truth of their squabbles anyway? "You are brothers and sisters. You must not fight with each other. Family. And that's that," was the refrain she struck over the years, despite her doubts, despite specific circumstances, evidence to the contrary, especially with Mead. She knew it was harsh but, as long as she was constant, it was the only solid ground she could find. Mrs. Walter William Bennett first, mother of the children second. "I love all my children equally," she would say when assailed with complaints that her behavior was unfair. "Equally," she would assert and leave the room. Had she continued to articulate the hierarchy she had built, Elizabeth herself would have placed a very distant third.

"Walter, please." She assumed the impatient tone of voice which usually roused his attention.

"Yes, Lizbeth?" he said distractedly as he scribbled into the journal.

"What *are* you doing?"

He tilted the journal toward her and flipped the cardboard insert card. "Filling out a subscription."

"Another subscription?"

He nodded, not looking up. "This one sounds very interesting. *Neural Engineering and Modular Robotics Design Newsletter.* I wonder if Rand knows about it."

"Walter, you can barely keep up with all the journals and magazines you're already getting." She heard her own exasperation.

"Now, Lizbeth, don't exaggerate. Besides I enjoy my reading."

"I'm hardly exaggerating. In fact, I'm afraid to open your study door lest I die of massive paper cuts due to an avalanche of your unread periodicals."

Walter chuckled as he continued to fill out the card.

"Walter, I know you want to keep up with the children." He looked at her askance. She knew she was on thin ice. "Their fields are fascinating. Complex. And fast paced. But," she hesitated, "You're working too hard. I worry about you, cooped up in that damn library. Why you even have to go there since you get almost every periodical known to man here, I'll never know." She softened her tone and her tact. "This is not how I thought we'd be spending our retirement years." He gave her a blank stare. "It's just, well, I wish we could spend more time together."

His face darkened. "I'm always home for dinner, Lizbeth. Besides, you're pretty busy yourself, with that computer of yours. And Mead's letters. Not to mention our finances."

"Yes," she agreed, "I am. But they don't take up all day." She took a long, quiet breath and watched as he put aside *Artificial Intelligence* and tried to disappear into the current issue of *Developmental Psychobiology*.

"Really, Walter," and his head responded to the sharpness in her voice, which surprised even her. "We need to make some plans. For our anniversary," she reminded him in reply to his questioning look.

"Yes, yes. Of course. Well, what would you like to do?" She hated when he demonstrated his annoyance in the slow, slight Southern drawl that he had lost years ago.

"Something simple. Intimate. Just our family and a few of our closest friends." She waited for an answer.

"That sounds fine with me."

"But Walter, what would *you* like to do?"

"Why, I've always relied on you to manage those types of affairs for us.

And you have always, if my memory serves me correctly, done an admirable job." She could see that he was attempting to strike a complimentary tone and avoid a confrontation.

"Walter," her tone grew chillier, "arranging a professional dinner gathering or a party for one of our children is vastly different from arranging the details of *our*," she paused to let her last word sink in, "*our* fiftieth wedding anniversary."

"I take your point. Well, how about a nice private dinner at one of our favorite restaurants? Would you like that?"

"Would *you* like that, Walter?" She felt a frustration that seemed disproportionate to his conciliatory posture. And just moments ago she had been feeling sorry for him and the children's assault. Sometimes she didn't understand herself.

"Yes, Lizbeth, I do believe I would like that."

"Good," Elizabeth clipped. "Shall we set the date to be the actual date of our anniversary?"

"Yes," he intoned with good humor. "That would seem to be right."

"Done. I'll broadcast an e-mail to the children tomorrow, and we can settle on a restaurant and the guest list later."

Walter nodded, pleased with his contribution and the speed of the decision-making process. He tacitly requested Elizabeth's permission to continue reading.

"We're done," she said. "You may read now."

* * *

Luce sat directly before her old friend and stared intently. Hungrily. She let her eyes slowly travel from the tip of her head down the long bridge of her nose, over the full lips, into the slight cleft of the chin. Luce never tired of looking at her face, at once intelligent and sensual. The light, coming diffusely from some unseen window, brushed softly against the translucent plane of her long cheek, lingered in a patch of almost pure white on the tip of her distinctive nose, sparkled on her earring, revealed a sheen of moisture on her full red lips. Against the dark brown tapestry that hung on the wall behind her, the light flashed on the collar of her white blouse, the shoulder of her peacock blue shawl and most spectacularly on the rim of her red hat.

The woman turned her head and looked at Luce over her right shoulder. Her eyes, slightly shaded beneath the wide rim of that fabulous hat, held a curious expression. Her lips parted as if on the verge of saying something. Luce could almost hear the thought behind those expressive eyes, could almost feel the first gentle exhalation as her lips formed the words to give shape and definition to the inchoate thought.

Luce was glad that they had the expansive gallery to themselves. She loved coming to the Metropolitan Museum on the one night a week it stayed open late. Fewer people in general and fewer people with whom to share *The Girl With A Red Hat*. Sitting now on a bench before the canvas, she felt replenished, restored. The space, the quietude, the familiar smell of old oils on old canvases, of polish on wooden floors, the sense that the same air had been breathed for a hundred years by hundreds of people finding their own special painting, brought a deep sense of pleasure. Her uneasiness at being back in New York, on the verge of another nerve-wracking show began to wane as Vermeer's quietude and luminosity seeped into her being.

She had been coming to this gallery for years, ever since she was a child of eight or nine. The first time was on a school field trip. The thousands of subsequent times were of her own volition.

There were many paintings which touched her, many painters who moved her. But she had loved the Vermeer from their first meeting. It was the clarity she loved, his way of capturing life, mid-moment, unembellished. Vermeer taught her to see life, to see her life and those around her. Clarity. Simplicity. Accuracy.

She also liked that Vermeer was lost for almost two hundred years after his death. There were many times in her early career before she gained visibility when his life was a source of encouragement to her. Now that she had financial success, and increasingly critical success, she remained touched by his obscurity. So little was known of him, the Sphinx of Delft. She liked that. She strongly felt that an artist's life shouldn't interfere with the viewer's appreciation and understanding of the work. Obscurity certainly helped in that regard. Now, sitting on a well worn leather bench, as her eyes drank in *The Girl With A Red Hat*, she knew all she needed to about Vermeer.

* * *

Mead sat on the fallen trunk of a baobab tree, a makeshift bench outside her hut. The evening air was rich, full of the varied life which surrounded the park resort. She slowly surveyed the vast plain that opened graciously before her. Moon glinted in the tall grasses. Acacia trees, blue-black shadows against a paler sky, clustered secretively along the plain, upon the rim of a distant hill. And beyond, encircled with clouds that shimmered in the moonlight stood Mount Kilimanjaro. She was happy to be at the park and happier to be alone. After arriving at the lodge, they had taken a late afternoon ride through the park seeing elephants, eland, lions, buffalo, hippos and a rare black rhino. The *coup de grace* had been a lake shore packed with flamingos. Roz and Linda's bickering had resumed over dinner in the lodge's restaurant but soon ended, as Roz was tired and clearly didn't have the energy to provoke.

"May I join you? Do you mind?" Linda tentatively inquired from behind.

"Oh," Mead hesitated. "Yeah. Sure." Linda sat down and for a few minutes there was silence.

"Thank God we had the good sense to at least get separate huts, huh?" Linda mused. Mead looked at Linda who smiled softly. Mead nodded in agreement.

"Look, Mead, I want to apologize. That crack about doctors being a health hazard, well, it hit the wrong target. I'm sorry." Exhaling a cynical laugh she said, "I had heard that Roz could be biting but I had no idea that she'd actually leave tooth marks." Mead retracted perceptibly. "Not everyone shares your high regard for her. But don't worry, Mead. Unlike Roz, I don't see anything wrong with actually trying to get along." They were quiet again. "God, Tim would love this. I wish he were here."

"It must be hard, these separations," Mead empathized.

"Yeah, they are hard. And getting harder." Her voice trailed off. After a while she shifted her body to face Mead. "So what's the story?"

Mead cocked her head. "About?"

"About this Peter." Mead sighed lowly and was quiet. "Must be serious," Linda ventured.

"Was serious."

"Past tense, huh?"

"Very past tense."

"No offense, Mead, but you seem awfully upset for something that's past tense. Care to talk about it?"

Mead glanced briefly at Linda, then stared deep into the open savanna, as though searching for some point upon which she could fix her sight.

"I met Peter in Boston. He was a friend of a friend. We were both residents. He's also in infectious diseases. We were friends for a while. Then dated. Then lovers. Then engaged." Her voice unraveled in the distance.

"Then?"

"Then we broke up."

"Why? What happened?"

Mead breathed in slowly, as though summoning energy. "Peter, as you will see first hand, is extremely charming. He's quite bright, quite talented, amusing. And, easy on the eye."

"Sounds like a pretty good package. I'm failing to see the problem here."

"Best of all, or worst of all, he really loves women." Linda tilted her head in question. Mead expanded, "He's one of those men who really understands and values women. I think he genuinely prefers women's company to men's. When we were just friends, I was amazed at how many women friends he had. And when we started to date I was, well, proud. All my friends were either very impressed or very jealous."

"This is sounding too damned perfect."

"Exactly. Peter loves women. *Really* loves women."

"Oh, I see," said Linda, responding to Mead's emphasis. "And a lot of them?"

"Bull's eye. When we were dating I thought, well, we're just dating. I can't very well cut him off from his friends, can I? When we got engaged I thought, well, surely he'd changed. Then two months before the wedding I found out he hadn't stopped."

"Geez, that's awful. How'd you find out?"

"He told me."

"Gotta admit, the bastard's honest."

"Yeah, a virtual knight in shining armor. Or is it *amour?* A real code of honor all right." Mead gave a short cynical laugh. "When push comes to shove, that is. He said he'd tried being monogamous, that he really wanted to be, but he just couldn't be. And he wanted me to hear it from him directly, didn't want to run the risk of my ever finding out from a third party."

"Did you ever consider trying to live with that?"

"Christ, Linda," Mead flared, "Now you sound like my mother. 'He's so wonderful, Mead, perfect in so many ways. Couldn't you just look the other way?'"

"No, no, don't get me wrong," Linda defended. "Hey, I wasn't even remotely suggesting that you should. I was just wondering if . . . if you could. I mean, some women can, you know. Like maybe your mother?"

"No, Linda, that's exactly the point. My mother never would tolerate that behavior. Never. And I couldn't either." Mead folded her arms over her chest.

"But you've remained friends?"

"In a weird way. Probably like a lot of former lovers, equal measures of extreme comfort mixed with equal measures of extreme discomfort."

"Do you still have contact?"

"I guess. From a distance. That's partly why I moved to Chicago. Nothing like a thousand miles to shore up your resolve."

"And now he's here, soon to be in our midst. Must be disconcerting."

"I have my trepidations, to be sure. We've gotten together for dinner a few times over the past two years, when I've been in Boston or we've both been in New York. And we've run into each other at some weddings of mutual friends. At a few conferences. Mostly it's been on the phone. But lately, lately I've just let the phone ring through. And if it's Peter, I just listen to him leaving a message then return his call when I'm sure he won't be home."

"Weakening?"

"No. Oh, I don't know. I don't think so. It's just that I haven't met anyone else. No one who even comes close to Peter."

"Tough break, Mead. I'm sorry."

"Yeah." Mead hugged her knees to her chest and squinted into the open plain of the night.

* * *

"Lizbeth?" Walter's voice echoing from the bathroom sounded hollow and steamy.

"Yes, Walter?" She looked up from her book as Walter emerged from the bathroom, pink from his hot tub, wrapped in a thick white terry cloth robe, toweling his wet head.

"I need a cut. Is it too late?"

Over her half glasses she caught his sheepish, beseeching grin.

"You're in luck," she yielded, shutting her book and placing it on her bedside table. "The barber's still open."

"Oh good." The bottom half of his long face slowly broke into a smile as she got out of bed and went to the medicine cabinet to get scissors, a comb and towels. He pulled the chair from her vanity table into the circle of her bedside reading lamp and sat down facing the mirror.

"Okay, buddy," she said looking at him in the mirror. "What's it going to be today? A flat top? Pompadour? Perhaps you're feeling adventurous – I could give you a terrific ridge of spikes in the middle of your head and color each one differently."

"Maybe next time. I think I'll just take my usual."

"Yes, probably better to wait for that one until you get your nose pierced. The usual it is. By the way," she nuzzled her face into the warm damp crook of his neck, "I love a man who can withstand the pressures of fashion." She breathed deeply of his scent.

"I'm sure you say that to all your customers."

"In this case, sir, you bet I do." She parted his white hair and combed it down. Then lifting each thin strand, she cut the edges in straight steady lines.

25

She had been giving him his haircuts for decades now. It was a ritual that had started in their early struggling days when he was in med school and she worked to pay the bills. They needed to save every penny, especially when Luce came along. They had kept the habit through subsequent years when Walter could easily have afforded a posh Upper East Side barber. For years, especially when the children were little, it was one of the few times they got to spend together.

She placed her hands on both sides of his head to straighten it, then looked for a long time into his face. He returned her gaze but without his glasses she knew she was just a blur to him. She loved his face, had always thought him extremely handsome. Even now, at seventy-five, he was extraordinarily attractive. And she loved his size, almost 6'3, and the mass of his broad shoulders. His contemporaries were stooped, shrunken with age. From behind, with his strapping presence and erect posture, Walter could easily pass for a man of forty.

Odd, she thought, standing behind him and alternately gazing at his image in the mirror and the large crown of his head, how habit can become ritual and ritual intimacy. I guess one just has to live long enough for the mundane to become revered.

But to her dismay, Elizabeth's sentiments were moving beyond the scope of her glib thoughts. Lately she had observed herself frequently feeling emotionally piqued, and with little provocation. She discounted it as some transient sentimentality, no doubt due to her recent seventieth birthday or their forthcoming anniversary. It will pass, she thought dismissively each time she suddenly found herself welling with tears. The underlying truth was that Elizabeth, realizing how finite time was, could feel each remaining grain rub against her interior surface as the sands inexorably fell in the hourglass of her life. And all of it – her life, her family, the surrounding world – had become so incredibly, painfully precious.

"Walter, Celia phoned today. She and Michael are taking a house on St. Kitts the last two weeks of February. Plenty of room, she says. They'd love for us to join them. This is the third time they've been. Celia says it's beautiful beyond words."

"I'm afraid that seminar on new drug combining for AIDS patients is the second week-end in February."

Elizabeth stopped mid-cut, her face a composition in disappointment. "Oh, but that's only one week-end. Celia and Michael will have the house for two weeks. Think of it," she said, bending to whisper in his ear, "Warm weather, sugary white sands, Calypso music." She shook her scissors like maracas and clicked a short rhythm with her tongue.

"Hmm, sounds good. But some of the best minds will be in attendance. Mead ought to hear a full and accurate summary of the proceedings. Also, there's a lecture on fuzzy systems."

"Walter," and her voice ran out of air.

"Lizbeth," he said, reaching for her hand, "Why don't you go. I'll join you if I can."

"I wouldn't think of going without you. It'd be no fun."

"Well, let me see," he intoned slowly in a way that made her hopeless, "what I can do."

She wanted to shout, "For God's sake, you're retired." But even in her frustration, she didn't want to bruise his ego or remind him of last summer. Instead she asked lightly, "Promise?"

"Promise. Say, Lizbeth, what does our daughter have to say today?"

"Walter," she stopped short, in a sudden fury, and hoped the heat of her gaze would scorch the top of his head. "We have two daughters. To whom do you refer?"

Walter, quickly recognizing his *faux pas* and the anger it elicited from his wife, drawled deliberately, "Now, you know that Mead is the one who's been writing almost every day. It's simply a matter of probability that you heard from Mead today. No need to get in a huff."

Elizabeth clenched her jaw and clutched the scissors tightly. Damn it, he could still provoke her, first with his insensitivity toward Luce and then his condescension toward her. "Don't patronize me, Walter. In the realm of probability, it is as likely that I would hear from Luce as I would from Mead. A call from San Francisco is every bit as probable as an e-mail from Africa. More probable in fact."

Walter, effectively silenced, gazed into his lap. Elizabeth, in icy fury, gave him a less than perfect cut.

* * *

Luce is searching, running madly through the hospital. She tries to find . . . who? Doctors and nurses brush by her, unaware. Should I be here, Luce wonders momentarily at the sight of these authoritative people. The doctor, that's who she needs to find. If only Luce could remember his name, his face. Luce is lost in what seems like endless corridors that appear directionless and only lead away. She is starting to get panicky but tries to retain her cool. Calm down, she coaches herself.

Suddenly the figure of a familiar person slips behind a corner. For an instant, Luce remembers. I'm searching for . . . but it's gone before she can hold it, like a slippery little fish between her fingers. If only she could find that doctor. Maybe someone at the nurses station could help. But how to find it, Luce wonders, feeling completely overwhelmed. She steps out of the stream of traffic in the corridor and leans against the cold blank space of the wall. No one notices her. She can't tell if she finds that disturbing or comforting. Maybe she should just stop one of these busy people, ask them . . . what? But now she finds that a soreness she was feeling in her throat has turned to a huge lump. She can't swallow, let alone speak. She feels as though she's beginning to choke. There isn't much time, she knows that.

Luce woke in a sweat. Disoriented, she laid in bed surveying her surroundings. In the small, stylish New York hotel room, thin blades of moonlight cut through the blinds and sliced the wall like prison bars. Getting out of bed, she raised the blinds to the top of the window frame, then got back into bed and pulled the covers tight to her chin, as much against her dream as the chilly midnight air.

Watching the wall fill with the slanting blue-black rhomboid shadows projected by the ambient neon lights of the city, Luce felt a mixture of despair and relief settle over her. The despair she felt was twofold, residual from the circumstances of her dream, despair that she had had that dream – again. The relief she felt was fragile, very fragile indeed. Escape from the terms of her dream to the terms of her present life was a narrow escape at best. The dream clung heavily. Her throat still felt constricted. Disgusted, she jumped out of bed, dressed and left her room in pursuit of coffee and the reassurance of life's pulse.

She roamed the streets aimlessly, aggressively bearing down on each block. The empty midnight hours wrapped around her like a tightening vise. As if by automatic pilot, she suddenly veered into the lobby of a mid-town hotel and headed for a bank of phones on the far wall.

"Hello?" Chris's voice on the other end was thick with sleep.

"Chris, it's Luce. Sorry to wake you up in the middle of the night."

"Luce. My God! Are you okay, Luce? Has anything happened out there?"

"I'm not out there. I'm here. In New York. Just got into town yesterday, as a matter of fact. I was going to call you later today. Look, the thing is, I can't really sleep. I was wondering if you still keep that spare key behind the fire extinguisher."

"Yeah, I do." The voice came through the receiver with tones of disbelief and incipient annoyance.

"Well, would it be okay? I mean, I really feel . . . Sorry, I know it's not a great time." Only with a friend of long standing would she take such liberties.

"Oh, go ahead. But give me a call, will you? We never talk anymore. I miss you."

"Yeah, promise. I'll call in a day or two and we'll set something up. Thanks, Chris. Sweet dreams."

Back on the street Luce hailed a cab. "Kent Avenue. By Metropolitan. Do you know where that is?"

The driver sneered at her over his shoulder. "Yeah, yeah." Luce leaned back into the torn black leather seat, her tautness sprung now that relief was imminent. She took off her gloves and rubbed her hands briskly. Her palms burned. She cupped them together, as if to save the energy.

At Kent she handed the driver a twenty and told him to keep the change. Opening the door and dashing up the stairs, she reached the fourth floor in short order. Stopping before #10, she looked at the fire extinguisher nailed to the wooden wall, then lifted the bottom. A single key fell onto the slatted floor. Picking it up, she inserted it in the rusty padlock, twisted and pulled it off. She threw the latch and opened the door. Stepping inside quickly, she closed the door throwing the dead bolt and using the padlock for extra insurance. Then she turned around.

Her shoulders fell in relief as she took in Chris's messy studio, inhaling the familiar smell of paint and gesso and canvas. A new set of feelings flooded her. This had been her first studio. Chris had been her first lover. Years later, when Luce moved to SoHo, she'd offered the space to Chris, who eagerly accepted.

Luce walked up to the easel where Chris had left a work-in-progress. It was electric, as most of Chris's work was, animated by rapid short brush strokes and jarring colors. Standing before such sheer chaos, she shuddered and took it off the easel, placing the face against the wall. She looked around and found a stretched canvas that had already been gessoed. Bless you, Chris, she thought. Her hands, the burning now a raging fire, worked quickly, finding the oils, handling the brushes. She stood before the canvas and in a second surrendered completely, losing herself to another, truer world. Now her breathing became slow and deep, her heartbeat steady and sure; now she descended from the high wire of agitation and angst and stepped onto the firm fecund land of her art. She was home.

Hours later, as the sun began to rise, she stood back and observed the finished canvas. It would be another in her *Searching for Grace* series, which had the critics raving. Like all the others, she would simply add the location to name it.

With a cup of coffee in hand, she slumped against the wall and studied her new painting. *Searching For Grace/Brooklyn Bridge* was all manner of cold gray and blue hues. In the middle ground the silhouette of a single figure, cornered by an expanse of empty bridge, leaned heavily upon the railing. The background was dominated by the bridge's south tower, a gray stone structure whose two arches appeared as vaulted clerestory windows in the open church of sky. Space and form, shadow and light merged moodily as the figure, unaware and unattainable, stared into the distance.

Luce had begun painting this series two years ago and the success it had met with astonished her. It was ironic to her that at her least self-conscious moment, at her most melancholic, her critical achievement should be its greatest.

As the new painting set, Luce recalled a review she had read several months ago.

"The *Searching For Grace* series embodies the spiritual longing of our time," the critic had written. "Each canvas is suffused with a powerful singular perspective. Frequently the viewer peers down an empty street at dusk or across a lonely bridge. These hermetic architectural settings are ubiquitous in the series and reminiscent of the emptiness so masterfully depicted by de Chirico.

"In each of Ms. Bennett's *Searching For Grace* paintings, the solitary figure mysteriously dominates the composition. The viewer, instructed by the sure hand of the artist, searches for a connection with this somber form, who seemingly ignores our presence, eludes our grasp. Is it our better self, a divine being, a state of grace? No matter. It symbolizes the deepest yearning in us all. An unmistakable chasm exists. The figure, never revealing its face to us, visually summarizes the late twentieth century individual's relationship to his Spirit/spirit.

"Arrested and enthralled by these haunted words, the viewer confronts some fundamental questions – Has God turned His back on me? Or perhaps more fundamental and chilling, Have I turned my back on myself? Fear and hunger are left commingling in the pit of our bellies as we ponder how to traverse the formidable space and connect with this enigmatic figure."

This critique, typical of other reviews, amused and baffled her mildly. She did not paint the series with intention or design. In fact, it was only after reading a similar review that she realized the empty street or bridge were indeed constant elements. Nor did she paint them to show the viewer his or her disconnected spirit or malnourished state of being. No, the paintings were creations from a dark and shadowy place. Neither consciousness nor intellect intervened.

Examining the series' latest addition, she felt oddly distanced. For the past two years painting did not offer joy or completion. She found no resolution or satisfaction. The process, as always, was beyond question. It was simply something she must do. But the finished product had become frustrating, inadequate. Painting these days was like a whistling kettle. Unable to turn off the flame, she could only occasionally lift the lid and let off steam.

* * *

The full white moon cutting across the great expanse of African sky distilled the essence of each earthbound object, etching its primitive shape in deep blue upon the valley floor.

"So how does he wind up coming to Africa?" Linda asked.

"On his way to Kitwell to follow up on the latest outbreak of Ebola. Then maybe on to Gabon. And he arrives with a few days to kill, just as we're leaving on this trip. Lousy timing, I know. What can I say? I'm sorry."

"Look, Mead, you can save your apologies with me. Roz was the one who wanted an all female climb, not me." After some time she asked, "Are you scared?"

Mead turned her head sharply to face Linda. "Of what?"

Linda hesitated then gestured in the direction of Kilimanjaro. "Of that, the mountain. Are you scared of climbing it?"

Perplexed Mead replied, "I hadn't thought about it, so I guess not. Are you?"

She sighed deeply, "Yeah."

"Why? I know there have been some people who have died in the ascent – like that guy who was incredibly overweight and had the heart attack. But you're in good shape."

"Have you ever climbed a 19,000-foot mountain before?"

"No. I've done some hiking in the high Sierra."

"It doesn't intimidate you at all, does it? Not conquering it, not making it just isn't a consideration for you, is it?" She didn't wait for an answer. "Well, it is for me. It's not about some quirky thing that might happen, you know, like a sudden rock slide or temperature change that might cause an injury or even my death. It's just about not making it, not finishing, not being able to do it."

31

Mead uncharacteristically extended her arm and put her hand lightly on Linda's shoulder. "The outfitter is from Seattle and has been doing this climb for years. We'll go slow, pace ourselves. As long as the altitude sickness is manageable, it'll be a breeze. Hundreds of people, most untrained, climb it every year. You'll make it."

"Roz would just love it if I didn't, I'm sure." She suddenly burst into a fit of laughter. Mead withdrew her hand. "Sorry, Mead," she said between laughs, "it just came to me. God that's so funny."

Mead was lost. "Look, I know that Roz doesn't fully approve – me just being a nurse. I know I don't cut it in her eyes. But, oh, how to explain this . . .?" Mead watched her trying to construct some acute, unassembled thought. "You see, I wanted to be a doctor. Ever since I was a little girl." Her tone was embarrassed. "God, I do believe I wanted that more than anything in the world. I had the grades. I'd done well on my MCATs." She was struggling with each word now. "I just couldn't bring myself to fill out the applications. I don't come from a wealthy family – pretty blue collar. Christ, I'm the first to even graduate college. Tim wanted to get married. My mother said 'As a nurse you'll always be able to support your children if anything ever happens to Tim. You'll have security and flexibility.' My father just continued to nap." She started to laugh again and Mead braced herself, but this time Linda pulled herself together. "So I flinched. I didn't go. And that damned mountain and that damn Roz are the med school I didn't attend." She sighed again and was quiet.

"I always knew I would be a doctor," said Mead, breaking the protracted silence. "Never any question." There was a hint of sarcasm in her voice that Linda, still absorbed with her own failure, didn't catch. "My father's a surgeon."

"To the manor born," Linda observed.

"Yeah, I guess. But by default. None of my older siblings wanted it. My sister Luce, the brightest, the one he had pinned all his hopes on full force, was the first to defect. In the middle of her junior year she switched pre-med for art. If my father wasn't an atheist, Luce's actions would be considered mortal sins. As it is, she was convicted of high treason and made to walk the plank. My brother Rand, who we all secretly knew was too damned nerdy to ever make it as a doctor, even in research, went into Artificial Intelligence and is happily ensconced at MIT tinkering with binary code ad infinitum. At least he didn't fall completely afield of science, so his offense, while major, is forgivable. Avery, my other brother, completed med school but opted for psychiatry. Hmmm, we all know real doctors don't practise psychiatry. So, by the time I came along, the path was pretty damned narrow." Mead felt Linda's stare, a mix of doubt and incomprehension.

Mead continued, "Have you ever seen sheep dog trials?" Now it was Linda's turn to be perplexed. She shook her head. "Well I saw quite a few during a summer I spent in Australia. Fascinating, really. And the dogs are magnificent." She turned her body toward Linda to explain. "You have a large fenced-in field. The dog owner has to stay in one spot and can only communicate with his or her dog via whistles or hand signals. They release three or four sheep, generally the barnyard stubborn variety, and the dog, without biting them, has to get the sheep through a series of obstacles – chutes and gates. Then the dog has to chase them into a pen that the owner closes.

"The dogs are great to watch. They swing wide or sidle close, crouch on their bellies or make a sudden darting run at the sheep. Whatever it takes to get them through the obstacles. I guess growing up felt more like a sheep dog trial than a manor." She paused and turned her body out toward the open savanna again, uncomfortable with how much she had disclosed.

"You're not happy as a doctor?"

"No, I am. My analogy's a little misleading. A little extreme. Besides, there are some sheep that are perfectly happy being penned."

"I wouldn't call infectious diseases a penned-in field. And your career hardly seems penned-in."

"No. But you know what I mean. The routine of it all. Back home. I get up, go to the hospital, do the rounds, meet with the residents, go to the lab, do the research, write the papers, go home and get four hours of sleep and start it all over again."

"I don't think doctors have a corner on the market for being overworked and bored." Mead felt some steel behind Linda's words.

"I guess not," she replied, but it was only a guess.

* * *

"Elizabeth, you look wonderful." Celia, Mrs. Michael John Hamilton, wife of Doctor Michael John Hamilton, another former president of the New York Surgeon's Academy, lightly took Elizabeth's hand and air-kissed her cheek. "Wonderful to see you, as always. You too, Walter. You're looking as gorgeous as ever."

"Why, thank you, Celia," Elizabeth blurted, stealing the compliment. "That's nice of you to say."

Walter, intervening in an age-old rivalry interjected, and in his most cavalier tones, "I do believe my dear Celia is right. Both Lizbeth and I are looking well tonight."

"Oh, Walter, please." Elizabeth stationed herself adamantly between Celia and Walter.

"Come now, Elizabeth, come with me and let me find you a glass of champagne. Your Walter is quite safe. Everyone knows you're a pit bull and none of us are eager to tangle with you." Celia locked arms with Elizabeth, pulling her into the flow of the party and casting a parting phrase at Walter over her bare shoulder. "No matter how attractive the potential prize."

Weaving their way through the crowd, thick with tuxedoed surgeons and their evening-gowned wives, Elizabeth admonished, "Despite your being somewhat younger than I, you're really too old for that coquettish behavior, Celia. It's unattractive and makes me feel quite embarrassed for you. And I hate feeling embarrassed for you. It's such a stretch."

"Walter would be heartbroken if I didn't fawn a little. I see we're in fine spirits tonight. Maybe we'll pass the champagne and go straight to the martinis."

"Not on your life."

The rivalry between Elizabeth and Celia was more bark than bite. In fact, Celia was one of the few other surgeons' wives whom Elizabeth trusted. Away from their husbands, they dropped the school girl banter and occasionally let their guards down. Over lobster clubs at the Arcadia or sherry at the San Moritz, they had shared a feeling of ennui with their roles and regret for their times, their lost opportunities. Celia was only ten years younger than Elizabeth. When they first met and Elizabeth was thirty-five, this seemed quite a chasm. At sixty, Celia was now a peer.

Taking two flutes from a passing tray and handing one to Elizabeth, Celia asked, "So, have you two decided on our little jaunt to St. Kitt's?"

"I really don't think now's a good time. Walter is so busy. Well, we both are."

"I know you are. That's precisely the point. You work too hard. You need a break – both of you. And although I know it's *verboten* to mention in Walter's presence, you are retired after all. You didn't go anywhere for your seventieth birthday. Really," she said shaking Elizabeth's arm gently, "You ought to live a little."

"Walter has an important seminar he doesn't want to miss."

"For two weeks?"

"And I have Mead's letters to compile and edit."

Celia rolled her eyes in disbelief. "I think you're both carrying this perverse work ethic of yours too far. Just when do you intend to have some fun?"

"Oh, look," Elizabeth said as she pointed across the room. "There he is, Dr. Paul Belker, the incoming president. Let's go over and you can introduce me." Celia, knowing the conversation had been terminated, followed in her wake.

"Dr. Belker. How are you this evening?"

A courtly man in his late forties, Dr. Belker bowed slightly. "Mrs. Hamilton, how nice to see you tonight."

"May I introduce Mrs. Walter William Bennett?"

"How do you do, Mrs. Bennett?"

"Elizabeth, please. Congratulations on your election."

"Thank you, I think. As they say, I think the first thing I should have done was to demand a recount."

"Elizabeth's husband was president of the Academy, oh, God, when was that? Help me out, Elizabeth."

"Actually, he was twice president. First in 1977 and then again in 1983. I think. Oh, thank God, here comes Walter. He can confirm my memory." She waved him to her side. "Walter, this is Dr. Paul Belker, the incoming president."

"Dr. Belker and I have met on several occasions." Walter spoke formally, assumed a professional posture. "How are you tonight?" They shook hands. "In fact, I quite enjoyed your lecture last year at the American Surgeons Meeting. Your data was quite intriguing, though your conclusion perhaps a trifle premature. Congratulations on your election. I'm sure you'll find it as I did, demanding but satisfying."

Dr. Belker stammered under his breath then asked, "Have either of you met my wife? Sandra, can you join us, please?" A very attractive woman in her early forties entered their circle. "Sandra, this is Celia Hamilton and Elizabeth and Walter Bennett."

"How do you do?" She extended a straight length of arm in Elizabeth's direction.

"We were just congratulating your husband on his new position," Celia said.

"He's a maniac. I don't know where he thinks he'll find the time." Her husband fidgeted with his cocktail napkin and shifted nervously from foot to foot.

Elizabeth tightened her grip on Sandra's hand, then clasped her hand onto Sandra's forearm as though not wanting her to get away. Beneath a charming smile she said, "Well, fortunately, as de facto head of the Auxiliary Wives Association, you'll be too busy to notice his dilemma."

Sandra pulled back immediately and gave Elizabeth a look of disdain. "I have my own surgery practice, Elizabeth. As well as teaching at N.Y.U. I'm afraid I haven't the time for auxiliary functions. I told Paul he was born just twenty years too late. The days of wife as secretary and useful appendage are over. Amputated if you will."

Paul laughed uncomfortably. "You must forgive Sandra. She enjoys being shockingly direct."

Red was rising at the base of Elizabeth's neck. "I have never been Walter's secretary. Or appendage. I have managed all of his business affairs, the financial end of his business. And our investment portfolio. I have never considered my role appended, if you will." She looked directly at Sandra, her smile never faltering.

Turning her attention toward Walter, Sandra said, "Dr. Bennett, do you recall that you supervised me during a period of my residency?"

"That's why you look so familiar." Walter warmed immediately. "I was wondering where I had seen you before."

"That was it. You were especially helpful with my first micro-laser surgery."

"Of course, it's all coming back to me. My, that was a complicated one. Especially for a first foray. But you performed commendably, as I recollect."

"Excuse us, please," Celia extricated Elizabeth as delicately as she could. "There's someone with whom Elizabeth and I simply must speak. Come, Lizzy." Walter and Sandra barely noticed their departure. Paul seized the opportunity to move to other social turf and nodded his good-bye.

"You're seething, Elizabeth. Here." Celia replaced their champagne flutes with a fresh ones. "Let's snoop around. Maybe we can find a private room."

"What on earth do I want a private room for?"

"To compose yourself? You're practically foaming at the mouth."

"God, Celia, how you do exaggerate. I'm perfectly fine. Don't fuss over me." She turned her back and headed deeper into the social fray.

* * *

From a distance, the figure, arms on the bridge railing, head slumped on her arms, seemed pitiful, forlorn. Above the zooming cars, the raw steel girders, the endlessly sprawling cities on either side, her presence was the smallest bit of punctuation on yet another day.

Luce, leaning against the railing, looked down. Immediately below were four lanes of traffic exchanging people between Manhattan and Brooklyn. Another one hundred feet below that, on the East river, a barge traveled out to sea while a cabin cruiser traveled in. She watched as the two captains waved greetings and sounded their horns. When they had passed, she stared into the face of the river, cold and inscrutable, and shivered. Pulling the collar of her tightly buttoned coat around her ears, she clapped her gloved hands together and stamped her feet. Oh God, hurry up, Ruthie, she thought. Please hurry.

Facing south she saw a ferry circle the Statue of Liberty. Beyond that, the erector set bridge arced into the sky. A mist covered the Palisades. It had been another gray day, biting and bleak. Looking down the empty streets of the financial district, over which the corporate towers hovered imperiously, she felt as though she had been painted into an Edward Hopper, so vapid, so despairing was the evening around her.

She hated being here. She didn't know why she had agreed to meet mid-bridge. But Ruthie's voice over the phone had sounded so warm, so infectious. Just like old times. Luce imagined standing mid-bridge, as she had many times before, having walked up from the subway. She could almost see them walking arm in arm, approaching her, laughing at some silly private joke.

"Hey, hey, don't jump." Luce felt a sudden pull from behind as Ruthie clasped her arms around her waist and pulled her away from the railing. "There," Ruthie said, "I've done my good deed for the day. Thank God. I love getting that crap out of the way." Ruthie, laughing huskily, stood back and held Luce at arm's length. "Shall I lie and say you look terrific? Geez, with the expression on that mug, I'd be doing you a favor if I pushed you. Am I on your insurance policy by the way?"

"It's good to see you, too, Ruthie." They embraced. .

"So, how do you think the dumpy old broad's looking?" She twirled around, holding her worn winter coat far from her body in mock model style. "Not too bad for sixty-something, huh?"

Luce deadpanned, "Not *too* bad."

"Oh, you smart ass. I should push you. I'm an old lady. Didn't your mother ever teach you to respect your elders? Don't hurt yourself thinking about it now. So where's your California tan?"

"San Francisco's fog belt."

"Oh, that explains your pasty look. Milton, who sends his regards," she raised her eyebrows and rolled her eyes, "for whatever that's worth, said, 'San Francisco, why did she have to move to where all the nuts and fruits are?' So I said, 'Well, they may all be nuts and fruits but that's gotta be better than all you boring morons.'"

"How is dear Miltie?"

"My own flesh, my own blood. Such a moron. He called me the other day to ask how the asshole was doing. I said 'Which asshole? I know so many. What, are we talking about your wife? Are we talking about my ex-sister-in-law?' 'No. No,' he says. 'I'm talking about the biggest asshole in the world.' 'Oh,' I say, 'Why didn't you say so to begin with and stop wasting my time? I got a postcard from our sister just yesterday.' Who, by the way, is on some Caribbean cruise, a different port every night and all that jazz. So how's Milton? Milton is green with envy that Pearl is off on the Love Boat, and, worst of all, spending her money. I said to him, I said, 'Milton, just get over yourself. First of all, she's going to spend every single penny that jerk left her. Secondly, she going to outlive us both by a hundred years. She's too mean to die.' So long story short, Milton's about the same. Are you hungry, honey?"

Luce had leaned against the bridge railing, as though blown back by the force of Ruthie's conversation.

Ruthie tucked her arm through Luce's. "I know, I know, I still talk too much. Let's get some dinner."

* * *

A loud banging on her hotel door awakened Mead abruptly. She sat bolt upright and snapped on the light. "Who's there?"

"Richard Gere." Peter's voice from the other side sounded surprisingly good. Damn him, she thought taking blurry aim and hurling a pillow at the door. "For God's sake, Peter, what time is it?"

"Time to open the door and say hello to your old friend Peter."

Mead went to the door and opened it reluctantly. Stooping to pick up her pillow Peter gallantly presented it to her, as though it were a special gift he had traveled miles to personally deliver. "By the way, Mite, you missed."

His wide awake, impish smile, that he now opened to full throttle, sent a wave of nausea through her sleepy system. "C'mon in." She turned and sat in the chair by her bed. "Couldn't you have waited till morning?"

"Hell of a welcome. I come thousands of miles, and that's all you have to say to me? 'Couldn't you have waited till morning?' I endure flights from hell, ground transport frustrations that only a third-world country can serve up, a series of convoluted disastrous events with the reception desk of this fine lodge straight out of Fellini and, longing to feast my eyes on a friendly face, all this weary traveler gets is 'Couldn't you have waited till morning?'"

Peter casually assumed Mead's spot in the bed and settled in, hands clasped behind his head. Mead, caving in as the vigor of his personality filled her room, sullenly said, "I didn't invite you, as you may recall." She watched him prop himself on his elbow and smile annoyingly. "And don't call me Mite."

His smile broadened. She resorted to another tactic. "Peter, dear Peter, it is so good to see you and so good of you to join me." She cocked her head and dropped her voice to a lower register. "Now will you leave. It's 1 a.m. Please?"

"You, my dear Mite, uh, Mead," he jumped enthusiastically out of her bed, "are as lovely and sweet as ever. Thank you for your gracious welcome. I am overcome and, prodded by your gentle suggestion, I think I will find respite in slumber." He bent to kiss her cheek and she darted out beneath his arm. "The mountain will call, and I must be up to the challenge of meeting nature head on. Till morning, *mon amie.*"

He waited at the door. "Good night, Peter." Satisfied, he blew her a kiss and shut the door behind him.

Mead tiptoed over and quietly threw the lock. Sighing, she collapsed back in her bed, face first. Sniffing his scent on her pillow, she exchanged it for the unused one on the other side of her bed, propped herself up and stared at the door.

* * *

"Yes," Elizabeth said, reaching for another flute of champagne, "Mead is on a hard assignment. Of course, they chose her and God knows how many they considered. You know, at her level it gets so political, the World Health Organization gets into the act, NIH, CDC All the medical politicos have to sprinkle their holy water of consent. She's recording her experiences in her *Kenyan Letters*. Well, that's just a working title, of course." The circle Elizabeth was holding hostage included Dr. and Mrs. Mark Thomason, Dr. and Mrs. Steven J. Parkins, a colleague of Walter's and Celia.

"Well, you must be very proud of her. We knew from the start that she was going places," Dr. Steven J. Parkins reminisced. "She always had superior gray matter. I still keep in touch with my old Alma Mater in Chicago. Believe me, they think highly of her there."

"I heard from a friend of a friend that the powers-that-be thought the paper she delivered at the last AIDS conference was so good they plan to offer her a luncheon keynote spot next year," Celia added.

"Well, it's all rumors at this point. Speculation. But nothing Mead does surprises me. Of course, I am editing her *Letters*. Just a temporary role until we find a satisfactory publisher. Sometimes I read her accounts and I am amazed and impressed and can't even imagine that she's my daughter."

"And how's your other daughter?" Beverly Thomason interjected. "I'm sorry, I read her name so often and I can't recall it right now."

"Luce. That would be Luce. She's doing quite well. Moved her studio out to San Francisco a few years ago. You know how these artists are. Steven,

39

I was wondering if I could impose on you to read some of Mead's *Letters*. It's terribly good. And terribly important. It would mean so much to us to have a doctor of your caliber give us some feedback."

"Why, of course, Elizabeth, I'd be happy to."

"I guess," Beverly persisted, "that you're thrilled with Luce's forthcoming show. When is it exactly?"

Elizabeth turned to face Beverly squarely and assumed a blithe tone. "Oh yes," she said, not missing a beat and assuming a proud countenance. "Very proud."

Over the past decade she had become deft at vague supportive conversations about her daughter's increasing notoriety. And she had developed an equally adroit facility for smoothly transitioning the conversation away from the topic of Luce.

Beverly, sensing Elizabeth's camouflaged discomfort, continued, "I thought of you this morning when I read about Luce in the Art and Leisure section. It must be wonderful to have her back in town. And to attend the opening night, well, it must be a thrill."

Elizabeth quickly steadied herself. Their relationship with Luce was a source of conversation and gossip among certain crowds. She pushed her feet more firmly to the floor to offset the internal swaying she felt. Beverly could just try and get her goat. Watch out, she thought and hoped her eyes conveyed the warning, be sure you want to take me on. Pleasantly she said, "We love Luce dearly, of course. But you must understand, Walter is a man of science. Well, we all are. We really don't know anything about art. Except, of course, that she's very good."

Celia cleared her throat. "The Bennetts are blessed unfairly, if you ask me. All their children are both gifted and successful. Elizabeth, look, here comes Walter." Turning her head she saw Walter headed directly toward her. "Excuse us." Celia grabbed Elizabeth's arm and once again pulled her from a trying, precariously balanced circle. "Looks like he needs another drink."

"He must be so proud, as well," Beverly shot in parting.

"Terribly," Elizabeth tossed over her shoulder. Lowering her voice she brusquely demanded, "Why the hell didn't you tell me Luce is in town?"

With nonchalant venom, Celia replied, "You've asked me on more than one occasion not to discuss Luce."

"Well, I never meant to the point of being fatally ambushed."

"Now who's exaggerating? You, dear Elizabeth, will never be fatally ambushed."

"Walter," Elizabeth smiled broadly, "are you enjoying yourself?"

* * *

"So," Ruthie looked up momentarily at Luce across the deli table and smiled. "I was worried that since you left New York you've lost touch." Luce looked quizzical. Ruthie resumed digging through the large burlap bag that served as purse, shopping bag, overnight case. "Here. Found it." She triumphantly pulled a copy of the *Weekly Sun* from her bag. The waitress cleared their plates and refilled their coffee cups. Luce, trying vainly to suppress her amusement, gave Ruthie a stern look.

"Okay, Miss Smarty Pants." Ruthie moved the pickle bowl, salt and pepper shakers and mustard jar aside, spreading the paper before her. "Did you know that WD-40 is an incredible cure for arthritis? Back pain? Stiff neck? See, you didn't, did you? They don't talk about things like this in San Fran, eh? I'd better hide this from Milton when he comes over for dinner on Tuesday. His wife will be washing WD-40 from his collars for weeks. Oh, here, look at this, Luce. A sweet pussy cat, the world's largest at 65 pounds. And growing! Don't think I want to clean out that litter box. Yikes! Boy raised by mountain goats – old story. Not even worth the space it's taking up here. This was a very touching story." She pointed emphatically to an article on the second page.

"A gal who received a heart transplant suddenly starts craving beer and junk food. Turns out her donor was a teenage boy. She sought his family out to learn more about him. Very moving. Very moving. Not sure I believe it, though. Of course, if she starts finding herself in the back seat of a car with a cheerleader, well, then I guess that would be proof. Hey, that'd be a nice sequel, don't you think? Maybe I should write the editor and suggest it. Oh, here's one. A doozy. Really big news. The reason why Elvis was so bright-eyed and bushy-tailed? He ate squirrel as a kid. Now this is not a joke, Luce. You can just wipe that smile off your face right now, young lady. I'm trying to keep you informed of important current events. You're in New York now. These are things you need to know if you hope to appear *savoir* and *au courant*. We don't want you being mistaken for a hayseed. "

"Thank you, Ruthie," Luce smirked.

"Okay, then listen up." Ruthie moistened her index finger and flipped the pages. "Big headline: 'Misery Makes You Smarter.' This is news? Oy. Uh, here is something everyone should know about. This alone is worth the cost of the paper. Did you know, Luce, that Coke machines can swallow you? Deadly, huh? Here's a story of a guy who got stuck in a Coke machine for five terrifying hours! Upside down no less. The fact that he happened to be breaking into the machine is a minor detail, I'm sure you'd agree. This poor schmuck has done us all a great community service. There's a moral. I don't know what the hell it is. You're a bright girl, you figure. Not now. Please. Later, in the privacy of your own hotel room. I for one am never going near a vending machine again, at least not alone. More coffee?"

Luce looked at Ruthie incredulously. She had forgotten what a character she was. She began to laugh. Ruthie joined in, and soon both had tears streaming down their faces. Taking off her glasses and wiping her eyes, Ruthie reached across the table and took Luce's hands into her own. "Oh, we've had some laughs, haven't we. Luce, Luce. It's so good to see you. I've been worried about you." She gave a squeeze.

Afraid to look up, Luce stared at Ruthie's hands, which covered her own. They were gnarled with arthritis and speckled with age spots. She pulled one of her hands free and placed it on top of Ruthie's. "Are you coming to the opening?" was all she could choke out.

"Is the Pope an unbelievable, outdated, pain in the ass? Of course, of course, I'm coming."

"Good. That's good. Thanks, Ruthie."

"Aah, just add it to the many things you owe me for. Which, I might remind you, is getting to be a very long list." Luce looked up and held Ruthie's gaze. Behind the feigned humor Luce recognized her own bittersweet sadness at meeting.

* * *

After a restless night, Mead was happy to check her watch and see it was 5 a.m. Close enough, she thought, getting out of bed and dressing quickly. Taking notebook, pen and flashlight, she padded out of her hut and tiptoed until she was well into the plain and clear of the other huts. Shining a path for herself with the small magna light, she wandered through the open savanna toward the small outcropping of acacias she had noticed with Linda the night before.

The globe of her flashlight revealed a wonderful variety of footprints. She observed the flat, round impressions left by a group of elephants and other prints from a slender four-toed creature that had traveled recently and in great number. Cresting the hill, she sat beneath a tree with her back to the game resort, opened her small note book and looked ahead. Kilimanjaro was all shades of gray and light blue as dawn approached. Even the ubiquitous band of clouds that encircled its three peaks was pale dove gray.

She put the pen to the paper, but nothing came. Her thoughts, usually so orderly and clear, so accessible, were unruly and defied expression. All she could do was curse her situation and the people around her who seemed the source of her agitation, of her tangled state. She closed the notebook and leaned heavily against the tree.

She found the expanse of land, with its vast open stretches, surprisingly appealing. Having been raised in New York and now living in Chicago, she was unaccustomed to such a horizontal view of life. The skyscrapers of New York and Chicago were vertical markings that were her unconscious reference points, a constant filter. I wonder, she thought, what the effect would be of such open living. As she sat quietly, as the rising sun reached her body, warmed her flesh and the surrounding air, she began to relax. God, she thought with amazement, it's just been slightly over a month since I arrived. A kaleidoscope of scenes appeared in her mind: arriving at the airport and the trip into Nairobi, her first view of it, the slightly dilapidated and miserably understocked hospital, the endless, imploring faces, evenings on the porch of the Norfolk Hotel, having "sundowners" with the other doctors, Roz or Linda, the few hours she caught to explore the city, the colonial streets and parks, the crowded markets.

She realized that she hadn't really had a chance to sort it all out. And the horror of disease, of plague juxtaposed against the thriving countryside with its rich diversity of animal and human life. The inextricable weave of doom and disaster with such stunning, pulsating beauty. The faces she saw up close, she could afford to examine with the permission allowed by the doctor-patient relationship, were usually withered and worn. The "slims", no longer as common a symptom among the HIV/AIDS patients she saw in Chicago, still existed in sub-Saharan Africa, which didn't have the life-prolonging techniques increasingly available in the Western world. Theirs were decimated faces, grotesque parodies of what they used to be. But the faces of the families who sat patiently in the crowded hospital lobby, or gathered round the death bed, were unbelievably beautiful faces to Mead. She could easily detect the structural and tonal differences among the Africans, although she could still identify only a few distinct tribes: the elegant Masai, the ebony Chugga (often said to be the most beautiful), and the Pokot with their copious and distinctive jewelry. New York, Chicago seemed galaxies away. Breathing deeply she thought, I like Africa. I like Africa very much.

* * *

Elizabeth slipped quietly out of bed. Fixing a cup of chamomile tea, she padded softly into the den and booted up her computer. Still provoked by Beverly's comments about Luce at the party, she was unable to sleep. Distressed more than she cared to be, and certainly more than she cared to admit, she sought something to read. In the dark of her den she opened the file *Kenyan Letters* and reread some of Mead's previous entries.

"I hired a cab this afternoon to drive out to the Nairobi National Park. Just eight miles out of the teeming city you find an authentic game preserve with lions, cheetahs, rhino, antelope, and hippos. It's wild to drive through the park and see all these animals wandering the plains, with the backdrop of Nairobi's rising skyline. I came across two cheetahs sunbathing, nonchalantly yawning as the city slowly moves to encroach on their territory. I thought of the Kenyans nonchalantly yawning as the HIV virus encroaches on their lives.

"I've taken to walking from Nairobi Hospital back to the dormitories of the University of Nairobi where they house us, taking different routes to become familiar with the city. Last evening I walked the full length of Kenyetta Avenue, a broad tri-part boulevard which the citizens are all very proud of, which is to say it is true old colonial western. There are two dividing strips that separate the three roads of Kenyetta Avenue. Late blooming jacaranda with its gorgeous purple blossoms interspersed with palms and the ubiquitous acacia line the streets. The people in their variety defy description: various tribes in their native dress, usually the bright colored kangas; high school girls all uniformed in blue skirts, blue blouses, black ties, white socks and black shoes; Muslims in their long hot gowns, the women in their black choudras; East Indians in their saris. It's an astonishing and colorful pageant. With the buzz that you'd expect of a big city, there is at times an odd sense of festival. But beneath the costumes, beneath the activity, beneath the rhythmic music accented with the joyful simplicity of the penny whistle lurks a plague, inevitable and gaining ground every minute.

"Despite HIV detection techniques that have been established procedure for almost a decade, most of the blood remains unscreened. All that tainted blood is being used for transfusions. Getting people to use clean, fresh needles is almost impossible. Mostly a question of resources. I heard of some Belgian nurses/ nuns who in their good-hearted attempts to inoculate against malaria, infected an entire village. They knew what the potential risks were. They made a calculated decision based on having only five syringes. And lost.

"Then there's a related complication – the increasing spread of multi-drug-resistant TB. This, beyond doubt, is the single biggest health threat.

"I read in a WHO newsletter that the U.S. spends $2.71 per person on HIV/AIDS, which is woefully inadequate. Here they spend just seven cents. Not surprisingly, the life expectancy, which was already pretty low at 52, is plummeting with the birth of HIV-infected babies. I keep getting the sense of a huge tidal wave, a tsunami, growing in strength, in height, in force along the coast of this entire continent and which will come crashing down over the next decade in a flood of blood and unimaginable death. How can they, how can we, remain so god damn complacent in the face of it? I shudder to think what it will finally take to decide to marshal our forces. And I wait. But this devil of a virus is so unstable, so damn clever in the mutating magic it performs, increasingly virulent and resistant, will the timing be sufficient I wonder?

"I work with a Dr. Birati Singh, a native of Kenya whose family is part of the great Indian merchant class that lives in Mombassa, along the coast. She went to university here in Nairobi and returned after going to med school in the UK. A remarkable woman. Extraordinary, really. Very quiet but so present. She works at the hospital then has a separate practice dealing with the sex workers. The trend lines are staggering. Did you know that 85% of all the commercial sex workers in this city are infected? She tries to implement educational programs and safe-sex procedures. But it's a difficult endeavor. As always, there's the economic consideration – lots of tourists come here for sex safaris. As you might imagine, there aren't a lot of employment opportunities for the people who flood the city from their tribal villages. And the resources are so paltry. She's modeling her program on one conducted in Kinshasa. It had initial results of lowering the infection rates among sex workers from 18% to 2%. But then, as is typical, without resources, without appropriate follow-through, the program fell completely by the wayside. She's trying to get a comparable program authorized and implemented here. It's a thankless, frustrating task. The government leaders are fairly unhelpful. None want to admit that it's really a problem – part denial, part economic necessity. If tourism fell off, Kenya would dry up. I honest to God don't know how Dr. Singh withstands this on a full-time basis.

"She invited me to dinner after a particularly long shift. I don't think either of us had slept for over twenty hours. She lives on the outskirts of the city, in an area called Parklands, where many of the Asians (as the Indians are called here) live. While her cook made us something to eat, we sat on her verandah listening to the occasional throaty roars of the lions in the wild. 'How do you do this?' I asked.

45

She has those deep brown, watery eyes that seem to overflow with wisdom and eternal patience, and when she talks she is almost mystically soft-spoken. 'Mead, we simply do what we must, what we can. There is no mystery.' I remain baffled."

Elizabeth tried to imagine, really imagine, what Mead was experiencing. She could sense that something was happening to her daughter, could almost hear interior shifts in between the words she silently read. She looked up and out of her window. The park was a midnight maze of shadows. The thinning snow had a blue cast. She sighed.

She worried for Mead. Beneath her tough exterior Elizabeth knew that she felt her work. Walter, for entirely different reasons, had adamantly opposed her going to Africa. Elizabeth suspected that his adamancy was due more to the fact that she had announced her decision rather than sought his counsel in making it. There had been several heated discussions at the beach house. "Let someone else do the dirty, tedious field work, Mead. You'll be much more valuable using your mind." He had wanted her to pursue an association with the Pasteur Institute. But Mead had been insistent, immediately rejecting his notions. "For God's sake, Daddy, why do I want to further bury myself in all those antiseptic labs?" Her brother Avery sniped, "Are we having a premature mid-life crisis or is this simply a death wish?" Walter had given him a disapproving look. "Mead, I just want you to be careful with your career. You need to be very careful."

Elizabeth recalled her own fear as she watched Mead rise off the white wicker love seat and, trembling with barely contained fury and distinct dislike, stand threateningly close to Walter. She gathered herself to full height, looked down on him and replied, her voice all ice, "First, as even the worst doctor knows, new strains that are not available to me in my research lab, are emerging in Africa. Secondly, unlike certain static fields of medicine, with which you have been more familiar," she paused deliberately, " the value of field work with a such a dynamic virus is key. Finally, *I'm* running my career. It's *my* work, *my* choices, *my* risks and, *my* rewards, should they occur." With that she turned and stepped off the porch, walking along the shore until she was a dot that Elizabeth could no longer distinguish. "I don't know why she has to play such a hero all the time," Avery said. Rand squinted through his glasses uncomfortably and disappeared into his robotics book. Luce quietly looked at her parents until Walter, visibly shaken, retreated to his bedroom.

Mead came back from her walk hours later in a conciliatory mood. She was able to hold her position but unable to hold a grudge, especially where

Walter was concerned. "Game of chess after dinner, Daddy?" An apology was never necessary. This was something she had learned from Walter, his behavior not his words. Once Walter saw that his cronies were impressed with Mead's career move, once he saw the stature accorded her position, he fell in line.

The memory of last summer still tired Elizabeth. She felt anew all the tension. And now Luce was in town. No call, no note. Elizabeth wasn't surprised, just caught off guard. Luce rarely contacted them anymore when she came into town for her shows. But this forthcoming opening, like the others, would indeed make for awkward social situations for the next month or two. Elizabeth went to the club chair, turned on the lamp and looked through the newspapers she had stacked on the ottoman. She rarely read the art section, usually just scanned it for the reassurance afforded when Luce wasn't mentioned. Now she opened it and thumbed her way through it. On the inside last page there was a two-column story on Luce. She heaved a sigh of relief when she saw that the painting they had photographed seemed to be a landscape. Thank God, she thought, no more embarrassing family portraits.

Luce's painting was a difficulty for Walter, for her. First, there was the betrayal and anger Walter felt when Luce left pre-med for art school. For five years their contact had been strained, infrequent. After much cajoling, Elizabeth managed to heal the wound of Walter's ego and they attended a small collectively organized exhibit that Luce was part of in Brooklyn. Is it possible, Elizabeth thought, was that almost twenty years ago? Luce, generally aloof, kept her distance that night as they walked through a convoluted run-down space largely filled with bad experimental art. When finally they came upon a cluster of three of Luce's paintings they were shocked in part because of Luce's forceful realistic style. As they stood before the works, as the reality of the content soaked in, their shock grew more profound.

The first, called *Conversation*, was a painting of Walter in his chair reading, oblivious to the presence of Elizabeth who, half-seated and leaning toward him, was entreating him for some form of acknowledgment. The second, *Marriage One*, showed Elizabeth and Walter standing at the farthest point of a long dim hallway. The third, *Family*, was a painting of Elizabeth in the center of the living room surrounded by Luce, Avery, Rand, and Mead as children, all pleading with her. In the distance Walter, his hand on the front door and back to them, was about to leave.

Elizabeth didn't know what she had expected to see in Luce's work. Her vague familiarity with painting had suggested perhaps large canvasses filled with abstract shapes and forms, although upon further reflection she did know that that seemed incompatible with Luce's personality. Maybe quiet landscapes, or, since she had been excellent at scientific illustration, perhaps paintings that found their roots in science: cells, amoebas, viruses.

It wasn't as though any of the scenes were objectionable. On the surface, they recounted ordinary events. But the atmosphere in which they were set, the expressions on the faces, were so piercingly sharp, so astutely, unforgivingly accurate. It had never occurred to her that Luce would so directly, so honestly paint the family, that their private lives would be her subject matter. As she stood before these paintings a sense of exposure overcame her, and turning slightly to steady herself on Walter's arm, she saw that he was having an equally violent reaction.

She felt as though someone had pulled her nighttime covers off and she had awoken to find an assembly of utter strangers gawking at her. Walter led her toward the door, next to which Luce stood placidly.

"This is not art," Walter spoke each word firmly, evenly, with ample spacing around them. "This is belligerent trespassing and juvenile exposé." He put his arm behind Elizabeth, and she could feel the restrained heat of his words propel her through the doorway. They walked down the small stoop and crossed the sidewalk.

"As surprising as this may seem to you," Luce's voice, gentle and, Elizabeth was fairly certain, without rancor, had followed them as they walked to the curb and hailed a taxi, "this is my life." As Walter was getting in, Luce reached her hand to block the closing door. Leaning into the cab she said, "It is not my intention to hurt anyone. But it is my life. Don't confuse that with betrayal." She stepped back and shut the cab door very softly.

Since then their contact was perfunctory at best. She and Walter had never discussed that evening. Elizabeth tried to understand but could never get beyond feeling like an unwilling model in Luce's presence.

Sipping the last of her tea Elizabeth guiltily wished that Luce could transfer her art business to San Francisco as well as her studio. It had been a secret relief to her when she had moved rather suddenly to San Francisco a few years ago. She was the source of too much conflict, too many hard feelings. Elizabeth loved Luce, had even visited her in San Francisco once. I love all my children equally, she heard herself saying, echoing through the tunnel of the years. But, she thought, some with more difficulty than others.

* * *

"Luce, you made it. Here we are at last." Jacob rose from the table and kissed

Luce on the cheek. "What will it be, Luce? Red? White?"

"You choose, Jacob. Everything ready?"

"As ready as it will ever be. Tina is planning another phone blitz to the press tomorrow – just a helpful reminder. But everything's been hung, rehung, and re-rehung. Oh, say, the catalog came in yesterday."

He mimed a long whistle, rolled his eyes and slowly waved his hand up and down in front of himself. "Very fine. No expense, believe me, was spared. It looks great."

Luce smiled. "Where's Ms. Right? Jenny? I thought I was going to meet her."

"She's got a business function. Cocktail party or something. She'll be along in a while."

"Good. I'm looking forward to meeting her."

"Luce," Jacob drew out the pronunciation of her name in a long, teasing way, "I have some good news." He raised his eyebrows and tilted his head in way that begged to be asked.

Luce took a sip of water, picked up the menu and said, "What's good here, anyway?"

"Luce!" This time he widened his eyes. "Don't do this to me."

"All right. If we must. What's your good news?"

He rested his arms on the table and slowly shook his head. "Have I ever mentioned to you what a pain in the ass you can be?"

She cocked her head, slowly scanned her eyes in the direction of the ceiling. "Ah, no, not this trip."

"You are. Gigantic. Why do I treat you so well?"

"Your commission?"

"Crass. A crass pain in the ass."

"Okay, okay. So what's the good news?"

Now it was Jacob's turn to play coy. Motioning to the menu, he indicated "Blackened East River bass is always good. Naturally blackened, as you no doubt know. Those oil spills are to *nouvelle cuisine* what Shake and Bake is to home cooking. Now that's a good thing about pollution you never hear about. Think what time it saves the chefs."

"Jacob, forgive me. *Mea culpa, mea culpa.* And tell me what the goddamn good news is."

"Oh, okay. Since you've asked. A major art museum located in the midwest may soon acquire a Luce Bennett." He paused. "Did I mention major?"

"Jacob." She grabbed his arm. "The Chicago Art Institute? Really?"

"Really. Unbelievable, huh?"

Luce sat back in her chair and let out a long breath. "Unbelievable? How about fabulous? Really? But what does this mean. You said *may* acquire. What does it mean?"

"I've spoken three times with the head curator. It's been to the acquisition board. And approved."

"So why the 'may'?"

"Well, there's a tiny infrastructure problem that may cost a little more than the facility maintenance budget can accommodate. If that's the case, the purchase may be delayed."

"What tiny infrastructure problem?"

"They need new plumbing."

Luce laughed. "Great. Toilets before art. There's probably more of a connection there than either of us cares to think about." She shook her head. "I'm definitely ready for that glass of wine." Jacob poured her a glass and settled back into his chair. "So, what are they buying, Jacob?"

"*Searching for Grace/Paris*. 'An eerie, lamentful commentary on the spiritual anguish of our times,' says the curator. Or something to that effect. It's ironic, I know. Every single one in that series sells. Is sold. Assuming they buy it. By the way, I doubled the price."

"You're kidding?"

Jacob shook his head. "They didn't bat an eye."

"God, it's weird how popular that series is."

"Whatever you think, the paintings do resonate for people. Haunting is actually a pretty apt word. The raw emotion combined with your technique, well, they are powerful."

"And you're really asking that price? Well, you'll be happy to know you'll soon have another to sell. *Searching for Grace/Brooklyn Bridge* has been added to the series. Once she dries."

Jacob chewed his lower lip. "I'm a little happy. A little sad. I know they're not easy to paint."

Luce shrugged her shoulders.

Jacob bent forward. "So, how have you been?"

"Not bad."

"And San Francisco, how's that working out?"

"Okay."

"Don't knock yourself out giving me too many details, Luce." Jacob smiled slyly.

Taking a deep breath Luce tried to harden herself. "I see you're bound and determined to have a heart-to-heart."

"Still have one, don't you?"

Luce winced then gave him a sharp look. "Sure feels like I do. Wish I didn't."

"Sorry, Luce. It's just that I worry about you. This is your home, this is where all your friends are, your support is. I hate thinking of you being so far away, so alone." Luce had no reply. "Look, I know it's hard, it must be hard. But you can't just step out of the stream of life."

"I'm painting, aren't I?"

"Yes. And well. And, as we both know, ironically your work has never received such positive critical attention."

"Is that an oxymoron – positive critical attention?"

"I mean, have you met anybody?"

"Jacob. Stop being such a Mama! I'm a grown woman. I can take care of myself. Besides, I don't want to meet anyone."

"Ah-ha, there, see, that's what worries me. You've shut down, cut yourself off. Luce . . . "

"Jacob, it's only been two years. Leave me alone."

"I understand." Luce shot him a look of skepticism. "I do. Well, I want to. Two years is a short time. On the other hand, life is short and two years is a long time."

"Thank you. That's very clear now."

"You know what I mean."

"And you, Jacob, know what I mean."

They had been friends for many years now, long enough to take liberties, occasionally to cross boundaries and certainly long enough to know when they were close to the brink and should back off.

"So, I guess that means that you don't want to hear about someone I recently met who I think you'd find interesting and attractive?"

Luce dropped her chin with disbelief onto her hand. She let her mouth fall slack and shook her head softly. "Good God, Jacob! What have we been talking about here? I don't want to meet anyone. Did I miss a major life lesson somewhere along the line? Is there an emotional actuarial chart that got handed out one day when I wasn't in school? After two years, you're definitely ready to move on. Am I really so obviously retarded? Look, Jacob, somewhere inside I know, I do, that you have my best interests at heart. But the reality is, I'm not ready. And anybody, no matter how interesting, attractive, bright, wonderful, etc., would only wilt in comparison. It wouldn't be fair. Can we talk about something else?"

Jacob sipped his wine then drummed his fingers on the white table cloth. "So how are you?" his voice softened. "I mean, really."

Luce looked at him, then looked around the restaurant. Why do friends

51

have to be so damned sincere and insinuating, she thought. She wished she were in San Francisco and longed for the undisturbed silence she had found there. Feeling the growing weight of his caring look, his expectation, she replied, "Honestly, I don't really know. I guess I'm pretty numb still. I'll be fine. I will. I guess I'm just slower than others."

Luce could see Jacob's frustration and offense. She had been dealing for two years now with people who wanted to sweep her into their arms, whisk her away from her pain, her depression. She had managed to avoid the embrace of most. Jacob was different, more persistent. And she cared more for him than others.

She knew he meant well, that he had no idea how fatiguing, deeply fatiguing it was for her to try to express herself. Now, watching him try to mask the entitlement he felt, she wished she could somehow find the words, the answer to satisfy him. But she respected him too much to feed him lies, which neither of them would tolerate anyway. So there they sat, sharing a wide open plain of love, separated by a deep, unnavigable chasm. She reached across the table and took his hands in hers.

"Thank you, Jacob. I know you care about me, want me to be happy. I'm just not. That's all. Not right now. And I can't shake it. Not yet."

"Luce, I wish I could do something."

"Not everything can be fixed."

"Should I be worried?" Both Luce and Jacob looked up at the source of that question, uttered in tones of warm, mock alarm.

"Jenny." With delight, Jacob sprang to his feet and kissed her sweetly. "You're early." Jenny turned toward Luce, grasping Luce's hand and enfolding it warmly in both of hers.

"I'm delighted to meet you. I've admired your work for a long time. Even before I met Jacob."

"Thank you. It's good to meet you, too."

As Jenny settled into her chair, Luce took her in. She was an attractive woman, late thirties with a thick mane of auburn hair that reached her shoulders. She had small but even features and a graceful demeanor. Luce liked her right away.

Over coffee, after much good-humored banter and exchange of the usual information, Jenny asked, "So what does the prodigal painter do with her time when she comes back to New York?"

"Not visit her prodigal family, I bet," Jacob intoned.

"Actually, I spent the day yesterday with Ruthie."

Jacob's face lit up. "How is Ruthie? Oh, Jenny, you wouldn't believe Ruthie. Truly an original."

52

"She'll be at the opening, Jacob, so you can renew your acquaintance."

"Who, if I might ask, is Ruthie?" Jenny looked from Luce to Jacob who seemed to be sharing a moment of covert discomfort. An awkward silence ensued. Jenny signaled the waiter for more coffee.

Luce and Jacob held each other's glance. They were at a moment, familiar, defining and yet, like everything else that used to be similar, painfully different. Looking into Jacob's eyes, Luce was sure he too was recalling the various times when the two of them, with Jacob's new girlfriend in tow, would reach a similar point in the conversation. On previous occasions Luce would impishly toy with disclosure while Jacob, all eyes on the third person, would wait expectantly for a reaction. If the dinner had not gone well, which is to say that the woman in question did not make the cut, the moment's importance would wane. If the woman had shown promise, Jacob would be on red alert awaiting a reaction. The unsuspecting woman had no idea how much that reaction would determine her future relationship with Jacob.

Now, habit, pattern and history hanging in the balance, Luce and Jacob continued to look at each other, each knowing, in a small, important way, that what was, was. Past tense. The defining moment had been redefined. Jenny, bewildered by the sadness which had suddenly engulfed them like a summer storm, pensively sipped her coffee. Luce broke the silence. "Ruthie's my mother-in-law, I guess you could say," she said, straightening her back and stretching her neck. "If you come to the opening you'll have a chance to meet her."

"I'm sure I'd like that." Jenny's response was soft, kind. She knew she was on delicate territory. Luce thought she saw her hesitate for a second. She continued. "I didn't know you were married, Luce."

Looking directly at Jacob, who returned the look with equal intensity, Luce said, "Was. I'm a widow. Have been for two years." She saw pain cloud his face and sorrow gather in the corner of his eyes. Is that what he feels, Luce wondered, or is he just mirroring my face?

"I'm so sorry. What did your husband die of?"

"Breast cancer." Luce turned to face Jenny. "Grace died of breast cancer."

Immediately Jenny reached for Luce's hand. "God, that's awful. How horrible for you." She started to say something else then decided against it.

Luce awkwardly retrieved her hand from Jenny. "Yeah, it's tough. Well, I think I'd best be going. Thanks for dinner, Jacob." Turning to Jenny, "It was good to meet you."

"Jacob speaks so often of you, Luce. I'm glad to finally meet you. I'll see you at the opening."

Luce just looked at her and shook her head.

"Hey, we'll see you back to your hotel." Jacob was on his feet and signaling the waiter for the check.

"Not necessary, dear heart. Really." She stood and they embraced, holding each other a little longer than usual. Standing on the tips of her toes she kissed his cheek, then turned to Jenny. "He worries too much."

"I know."

"Good night."

Jacob remained standing and watched expectantly as Luce turned and walked through the crowded room and out the front door. His hopes were realized when Luce looked back through the large pane glass window and half gestured a feeble wave in his direction. Almost collapsing into his chair, and staring at the now empty window, he said, "God, I do worry about her. I wish I could do something."

Jenny put her hand on his arm. "You love her. You're a good friend. Sometimes that's all you can do. And sometimes, with a person as private as I suspect Luce is, leaving her alone is the very best you can do. Cognac?" He sighed his consent.

In the street Luce felt a wave of nausea. She was caught in the grip of two forces. An overwhelming sense of claustrophobia overtook her. In an instant the space she occupied, the wide, bustling street, her very life seemed small and constricted. Simultaneously, the street, the world, the edges of her being seemed incredibly large, endless, porous. Rounding the corner, she stepped out of the blur of sidewalk traffic and slumped against a cold brick wall. Her throat tightened. Her body was covered with the sheen of cold sweat. She felt some nefarious, omnipresent g-forces pressing intensely on her. She wasn't sure if the forces she felt were about to compress her into a small piece of carbon that would be mindlessly kicked into the gutter or if she was about to be ripped asunder and scattered into the atmosphere. Leaning her head against the wall, Luce shut her eyes and tried to breathe.

PART TWO

Entering the lodge restaurant, Mead spotted Roz and Linda at a table, backs toward her and obviously enjoying Peter's company. Steeling herself, she joined them.

"Good morning, Sunshine." Peter was annoyingly cheerful.

"I see you've all met," Mead observed tersely.

"Indeed. Male intuition, I guess." He gestured around the empty restaurant. "I was able to find them right away." Roz and Linda laughed. "Beautiful day, huh?" Mead looked past him as she sat down.

"Mead, why didn't you tell us Peter was such a cowboy?" Roz was ebullient.

"Somehow I suspected you'd find out. The news of Peter riding herd on bacteria, viruses and parasites just can't be kept secret for long."

"We're on vacation. Let's not let shop talk hamper our fun and adventure." Peter fixed a cup of coffee, no sugar and a little milk, and set it triumphantly in front of her. "Still take your coffee this way I trust."

Mead stared blankly at the cup, then at Peter.

"Well, I've just been fascinated listening to his adventures in Venezuela, Bosnia, Africa. How many times have you been here?" Roz seemed to have completely forgotten her resentment for Peter's intrusion. Mead was not surprised. Linda gave Mead a knowing glance.

"Hmm, five or six. I've passed through Nairobi several times but this is my first stay in East Africa. Fortunate to have found such great company." He offered an expansive smile to all three women.

"And you've personally worked with Lassa, Marburg and Ebola?"

"Yeah, and a few other hemorrhagic viruses the CDC's still trying to identify."

"Doesn't it scare the bejesus out of you? It would me." Roz was rapt.

"First few times are the worst. I'll never forget my first field trip. It was to the Democratic Republic of the Congo. We'd heard about some mysterious hemorrhaging deaths up river country and had gone to investigate. Took a small plane for half a day. Later that night we boarded a boat and rode up river for almost three days. The first night I thought I was hallucinating. All the branches overhead seemed alive. And the logs along the banks, too. Everything was moving. I thought I was delirious. Next morning I realized that the trees were full of moving snakes and what I thought were logs were

55

crocodiles floating in the river.

"When we got to the village it was completely deserted except for one old woman. The guide asked her if there had been any deaths in the village. She took us to a large round mud hut. Inside, sitting upright, propped against the wall, eyes completely wide open, were fifteen corpses. She, or someone, had stuffed their noses and ears with cloth. It was so bizarre. Each one had a different pattern of cloth. It was like a room full of limp Raggedy Ann dolls. Everyone else had fled. That was a bear, trying to track them down." He paused to take a sip of his coffee.

"Of course, you're always scared. Be a fool if you weren't. Especially after the autopsies, and you see what a complete meltdown of every organ it is. These are lethal little buggers to be dealing with. When you've been exposed there's only a 50-50 chance you'll survive."

"Must make your parents wish you'd become a dentist," Roz said, looking at Peter as though she had been struck by gale force winds.

"Yeah, they get pretty worried," Peter said, paying close attention to Mead. "But, for me, I think life is a risk. I could just as easily get killed crossing a street or gunned down at my local ATM. All for a couple of twenties, right? No guarantees. Right, Mite?"

"Oh, but to go at the hands of one of those viruses. Gads – to crash and bleed out. Too violent and exotic for me." Mead watched Roz fall under his spell.

"I'd definitely prefer an exotic exit to a mundane one." Peter hailed a man who entered the restaurant. He turned in Mead's direction. "Hope you don't mind, Mite, I brought a friend along."

"The more the merrier," Roz almost chirped.

"Not at all, Peter," Mead replied coolly.

"This is Gil. Gil, this is Roz, Linda and Mead."

Hellos were exchanged. Gil, a wiry man with dark brown hair, dark hazel eyes behind glasses, an olive complexion, bowed slightly and, with genuine reticence, said, "Sorry to be intruding on your climb." He had the hallmark permanent stoop of very tall people. "I'm very glad to meet you, though," he said, looking directly at Mead. She suspiciously wondered what Peter had told Gil to provoke such a specific interest.

"Gil, what did I tell you, the blame is all mine. Truly. Sit," Peter happily commanded, kicking a chair in his direction.

"Let's stop with the blame already. Coffee?" Roz graciously asked, pouring Gil a cup of coffee.

"No thanks. I just came to tell you the outfitter's arrived."

"Terrific. Let's get started." Peter stood and rubbed his hands together

56

enthusiastically. "Everyone ready?"

"Absolutely," Roz said. "Let's get this show on the road."

"You all go ahead." Mead continued to sit. "I'll just finish my coffee."

Peter, one hand on the table and the other on the back of Mead's chair, bent and asked solicitously, "Can I get your gear from your hut for you?"

"I already did that, Peter. It's on the porch of the lodge."

"Well, I'll load it up for you then." Peter slowly raised himself to full height, smiling ingratiatingly at Mead.

"I'll keep you company, Mead. I could use another cup myself." Linda refilled Mead's cup and her own as Peter, Roz and Gil left. At the door Gil crouched under the door jamb, looked over his shoulder at them and smiled apologetically before exiting.

Mead sighed as Linda broke into a quiet round of laughter. "Unbelievable," Mead said, shaking her head.

"Who's the scarecrow?" Linda asked.

"Haven't a clue. Peter has a way of acquiring an entourage – effortlessly. I can't tell if yet another interloper is an improvement or a disaster."

"I must say, Roz is taking it all very well. I'm proud of her," Linda chuckled. "She's hiding her disappointment superbly."

"Yeah, she's bearing up admirably, all right."

"Whew, I see what you mean about Peter." Linda widened her eyes and exhaled a soft stream of admiration. "Quite a guy."

"As a doctor, I'm always cautious about a diagnosis. But I'm afraid charismatic is definitely the condition. Terminally charismatic."

"I'll say. I see what you're up against." She sipped her coffee thoughtfully. Leaning over the table to Mead she whispered, "Are you going to be okay?"

"Let's just say if I make it through the next week, I can make it through anything. Hemorrhagic fevers excepted. Thanks for asking. And you?"

"Oh, I'm so taken with Roz's new role as hostess, I wouldn't miss her performance for the world. I'd probably follow her up Annapurna at this rate." They exchanged amused grins. Taking a breath, Linda asked, "Ready?"

"As ready as I'll ever be. To the top it is."

They had gotten into a caravan of Land Rovers and driven through the game park for over an hour. As they drove over the dry, scrubby plains they had seen wildebeest calving, clusters of zebras dancing in the dust, elephants plodding sorrowfully along, a few eland and a golden jackal. Tucked along the lip of the large lake were spoonbills, avocets, flamingos, sacred ibis and white crowned plover.

Leaving the park behind, they had returned to the main road, the Great

North Road, which ran from Cape Town to Cairo. They passed Masai bombas, several of which had roadside stands where men and women in native dress hawked wood carvings, beads and mock swords. A handful of naked teenage boys, caked in white powder, waved to them. "What gives?" Roz had asked. "Ritual circumcision." Gil had responded, and Roz smiled lewdly while Linda winced. Skirting the town of Arusha they had continued on to the base of Mount Kilimanjaro. Shambas, small native farms growing coffee and bananas in the rich volcanic lower slopes, lined their initial approach. Then they drove over another dirt road that soon became a thin line connecting increasingly deep and frequent craters and which finally disappeared into the thick, uncut bush. Once in the forest zone the caravan had stopped at a trail head.

Now, at 6,700 feet, they gathered around Mary Silver, a tall, well-seasoned woman from Seattle.

"The key," the outfitter said, "is to move slowly." Surrounded by palms, sycamore figs and other trees draped with wispy lime-green Spanish moss, they listened to her no-nonsense instructions, punctuated by the calls of colobus and blue monkeys in the upper reaches of the forest roof.

"I've climbed this mountain dozens of times, and usually make the trek once a year. For sentimental reasons mostly. This was my first mountain. It's a piece of cake. Really. But whether it's Kilimanjaro or Everest, the key is pacing. It's deep sea diving – in reverse and to a greater degree. But I don't have to tell this crowd about the science of it. If you go slowly you'll give your body a chance to acclimatise to the changing oxygen levels. The slower you go, the more you acclimatise, the less severe your altitude sickness is likely to be. The fewer flowers you'll wind up feeding. Questions?"

She surveyed the small group slowly, her hard gaze assessing each person. Mead and Linda sat on the ground in front of her, listening attentively, eager first-row students. Peter leaned nonchalantly against a Land Rover, sure of his grade. Roz stood nearby, ready to cut class at a moment's notice. Gil leaned awkwardly against a tree and nervously fingered a blade of grass, the newcomer, shy and withdrawn.

"This is the highest mountain in the world that's not part of a range. 19,340 feet. There are three peaks to Kilimanjaro – Shira, Mawenzi and Kibo. Kibo's the tallest and its highest point is Uhuru. That's where we're headed. Now about 11,000 people attempt to climb Kilimanjaro every year. 90% of the folks take the Marangu, the main trail on the eastern side. It has all the charm of the Santa Monica freeway at rush hour. Not even worth your money. Most folks don't allow enough time. They think they'll breeze right on up and allow only a couple or three nights to make the trek. Fools. Only 10%

make it to the top. So, we're taking the slower western ascent – a lot prettier and a little gentler. You get to the top just the same.

"Now there are five zones to the mountain. We've already gone through the first, the lower slopes. We're in the forest zone. After this we'll hit the Heath and Moorland, which is Lower Alpine, then Highland, which is High Alpine, and then the Summit. Altogether we'll travel about twenty-five miles up via the Shira Plateau. Should take us four nights up and two nights down. That's gravity for you." She paused and smiled, amused by the earth's humor.

"Today we'll get a leisurely start and hike about 2,000 feet. Give everyone time to find their rhythm. We'll still be in the forest zone when we set up camp tonight. This is the best zone for seeing animals so no point in rushing. Mbiti here, our lead guide, said he saw a leopard two weeks ago when he went up with another group. Birds are great, too. Make sure your rain ponchos are near the top of your packs, though. We'll definitely be getting wet.

"Tomorrow we'll be covering the Lower Alpine. You'll see fields of heather, everlasting wild flowers and lots of open grasslands. If all goes well we'll make camp at about 12,200 feet. Probably the single best day of hiking. It's a breeze to climb over 4,000 feet.

"Then, it'll be time to get down to business. The next day we'll cover over 3000 feet and camp at 15,300. We'll be in the Higher Alpine, very thin vegetation, more like tundra. Only green you'll see will be moss and lichen. Views are nice, though. You might start getting oxygen hungry 'bout then.

"Fourth day up separates the women from the girls, the men from the boys. The upper Alpine gets pretty steep, lots of loose volcanic rock. And snow. Weather permitting, we'll have some mighty fine views. Otherwise get ready for a complete white out. Fog and clouds can swallow you up there. And in a snap. We'll park at around 18,500. Single hardest day on the road. Sad to say, most who turn tail do it within five to six hundred feet of the summit. Funny, huh?

"Last day up is technically a piece of cake and actually only takes the morning. We'll cover the final 800 feet and get to the top by noon. Won't require any fancy foot work but you'll find you'll probably be exhausted so just to keep moving will be a challenge."

Mead glanced at Linda, who had paled considerably. She leaned against her, and gave an encouraging smile. Mead could see fear glaze her eyes. "You'll be fine," she whispered.

Mary stretched her arms into the sky and yawned. "Then, it's all downhill. We'll take the Marangu back. After five days and four nights, I dare say, you'll have had your fill of Kili. Two nights is all it'll take to return to planet Earth." She chuckled again and shook her head. Gravity amused her greatly.

"There's not much you can do about the insomnia – goes with the territory, I'm afraid. At the end of each day we'll climb an extra few hundred feet, hang out for a while then back track to the camp. 'Climb high, sleep low,' some say. Might help. If any one brought diamox you can try that, too.

"As for the altitude sickness, well, it's a fickle thing. Never can tell who will or won't get it. I'd wager everyone here will get a touch of it. Just depends whether or not it will knock any of you completely off your pins. If you're going to get it, it'll kick in day after tomorrow when we break through 13,000 feet. Just pay attention to your body. Headaches are part and parcel. You might feel a mild agitation and a little giddy. Pulse might pick up. If it progresses you'll find yourself losing concentration. The danger is that you can lose your judgment. With some of the sheerer terrain we'll be covering higher up, that could be a problem. Real problem with it, though, is that it can come on quickly. One minute you're fine, then kabam! and you think you're going to die. Maybe even want to. Severe cases can cause blackouts, but we'll be traveling in tight formation and I'll be keeping a close eye.

"One of the things about Kilimanjaro is that the days are as hot as hot can be, the nights can be like the coldest winter you've ever known. A sudden blizzard can move in. Bam – white out. All while the folks on the plains are sweating. Just never know what's going to hit. Got to be prepared, got to keep an eye out," she tapped her right eye with a finger, "all the time."

Mead wrapped her arm around Linda, who was definitely sagging. She felt Peter's eyes upon her and gave a quick confirming look over her shoulder. He was poised, ready to catch her gaze and ricochet a huge smile in her direction. She had seen that smile before. It was the smile he used in group settings when he wanted politely to exclude the others and create a personal bridge just to her. She instantly read the "Isn't life great? Aren't we two going to have a terrific adventure?" message it telegraphed, and she tried to stay expressionless. Turning her head slightly, she saw Roz, keyed up with excitement, a bright-eyed horse at the gate, champing at the bit. Mead continued her pan to include Gil. Crouched on the forest floor, his spindly legs and thin arms formed all manner of fleshy angles which protruded sharply from his safari shorts and shirt. He swallowed a smile, then looked at the ground. Returning her gaze to Mary, Mead thought, God, what a crew. She gave Linda a squeeze, as much to bolster herself as Linda.

"Okay, a few rules of the road. Stay together. No individual side trips. I want to be able to see everyone at a single glance.

"We'll start each day's hike at dawn. The porters will wake you up an hour beforehand and feed you breakfast. You're going to need to eat about 4,000 calories a day. Drink lots of fluids. At all the breaks and along the way.

As often as you can. It helps. We'll stop frequently for breaks. The porters, of course, will scoot ahead and set up lunch as well as our night camp." Mead looked at the group of five African men who stood behind Mary. They were a scrappy assortment, each wearing a different version of Western apparel, which Mead suspected had been left behind by previous climbers. One man sported a worn pair of GAP khakis, fraying at the cuffs, holes in both knees with a sweatshirt that had a map of the Paris Metro.

"All you have to do is move your feet. Final rule – there's no pride in pushing yourself beyond your limits. And there's no dishonor in calling it quits. High altitudes aren't for everyone. I expect each one of you will wind up communing with nature at some juncture. The point is that at any point you can change your mind and turn down the mountain. In fact, it's a courtesy to the rest of us not to be held back. When you keep going up when your body screams 'down' – that's a problem. And believe me folks, it will only get worse. Level with yourself. Level with me. That's all I ask.

"Okay, if there aren't any questions, then let's hit it – slowly. As the natives say: *Pole Pole*."

* * *

Luce ducked into the Catholic church mid-block on 46th. She hadn't even noticed the name of it. When she opened the heavy wooden doors, the warm air, laden with the aroma of incense and burning candles, hit her face like a holy trade wind. She stood quietly just inside the entrance for a moment, letting her eyes adjust to the darkness, then taking in the long shadowy nave that led to a brightly lit altar. It was still decorated with red and white poinsettias, holly and wreaths of Christmas. Three other people occupied the cavernous church. She walked slowly mid-way down the aisle and took a seat on the hard wooden bench.

Luce had acquired this sudden and surprising habit of visiting churches in the last two years. Like many of her newfound habits, she didn't understand it and didn't have the energy to fight it or to think about it. Growing up in the spiritually antiseptic environment of her parents' atheism, she found she rather liked sitting in these religious structures. The smells, the quiet, the visuals all had a calming effect.

The builders of the first Gothic cathedrals were right, she thought. If I can't know God, then at least, through the contrivance of vaulted space, ascending line, color and smell, I can experience something like God.

The building she found herself in was pseudo-Gothic. The ceiling vaulted above her some sixty feet, and she could see the paint peeling. The spotlighted

61

stations of the cross, the blue votive candles shimmering in the distance at the Virgin's feet, the stain glass triptych above the altar, catching the remnant shafts of the winter afternoon – all of it, the iconography, the colors, the lights, the smells, all fed her in a way she did not understand.

She looked around and noticed a young black man standing by a crucifix. His head was bowed and he held the feet of the crucified Jesus. An old woman was kneeling and bent over a pew in front of her, with shoulders drooped in pain and longing. Farther to her right, a balding man sat erect and expressionless as tears streamed down his face. These people were simultaneously comrades and strangers to her. They were mysteries to her, the real mysteries of faith: people who silently and singularly brought the moments of their lives to these spaces, who whispered prayers under their breath to the unknown, who genuflected before the unseen, then left, in as much pain and sorrow as before, into the city street. She liked mingling with this small community and felt oddly connected.

Her own parents had exposed their children to myriad religions and various belief systems. Each holiday was a short academic course, one year in Christianity, one year in Buddhism, one in Hinduism, and on and on. But, as with any course taught by unenthusiastic skeptics, it all seemed wearisome and vapid, constructed to ultimately expose the bare cupboard.

Luce leaned her head back and caught a magnificent blue line in the stain glass rosetta above, a simple blue line that shot through the panes of ochre-red and burst through with unrestrained vibrancy. Color, Luce thought, that's what touches my spirit. It was why she so liked the winter season, when colors stood out against the monochromatic gray days and dark nights.

Now she studied that frame of blue stained glass, almost cobalt, as a sliver of waning light shivered behind it. The blue was so familiar to her. She continued to gaze at it, then closed her eyes. Slowly, slowly the canvas began to emerge before her mental eye.

It was a blue canvas, cobalt blue. Dark around the edges. At the center, in a protective bubble, was the small village from the past, a yellow crescent moon burning brightly above. A happy village, destined always to be brilliant, always to be a memory. Painfully untouchable in the distance. Floating in space in the upper right-hand corner were the lovers, wrapped in the leaves of the past, ever green. In the lower right-hand corner the beloved, wiping a tear from her cheek, sad to be parted, sad to be departed. And the painter, in the lower left-hand corner, with a head turned completely upside down by grief, held brushes but could not paint.

Luce had seen that canvas at the Georges Pompidou Center when she last went to Paris. "Everything turns black in my eyes," wrote Chagall on the day his beloved Bella, wife of thirty years, died. He laid down his brushes and paint. For almost a year he too was dead, unable to paint. *Around Her* was one of the first works Chagall had completed when he surfaced from his grief.

Now, looking at the cobalt blue glass, Luce felt the sadness and longing press heavier upon her spirit. Her past, like the memory of the village in *Around Her*, burned brightly, out of reach. Emptiness, complete and utter emptiness, was all she could touch.

* * *

Beneath the dense canopy of trees, Mead occasionally caught sight of a small patch of sky. It was such a light blue it was almost white. The monkeys and birds offered a constant antiphon above. Mary had said this was the best trail for wildlife, and already they had caught a momentary glimpse of an olive baboon as well as several darting bushbucks. Surveying the surrounding forest, Mead was sure that every shade of green in the world must be within her view.

The lower altitudes still afforded everyone the chance for conversation, and they had randomly fallen into groups of two or three over the course of the day. Mead had managed not to be alone with Peter but now, with Gil and Roz ahead of her and Linda and Mary behind, Peter seized the moment and fell into step with her. His excitement was palpable.

"So, Mite, how do you like Nairobi and the great Continent?"

"I like it. To my own surprise, I like it." Keeping her eyes on the trail that ran through the abundant thicket, she could feel Peter's searching eyes hot upon her cheek.

"Doesn't surprise me." He was buoyant, at once confident and smug.

"No?"

"No, I suspected a cowgirl lurked beneath that starched white lab coat of yours. I'm glad you made the move. It's good for you to get out of the lab. Good professionally, too. Field work is always a plus on the vitae." His enthusiasm for her career outweighed his condescension, and she decided to ignore the latter.

"You know, Peter, I have to agree with you."

"Hey, why the surprised tone of voice? If I remember correctly, we agreed on most things." Mead kept silent. "With one exception." His tone was intentionally confessional, penitent. Mead quietly fought the urge to look him in the eyes. "How's the hospital?" he asked.

"Good. There are some top-notch permanent staff. Incredibly dedicated, as you can imagine. A few interesting doctors on rotation from France and Belgium. The hospital itself is pretty rudimentary. But not as bad as I'd expected."

"And the patients?" He dashed ahead a few feet to hold a drooping branch off the trail for her.

"Thanks. Overwhelming. In number and intensity. Not enough, not enough of anything for anyone."

"It's an eye-opening experience to leave the hallowed halls of western medicine, eh?"

"I'll say. By the time most of them reach the hospital, they're too far gone. And less than nothing can be done for them."

"Makes you long for a simple case of Girardia."

"The other day I had two German tourists in. They'd gotten friendly with some citizens on the city bus and had eaten some cookies they'd been offered. And some juice."

"KO-ed them, I bet. Guess they didn't bother to read any of the travel advisories before they left the fatherland."

"When they came to, at the end of the line, everything was gone – wallets, jewelry, cameras."

"And new-found friends."

"But at least I was able to treat them, be annoyed at their naiveté¢ and point them in the direction of the German embassy. Where do I point the Africans?" She turned to look at him with a glance that simultaneously revealed an imploring question and an overwhelming frustration. Fearing she had shown too much in her otherwise controlled countenance, she averted her gaze. But she could tell by the empathy his tone assumed that he had seen. She wondered if it was the emotional revelation or just that he had seen the chink in her armor that spurred him into a supportive, helpful tone.

"The numbers are staggering, aren't they?" His spoke with care. "I downloaded a Sub-Saharan HealthNet report before I left Boston two days ago. Cholera, dengue, malaria, meningitis. In Nigeria case fatality rates for meningitis are as high as 34% – mostly kids. The number of cases reported in the first two months of this year alone are greater than all of the annual figures for previous years. One million people need to be vaccinated against Yellow Fever in Liberia, which is in utter chaos. One million. And with eighteen million – and counting – HIV/AIDS infections making so many immunodepressed, well, just throw in TB and . . . "

"We're losing the war."

"Mead, you didn't have to leave Chicago to learn that."

"No. But seeing it is entirely different, Peter."

"Yeah." His voice drifted to a lower register of compassion. "I know what you mean." Sensing her gloom, he fell into a silence. Finally he said, with an intimacy that she found both aggravatingly presumptuous and sweetly sentimental, "Funny, huh, I have to hike Kilimanjaro to have a conversation with you?"

"I return your e-mail. And your phone calls." Mead cracked, wanting firmer emotional terrain beneath her.

"Whoa, a little defensive? Yeah, you do. But we still haven't talked, really talked, in months." He stopped and turned his body to face her, blocking the trail.

"Peter, there's nothing to say." Mead cast a downward glance.

Bending over so that he was face-to-face with her he said in tones she thought were skillfully tinted with tenderness and remorse, "I think there is. It's really good to see you, Mead." Then, slowly taking her in from head to toe, he shifted to an entirely different level. "You look great." His fingers softly traveled the plane of her cheek, the rise of her lips.

"If you don't mind." Stepping back, she gestured ahead to where the others were stopping for a break.

"Mead, I miss you. Do you know that? Do you have any idea how much I miss you?"

"I'd rather not have a heart-to-heart, Peter," she said resolutely, trying to brush by him. "Not here. Not now."

Peter grabbed her arm gently and looked chagrined. "You don't believe me, do you? I can see it in your eyes."

He sighed and ran his hand through his hair. Relenting sweetly he said, "You're right, of course. This is not the time." He gave her another full body glance. "Later. We'll talk later."

Releasing her arm, he walked into the group of resting trekkers and asked gregariously, "How's everybody doing?" As Mead watched Peter attend to everyone, she felt her sphere deflate like a balloon, her pulse slacken from a gallop, as a poignant relief engulfed her. Damn it, she thought, trying to brush the heat from her cheeks, this is going to be harder than I thought. And worse than I feared.

* * *

"Taxi." A cab slowed to the corner of 6th Ave and First. Jacob watched as two skinheads jumped into the cab he had flagged. Two empty cabs flew by, ignoring his frantic wave. As his gloved hand fell in defeat, he looked feebly at Luce who stood on the corner swallowing a smirk. "I must have done something wrong last incarnation."

"More likely our waiter put out an APB that you're a lousy tipper with attitude."

"For God's sake, Luce," Jacob protested, "all I did was ask them to change that damned CD."

"Jacob, what you said, as I specifically recall, was 'Can't you play something besides the *New Delhi Fly Swarm Song?*' A little offensive, dear, even for a culture that's had that song on their top forty for a couple of aeons."

"Every time I eat at that Indian restaurant, it's the same damned song. I feel like I need to swat my face all the time."

"Plus you left a measly tip."

"Did not." He cringed at the impossibility of such an act.

"Did. The point is, your name and face will live in infamy in this neighborhood. We'll never get a cab so let's just walk."

Luce slipped her arm through his, hoping to abate his sulking. They walked along the crowded street toward Broadway and back to the gallery where Jacob had a hectic afternoon. It was a clear, crisp day. She was happy to be in Jacob's company, surrounded by the city street on a busy, bright afternoon.

Luce started to hum the tune that had driven Jacob crazy in the Indian restaurant. He put a gloved hand over her mouth and grimaced broadly. "Please. Torture me if you must, but just don't sing." Smiling, Luce mock punched him in the arm then tightened her hold.

"I may have found the perfect buyer for your *#19/Autumn.*" At the corner of 2nd, Jacob maneuvered skillfully to avoid stepping into a black puddle of melted snow with his Kenneth Cole loafers.

"Really?"

"Yes, through our Rome dealer. Meets the criteria anyway – i.e., private collection, out of the country."

"Good. That sure has taken a while."

"Three years. Brrr. God, it's cold." He peered longingly into the street for an empty cab. "I still think you're overly cautious about that series."

"Perhaps, but I feel better knowing the three paintings are out of the U.S. Better to be safe."

"Think you'll finish off that series soon?"

"I don't know. You know how I feel about it . . . "

"Passionately ambivalent?"

Luce smiled. "True, I am oddly attached. After I paint the *#19/Winter* the cycle will be complete. I'm not sure I'm ready for that. Besides, I'm not sure it's *Winter* yet for *#19*."

"You know, Luce, that's about the most optimistic thing I've heard you say in months."

"Oh, stop it, Jacob. You've really developed a flair for the dramatic."

"How come you never call any of your old friends when you come to town? Chris called me yesterday saying you had promised to call. And hadn't."

Luce tried to brush off the accusation. "Too busy. I will. Soon." Out of the corner of her eye she saw his doubting expression and steeled herself for another barrage. But he changed his tack.

"I wish you would move back."

"Jacob, please don't get started on that again. And don't be insulted, but there's nothing for me here."

"That's crazy, Luce. Everything is here, your whole life, all your friends, your profession, me."

"San Francisco's beginning to grow on me."

"Yes, I can tell you love it there. That's probably why in the past two years you've spent eight months in Europe, six months in Mexico, one summer in Maine. Let's see, with a week here and there, you've probably spent another month or two in New York. That would make about six months you've spent in San Francisco. Maybe."

"It takes a while to adjust."

"Look, Luce, just because you and Grace were planning on moving there doesn't mean you have to live there. It's crazy."

"You're repeating yourself, Jacob. Maybe you should have that checked next physical. You know, I like Jenny."

"Don't change the subject. She likes you, too. You know no one there. How can you stand that?"

"She seems solid. Mature but not jaded."

"She is. It must be so lonely out there. It's not healthy for you to be so alone."

"After the lunch you just ate, you're telling me what healthy is? Jenny seems to genuinely care for you. That's good."

"I think she does. Just because Grace is dead doesn't mean you have to bury yourself in some geographical crypt."

Luce paused their walking long enough to glower darkly at him then continued. "She has beautiful skin, so creamy. And that auburn hair is luscious."

"She's gorgeous. Maybe you should paint her – your first portrait when you return to New York?"

Luce, slyly casting him a sideways glance, said "I'm still in my landscape period – window on the soul kind of thing. And with you doubling the prices, I have no motivation to try portraits again."

"I miss you, Luce."

"Ditto. The two of you make a great looking couple."

"I'd like to marry her. I think. If she'll have me. I think. The three of us could go to movies, play Canasta . . . "

"You hate Canasta."

" . . . take that house on the island together . . . "

"The one you swore you'd never go back to after that $400 plumbing bill?"

" . . . gossip viciously about our enemies and acquaintances."

"Sounds fun. I'm sure Jenny would love having a third wheel around."

"Grace never minded having me around. Did she?"

"No. But that was different."

Jacob stopped up short and indignantly asked, "Why?"

"Because it was." Luce continued walking, tugging him along.

"Excuse me, Luce, but that's bull."

"So have you introduced her to your parents?"

Jacob took a few giant steps to get in front of her then grabbed her by the shoulders. "I'd like to shake the hell out of you. Maybe I should have you exorcised."

Luce looked at him, then out across the traffic, dropping her head onto his left arm. "I don't want to be exorcised, Jacob. Grace was the best thing that ever happened to me. I don't want less of her, I want more of her."

With his index finger under her chin, Jacob gently turned her head to face him. "Not possible, sweetheart. That's not possible, no matter where you live. No matter where you go. That's just not going to happen. You need to get on with it."

A tear slowly rolled down her cheek. "Don't want to."

Jacob traced the tear dry with his finger. "I know." He pulled her into the circle of his arms. "But you have to." He rested his cheek against her head. "You really have to."

Around them pulsed the city – vibrant and oblivious.

* * *

Mead had gone straight to her tent after dinner, feigning fatigue, and spent most of the night listening to the sounds of the forest and remembering her years with Peter. She forced herself to counter each happy memory with the memory of that morning, just weeks before their wedding, when he interrupted her on morning rounds and took her into an empty supply closet. There, shaky and sweating, he told her about the women. At first she thought it was a joke but realized it was true when she smelled his fear. She forced herself to remember, as she found out later, that he had had his crisis of conscience because he had gotten involved with a female colleague, a mutual acquaintance. Melanie had wanted more than just a roll in the hay and was willing to go to considerable lengths to turn events to her favor, to get Mead out of the picture. Peter knew he'd have at least a shot, small though it was, if he told Mead directly. She had never seen him so unhinged, so desperate. He had bruised her forearm, so tightly had he tried to hold her in place. "Get out of here, Peter," she had said in a tone that was all knives, razors and broken glass. "Get the fuck out of here *now*."

A cacophony of birds woke her from a brief, angry sleep. Damn, she said to herself, he's charmed himself right back into my life. And I let him. Am I so unhappy, so hopeless, that I would actually consider getting involved with him again? Disgusted with herself, she pulled on her sweatshirt and leapt out of the tent.

A mist was lifting. Shafts of sun filtered through, etched with the flight of iridescent blue dragonflies. The morning smelled rich and promising. Heartened, she headed toward the mess tent where she found only Peter and Gil. She tried to keep Peter at bay by engaging Gil. When he left, she took her tea back to her tent. "Stay a moment," Peter had pleaded. "No, got to get myself together." His expression was wistful. Christ, she thought, jamming her gear back into her pack, I'm almost imprisoned. She was relieved when she heard Mary's call to assemble.

Now, after four hours of rigorous hiking, she felt better. They were ascending through the lower Alpine zone, what Mary had termed the heath area. Clumps of giant heather, some reaching thirty feet in height, grew in the grasslands. Protea, with their durable, pre-historic beauty, and fiery red-hot pokers abounded. Oversized lobelia, odd plants with long spidery hair that looked as if they had been hijacked from the set of *Fantasia*, marched across the landscape like botanical Sufis. It was a wide open meadow, and the blistering sun sparkled in the tussocks of grass. Below, Mead could see the flat, golden plains of Kenya and Tanzania, dotted with herds that she was unable to identify, even with her binoculars. An occasional black-and-white kite swooped soundlessly overhead. Gil was hiking just a few paces behind her.

"So, how do you know Peter?" she asked.

"I'm a photographer. Worked with him on one of his field trips in Nigeria a few years back."

"A medical photographer?"

"Oh no. No. I'm really just an amateur. I manage my mother's land in northwest Kenya. But I offer my services as a photographer, mostly for wildlife, when there's a need. It was just a fluke that I hooked up with Peter. A friend of a friend type of thing."

She noticed he spoke with an accent she couldn't quite peg. His diction was quite precise and his cadence had a lilt. It wasn't Kenyan. "Wildlife, huh? Sounds interesting. Safaris? That kind of thing?"

Something flashed across his face but he quickly resumed a polite expression. "No. I work mostly with environmentalists – you know, the freelancer for *National Geographic* who's tracking the further demise of rhinos or the growth of poaching, the academic who's gotten a grant to study the effect of war on animals."

"Oh, less interesting then, more depressing."

"Quite. I've just finished a project dealing with the impact of the Western medical research industry on African monkey populations. Heinous really. Devastating results, you know."

Mead looked at him askance to confirm she hadn't misunderstood his message. His expression in profile was polite but resolute. They hiked in silence for some time. In his slow loping gait Mead thought he was walking uncomfortably close to her. There was something in his silence she found disconcerting and she sensed he wanted to say something. They both began to speak at the same time, then laughed.

"Please," he said softly. "You first."

"I was going to ask about northwest Kenya and your mother's land."

"It's beautiful country, out along the Great Rift. Marvelous sense of space. Wonderful outlooks. Gorgeous. I consider myself very lucky to have grown up there."

"Do you live there now?"

"Part of the time. About fifteen years ago my mother set up a foundation for wildlife and turned our land into a preserve. We have a lot of species, but the most endangered are the elephants and rhinos. I help manage the preserve. And I train the locals on how to combat poachers. But we also have a house outside of Nairobi where we work mostly on the foundation. These days I spend about half my time in each locale. The rift valley is incredible, though. You should definitely see that region of Kenya before you leave."

"Yes, I'm sure I'd like to if I can find the time." Again they lapsed into silence, then Mead, remembering that he had had a question minutes earlier said, "What were you going to ask?"

He hesitated, looked at her intently then paused again. "I wasn't going

70

to ask anything really. I was just going to say how much I was looking forward to meeting you."

"Why?" she bluntly quizzed, wondering if this was turning into a pickup.

"Well, when I first met Peter and found out that he knew you, I was intrigued. Then when he called and asked if I could meet him in Nairobi and fly down here to join you, I jumped at the chance."

Mead had stopped dead in her tracks some yards back. Now Gil turned to face her. "Have I said something wrong?"

"I'm a little confused here, Gil. Why would you want to meet me? Unless you happened to catch my important, but nonetheless turgid, article in the *Journal of the National Institute of Allergy and Infectious Diseases*, I'm really not much of a celebrity."

A look of complete embarrassment enveloped him. She suspected that had he not already been red from the hike, his long, thoughtful face would have turned beet red. "Help me out a bit, Gil."

"You see, I've never done this before. I'm making a mess of it, aren't I? It's just that I am, well, my mother, too," he pushed his glasses up the bridge of his prominent nose, "we're such enormous admirers of your sister Luce that, well, I was really anxious to meet you."

Mead felt as though the air had been knocked out of her. She put her hands on her hips, looked down and kicked at the trail.

"Have I insulted you?" Gil asked, plainly distressed.

She twisted her head in his direction then grimaced. "No. I don't know, maybe you have. Not many in my circle even know of my sister. I guess I'm a little surprised. Didn't expect to be hiking Kilimanjaro with an autograph hound." He visibly retracted. She shook her head. "Sorry, that was a little harsh."

From behind she heard Mary yell, "We're on your tail. Pick it up."

When Mary and Linda were abreast of them Mead motioned them ahead. "We'll be caboose. Go on."

Mary narrowed her eyes and astutely appraised the scene. "Everything okay here?"

"Fine, just catching my breath. We'll be right behind you."

"Awfully sorry, Mead," Gil murmured, "Didn't mean to say the wrong thing. Certainly didn't mean to embarrass you."

"I'm not embarrassed," she lied, angry that her reaction was so transparent. Then, trying to strike a blasé tone, she began, "I hate to disappoint you, Gil, but I don't really know much about art, especially Luce's." He shot her a look of consternation. "I guess that sounds strange but, well, all of my family is in some branch of science, except for Luce. And science dominates." Gil continued to look perplexed. "The truth is that we don't really follow her career much."

He was utterly confused. "Are you estranged? I mean, I know this is none of my business but . . . what exactly are you saying? You don't talk with her?"

"No. We all talk. Well, she's pretty quiet so . . . But, mostly only at family gatherings that my mother foists upon us resentful siblings once or twice a year."

"That's it?" His eyes widened with bafflement.

"Yes, that's it." Mead defensively continued, "None of us are really that close. It's just that, except for Luce, we're all in some field of the sciences. We have something in common. Look, I don't even know why I'm telling you. This is a family matter. You know, private."

"Oh, right. I understand. It's just that," he persisted, "well, I guess I don't understand. It's not just that she's such a wonderful painter, it's more that I come from such a close family. I can't imagine, for instance, not knowing about my sister Sonia's life."

"I didn't say I don't know anything about her life. I thought we were talking about her work."

"Oh, then you do know something about her life?"

"Well, she's ten years older than I am. I was still a kid when she went off to college," Mead said begrudgingly.

Sensing her extreme discomfort and the thin ice beneath them, Gil said, "Say, I'm awfully sorry I brought this discussion up. I assumed . . . I certainly didn't mean to pry. It's just that, as I said, we love her work."

They walked on a bit. Mead, sensing the ball was in her court and anxious to show that she was unperturbed, inquired, "So, you know Luce's work pretty well then?"

"Yes, in fact, my mother owns several pieces. She keeps them at our Nairobi house. Perhaps you'd like to see them sometime."

"Perhaps." After a long pause Mead asked, "Why exactly do you like them?"

"Well, your sister's style is very strong, very representational yet very personal. It's all subjective, a matter of personal taste of course, but so much art is abstract or expressionistic. While I like some of that style, I think there's an anonymity in it all. Many painters hide behind their work, preferring to have the viewer tell them what is there, what they see. Your sister is so present, so clear in what she says."

"Sounds like my parents' worst fears come true." She offered a paltry grin and a soft sigh.

"Her portraits are honest. Nothing is compromised. I especially like . . ." His words fell off a sudden cliff.

Mead cocked her head, knowing that something was being withheld. "What were you going to say, Gil?"

"Just that I like her artistic courage," he fumbled.

"Finish what you were really going to say. Please." She knew she was demanding, not requesting.

"There's one in particular of you that I especially like." His voice tapered off apologetically.

Mead felt as though she had been slammed against a wall. Here, thousands of miles from home, on the slope of a goddamn mountain, she was known by a total stranger. What other deeply personal details of her life would she find captured in Luce's oils, hanging in a stranger's living room or office or foyer? The notion made her distinctly uncomfortable, as though her life was a stained slide beneath someone else's microscope. Gil saw the fury gather in her eyes. He drew a long breath then, intentionally changing gears, asked, "How long will you be in Kenya?"

"The exchange I'm on is for three months. Two more to go," she stammered, clearly elsewhere.

He waited, giving her time. "Peter says you live in Chicago. This must be a bit of change for you."

"Yes, it is," she said, distracted.

"Kenya is a fascinating country." He paused, then continued, "I was born here. The first in my family to be born in Africa." He glanced to see if she was paying attention. "My mother was pregnant with me when she and my father moved here from Italy."

She turned to look at him then slowly asked, "Why did they do that?"

"Growing up in Italy, Africa seemed so extremely different to them, especially my mother. Exotic. Frightening. Fascinating. I think that's what attracted them. And they both had enough sense of adventure to find how exactly how different. My mother knew from the time she was a school girl in Florence that she would ultimately live here. My father was interested. And willing. But it was my mother's passion that pushed them. As a school child she'd walk through the streets of Florence, surrounded by the art and architecture of Michaelangelo and Giotto, Ghilberti, my namesake, and Brunelleshi, fantasizing mud huts in Africa."

"Is your father still happy he made the move?"

"My father's dead. Unfortunately, he died before I was born. A few months after my parents had arrived here."

Mead shaped her brow with sympathy. "Too bad."

"It was too bad. You see," he disclosed, "he was killed by elephants."

"Really?" Mead exclaimed incredulously, then searched for a more appropriate reaction. "How awful."

"Yes, it was awful. Quite shocking, really. He'd been hunting and had just shot and killed another elephant. The two surviving elephants that were traveling with the one my father shot turned and stampeded him."

"My God, I'm sorry, Gil, but that just seems so unimaginable." She looked at him now with fresh eyes. He was obviously uncomfortable but oddly determined. What an amazing childhood he must have had, she thought, while visions of her urban upbringing flashed in her mind.

"Yes. It is. When my parents first moved here wild game safaris of the killing variety were still very much in vogue. It's only been in the last twenty years, fairly recent in the scheme of things, that we've started to develop a different consciousness about the wildlife. Even my mother, who never killed an animal or much cared for killing, didn't really think of it as immoral at the time. Although she vowed then that there would be no more hunting."

"It must have been awfully tough on her."

"It was. Her friends tell me that she went into a severe period of mourning. Except for my older sister, she would see no one except the workers. But she's an amazing woman. Incredibly strong. She's told me she never once thought of leaving. And I know that's true. I try to imagine what it must have been like for her, all alone with a young daughter and me on the way, her husband killed by the very creatures she had dreamed of all her life. But, to survive here, indeed to thrive here, you must be strong."

During Gil's recounting they had both stopped hiking and now an awkward moment ensued as they continued to look at each other after the words had stopped. Mead suspected that Gil had been disclosing details of his life to make her feel more comfortable, less exposed. She saw in his face a genuine love for his mother, for his country. There's something else, Mead thought. Kindness. Yes, I'd call that kindness. "Your mother must love it here."

"Oh, yes, she definitely does. To stay here you have to. But then again, there's much to love."

From above fell Mary's shouts, "You're falling behind back there. Pick it up."

* * *

It was all as she had remembered, the neat row of well-heeled buildings on a quiet residential block. The one she now watched so intently was truly a handsome building – a blue gray Georgian structure, three stories with black trim. A black cloth awning covered the landing at the top of three marble stairs that led to the front gate. The gate itself was a tasteful piece of metalwork with a slight Japanese flair, finely done so that security and art melded in an aesthetically pleasing, unobtrusive way. The door behind the gate was largely beveled glass with black lacquer trim and an elegant brass handle. The beveled glass offered a view into the lobby, which even from a distance had an aura of assured and discrete warmth. A fine red Persian rug lay on well polished white tiles. A palm, potted in a large porcelain blue-and-white Ginger Jar, stood against an oyster wall. A staircase with a plush oriental runner could partially be seen. The thick banister in oyster enamel vanished to the second floor.

Outside the gate hung a brass plaque with the street number #19. Beneath that were three buzzers. The face of the building was subdued but carefully attended to. Each of the three floors had two large windows facing the street. On the third floor a set of plantation shutters, slats open and the shutters slightly ajar, could be seen. At the base of the windows on the third floor were planter boxes, now empty.

It was, Luce thought, just as she had observed over the past ten years. She found that oddly comforting. If, as she now did with her two hands, one blocked out the hideous and cold modern atrocity to the right and cropped the skyscrapers that sprouted like unruly weeds from the roof, it was a block that had a sense of timelessness – parked cars and traffic excepted. A Japanese maple grew on the sidewalk, protectively fenced by iron work from the same hand as the gate. Dusted now with thin lines of snow; Luce had seen it in all its seasons.

The small bistro in which she sat, one table removed from the window, was across the street and one building down from #19. Luce, keeping her gaze fixed on the building as she ordered another glass of wine, sketched the scene on a cocktail napkin with a black felt pen. The napkin had tears where the fine point of the pen had ripped it and dark blots where the ink had gathered in uneven circles.

Halfway through Luce's second glass of wine, she saw a taxi slow before #19. A tall man leaned forward and paid the driver. Getting out he stood in the street a moment, looking to the top floor. From the back, wearing a black cashmere coat, he seemed a well-built man of forty. His posture spoke of determination, solid and strong. He tipped the brim of his black Fedora ever so slightly in an upward direction and jauntily climbed the front steps and rang one of the buzzers. Eagerly opening the front gate and then the glass door, Luce's father crossed the lobby and ascended the stairs two at a time, disappearing off the canvas of her view.

Shoving the napkin she had sketched on deep into her coat pocket, Luce paid her bill and left. At the door she turned down the block, away from #19 and walked to the corner. Hailing a cab, she tossed the wadded cocktail napkin into a trash can on the curb before sliding into the back seat.

* * *

Mead stood on the edge of the mountain at 12,000 feet, clicked a final shot, then let her camera drop on its strap around her neck. Cherishing her limited solitude, she took one last glance, then headed back to the mess tent. From a few paces away she caught bits and pieces of the conversation. The topic was AIDS.

She entered the tent and took a seat next to Linda. Peter gave her a look of studied concern.

"So what's the history on it?" Gil asked Peter, pouring himself a cup of coffee and offering Roz a refill. "Might as well," she grumbled, "since sleep is impossible anyway." They were sitting around the table, and the dinner plates had been cleared away. It was their second night.

"Mead, I believe this is your specialty," Peter proudly deferred. Roz's face fell in disappointment.

Mead reluctantly began. "There are several versions, indicative of an altogether different problem. One takes place in Lukunya, a village on the Ugandan-Tanzanian border. 1983. It seems a trader from Uganda had come through the village selling cloth for kangas. There was a pattern, Juliana – which is what the disease was called for a while – the village women found particularly attractive. Several, having no money, traded sex for cloth.

"In a few months one of the young girls got sick – no appetite, vomiting, severe diarrhea. She wasted away, grew so weak she had to be carried around like a baby. Before she died, shortly thereafter, several other women who had traded sex came down with the same symptoms.

"Because of the earlier wars, in 1978 and 1979, there was bad blood between the Tanzanians and Ugandans. The villagers were sure that the Ugandan trader had been a witch, sending a curse. When the local shamans couldn't heal any of them, people were sure that it was retribution for the women having consorted with the enemy."

"I'm afraid it's not unusual for tribal people to see sickness as punishment." Gil seemed apologetic.

"Don't limit yourself to the tribal people. It's just typical behavior." Peter piped in. "Do you know that in the fifteenth century there was a horrible disease in England called the Sweats – so named because the victim sweated profusely and died. Vile painful thing – came on suddenly and killed the victim, all within twenty-four hours. The French were sure it was retribution for English wars against them. For some crazy reason, the French were immune"

"Probably their foie gras and beaujolais. Cures for almost anything that ails you. Say, have you ever been to Paris, Peter?" Roz asked. "Fabulous city."

"What's the other version, Mead?" Linda prodded, giving Roz an evil look.

"It's called Robber's Disease. Similar themes, slightly different details. This one takes place in Kasenero, Uganda, a village along Lake Victoria better known for its smuggling industry than fishing. As their economy soared, bars, hotels and breweries sprang up. And prostitutes. It was a freewheeling boom town. Traders partook of the local delights, bringing AIDS back to Tanzania. And Kenya. And Rwanda. And all the surrounding countries. Seventeen villagers, smugglers, came down with AIDS. At first people said they were stricken as retribution for consorting with the Tanzanians. People also felt they were getting their comeuppance for the sins of robbing and smuggling."

"Juliana or robber, whatever you call it, the point is," Roz said, "that AIDS originated here."

"Not necessarily," Mead countered. "There are a handful of suspicious cases in the U.S. and elsewhere that refute that theory. The most controversial, and compelling, is of a sixteen-year-old boy in St. Louis in 1968 who seemed to have no immune defenses and virtually melted away, dying the following year. He went on the books as a medical mystery, but researchers began to speculate in the early 1980s that he had AIDS. Blood and lymph samples had been frozen and were tested in 1987. He was positive."

"That's hardly conclusive," Roz argued.

"No, you're right," Mead conceded. " It's not. There are a lot of theories."

"Roz," Linda exclaimed with thinly veiled disgust, "what does it matter? The city dwellers say it came from the country, the rural folk say from the city. Men say from women, women say from men. Many think it's a white plot. The point is, it doesn't matter. There's a doctor at the hospital, Jane Kapito – I think you'd really like her, Mead – who says, 'There's a snake in the house. What does it matter how it got in? We need to get it out.'"

"Linda, for your professional edification, from an epidemiological perspective, it matters quite a bit," Roz said, trying to regain face.

"So how did they finally figure out it was AIDS?" Gil asked.

"A couple of doctors at a small hospital in Tanzania, the true heroes of the story as far as I'm concerned, were convinced that this was something entirely new. Eventually, they scraped enough money together to send one of them to Muhimbili Med School in the Dar Es Salaam, on the coast.

"There in the medical library, flipping through *The New England Journal of Medicine,* this rural doctor came across Gottlieb's findings dealing with gay men in L.A. Except for the differing client populations, it seemed to be the same disease."

"Imagine," Linda said, "being in Dar Es Salaam and reading *The New England Journal of Medicine?* That's just wild."

Roz rolled her eyes and in an aside to Peter said, "Guess she hasn't been to the Small World Pavilion at Disneyland."

"Roz, it's too bad you're so damned jaded," Linda jabbed back, "but I happen to think it's amazing." Roz recoiled. Mead was glad to see Linda feisty, even if it was due to sunburn she'd recently acquired.

"Who's Gottleib? And what do you mean by differing client populations, Mead?" Gil inquired, maneuvering the conversation away from Roz and Linda's sparring.

"Gottleib is a doctor who was working at U.C.L.A./Med Center back in 1989 who got involved with the first cases of AIDS. He started seeing patients with similar severe symptoms: they were ashen, extremely thin, mouths full of a fungal infection like cottage-cheese, uncontrollable coughing, lung pain. It looked like pneumonia, but it was really unusual for white, healthy males to be demonstrating these symptoms. In L.A., Gil, as with most of the U.S., the patients were all initially gay men. In Africa they were all heterosexual." She paused. "But back to these local Tanzanian doctors. Eventually, after much political brouhaha, pleading and working the government channels, they contacted the CDC and were authorized to send in a sample. Their suspicions were confirmed and the rest, as we say, is history." Mead sighed.

"I remember those early years," Gil recollected. "Word of a new killing disease spread like wildfire. And villagers knew that it was incurable. Many who got sick killed themselves rather than face the way they'd seen others die. For a while local stores couldn't keep Thiodan in stock."

Roz tilted her head in question. "Which is?"

"A pesticide. We had to put all of our agricultural supplies under lock and key – they'd try anything."

"Did you come across any injectionists?" Mead asked.

"No, I only heard of them."

Roz smiled coyly at Peter. "I feel so out in left field. Guess there hasn't been a run of dermatitis in these parts."

Linda's jaw dropped. "You are really pathetic, Roz. I think you have dermatitis of the brain."

"I was just joking. You can calm down, Linda, before you even get started. Just a joke. So," she continued with forced interest, "Tell me. What was an injectionist?"

"Is. Apparently they're still around." Mead looked to Gil for corroboration and he nodded. "A cross between a witch doctor and a snake-oil salesman. Black market stuff. A guy gets a hold of some syringes . . . "

"More likely a syringe. One single syringe," Linda interrupted.

"Right," Mead proceeded. "A syringe and some black market antibiotics. Or, just some liquid concoction."

"We've had a couple of cases at Misericordia," Linda explained. "Well-meaning mothers take their families into the fields, where these guys hang out and inject them against everything and anything. Needless to say, they have zip medical training. And no sterilization, of course. It's really sad."

"Life is sad," Roz quipped.

Linda swiveled her body away from Roz and crossed her legs. "Don't get yourself too worked up, Roz. You're about to choke on your milk of human kindness."

"Simple fact. Per the Buddha, 'Life is suffering' – in case you hadn't noticed while you were changing bedpans, Linda." Roz idly ran her finger around the rim of her cup. Then, with an air of contrition, she murmured, "No wonder they say Africa's lost." Linda, fuming, shot her a skeptical look.

"Who says?" Gil asked. Roz just gave him a look of disbelief. Gil persisted, "Who?"

"Established medicine," Mead droned. "And, in this case, they're probably right."

"Might," Peter said, then quickly explained. "Not you, Mite. Might as in m-i-g-h-t. Might be right. As long as we're still breathing, there's hope."

"Oh, please, " Mead turned her head and couldn't resist smiling. "Since when did you become an optimist?"

"Mead, I'm surprised. I thought you knew me better. I just don't give up so easily."

An awkward moment ensued as Peter stared Mead down in the soft glow of the kerosene lamp.

"How did you come to specialize in AIDS, Mead?" Gil asked, trying to right the capsized conversation.

Mead and Peter exchanged complicitous glances. "Well, a number of things happened." Mead raised her brow and sighed.

"Hey, play fair," Roz asserted. "No private jokes. Let's hear it."

"It's nothing private really," Mead said shortly. "Certainly not a joke. Or even that interesting."

"Don't undersell yourself, Mead." Peter was all encouragement.

"I, for one, would like to hear the story." Linda turned to Mead sincerely.

"Well, I was in pre-med when AIDS was first identified in the U.S. There was still a lot of arrogance at the time among the medical establishment that infectious diseases were about to become a thing of the past. And, I have to say, I was fascinated the first time I looked through a microscope. A whole new world was revealed, and I wanted to know everything I could about it."

"That's not what you and Peter were exchanging looks about," Roz said. "Come clean."

"My father's a surgeon. He wanted to pass the family scalpel to me. I chose otherwise."

"That's a tad understated," Peter said. "Walter, Mead's father, is a pretty powerful personality. I think that's a fair assessment, wouldn't you say?" Mead nodded. "In fact, Walter makes Ghengis Kahn look like a pussy cat. Point is, not too many cross him. Mead had a friend, Tommy. Actually her sister's best friend from college."

Mead explained about Tommy. "He was like an older brother to me, really. Better, though. Always forcing Luce to include me on their outings. Always asking me how I was. Never speaking down to me. He was very special and a good friend. I used to call him long distance and he'd always talk to me. Or call me back. That's different, huh, college guy taking the time to talk to a kid."

"And years later," Peter continued, "he was, unfortunately, one of the first AIDS cases in New York. Daddy did not want his youngest daughter consorting with a man who had that homosexual cancer, much less directing her very promising career toward such an end." Mead shrugged. "And so, the first line in the sand was drawn between them. When Mead did not flinch and crossed it, Walter began to get a sense of who he was dealing with." Peter paused to give Mead an admiring smile. "Mead launched a very successful career. As well as a successful defense against Walter."

"You know, Mead," Gil began hesitantly. "I think . . . "

"Out with it, man," Roz demanded harshly.

Gil gave Roz a disapproving look before directing his comments to Mead. "Well, I think I may have seen him, this Tommy." Heads turned. "I mean, a painting of him. There's a series your sister did, oh, perhaps a decade ago, although I saw them in Rome about four or five years ago, called the *Neon Plague*. There is this blond guy, tall, rather good looking, small cleft in his chin . . . "

"Sounds like Tommy," Mead was stunned.

"It was a controversial series when it came out, beautifully done but overwhelming. Very explicit. You know that this guy, young, good-looking, is dying. And suffering. All done in a very austere blue-white hospital room with that cold florescent lighting. And in each painting you can see the city through the hospital room window. So there's an incredible contrast of his isolation and imminent death with the city that is so busy, so alive. Especially the ones done at night when the city lights are burning bright and the neon is flashing."

Mead sat dumbfounded. Gil looked uncomfortably into his hands, then at Mead. Linda gave Peter a questioning glance but he only shrugged.

"Wait a second," Roz demanded. "Your sister is a painter?"

"And a good one," Gill insisted. Mead looked at him briefly. "Perhaps I shouldn't have said anything," he recanted quietly. "Sorry."

"How come you didn't tell me? I'm always looking for a good investment."

"Stick with jewelry, Roz." Linda's icy tone silenced her instantly.

Mead, hand against her head to brace it, sat in a silent stupor, locked in a gaze with Gil. Peter tried to intervene. "The other side of it, as Mead already alluded to, is the excitement of the microbial world. As I recall your telling me," Peter looked at Mead, a million miles away, and placed a consoling, distracting hand on her arm, "the microbes were a new universe. And Mead, unlike some in the medical establishment at the time, never underestimated them. She started to study the history of disease and came to the conclusion that the war would not be easily won. If ever. AIDS is her specialty. Microbes are her passion." He paused. "Are you okay?"

"Yeah," Mead's voice was small. Again she was overwhelmed by this stranger who was privy to scenes of her life, who knew more about her sister than she did. She tried to hobble together a suitable cover. "I guess I just haven't thought about Tommy in a long time." An uneasy moment followed until she spoke again, curiosity prevailing over embarrassment, "An entire series? That's amazing. How many are there?"

"I don't really know – five? Ten? My mother might know, might have it in a catalog somewhere," he responded cautiously. "They were critically acclaimed but didn't sell well. As you might imagine." A pall fell over the table.

"I do believe,' Linda said, rising, "it's time to turn in."

"Good idea," Mead said, standing quickly, eager for an out. " I think I'll follow your lead. Good night."

Peter grabbed Mead's hand as she left the tent, brushing her hand with his lips, offering comfort with his eyes, "You sure you're okay? Can I do anything?"

"Thanks, Peter." Touched by his concern, she let herself briefly hold his hand before releasing it. "I'm okay." She left, following the circle of Linda's flashlight.

Roz watched through the open tent flaps until the flashlight turned out of view. "Well, gents, looks like we're getting down to critical mass. Happens at every party." Roz stared from Peter to Gil. "Who's man enough for another cup of java?"

Peter and Gil looked at each other and smiled. Both extended their cups to Roz.

* * *

Luce leaned into the cold concrete balustrade at Cherry Hill. Central Park was a grimy wash of gray white. She looked into the empty field remembering warmer, brighter days of summer picnics, summer concerts.

Having walked all afternoon, she paused. Not to rest, for there was no rest. Just to pause. Left alone, the city was a ghost town for her, more desolate than any dry and wind-blown western town conjured by black-and-white movies of the fifties.

Through the scrim of her memory Luce saw the shadows of her former life as she walked, endlessly walked, the city streets. At this corner, a piqued Grace glancing feverishly at her watch spots Luce coming and tries to submerge her initial reaction of joy beneath a veneer of chastisement; through this restaurant window she can see the two of them dining with friends, later in their relationship, when the fire of passion had cooled to the comfortable warmth of intimacy; here was the jewelry shop where she had bought Grace a ring, agonizing for two full months before their second anniversary; this furniture store was where they'd made their first joint purchase, quickly buying something they both liked, as though that would be a sure-fire cornerstone, an emotional insurance policy.

Had this been her life, she wondered? What now appeared disembodied, elusive, ephemeral? Balinese puppetry, no more. The lithesome shards of the past dancing upon the thin white screen of her present? Did that time still exist, elsewhere, just beyond her reach? Like fireflies caught in a jar, the flash, the heat of each memory was fading.

She hated that, the slow dulling that removed the acute shine, leaving a flat filmy patina and pain. She railed against it. That was her life, who she was, where she wanted to be. She longed to pierce the screen, slice it viciously with a slash of her hand, break through, return. But there was no escape from the cruel isolation of her present.

82

"I feel our lives have changed irrevocably." Grace had said, beaten. They were slumped in opposing corners of the living room sofa. "I wonder if I will ever be able to see life with a B.T.N. perspective again."

"What's B.T.N.?" Luce dug for the energy to talk. All she wanted to do was crawl back in bed, where they had spent the past two days.

"Before The News. Now we're in A.T.N. – After The News. A whole new country."

Luce watched Grace, gray shades of defeat and despair, twirl the fringe on the sofa pillow she hugged across her chest. She couldn't believe it had been only eight days ago when Grace, stocking feet, oversized tee-shirt, stumbled into the kitchen. Luce, caught off guard by the look of fear on Grace's face, noteworthy for its rare appearance, stopped grinding coffee. "I've found a lump," was all she had said, all she could say before her throat constricted shut. Somewhere in the past few days there had been a visit to the doctor's, visits to labs, back to the doctor to sit in her sunny office and get the news. It had been a disconcerting continuum of sleepless nights and midnight conversations that all began and ended with "What if?" A time when fear flattened hope, denial arm-wrestled reality, a time of acute numbness coupled with acute perception, a time when Luce, standing somewhere outside herself, constantly observed the essential preciousness of their ordinary life.

"Luce, promise me you'll be okay."

And Luce, digging deeper, rasped, "I'll be fine."

Propping her elbows on the balustrade, Luce thought, You're wrong, Grace. Before The News and After The News aren't two separate countries. They're joined, a single borderless continent, completely lost to me now.

* * *

After tossing and turning for almost an hour, Mead slipped out of her tent. She heard the low murmur of voices around the dining table and quietly walked in the other direction. About thirty yards from their encampment she found a clump of Senecios trees, prehistoric forms in the dead of night, and sat down. As uncomfortable as it was leaning against the prickly bark, it was a relief to be out of her small, airless tent, crowded by this sudden unexpected burst of feeling and memory.

Was it only two weeks ago she had casually projected a spirited, all-women mountain climb up Kilimanjaro, a climb she was sure would refresh her from the travails of doctoring in Nairobi? Now, entangled with the past, the mountain which she had hoped would be a solid ramp to some new height, some new source of oxygen, was a suffocating landslide of rocks from her shifting past. She took a deep breath and tried to tease it all apart.

Imposing order on what felt utterly chaotic, she methodically grouped her thoughts into distinct categories. First, she thought, there's Peter. He was obviously trying very hard to reconnect with her, to support her, to champion and charm her, going out of his way to show that he could change, had changed. As she peered into the black panorama of the distance, memories like phantoms, paraded by: walks along the Charles River during their courtship; passionate afternoons stolen from their busy schedules when they met at his or her apartment; a few rare backpacking trips; late night conversations over bad coffee in empty hospital cafeterias. She recalled a few dinner parties in New York when her parents, but especially Walter, exuded pride at their future son-in-law, even clasped his arm in an odd show of ownership in front of his cronies. He was eminently acceptable. Even more, he was a real prize. And now? she asked herself. There's a chink in my resolve, but a chink is all he needs. He's winning.

Acknowledging that defeat she moved quickly to Gil. Well, it's not Gil per se, she mused. He seems pretty innocuous. Which only makes what he's brought up for me more remarkable. Here I am, 15,000 feet above sea level, thousands of miles from San Francisco and finding out about my sister and her paintings from a virtual stranger. Shame tugged at her. She immediately dismissed this as unproductive. Jealousy soon followed. Then possession. How could she paint Tommy dying?

So Gil leads me back to not only Luce but to Tommy. And now that she was alone, just his name, a soundless whisper in her mind, caused a flood of memories that moved so fast she could barely keep up with the fleeting, fragmentary images: skating at Rockefeller Center, visiting the Met, going to a Talking Heads concert, Tommy shouting with mock anger as they stood at the co-op door, "Hurry up, Mead or we'll book without you."

Luce had never instigated Mead's joining them, but she never seemed to mind. In fact, thinking about it these many years later, Mead wondered if Tommy wasn't a necessary emissary between Luce and Mead, Luce and her parents. Tommy, ready with a laugh, had a sweet teasing way that seemed to ingratiate him with this otherwise cool and aloof assembly. He could take liberties with them that they would otherwise find appalling. He softened their edges, pierced their protective bubbles. All with good humor, all with a genuine warmth. And when he was with them they sometimes thought the warmth was theirs, intrinsic, not generously superimposed.

She and Tommy would sit up in the kitchen after everyone else had gone to bed, talking into the early hours. He would ask her questions about her life. At first she found his probing impolite and didn't know how to respond. To talk, really talk, violated some unwritten code. But he would drag it out of her – who she had crushes on, what it was like being the baby with all the other kids at school, what she wanted to be when she grew up. She could talk to him about anything. Even Luce.

Mead had known from their first meeting that he was gay. Still, she appreciated it when he took her aside one afternoon when she was fourteen to tell her himself. He treated her honestly and with respect, which only increased her love for him.

Walter and Elizabeth had feigned shock when they learned his diagnosis years later. While they never retracted their hospitality, they didn't have to. Tommy's visits to the co-op had fallen off by then. Luce had her own place down in the Village where they met, and Mead was in Boston at college. Her stomach tightened with anger, her face streaked with tears. She quickly pushed aside any further memories, slamming the vault door shut.

This left Luce. Besides Tommy there were portraits of Mead. What else did Luce disclose in her oils? The anger she had felt that afternoon abated. Now there was a speck of curiosity. Beyond the content of her work, Mead wondered, why have I never seen her paintings?

Then she remembered the evening that her parents had returned to the co-op after attending Luce's first show. Her father, always imperious and distant, was a seething glacier. He went directly to his study, while Elizabeth paced nervously, fitfully. "How was it, Mom?"

"Horrible," she had answered. "Just horrible. I don't know how she can be so cruel, how she can do this to us." It was never discussed again but the censure was complete. Mead had never, before, or since, seen anything disturb them both so profoundly.

And Luce, what to think about Luce? Somehow meeting Gil had given reality to the fact Mead distantly acknowledged that her sister was a success in her own right, in a different world. For the first time ever, Mead wondered how it must feel for Luce to attend the annual clan gathering and never hear mention of art or her career. Or worse, to know that beneath the surface there was a decided prohibition about it. That there was no mention of Luce's personal life was not surprising or provocative. Few details of any of their lives were ever exchanged. In fact, Mead recollected that at the beach last summer no one had mentioned Peter's resounding absence. Always on egg shells, she sighed, always at arm's length.

But now, curiously, Mead wanted to know more about Luce, what she painted, why she moved to San Francisco. How is it, she wondered more than slightly mystified, that there are such gaping holes between us?

Mead took a couple of deep breaths. The crisp evening air, the mental exercise, the crying had succeeded. She felt slightly restored. But what to do, she thought, about Peter, contrite and howling at her door? Not going to figure it out in one evening, she said, steadying herself. Take your time. Ironic, she thought, rubbing together her hands, which had begun to swell with the higher altitude, I'll be happy to be back in Nairobi. The exercise of climbing, especially now that they had hit the steeper grade and could not easily converse, left her with too much time to be with herself. And the company she had found herself in had churned her usually calm mental waters. Like a host besieged, she felt invaded from all sides.

She thought of Nairobi, teeming with disease. And just as quickly, she flashed on an image of herself in her clean, well-funded, high-tech lab in Chicago, pondering the virus. Either way, she was fascinated, enthralled by infectious diseases and the precariousness they lent life. It was what fundamentally interested her in her research work, the notion of disaster held in check by chance, some intentional effort, or an unaccountable assist from nature. It was a wafer thin balance, which had broken with AIDS and other infectious diseases. Now she was in the thick of it, in the trenches, on the other side. She, like the virus, had crossed a line.

Looking across the encampment she noticed the kerosene lamp was doused and the low chatter, which had been a constant backdrop to her musing, had stopped. She started to rise when she recognized the shadowy figures of Roz and Peter walking back from the mess tent. She waited, not wanting to have to talk with anyone or reveal her tear-stained face. As she leaned against the tree trunk, half crouched, she watched them stop in front of Roz's tent. Roz slipped in and a moment later, after checking over his shoulder, Peter slipped in, too.

The sound of the zipper closing the front flaps was a buzz saw gashing the night.

* * *

The flicker of a threesome crossing several feet in front of her snapped Luce out of her reverie. She watched the group, obviously a daughter, mid-thirties, and visiting parents in tow. The daughter stopped her parents in front of the statue of Bethesda and uncased her automatic camera. They put down their

86

many shopping bags, chock full of post-holiday bargains. The daughter set about arranging them, angling them this way, turning them that way, waiting for a clear frame. It was a cozy scene, the parents laughing benignly, slightly embarrassed to be such apparent tourists. Luce felt a pang, usually buried beyond exhuming. Family. The warmth of a family circle.

After the daughter snapped her parents, the father insisted on capturing mother and daughter. Luce, eyes narrowed, watched, always a voyeur on the parent-daughter relationships. She saw the two move closer, at the father's coaxing. She watched as they lightly arced their arms about each other. She noted the subtle slant of the mother away from the daughter, the daughter's taut smile and how they both rapidly dropped their arms the instant the shutter clicked closed, as though gratefully released. She heard the mother's voice, perfunctory and flat, ask "Which way now?" and saw the daughter soundlessly point. Family, Luce sighed, and tried to re-bury the pang.

Up above, ten or so blocks away, her parents probably sat in their living room, in opposing club chairs, behind their respective book or magazine. So close. So far.

"Luce," Grace had said one evening over dinner, "let's have your parents to dinner."

Luce reeled back in her chair and stared at the alien who had invaded Grace's body. "No."

"Luce, I've known you for almost three years. I'd like to meet them."

"Grace, I've known them all my life. I wish I'd never met them."

"Be serious. These are your parents, after all. You know, Mom and Dad."

"No. It's a bad idea."

"I know, let's have them to Seder . . . "

"Bad to worse. Were you and Ruthie smoking pot this afternoon?"

" . . . with Ruthie, Pearl and Irv, Milton and . . . "

"Worse to worst. In record time. No way."

"Luce," she drew out her name in a pleading way, "are you embarrassed by me?"

"No," she said emphatically. "You know that. I'm embarrassed by them."

"Well, hey, if it's an Embarrassing Parents Contest, we should definitely enter Ruthie."

"No offense, but she's bush league. Grace, it is true that I do not want to invite my parents to dinner. It is equally true that they would never come. And . . . "

"You'll never know until you ask."

". . . And, should hell freeze over, pigs start to fly, and they came, they would have a miserable time. As would we."

"Luce, I just can't believe that they're really as bad as you think. People change, mellow. Especially as they get older."

"Not Dr. and Mrs. Bennett. They've calcified."

"What on earth does that mean? Calcified?"

"If you knew them you'd know."

" See, that's what I mean. I have no frame of reference."

"No."

"Okay," Grace retreated. "What about Mead?"

"What about Mead?"

"Let's have her to dinner." Luce stared incomprehensibly at Grace, who leaned closer over the dinner table. "I want to meet somebody in your family, see what they're like. I want to understand your background better. Don't look so shocked. You know, Luce, in many parts of the world this would not be considered a bizarre request." Luce leaned back into her chair and sighed. Grace leaned forward. "Please, Luce."

"Okay," she relented, regretting it immediately.

Later in the study she picked up the phone to call Jacob. Grace, in the kitchen, was talking to Ruthie.

"So, it worked like a charm. I insisted on the parents and settled for Mead."

"How did you get to be such a devious person? My own daughter."

"I think you just answered your own question, Ma."

"Smart ass. Why you never went into law I'll never understand. You'd be a very rich woman. Better yet, I'd have a rich daughter. I just hope this doesn't backfire on you.

"Ma, they're sisters. They should know each other. Talk to each other. Go shopping together. You know, things like that."

"And what if she's like Pearl. In case you haven't noticed, not all sisters get along, Ms. Know-It-All."

"I suppose that's why we moved in next door to your sister when I was five. I suppose that's why you still live next door. You and Pearl love each other. You just love to fight. If that's what happens, well, at least Luce will have someone to fight with."

"Don't get me wrong, Grace, you know I love Luce. But in these matters she is a little retarded. If her sister's the same way, it could be a very awful evening. Oops, the door. Probably your Aunt Pearl come to show me her latest jewel. Oy."

"I'll call tomorrow, Ma."

"Okay. We're still on for the movies on Saturday?"

"You bet. Your turn to pay."

"What a brat. Didn't paying for your college count? Gotta go."

"Love you."

"Love you, too."

Luce gently hung up the phone and sat down at the desk. She was flattered that anyone would go to such lengths to manipulate her and afraid that Grace would be disappointed. She picked up a picture frame of Grace and Ruthie. It was a double frame. In one photo they faced each other, broad smiles, clowning. Luce could imagine the irreverent conversation. "You are such a pain in the ass," Ruthie would be saying. "I learned from the best, Ma," Grace would laugh. In the other photo they leaned against the railing of the Brooklyn Bridge as a summer sun set, Grace's arms looped tightly around Ruthie's waist, her head resting on Ruthie's shoulder, Ruthie's hand on Grace's cheek. The love that flowed so freely, expressed itself so easily, was a foreign language to Luce.

"You wanna know what family is, Luce, when it's good, anyway?" Ruthie had joked at one of their endless tribal gatherings. "Family is when you love someone, even though you have to." Grace had rolled her eyes and shouted into Pearl's kitchen, "That's it. She's over the edge. No more brewskis for Ruthie."

* * *

Mead, Elizabeth thought, leaning back into her club chair, should be two days away from the summit of the mountain now. She put a marker in the book she was reading on East Africa, shut it and placed it in her lap. Surrounding the warm mug of tea with her hands, she sipped slowly, letting thoughts of her youngest daughter float over her like waves of orange spice.

She had bought the book on Africa, yet another, yesterday at the Barnes & Noble downtown. She had perused the travel section looking for anything and everything on Kenya, Tanzania, Mount Kilimanjaro. By now she knew most of the books, having either checked them out of the library or purchased them. A young man had asked if she needed assistance. "My daughter is in Africa," she spewed. "She is a doctor and she and several women friends are climbing Mount Kilimanjaro." The clerk was stoned and gave her a dull expression. "She's a doctor of infectious diseases. AIDS is her specialty."

"Oh, AIDS, all our books about AIDS are against the wall," he rallied. She demurely thanked him for his help and took the book to the register.

Such an adventure, she thought, closing her eyes and envisioning the mountain, three degrees south of the equator, rising from the flat dry plain to a snow capped culmination. Hemingway had described it as "wide as all the world, great, high and unbelievably white in the sun, was the square top of Kilimanjaro." Classified as a dormant volcano, Kilimanjaro had an extensive crater at its peak. The shape of Mead, upright and resolute with the mountain's sharp incline slanting downward from her feet, dominated Elizabeth's inner vision.

Elizabeth looked at the stack of books on the reading table: *Out of Africa, West with The Night, The Best Game Parks of Africa, The Collected Hemingway.* She had been reading the section from *The Green Hills of Africa.* Of course, times had changed. Still, the excitement and scale of these African stories stirred Elizabeth, and she thought that Mead was leading her own expedition, although her prey was microbes, not game. Sometime during the previous restless night she had flicked on her reading lamp and read *The Snows of Kilimanjaro.* She shivered at the thought of it. It had been years since she had read it and the short story had left an annoying sense of foreboding. Thank God she's not in any little planes!

What a thrill it must be for Mead, such a sense of triumph! Thousands of miles away Elizabeth filled with pride and marveled at her daughter. The thought of these three women, with a woman outfitter, tackling such an expedition, was awesome to Elizabeth. "Really, Mother, no need to gush. It's just a protracted hike. Views should be nice, though," Mead had e-mailed in her customary low-key fashion.

She picked up her book again and studied the map. With her index finger, blue veins beneath papery skin, she gently caressed the route from Nairobi southeast to Mount Kilimanjaro State Park. Laying her entire hand over the coast of east Africa, she longed for her daughter's well being.

The opposing page had a black-and-white photo of a road passing through a Masai bombas. The road was flanked with a few thatched-roofed huts and Masai in native dress riding bikes, herding cattle, and driving overloaded donkey carts. To think, Elizabeth mused, that that village is choking with activity as Mead climbs closer and closer to the apex of Kilimanjaro.

She took off her glasses, closed her tired eyes and leaned her head back into the chair. It had been a difficult night. She had tossed and turned. Intrusive thoughts of Luce would not be stilled. What should she do about her? Guilt had left her with a dull headache and she rubbed her temples. Elizabeth hadn't mentioned Luce's presence in New York to Walter. What would be the point? It would only further complicate a strained situation. And, Walter, poor dear, she worried, he's so distracted, working himself too hard. Suddenly she lurched forward. I'll do it, she thought, I'll just do it. She rose and strode to the desk with a rare impulsiveness, opened the middle drawer and pulled out the phone book. Finding the number she sought, she quickly dialed.

"Malowitz Gallery." The voice on the other end was young, affected, a touch arrogant. Elizabeth instantly felt a deep sense of intrusion. "Hello. I was wondering if Luce Bennett might be available." She tried to sound casual, disinterested.

"Who's calling?"

She hesitated. "An acquaintance."

"Sorry, not here yet. She will be here for the show and stops by fairly often. I can leave her a message. What's your name and number?"

"Oh, no. No bother. I'll call her later . . . " She quickly hung up the phone, put the phone book away and returned to her club chair. She clasped her fingers around the mug hoping the warmth would stop their slight trembling. Damn it to hell, she thought, not sure what or why she was cursing. She placed her book on the top of the stack and clicked on CNN.

As some inane congressman droned on about getting back on track with some partisan agenda, Elizabeth angrily wondered what she would have said, anyway. "Oh, Luce, I read you were in town. Have time for lunch?" No. "Luce, by luck someone at a recent party mentioned you were in town. Care to stop up for dinner?" Worse still.

What did she want with her oldest child anyway? What? Agitated, she clicked off the TV and went to her computer. Maybe there'd be news from Rand or Avery. She booted up and heard her computer say, in a way she still found disconcerting, "You have mail." She went to her box and opened her new message, addressed to EBennett, from Chad. What is this?, she wondered.

To: EBennett
Fr: Chad
What happened? Last thing I remember I was nuzzling my head in your breasts. Then you were gone. Where did you go?

Elizabeth was shocked and quickly typed a response. "You have the wrong person, young man. Try again . . . ELSEWHERE." She deleted the message immediately. What was happening to the world, she groaned. Angrily, she exited and sat back down in her club chair. With a deep sigh, she opened the book and minutely studied the map.

* * *

"Roz," Peter shouted solicitously to where Roz had propped herself against a boulder, "can I bring you any pasta?" She emphatically shook her head and waved him away.

They had stopped for lunch on the third day. Mary, preferring solitude and exploration, left them alone. Roz, who had been suddenly hit by altitude sickness mid-morning, slumped lifelessly against the boulder. Her catatonic staring was punctuated by hasty retreats to commune with nature, privately. The climb was beginning to fray everyone's nerves. Mead, although still reeling, was intent on not disclosing what she had seen the previous night and struggled to maintain an unruffled facade. Now she sat on a blanket with Linda, Gil and Peter. They all nibbled at their lunch, except for Peter who ate heartily.

"Is there any progress with the Ebola virus you're hunting?" Gil asked.

"No, not really. We don't yet know what the natural host reservoir for the virus is. It completely destroys its host – its favorite being humans. But after an outbreak it goes somewhere, to something, which it doesn't destroy. That's what we're looking for and that's what we can't find."

"Ebola is one of the new diseases." Mead directed her comments to Gil, attempting a cool, professional tone. "A sign of a relatively new disease is that it's fatal – the host and parasite are new acquaintances. And the parasite hasn't yet learned how to devour its host without killing it entirely. The parasite is selfish - but not too smart."

"Not yet anyway," Peter beamed and Mead felt her stomach turn. "The notion is that what begins as parasitism ends as symbiosis. There's actually a certain beauty to it."

"Peter," Mead fired, "parasitism, microbial or human, is not a benign activity, much less beautiful." A stunned look quickly darkened Peter's face. Mead, holding the upper hand, continued, "But there are things far worse than new diseases like Ebola, Gil. In a way, Ebola and similar diseases are more medical theatrics. They're deadly, and highly dramatic, but they're not responsible for the majority of deaths. It's the old ones, the ones we long thought were under control, that are re-emerging. Diseases like TB, dengue fever, diphtheria are returning with a renewed virulence. You see, Gil, these microbes can cross all borders. And they are incredible at adapting. Which means, give them enough time and they can soon become immune to a previously successful drug treatment."

"Or, like some strains found in drinking water in several U.S. cities, they can even live in chlorine.

Now that's when you need to start paying some attention," Linda mused.

"How about get scared shitless?" Roz said. She joined the group, albeit on shaky legs.

"That would also be appropriate. You okay?" Linda shielded her eyes to look at Roz. "You look a little green around the gills."

"I'm fine," she clipped.

"You know," Gil said, "the ironic thing is how much the independence of the countries seems to have played a role in all of this. Don't get me wrong. I'm not suggesting we return to any of the old colonialism. But ever since all of these countries have assumed independence, everything is out of balance. The people leave the villages in droves for the cities. There's no work there so they wind up festering, living in the worst imaginable conditions. Have you seen Sofia Town yet, Mead?" She shook her head. "Deplorable. Sofia Town makes poverty seem posh."

"Then there are the wars that take such a toll," Mead interjected. "Right here in Tanzania they're dealing with half a million refugees from the Rwanda-Burundi conflict. Here's one of the poorest countries on the face of the earth, with a life expectancy of forty-two years, deluged by a flood of people just wanting safety."

"It's happening everywhere," Gil observed. "Not just Rwanda or Burundi. Or Liberia or Somalia. Look at Sierra Leone. Ten thousand people have died in their civil war. Over a million people have been forced to flee their homes."

"Where's the leadership? Where are the peace makers?" Linda asked.

"In the counting house counting out their money." Roz gave Linda a look of disbelief and shook her head.

"Good question, Linda," Gil replied. "In Sierra Leone they just had a presidential election. The rebel leaders ordered a boycott of it. Voters who didn't co-operate had their hands cut off. The rebels even use hot irons to brand 'no election' on the backs of some who defied the boycott."

"That's disgusting. How can anyone be so brutal?" Linda was aghast.

"Hello? Where have you been, on an extended visit to Girl Scout Camp?" Roz retorted. Altitude sickness was a vicious fuel.

"Some of these leaders are pretty vile," Gil said. "And most do have either Italian villas or Swiss bank accounts."

"It's such a morass," Peter said. "Look how long it's taken to get the leaders to talk openly about the problem of AIDS. They deliberately suppressed data to minimize the situation."

"As a famous politician once said, 'You cannot believe how much you have to deceive a nation in order to govern it.'"

Linda looked up. "Who said that, Gil?"

"Hitler. *Mein Kampf.*"

Peter laughed, "That's a good one. It goes right up there with 'Work makes men free.' – The welcoming inscription at Auschwitz."

"Is this the party game of the new millennia? Endless discussion about our imminent demise as a species?" Roz was getting testy. And greener.

"Or maybe it's just age," Linda offered. "Does it make you any happier to think of a bar full of twenty-somethings somewhere dancing and drinking themselves into delirium, happily oblivious to our inevitable doom?"

"Knowledge may be power but it isn't necessarily fun," Roz retorted.

"Good point," Linda granted.

"Excuse me," Roz hurriedly said, a darker shade of green. "Again," and staggered off.

They watched her disappear behind the boulders. Peter, trying to engage Mead, deferentially asked,

"So what do you make, Dr. Bennett, of the recent correlation between lack of circumcision and HIV infections in the Sub-Saharan AIDS belt?"

She gathered her lunch plate and rose. Over her shoulder she tossed, "Not much. Interesting correlation of data but no real science behind it yet." Her tone was coldly authoritative, condescendingly brusque. She walked off, feeling the slap of her words on Peter's cheek.

* * *

The late afternoon sun, captured in the large picture window on the top floor, appeared to Luce, from the bench in the small park below, like a blazing trapezoid, sizzling with flames of orange, yellow and red. It seared her vision and Luce could only tentatively look at it. Below, on the ground floor, across the street from the park in which she now stood, was Mary's Market, a small corner grocery store, Lee's Laundry and The Great Wall, the worst Chinese food in the world. A montage of people she had seen on this street over the years appeared before her: the local theater legend clad in yesterday's sweats, cigarette drooping from her lips, miniature poodle cradled lovingly in her arms; Mr. Tennebaum, a lithographer with a thick German accent, always dapper, living with the memory and guilt of surviving the Holocaust; Françoise, a vibrant young drag queen who performed in a local dive and spoke French with an accent firmly rooted in Ohio. Luce shivered with the chill of memory.

"I could move in with you. Or you could move in with Ruthie and me. Or we could find a new place together," Grace had suggested after they had known each other a year.

"Or we could continue as we are, get to know each other better." They sat in the park drinking coffee, reading the *Sunday Times* and soaking up the early rays of a sunny Spring morning.

"You sure know how to work your brakes, Luce. We can continue to get to know each other while living together."

"I'm thirty-four. I should know how to work my brakes."

"Well, I'm almost thirty-two."

"Exactly."

"I presume you think you've just said something clever? Hmm, I think that an audit is what we need. Shall I review the situation?"

"Would my saying no stop you? Please, audit away." Luce blew on her coffee then sipped gingerly from the hot paper cup.

"We've known each other for almost a year. You have no communicable diseases, except a slight tendency toward bleakness and despair, which on you has some charm and for which I seem to be developing an immunity. You have no disgusting personal habits - very important. Good dental hygiene. An interesting, if small, social circle. You're very sexy, don't talk much, do not have an intrusive family - big plus. And you have never asked to borrow money. Perfect."

"I am flattered, Grace. Almost embarrassed to think my charms are so obvious. Have you done this before - you're so very smooth?"

"Small blemish - you're a little too glib for my taste. But since you're not much of a talker it's not too big a deal." Luce smiled. "Your Cheshire smile could, say in a decade or two, become a little irritating. But for now, I still find it amusing and am willing to ignore the condescension."

"Ow. I see your inventory is beginning to turn up some negatives."

"I thought that'd make you happy - a woman like yourself. Knowing that I have a balanced view, I mean. I only aim to please."

"I'm almost ecstatic."

"Yes, I can tell. That crease on your brow is about to burst into a full blown smirk. Try to get a grip, Luce. We are in public. As for me," she continued undaunted, "I am self-sufficient and easily entertained."

"Thanks a lot."

"By which I mean, that, when I have lost my dearly beloved for weeks on end to painting, I can amuse myself."

"A decent retrieve. I'll let it pass."

"I am loyal and true."

"Good girl, Fido."

"I do have a mother."

"Yes, no denying you do. However, I actually like Ruthie."

"Yes, a serious omission from my assessment of you. Several girlfriends fled mid-borscht. You stayed the whole meal. Perhaps I should be concerned. But this is not about Ruthie. To continue, I have never read a self-help book in my life, I have no inner child who'll crowd us, I know nothing about art so I'll never interfere, I cook - thank God, I am boringly stable and of healthy Russian peasant stock."

"Well, not exactly how I would have summarized things."

"Luce, I'd be an old lady if I waited for you to summarize things. Fortunately, I bear no grudge."

"Please."

"Overstated but true. Last but not least, I'm crazy about you. You have, on occasion, let some interest in me seep through that placid exterior of yours which I interpret as you being crazy about me - in your own wild way. So, there you have it. I rest my case."

"A stunning, conclusive presentation of the evidence. What can I say?"

"Perhaps that you love me, too? Of course, that'd be a pretty bold step so maybe you could just nod your head and stamp your foot. "

Luce sat on the park bench, paused a moment then nodded her head.

"You are hopeless." Grace, hurt, tried to strike a light tone.

Luce reached over, put her hand behind Grace's head and pulled her close. "Grace, I do love you," she whispered through her curls, "Too."

Luce, leaning against the cold chain link fence, looked up to the window of the apartment they had shared, then at the empty bench and put her gloved hands over her eyes, as though to hold her memories.

* * *

Perched on a large volcanic rock, Mead watched the moon traverse the ink black sky. Dinner on their fourth night had been a paltry affair. No one had much of an appetite. The successive days of hiking, the drop in temperature and the increased altitude were taking a toll on almost everyone. The precarious camaraderie the group had found on the preceding nights was reduced to bare civility. Roz especially was having a bad time and her nausea seemed to be growing more severe. She had enlisted the porters to move her tent to the periphery of the encampment hoping the additional twenty yards would afford more privacy. Gil seemed more withdrawn and Linda's worsening sunburn made her short tempered. Only Peter, Mary and the porters seemed to be getting full nights' sleep.

It had been, as Mary had warned them, a hard day of hiking. The incline had become significantly steeper and right after lunch they hit snow. Mead, immobilized by the sight of Peter entering Roz's tent, had spent much of the previous night slumped against the tree. Even after Peter sneaked back to his own tent, Mead could not move. Right before dawn she managed to pull herself up and go to her tent. All day she had felt numb and sick to her stomach. Due to the rigor of the climb, there had been little opportunity to talk with one another and for that Mead was grateful. Despite the hours to herself, no thoughts entered her head, only the sound of the tent zipper, with each crush of her boot, lacerating the snow.

On a mid-morning break Mary had demonstrated a new technique for hiking up the steeper, rockier slopes - the lock step method. After each step the knee of the uphill leg was locked in order to put the weight on the leg bone and not the muscle, letting the other leg rest. Each step required a few seconds' pause. Even so, it was an exhausting process.

Studying the scene Mead thought the landscape had a lunar quality. The snow was powdery and dry. The dark lava rocks could easily have been moon boulders. Kerosene lanterns burned in the blue tents which dotted the land with eerie blue triangles. With the onset of dark everything seemed so sparse and essential, so spacious and remote.

She saw the silhouette of Peter, vital even as a shadow on the snow, approaching. The sense of controlled agitation and fury that had been simmering within for the past 24 hours now turned to icy dread. She still didn't know what, if anything, she would say to him.

"I thought you might want a bit of tea to warm you up - decaf." He handed her two cups and poured them both tea from a thermos. "There, that's better. Beautiful night, eh?" His voice was dulcet as he gazed into the starry sky.

"Yes," she said evenly, refusing to be drawn out.

"Too bad about Roz, huh? She's in pretty sorry shape."

"Too bad." She idly wondered if her tenor held even a sliver of concern.

"How are you holding up?" He leaned toward her tenderly.

"Not bad," she said scooting away from him. "Could use a little more sleep - but that's always the case."

"Our sleepless days in residency seem to be good training for mountain climbing." For a while they were quiet, then, as Mead had anticipated, Peter spoke. "Feel like talking?"

"No."

"Mind if I do?" He took her silence for consent. "I've done a lot of thinking since you moved to Chicago. A lot of time to think. A lot to think about. It's funny, Mead, because when I think us, it's never because we were doing anything really exciting or interesting. We were too busy for that in those days. Lucky just to get over to the Square to catch a first run movie. No, what I think about is just how good it was being with you, talking with you, sharing our lives. And our work. I really miss being able to share our work. There's no one else in your league. No one even comes close." He paused to check her reaction. Her face was blank. "I realize now how very special you are, not that I didn't know before, but I get it. Really get it. The bottom line is that I miss you. Mead," he paused dramatically, smiled broadly, "I want another chance."

Mead looked into the deep black sky and sighed. She had decided not to speak the truth, and for the moment, skip the accusations and acrimony. "Peter, I'd be lying if I said I didn't miss you. I do."

"Well that's a start. That's good."

"No it's not."

"But, Mead . . ."

"I've done a lot of thinking, too. Especially these past days, having you around, seeing you, talking with you. You know what? It makes me realize how angry I am."

"Angry, what for? Have I done something the past few days?" The pose he struck of contrived innocence filled her with repugnance. And amazement.

"Yeah, you've been yourself - in every way." She waited to assess his response, which was neutral, then continued. "You've been, among other things, utterly charming, bright, sweet, attentive. You don't get credit for your good looks - those you can't help. I see so clearly how I fell in love with you."

"This isn't good? Sounds good to me." He assumed that boyish gee-whiz look he knew was usually effective.

"No. It isn't good. Because it makes me ache for something that will only cause me more pain. I'm not willing to do that."

"You know," he said, voice tinged slightly with self-righteousness, "I didn't have to tell you about those other women. Don't I get some credit? "

He really does like high risk, she thought, shocked at the boldness of his move, his lie. No wonder he's a microbial cowboy. For the first time she understood that it wasn't hunting the deadly virus or finding it that thrilled him. It was standing on the edge, taunting the virus. For a moment she was tempted to throw the carbolic acid of truth into his face. But she knew where she was going and knew she would get there just the same without the addition of recent corroborating evidence. "No you didn't have to tell me. But," and she drew out the silence for a few uncomfortable moments, "You do not get any credit. What am I supposed to do? Thank you for being so magnanimous about your character defects? You saved me from a painful future. Thanks. You also cut me off from a promising future."

"This is so screwed up. I was trying to do the right thing."

She was appalled. "Damn it, Peter, don't you understand? I could never trust you. Never. Do you have any idea how corrosive that is?"

"Mead, listen to me," he reached for her hand which she instantly withdrew, "We're good together. You know that. Deep down you can't deny that we're very good together."

"Peter, you're incredible. Have you heard one word I've said?"

"Mead, I only know that I love you. I think you still love me." He hung his head bashfully. "At least I hope you still do. We could have a wonderful life together."

Had he always been so obvious, Mead wondered? And I so blind? Disgust rose at the back of her throat.

"Won't you consider getting back together?" he pleaded. She suddenly wondered what all this effort was about, why he was so intent. She quickly concluded that it probably had little to do with her. "No," she said simply. He paused to scrutinize her face. If he had any suspicions or wanted to ask the question, Mead knew her expression held the answer.

"Is there someone else?" he asked.

She almost choked. "No."

He stood and seemed at a loss, shifting his weight from one foot to the other, brushing his hand through his thick head of hair. "Mead . . ."His voice made her name a question. "You really won't consider getting back together?"

Leveling her gaze directly at him she said a very solid tone, "No." Could he, she wondered, really be surprised? Unbelievable. "Peter, don't you get it?" she asked sharply, "I already have. I've made my decision - twice now. I won't make it again."

Peter looked at her, bit his lower lip, slowly nodded his head, turned and walked away.

She felt so vacuous she was almost surprised that he didn't bounce weightlessly away as she watched him cross the barren moonlit slope. She thought she heard a bell ringing but it was only the empty mountain wind whistling in her ears.

* * *

The ringing phone pierced the tense quiet of the darkened hotel room. Reluctantly she picked it up.

"Luce, Tina here. Look, Jacob's getting a little squirrelly. Are you ready? Are you leaving soon?" Luce held the receiver away from her ear to lessen the level of panic she heard in Tina's voice.

"Almost ready. Tell Jacob I will be there. Shortly." She used pedantic, measured tones against Tina's barrage.

"Luce, please don't dawdle. You know how he is and a couple of the key reviewers are coming early and can only stay for a short while. And . . ."

"Yes, yes. I understand, Tina. I'm almost ready. Just give me a few minutes to finish and I'm on my way."

"Okay. But hurry. Please."

"Yes. Of course."

Luce hung up the phone and continued to sit in the over-stylized chair by the undersized round table that passed as a desk, fully dressed, ready to go, unable to get up. I wish I were dead, she thought.

It wasn't just the fear of the show that immobilized Luce, turned her legs to lead. She had had many shows and while they all made her feel uncomfortable and vulnerable, she had learned how to get through them. While she was hardly adept, she could hold a conversation with a critic or reviewer, schmooz with a potential buyer. Best of all she had learned how to talk about her work in abstract terms, in a zone she kept at some distance from her heart. And it wasn't that this show had taken on a new significance with the recent positive reviews and notice of her. It wasn't even that this was the first show since Grace's death. It was the stinging accumulation of these factors. Her professional success heightened the contrast of her personal emptiness and despair and pointed acutely, irrevocably to the loss she felt. For every professional achievement, she felt a commensurate hole in her personal life. And the imminent contrast showed how small and finite and tasteless pain made her life.

She knew she would not kill herself, that was not even up for discussion. On a fundamental level, having been raised in the even-keeled moral environment of her parents' atheism, it was simply not an option.

But, if she were to die, she would not mind. "I don't mind dying," Grace had whispered frailly, "but I do mind leaving you," and at that precise moment, Luce sitting on the edge of the bed, leaning to hear her words, could have slapped Grace, so violent was the anger that surged in her body and took her by the throat. But now, two dry years later, Luce understood.

She had arrived, via a different disease, at the same point. Overwhelming sorrow had taken her by a different route but at last, exhausted by pain, she understood Grace's words. For all her selfish exhortations to Grace to fight, to survive, to live, Luce would not mind dying, so flat had life become. She would welcome the relief, the lifting of the weight of sorrow and grief, the end of loneliness. Misogyny aside, she envied Indian wives who could throw themselves on burning biers, Pharaoh's wives who had walked through dark and convoluted tunnels to be with the one they loved. She did not believe in an after life but she did believe in a life no longer worth living. It was what she faced every day. Hanging on, marking time, simply enduring became all the more difficult as a result.

The phone rang again. In the dark hotel room the red light on the phone quivered with each ring. She watched it blankly then finally reached to pick up the receiver. "Tina, I am on my way," she said.

"Luce, is that you?" a warm voice asked.

"Yes, who's this?"

"Jenny. I'm so glad I caught you. I just left work, right around the corner from you. And I thought I'd take a chance and see if you were still here. I thought we might take a cab together to the gallery."

"Oh, ah, okay."

"I'm in the lobby."

"Be right down." Luce hung up the phone very softly, lifted her leaden body very slowly and, getting her coat, left the dark hotel room very reluctantly.

* * *

In the glare of the blinding snow, Mead leaned into the precipitous incline of the mountain and took a swig of water. They had started their ascent through the second part of Western Breach that morning and the temperatures had remained cold despite the sun overhead. The trail was definitely more arduous now, and Mead could feel her own uncomfortable swelling as capillaries and veins constricted. At this altitude they were taking in half the amount of oxygen they usually did at sea level and her chest tightened. It was disconcerting to feel such a hunger for oxygen, to breath and not get a full breath. Headache, nausea, shortness of breath. Is it altitude sickness, she mused, or just life sickness? She rubbed her temples trying to alleviate the dull pounding.

They had taken more breaks than usual. Roz, dehydrated from her frequent bouts of vomiting, was definitely slowing them down, her pace a labored crawl up the sloping white face of the mountain. While all had remained quiet on the topic, eye contact among the more upright trekkers suggested wariness and growing impatience. Mary had laid down the law right after breakfast. "Roz, your buddies are being polite, and it's their decision, but personally I think you'd better head back. We're about to hit some of the roughest terrain." Roz had adamantly shook her head and dragged herself along. The quiet morning climb had been punctuated by Mary's exhortations

101

to Roz: "Keep going, Doc, keep going. You wouldn't stop mid-surgery, would you? Don't stop now." Roz attempted to counter these pointed entreaties, and correct Mary's notions of her practice, with snide words and dirty looks but could only muster slight grimaces and feeble grunts.

"Okay now, everyone, listen up," Mary stood mid-group. Mbiti and two other guides were leading, followed by Mead, Linda and Gil. Mary came next, then Roz and Peter. "The section we're about to hit I call Buddhist Meditation. It's going to require complete concentration. You need to think, people, about each move you make. Be fully alert and attentive. We're going to be scaling a narrow sluice that's all rock, snow and ice. Slippery and tricky. Take it slow. Make each step a sure one. I recommend that you not look up, and certainly don't look ahead. You're all getting tired and it will only discourage you. Keep your eyes on your feet and the small patch of mountain you're hiking. One step at a time, slow and steady, and we'll all make it up."

Mary, in roll call fashion, asked everyone how they were faring. She didn't include Mbiti and the two other guides who were some twenty feet ahead smoking cigarettes. "Mead?"

"Except for the jack hammering in my head, couldn't be better."

"Linda?"

"I'm okay. This sun is a killer though. Even with these glasses, looking at the snow feels like a knife through the pupils."

"Gil, my man?"

"Well enough, thanks."

"Roz?" Roz could barely lift her hand to her head in a limp salute. "Peter, I don't even have to ask. I want you stay close behind Roz. She might need assistance through this next pass.

"You guys don't know how lucky you are. Here we are at 16,000 feet. Storms can come up in a heart beat. Temperatures can plummet. And look at us, we're just having a beautiful day. Somebody's smiling on us. Okay, if everyone's ready, let's continue our stroll."

All morning Mead had entertained fantasies of abruptly stopping, turning around and simply letting herself slide to the bottom. The thought of a quick get-away, no matter how ungraceful, was tempting. But the rhythmic sound of Linda's climbing behind her had spurred her on. Now, at a forty-five degree angle to the mountainside, she let her mind go blank and studied each bit of treacherous slope before her. A few times her stomach dropped as she slipped her footing. The image of a chain reaction spill down the jagged sluice was enough to refocus her concentration.

From below the air filled with sudden shrieks and squeals of pain which cracked the blue-white quiet into a thousand splintering pieces. Mead instinctively dropped onto her stomach and grasped a nearby ledge, holding on for dear life. She listened to the sound of feet frantically slipping over rock, followed by a loud, prolonged rumbling as bodies tumbled and scraped down the mountain.

"Oh, my God," she heard Roz shout.

Peter's panicked voice rose up, "Hold on. Try to get a grip."

"Mbiti," Mary shouted, "Stop. Quick, come down here. Hurry."

Mead rammed her body into the rocky wall to make way for Mbiti and the two other guides who half-scampered, half-slid down the narrow pass. More rumbling, more shouts, a loud sickening thud, then a dreadful quiet prevailed.

"Mead," Linda's voice was thick with terror, "What's going on? Oh, my God. Are we going to die up here?"

The section of the sluice they were now in snaked up the mountain and Mead, had she had the courage and solidity of spirit to turn her head, would not have been able to see below. "I don't know, Linda. Sounds like they've taken a fall. Try to keep calm. Gil, are you okay? Can you see anything?"

From twenty feet below Gil's voice answered, "I'm all right but I can't see a thing. Keep where you are. I'm going to slide down. I'll be back and give you a report."

Mead dug her gloved fingers into the stony ledge and tried to lift herself up onto a firmer spit of the pass.

"Mead, I'm loosing my grip. I'm going to fall."

Mead could hear the panic precipitating an attack of hyperventilation. "Linda," Mead's voice was emphatic, commanding, "You're not going to fall. Hold on. I'm coming to you. Keep your grasp." Mead, belly down, tumbled toward Linda. The ice and rock pulled up her gortex jacket, scraped her stomach and accelerated her slide.

"Watch out," Linda yelled as Mead's boots came flying at her, pummeling her face. Now flipping over Linda, they both somersaulted backward some fifteen yards before Mead was able to slow their slide with her hand and turn her body horizontally in the rocky chute. Her glove was shredded. Stretching full length, neck pressing into one side of the pass, feet digging into the other, she jammed herself across the width of the sluice. Linda careened violently into her but the wedge Mead had made of herself held them both. Mead watched the sky twirl several times before coming to a halt.

She automatically took a physical inventory from head to toe. She was okay, bruised, stiff and a little bloodied, but all parts felt operable. "Linda, are you okay?"

Linda put her hands over her face, "I want down."

"Hold still, okay? I'm going to do a quick check, make sure nothing's broken." Slowly dislodging herself from beneath Linda, Mead took off her gloves and pried Linda's hands from her face. The force of their fall had ripped Linda's sun glasses from her face. "Jesus," Mead said looking at Linda's swollen face, "Can you open that eye?" Linda moaned but gradually opened her right eye. "That's going to be a shiner. Sorry." Mead placed her hands on Linda's head and proceeded to work her way down her body checking for breaks.

"Ouch," Linda cried when Mead touched her leg.

"Just a bad bruise. Lucky it's the femur. You're fine. Here, try to sit up." Groggily, she sat up and slumped against the wall of the pass. Mead, frustrated to be blinded by the terrain, shouted, "What's going on down there?" No answer. Linda's face filled with fear. "Let's just stay here for the moment," Mead advised. Linda began to shake. In minutes her body was rattling full bore. "Christ, Linda," Mead shouted, afraid that she was going into shock and hypothermia, "Stay with me." She rolled Linda full length and laid on top of her, vigorously rubbing her body trying to keep her circulation going.

"Christ, you're hurting me. Will you get off of me. Jesus."

Mead backed off slowly, carefully checking Linda's eyes for signs. Pulling away from Mead, she said, "I tell you I'm okay."

Ten minutes later they heard the steady steps of someone approaching. "Who's there?" Mead asked.

"Mary." Her voice was flat, angry.

Mead waited until she reached them before asking, "What the hell's happened, Mary?"

"Roz," she replied acidly, "is what the hell's happened. "God damn pig-headed debutante has no business climbing this mountain." She sighed heavily. "Sorry, guess I shouldn't talk about your friend that way. What happened to you two?" She leveled a tough, ruthless gaze at them.

"We took a little spill," Mead minimized.

Mary motioned toward Linda's eye. "What the hell did you do? Punch her?"

"Doctors, Mary, are a dangerous lot." Linda gingerly wiped her eye with a handful of snow.

"You okay?" Mary bent in concern.

"Yeah, a little bruised, a little shaken," Mead said. "Other than that, we're fine."

Mary took a deep breath. "Well, it's turkey time. You two have to decide if you want to continue or if you want to follow the others down the mountain."

"Mary, tell us what happened, for God's sake," Linda roared.

"Roz lost her footing. I knew she was headed for a fall. Flattened Peter. Don't know how she managed it but somehow they spun out of the sluice and over the edge. Took about a fifteen-foot fall. Thank God they fell on snow pack. Could have been worse. Much worse." Mead could see Mary was shaken. "Peter's okay but Roz seems to have broken her ankle. They're down below now. Peter's packing it with snow." She shook her head with disgust. "Never, never have I come across one like that. Saw it coming the moment I laid eyes on her. Just had a feeling in my gut. Well, what's it going to be, gals? Peter, Gil, Mbiti and one of the other guides are going to take her down. They're rigging up a makeshift gurney as we speak. Guess Gil plans to fly her back to Nairobi for treatment. We can either head up. Or head down. Your money, your call."

Stunned, Mead and Linda exchanged glances. "What do you think, Linda? I'll go whichever way you decide."

"Are you sure about that?"

Mead nodded. "'You took the body blows."

"If you asked me," Mary interjected, "I'd say we're awful damn close. Linda, if you can haul that body of yours some more, well, it'd be a shame . . ."

Linda looked up the sluice, then down. "Then I say up."

Mead, surprised by her decision, smiled. "Up it is."

"Mary, there is a Holiday Inn up there, right? Comfy bed, hot shower, room service?"

"Hon, if there is, I'll fight you for the last room. All right then. That's decided. You two stay here. No point in us all retracing our steps. I'm going back down to get this mess squared away. I'll be back in about a twenty or so minutes. You have enough water?" Mead checked their supply. "We're fine."

"Okay, then, I'll be back." She started to slide down the pass, then stopped herself with her hand against the wall and turned, "Any parting messages?"

They exchanged glances and Linda shook her head. Weary and wary, Mead leaned against the hard wall of the sluice. What to say, she wondered. Her suspicion of Peter's true motivation for going with Roz was an acid burning her gut. A cabal of anger, hurt, insult and disappointment pounded her chest.

Then, just as quickly, everything was washed away by loss. She knew she would not be seeing Peter again, that this truly was good-bye. Appropriate that it should be happening through an intermediary. The sound of the tent zipper ripped through her head. She looked at Mary and said, "No, none that I can think of."

They stayed on the cold, hard ground for some time in silence. After a while Linda leaned into Mead. "You okay, Mead?"

"Sure. And you?"

"You know, I do believe I am going to make it to the top."

Mead smiled. "I do believe you are."

"You're neither one of you going to be making anything unless we get our asses in gear," Mary's voice preceded her up the sluice. Fred, the remaining guide, took lead position. "You might want to take one last peek at that blue sky. For the next six hours we're only going to be looking at our toes. Okay? Well, let's get a move on. We need to make up some serious lost time."

* * *

"There you are," Jacob said taking a flute of champagne off a tray and handing it to Luce as she entered.

"Where," he smiled sweetly and lowered his voice, "the hell have you been? Hello Jenny." He leaned to kiss her. Jenny motioned that she was going to put her coat away and took Luce's as well.

"Thanks, Jenny," Luce said watching her walk away. "I really do like her, Jacob."

"Luce you are a half an hour late. The *Art Review Quarterly* editor has been patiently pacing the gallery. The PR Director of a large high tech company was very interested in meeting you, but couldn't stay any longer. A big sale – gone."

"Jacob, scowling is most unattractive. Didn't your mother ever tell you your face could freeze like that?"

"Luce, I am delighted to see you are in good spirits. It will be ever so helpful for the few remaining moments of your show."

"Let's not exaggerate. But I am sorry, Jacob. Traffic was terrible. And I did get a bit of a late start. I'll go talk to the editor right away."

"If it wouldn't inconvenience you. And on the way, would you tell Ruthie she doesn't have to load up her purse with hors d'oeuvres? I will be happy to send her home with a plate."

Luce smiled, put a hand on his back and tiptoed to kiss him. "I am sorry, Jacob. I promise to get to all the luminaries."

"Oh-la-la, don't we look very chick tonight? Nice threads. Say, Luce, I've been looking at your paintings, you're not a well woman. These are very sad paintings. Truly. But I'm a little puzzled. I overheard someone say that they're full of beautiful ants. Am I crazy? I don't see any ants, beautiful, ugly or otherwise. Luce, why would you want to paint ants anyway?"

"I think you mean angst, Ruthie."

"Whatever, you need help. I've got a great 900 line for a good psychic. I'm serious. I'm worried. All these *Searching For Grace* paintings, Luce this is not good. Not good. Your highway ones are nice, well, nice if you like looking at highways. Funny thing, these customers here tonight seem very high brow. I guess only the filthy rich would want to have a picture of a highway in their living room. For me, I waited on a list for years to get an apartment on the back of the building so I didn't have to see all that traffic. Who can explain what money does to you? And speaking of money, I think your printer made a big mistake. Did you see this price list?" she whistled. "Are you for real with asking that many smacker-roos for one of your paintings? If so, I'm gonna start being nice to you. To hell with Pearl. Who needs a pain in the ass sister when . . ."

"Excuse me, Ruthie. There's some one I have to talk to right now. I'll catch up with you in a few minutes."

"Hey, Miss Big Shot, I know you're working. I'm fine, I'll just look around. Try to find me a rich husband with one foot in the grave and the other on a banana peel. Go. Go. I'm having a great time. And whenever anyone asks me how I know you I tell them you're my fairy god daughter. Good one, huh? Go. Go. Don't worry about me. Love this stuff," she raised her flute to Luce. "What do you call this? Cold Duck? Tasty. The food's great, too. I'll see ya later."

"Oh, and Ruthie, Jacob said he'll be happy to give you an extra plate of hors d'ouevres when you leave."

She leaned down and whispered confidentially, "I think he's worried that you'll make a mess of your purse."

"Ha, this old thing! Well, that's very nice, though. And, Luce, when you come back I've got a hot tip for you. Very hot. Just off the press, if you know what I mean. I'll give you a hint - pizza delivery boys are not what you'd think." She offered Luce an exaggerated wink.

Luce walked past the chamber quartet and toward the editor while watching Ruthie pull canapés from her purse. Seeing the editor, she paused to brace herself. Then, with a newly applied smile, walked toward him.

Jenny found Jacob and took the champagne he extended. "Thanks," he said, as they watched Luce talking with the reviewer. "I owe you one."

"No problem. I was only too happy to help. Once I left here I had a hell of a time getting a cab uptown, given the time of night. But he waited at the hotel so that was a help. You were absolutely right, she needed a kick start."

107

"What did you say to her to put her in such a good mood?"

"I didn't say much. Just listened. At the risk of making you angry, want some unsolicited advice?"

She turned to watch him nervously stroke his lower face. "Why not?"

"Stop coming at her with your solutions. Give her some space."

"And watch her completely miss seeing a life preserver that's just the other side of the wave?" His voice was brittle.

"Ooops." She looked at him, arched her eyebrows and swallowed hard. "Remind me never to give you unsolicited advice."

"With pleasure." He bent and kissed her on the cheek. "I still owe you one, though."

* * *

"Well, how does the top of Africa feel?" Mary asked. They had spent the past two hours scaling the Great Northern Glacier, a huge ice-blue curtain that draped the mountain top . Now at 19,340 feet they stood next to an understated rectangular sign that read "You have reached the Uhuru Peak - the highest point in Africa". Mead deferred to Linda.

"Great. To tell you the truth, it feels pretty damn great. Excruciating pain aside, of course. How 'bout you, Mead?"

"Ask me when we're back at sea level."

Mary laughed, "There're some interesting things to see if you want to nose around, the Reusch Crater has some vents that steam and belch sulfuric gas. There's an ash cone not too far away. Fascinating topography. We usually stay at the summit about an hour."

"At the risk of sounding lazy," Linda said, sinking into the snowy mountain top, "I think I'm just going to sit right here, so I don't have to walk an unnecessary inch, and enjoy the view - with the one eye I can still see out of, that is." She gave Mead a sidelong smile and Mead grimaced another apology.

"Sounds good to me." Mead started to squat. "Mind if I join you?"

"Not at all."

"All right then, I'm going to check it out. Be back in an hour. Oh, by the by, I generally offer this to my surviving climbers." Mary pulled out a split of champagne. "You'll stay put?"

Mead and Linda exchanged a glance then chuckled. "Mary," Mead said solemnly, "You can count on it."

"But you can take the car keys if you don't trust us, Mom," Linda offered.

As Mary walked off Mead popped the cork and poured champagne into two cups Linda had pulled from her knapsack. "Say, Mary," Linda called out,

"What exactly does Uhuru mean, anyway?" Without turning, Mary shouted over her shoulder, "Freedom." They exchanged glances as Mead extended her hand to Linda.

"Congratulations. You made it."

"Thanks, Mead." She took a long drink and coughed. "Here's to you. You made it, too."

"Yeah, I guess I did." They clicked their plastic cups together.

"No guessing about it." Linda gave her a hard stare. "You did. Not easy given the circumstances, especially with Peter . . . and Roz."

"What do you mean?" Mead's face was an empty slate.

"Who are you kidding? Not me, that's for sure. With seven tents pitched within fifteen feet of each other, a limited number of hiking boot brands, it only takes a crunch or two on the ground and a confirming peep out the bottom of the tent fly by this insomniac to put it together. Must have been hard. You handled it well."

Mead sighed. "Well, facts are facts. Any weakening resolve? A thing of the past."

"Oh, c'mon, Mead. Drop the stoicism. Christ, your White Knight, uh, your fallen White Knight, reinserts himself in your life only to screw Roz right before your eyes. This is not like being stood up for a date. This is a fucking big deal, no pun intended. I'm royally pissed and I was never engaged to the schmuck!"

"He is a bastard, huh?"

"Charming, handsome, virile, first class variety. I might have been tempted to shove him off a cliff myself - if Roz hadn't beaten me to the punch. I think I would have picked a better spot, something a little steeper. A little slip during the first part of the Western Breach and off he goes. So long, heart break."

"Not quite my style. However," she slowly grinned, "Not necessarily a bad idea."

"Well, for what it's worth, I am sorry."

"Thanks, Linda, but don't be. I never regret having clarity. Sometimes the price tag's a little high, but . . . Anyway, it's partially my own fault."

"What?" Linda practically screamed, outraged.

"I should have put a stop to it before it even began. I should never have let him come."

"Mead, we'll let it be our little secret that you're not perfect. Although, it does give me a bit of pleasure." She hesitated, "You know, we don't always approve of who, or what, we want. It's a bitch, huh?"

Mead nodded her head then swiveled around so that they sat back to back. They sat in silence, each lost in her own thoughts of the past few days, each looking at the glacial snow, billowy white clouds which encircled the summit and the endless blue sky above, sipping champagne.

"Mead?"

"Yeah?"

"Can I ask you a favor?"

"Sure."

Linda hesitated. "Will you write a letter of recommendation for me. I've decided to apply to med school when I get home."

Mead twisted her head and smiled. "You bet I will. That's a good move, Linda. You'll make a great doctor."

"Think so?"

"Know so."

"Thanks. You know what? I think so, too. At least Tim will be glad to have me home for awhile." She paused then asked, "Are you glad you climbed this sucker?"

Mead took a deep breath. "Yes, I am."

"Me, too. Well, perhaps we should offer a toast to our catalyst. Or is that pushing it?"

"No, not at all. She was just a bit player in my drama with Peter. Good idea. To Roz, ah . . ." Mead turned and lifted her shoulders in question, seeking guidance from Linda, then succumbed to her feelings. "On second thoughts that is pushing it." Mead jumped to her feet. "I know," she said pulling Linda into a standing position, "To Africa."

"To Africa." They each held their glass high.

"Better still," Linda added, "How 'bout to freedom."

"Yeah," Mead said, "That's the one. Uhuru – to freedom." They solemnly rotated a complete circle, touched their cups together and drank.

* * *

"I have a surprise for you," Jacob had said over the phone.

"And what might that be?" Luce forced a tone of curiosity.

"Best if I show you rather than tell you," Jacob playfully responded.

"Okay," Luce lapsed into silence.

"Luce," Jacob, exasperated, almost shouted. "Could you feign a little interest here?"

"Sorry, Jacob, I was still reading the paper," she lied, as she hugged the hotel bed pillow closer and muted the TV weather station. Trying to muster enthusiasm she asked, "What's my surprise?"

110

"That's better. Still pretty lame, though. Your flight's mid-afternoon, right? Can you meet later this morning at the gallery?"

"Sure. See you then. Oh, and Jacob," she dead-panned, "I can hardly wait."

"Pitiful, Luce, you're really pitiful. Why do I even bother? Bye."

Now they stood on the sidewalk before the SoHo building where Luce's old studio was. Arms firmly clasped over her chest and feet planted into the cement, she acidly asked him, "What exactly are we doing here, Jacob?"

"Why are you so god damn resistant? Just come inside with me," he said, pulling a hand free and tugging her into the building. In the freight elevator going up, scrunched into the corner, she steamed while Jacob ignored her and sang an insipid tune. At the top floor Jacob pushed back the elevator gate and pulled her into the empty space of her former studio.

Sunlight streamed in from the floor to ceiling architectural windows and the huge skylight. The space ran the entire length of the building and had windows on three sides. "Why are you doing this to me, Jacob?"

"*For* you, Luce. That's a distinction. Look," he said walking toward the far end, "I've talked with the landlord and he's willing to have the bathroom renovated. And a little kitchen put in. That'd be nice, huh?"

"What happened to the guy who took it after me?"

"Took a faculty post somewhere. Looks good, doesn't it? You have to admit, it's some of the best studio space in town."

Luce began to walk the length of the worn, paint-splattered hard wood floors. "Yeah, it does look good."

"The landlord said he'd wait and give you first choice on the space. Guess he has a soft spot for you."

"That bastard?" Luce responded dubiously. "We did nothing but fight."

"All right, I paid him. But just one month's rent. To give you some time." Jacob was mischievously pleased with himself. Luce forced a smile. "Thank you, Jacob."

"Well?"

"I'll have to think about it."

"What's to think? You could . . ."

"Jacob," she said from the opposite side of the room, "Would you mind leaving me alone for awhile?" He started to sulk. "Please?"

"Okay." He headed for the elevator, then paused. "You'll stop back by the gallery before you leave?"

"Have to, my bags are there."

"Oh, yeah," he scratched his head. "Forgot."

Then seeing his disappointment linger she said, "Thanks, Jacob. You're a sweetheart. And a good friend." He clownishly bobbed his head back and forth. "You are."

The elevator bumped its way down the floors as Luce slumped against the wall into a patch of sun. Overcome with fatigue, she stretched her body fully on the warm floor, shutting her eyes to the present, sliding effortlessly into the past.

"So, this is your studio? Hmm, very comfy. A home away from home I see." Grace had invited Luce to invite her to Luce's studio and stood in the middle of the room circling slowly. "So these are your paintings?"

"The same."

"Hmm. I suppose," she said coyly, "that I wouldn't find numbers beneath the paint, you know, one for red, two for blue?"

"Nope. Not this batch anyway."

"And I guess that you don't do many of those saucer-eyed third world kids."

"No, not many."

"Too bad. Among my faves. Right after black velvet Jesuses."

"Mine, too. I'm working my way up to them."

"Well, don't despair, you seem to show some talent. You might get there yet."

"You've done a pretty good job of keeping your art expertise a secret."

"Yeah, well, I don't like to brag but I've seen the best Woolworth's has to offer. Don't like to gloat. Not everyone's had my cultural advantages. Mind if I look around a little?"

"Please, go ahead."

"Thanks." She fell into a quiet mood and slowly made her way through the studio carefully looking at canvases which were hung and flipping through those Luce had stacked against the walls. It was their third date. Over the course of the previous two evenings they had spent together, Luce had found herself alternately amused, intrigued and horrified by this woman who friends had introduced her to. Last week, on their second date, Grace had begun the dinner conversation, proclaiming more than asking, "Shall I tell you what's going on for me here or would you like to go first?"

"Please," Luce had deferred, amused by her directness, her bravada. "By all means, you go first."

"Kitzel."

"Kitzel?"

"Yiddish for chemistry."

Luce waited, then smiled. "Chemistry?"

"Chemistry."

"That's it?"

"That's everything."

"I see." Luce had been delighted by Grace's sense of science.

"I have it for you."

"I see."

"Do you? Well, you don't have to say."

"I don't think I will. Not yet."

"No. I didn't think you would."

"No? Why?"

"Because you're decidedly upper East side. Very button down, very reserved. Me, I'm Brooklyn through and through."

"I see."

"I bet you do. I won't hold your origins against you." She smiled.

"Thanks. Very generous of you."

"Ruthie, my mother, says 'Wherever you go, there you are.'"

"Well, can't very well argue with that."

"And here we are."

"Indeed."

"Should we order?"

"That would be best."

One week later, Luce watched as Grace walked from a stack of paintings back to those hung on the long wall. She liked the way Grace's shoulders preceded her body, the way her hair, a tangle of curls, framed her oval face. Following to where Grace stood intently before two works, Luce said, "You not only get to see my studio, you get to meet my family. The one below is my parents."

"I see where you get your bubbly demeanor." Luce laughed. "*Doctor 1.*" Grace read the title penciled on the wall of the above painting. "Who's this?"

"My sister, Mead. It's painted from a photo I took of her last summer at my parents' beach house."

Grace shot Luce a look over her shoulder. "Mead? That's a name?"

"I guess we do have unusual names. There're also my brothers Rand and Avery."

"Geez, you sound like a bunch of escapees from *Atlas Shrugged*. What did your parents have against you anyway?"

"My father was into individuality."

"Well, Mead looks like she fits that bill. She seems pretty determined."

113

"She is that and more."

"And a doctor?"

"Will be. She's finishing up her residency."

"Are you two close?"

"No, not really. She's ten years younger. But I'm an admirer of hers. And I'm rooting for her."

"Rooting for her, huh? Gosh, Sis, don't knock yourself out."

"How about you," Luce shifted the focus, "Do you have siblings?"

"No, just my mom and me. Ruthie divorced when I was about five and never remarried. But my uncle Milton and aunt Pearl each have kids, so I have lots of cousins. Always wanted a sister, though. Being an only kid gets lonely. Hey, do you want to paint me?"

Luce was taken aback. "Uh, sure."

"Where do I sit? Here?" she said patting a stool that sat before Luce's easel.

"Now?"

"Why not?"

"Well, it generally takes some time."

"I don't mind."

"I mean, several sessions."

"I can make myself available."

"Well, all right. Let me just get a fresh canvas." For the next few minutes Luce searched and found a canvas, then framed it in the easel, and set up her paints. Ready, she looked up and saw Grace sitting on the stool stark naked.

"What are you doing?" Luce exclaimed, flustered.

"What do you mean, 'What am I doing?' I thought you were going to paint me."

"But I never said I wanted to paint you nude."

"No, you didn't." Grace paused. "I want you to paint me nude."

Luce took a moment to compose herself. "Okay," she said quietly. "Please sit still." She took Grace in, head to toe, circling slowly around the stool. A summer evening sun shaded her skin golden pink and stood in small pools of her collar bones. She noted the curl of her shoulders, like gentle waves about to shudder upon the shore, the plane of her back, which tapered sweetly into her waist, the distinct triangle of her sacrum. "Okay," she said, now in full control, now in another mode. "Turn your knees a little to the left. Good. Sit up straight and twist your upper torso toward the right. Now your head, tilt it a little. Other way. Like this." Luce held her hand at the desired angle for Grace to mimic.

"That's it." Luce began to work her paints, stroking in the outline of

114

Grace against the large windows through which the city formed a backdrop.

"I see all I have to do to shake that composure is undress. I'll file that away for future reference."

"Hold still please. No talking."

"Got any music?"

"No. Prefer quiet," Luce chastised.

"Not even a radio?" Grace persisted.

Luce grimaced then turned on the radio behind her.

"Mind changing the station?"

"You don't like classical? You'd prefer . . .?"

"Jazz will do nicely." Grace smiled while Luce adjusted the tuner. "There. Stop. That's perfect."

"Are you ready now?" Luce asked. Grace nodded her head. "Please don't move."

Luce worked quickly. After twenty minutes she looked at Grace. "Need a break?" From the radio came the voices of Ella and Louie:

Under a blanket of blue
Just you and I beneath the stars
Wrapped in the arms of sweet romance
The night is ours

Under a blanket of blue
Let me be thrilled by all your charms
Darling, I know my heart will dance
Within your arms.

A summer's night magic
Enthralling me so,
The night would be tragic
If you weren't here
To share it, my dear.

Covered with heaven above
Let's dream a dream of love for two
Wrapped in the arms of sweet romance
Under a blanket of blue

"Luce, come here."

Luce walked toward her and stopped about a foot away. "Are you always so provocative, Grace? So sure of yourself? So bold?"

Grace looked down, smiled, then looked directly into Luce's eyes. "No." She reached for Luce's hands and turned them palm up. "Nice hands. Very nice." She buried her face in Luce's hands and breathed deeply. Standing up she said, "You'll come to learn, Luce, that I truly love you." She clasped Luce's hands behind her naked back. "You will."

As Luce lay in the empty studio she could almost feel the warmth of Grace's touch upon her back but it was just the weak winter sun on its way down the sky.

PART THREE

"So, Mead," Dr. Jane Kapito's voice was soft with irony, her natural lilting cadence disconcertingly musical in the present setting, "This is Z59.5 – firsthand." She opened her arms to encompass the squalor that surrounded them. Mead slowly swiveled her head, taking in the sights, sounds and smells of Sofia Town. To buttress herself, she leaned against the small car they had driven from downtown Nairobi. The flinty sun reflecting off the small corrugated steel houses was stinging, as though the reality of Sofia Town was not sufficiently painful. Despite the glare, Mead removed her sunglasses. Already feeling the intruder, it seemed doubly impolite to hide behind dark glasses. The sounds of people's lives rubbing uncomfortably, unnaturally close to one another was a constant drone. She immediately thought of the interior of one of the massive termite hills she'd seen while driving across the open plains. A termite hill gone mad.

What passed for houses were in actuality domino rows of lean-tos, each sharing a wall with the neighboring house. The materials ranged from sheets of rusting corrugated steel, to ripped plastic tarping, to thin plywood strips and bolts of used fabric. One good storm would wipe out the entire town.

People crowded the hard, tired dirt streets, and the living seemed to spill out of each house into the alleys. In front of one shack an older woman sat beneath a torn black umbrella peddling colorless tomatoes spread before her on a hand-woven mat. At the next house, a girl no more than six, wearing layers of red and orange rags, carried a baby on her back, a frayed dirty towel her sling. She stood near another girl, perhaps eight or nine, who wore a coral dress smudged with dirt, obviously discarded by a wealthy family in the Nairobi suburbs. Silver beads, earrings and a bracelet completed the outfit. She knelt by a beaten pot placed over randomly strewn rocks and two paltry branches that smoldered and smoked, stirring some formless soupy mix. In another world, with the dress just back from the corner cleaner's, with new white laced-trimmed socks and patent leather shoes, she might be on her way to Sunday church. Here she was on her way to nowhere.

Older girls milled aimlessly in the background, leaning against poles, sitting in the meager patches of shade. Two women sat on a folded rattan curtain that served as a front porch, their beautiful dark features sculpted with suspicion as they eyed Mead. A man pulling a dented trash can, which rested on a handmade dolly of branches and two small tricycle wheels, sold water. The only other source of water seemed to be the muddy puddles left by the previous day's rain. A young boy, skull dramatically outlined by the hand of malnutrition, cuddled a puppy. An occasional bike rattled down the small rutted street. Apart from that, everyone and everything seemed lifeless, enervated by the relentless sun, by the relentless poverty. Mead looked down one street, then another. Sofia Town sprawled endlessly. Mead felt each piece of sensory information, the visuals, the smells, as a series of soft body blows. Chicago, with its lake view condo, sprawling hospital complex and clean, high-tech research lab, seemed light years away. Beneath the heat, she felt herself crumple.

Mead watched and listened as Jane spoke to the women. They answered her questions listlessly, batting flies from their faces. Linda had introduced Mead to Jane Kapito, a doctor at Misericordia Hospital, upon their return from the climb a week ago, and Mead had readily accepted Jane's offer to accompany her on rounds through Sofia Town. Jane was a commanding woman whose directness Mead admired – once she found her footing.

"I'm a pediatrician by training, Mead. As a pediatrician in Africa, we are of course used to our children dying. These days we must all treat AIDS. But AIDS is just one more thing. I am HIV-positive, too. Yes," she said in response to the snap of Mead's head when she heard those words, "you have heard my words correctly. My husband and I lived for many years in Kisimu, on Lake Victoria. I was doctor at a small health clinic. I doctored for four days and farmed for three. My husband was a regional education minister. One day, coming back from a visit to Kericho, he was in a very bad car accident and required blood. Of course, we were worried by the blood supply, because they do not test. So, as is customary these days, our family members donated blood for him. One year later his younger brother died of AIDS. We knew then what was in store. He was a good man, Mead. So full of life. He felt very badly that I was infected, too. The suffering, the death, well, that is most difficult to be sure. But there is a clarity that walks hand in hand with imminent death. We decided we wanted to spend our time providing help where it was most urgently needed.

"And so we came to Nairobi. He died last year. I made a sacred vow to my god and to myself to do what I could to help, however I can.

"Life can be – how do you say? – ironic, Mead. As a student I attended medical school in Belgrade, rather than here, hoping I would get a better post in the city. Instead I was assigned to a rural area and now Misericordia cannot even afford to pay me a full wage. Without the supplies, the equipment, I might just as well have studied a Red Cross first aid book."

Jane waved Mead to join her, and they walked down the street. The stench of garbage and human waste was repelling, and Mead had to concentrate to minimize the waves of nausea lapping in her stomach. They passed through a small town center dominated by an open air market where the vendors had little to sell and the buyers little money with which to purchase. In the middle was a maze of billboards covered with photos of children. Women, refugees from warring countries, clustered around the maze, slowly searching the photos, studying each face, trying to recognize a look in the eyes or a distinguishing feature of a child lost in some war two or five or ten years ago.

They turned down a side street. "Here we are," Jane said stopping before an entrance that had a battered piece of cardboard for a door. "Jambo," she called gently. A rustling sound was heard, then a small hand reached from behind and pulled back the cardboard door. Jane smiled at the little girl, cupped her cheek and entered. "Come in, Mead," she said to Mead who wondered how she, Jane and a small child could possibly fit inside the tiny house. As Mead stooped to enter, she was blinded by the dark, windowless interior of the smoky house. As her eyes adjusted she saw the forms of a woman and two other children sitting in two chairs against the wall. The entire enclosure could accommodate only a full-size bed, the two chairs and a narrow space for walking.

Jane spoke in Swahili, translating for Mead as she spoke. "I have told them that you are a specialist from America and that you will examine them." Jane stepped aside and sat on the bed. Mead moved toward the mother. She was skeletal, with vacant eyes, ulcerated lips and small sores dotting her skin. Mead, examining her, could feel the overpowering fatigue that wilted her body. The woman spoke and Jane translated, "I feel like I am a hundred years old."

"What's your name?" Mead asked, pressing her hands lightly against the woman's throat for fear she'd snap under too much pressure.

"Bila," she replied.

"And these are your children?"

"These are my children who are still alive. My eldest daughter has already gone to heaven."

Mead twisted her head in question to Jane, who nodded that the daughter had died of AIDS. Attempting to ascertain possible dementia, Mead asked, "Bila, how many children do you have?"

Her voice, a wisp of smoke, "I have some children." Again Mead searched Jane's face for understanding. Jane was clearly dismissive.

"Ask if I might take blood samples, please." Mead, anxious to do something, examined Bila's emaciated arm for a suitable spot then gently pricked her dark skin with a needle. She worked quietly and quickly, offering awkward smiles and empty squeezes to the three wide-eyed children who smiled shyly. The wall behind them was decorated with clippings from glossy magazines, color advertisements for TVs, stoves, stereos and washers and dryers. There was also a travel brochure for an expensive resort at the Seychelles. The hut was stifling, and Mead was eager to leave. Even the putrid air outside would be a relief.

As they stood to leave, Bila summoned the energy to focus her eyes and, with a strength that surprised Mead, grab her hand. In a faltering voice she asked Mead, "Have you medicines? I'm trying to live to take care of my children. After I die there will be no one to watch over them. Who will take care of the children?"

Mead felt her stomach fall, all words fly out of her brain. Never had someone begged her for life. She was completely unprepared and struck immobile by the raw request.

Jane went to Bila's side and pulled her into a big embrace, "I promise you, Bila, that I will see that your children are taken care of. Here, it is better that you lie down on the bed now." She gently helped her recline. "I will be back next week." She left a large parcel on the corner of the bed. "I will bring more food, too."

Outside Mead, unnerved and rattled to be so unnerved, asked, "Is there a husband, Jane?"

"Yes, I met him once. He too has AIDS but he does not like to be around when I visit. He is, as he has told me, both married and single. Do not look so, this is not uncommon."

"All of the children are infected." She strove for her professional, neutral voice.

"Yes, I know. Bila has had very bad luck in this life."

"You knew I asked how many children she had to check for dementia. What happened? Did I say something wrong?"

"It is an old superstition, older than AIDS, that women don't tell you how many children they have, lest the trickster overhear and take another, or all of them, away."

"What do you do for her?" Mead asked.

"What can I do for her? We have no medicines. Even if we did, she could not afford them. How much does AZT cost one of your U.S. patients?"

"About $6,000 a year."

"And your new protease inhibitors?"

"Probably close to $12,000, maybe $15,000, a year."

"Our annual health budget per person is $4.00." She shrugged despondently. "I try to lessen her pain, I treat her with dignity and compassion. I pray, I pray very hard, for a speedy death."

They walked in silence for some time, occasionally stopping by another house, examining the people. At one home they were offered juice and Mead observed as both the host and Jane spilled some on the ground. Mead followed suit. Later she asked the purpose. "African etiquette. We always offer a portion of our food and drink to the ancestors."

After the last visit, where Jane was clearly upset by the news that a child had died since her visit last week, she sighed deeply. "Many Africans believe that the most powerful God created the universe but that he turned the everyday management over to a group of lackeys. I think there is much evidence that this is so, don't you?" She didn't wait for a reply. "It is hard to minister to my people sometimes, Mead, knowing that so much of what ails them, pushes them toward death, has a solution that we can simply not afford. Meningitis has a vaccine we cannot afford, diarrhea requires inexpensive rehydration salts we cannot afford, AIDS requires condoms we cannot afford. Forgive me, but sometimes I wish that these diseases killed faster. That would be a kindness."

They got back in Jane's small car, locked the doors against the threat of car-jacking, and drove back to the city center of Nairobi. They passed the Kenyetta International Conference Center, a beautiful modern complex with a circular high rise, rode along Kenyetta Avenue with its mix of majestic, colonial buildings, remnants of the British reign, to the modern office, hotel and industrial complexes.

Exhausted, Mead leaned her head against the closed window. Z59.5, she thought, extreme poverty. The code used by the World Health Organization in its annual Executive Report to identify the biggest killer and greatest cause of ill-health and suffering around the world. Z59.5 – the main reason why babies are not vaccinated, why clean water and sanitation are not provided, why drugs are not available, why mothers die in childbirth and children die in childhood. Sofia Town could well be a global capital. The simple, innocuous code was woefully inadequate for portraying the scope of the problem, for depicting the very human expressions on the very human victims. Z59.5 – a four-digit alpha-numeric designation, at the end of the alphabet, at the end of the line.

Beneath dark glasses, Mead heavily shut her eyes against the day.

* * *

The weak winter sun filtered softly through the study window, slanted soundlessly against the wall where years of photos hung like trophies, slipped quietly off the window sill, spilled milkily over the floor and curled around Elizabeth's feet. Alone at mid-morning, she read:

> Back in Nairobi. Climb was fine. Much work to catch up on. Will fill you in later.
> Love, Mead.
> P.S. I've tried to e-mail Luce. No response. Is she back in SF? Pls call and tell her to check her mail.

Then she reread the brief e-mail. It was so cursory, so perfunctory it shocked her. Where were the details? Where was the sense of exultation? The excitement? She printed a copy, as though the message in physical form might be more revealing. She had waited more than two weeks for news, for details of Mead's trip, her climb, her great adventure. The few choppy sentences were vastly disappointing.

Holding the e-mail, she went to the window and gazed into the tired park. The bustle of the holiday season was over, kids back in school. The park was filled with people briskly, purposefully walking toward some destination or professional walkers with herds of dogs in tow. Elizabeth tried to read between the lines, scrutinize between the words. There's more, she thought. There must be more. "Climb was fine." Surely this would not be her complete recounting?

Her eyes traveled to the P.S. Elizabeth was surprised, disconcerted. To her knowledge her daughters didn't correspond. Why now? Was something going on? Was the mail that should have been sent to Elizabeth, bursting with detail, interesting observations, intriguing asides, sent to Luce when . . . ? Elizabeth caught herself. When what? she demanded. When it should have been sent to me. Elizabeth, you're being ridiculous. Just stop. She shook herself slightly and returned to her computer.

She should edit Mead's *Letters*. Having gotten Steven to agree to read them, she really should get them to him soon. Perhaps he could write a foreword. She had so hoped to include parts of the climb. Such a wonderful metaphor, she thought, such terrific imagery: Mead's struggle up the mountain, Mead standing atop the peak surveying the continent. Elizabeth had planned to weave Mead's thoughts and observations into the larger fabric of her medical work. But now she felt deflated.

She turned and propped herself against the window sill, studying the wall of photos. Shafts of weak sun, muted and filled with a thousand free-floating particles, illuminated the collection. Here, in judiciously selected frames, meticulously arranged for maximum chronological comprehension, were the moments of her past fifty years, frozen and silent. Her life, beginning in black-and-white, as a young bride and continuing to reach full color as a mother surrounded by her four grown children. Why did the reality feel like the reverse, a journey from a past of color to a present of black-and-white? A dreadful sense of foreboding grabbed her by the throat. I'm going to die, she thought, panic-stricken. Ice filled her veins. Her heart began to gallop. She took a deep breath. Of course you're going to die, she replied with a degree of impatience, you foolish woman. But not today.

As quickly as the fear had arrived a moment of sharp clarity descended. Who can I talk to about my own impending death? she wondered. She thought she was being practical, not morbid. Here she was at seventy. She couldn't, wouldn't live forever. Of course she and Walter had carefully planned for all the surrounding details – current wills, living wills, their financial affairs were in excellent order. But with whom could she talk about the fact that this would all be over – sooner rather than later? She wanted to talk with someone, to put the many years in some form of orderly perspective, to sort out the varying and often contradictory feelings she had about her own eventual end. Not to share, or impart, any words of wisdom but rather to find out what she thought about it all. It certainly had not been what she had expected. Who, though? Not Walter, for sure. Or her sons. Luce? Unlikely. With her career at dizzying new heights, Elizabeth imagined her life one art soiree after another. And Mead, Mead's profession is death. Surely she didn't want to talk about it in her spare time. No one, she thought. There is no one.

This line of thinking must be because of Mr. Heinz. Eddy, the doorman, had told her about him just yesterday. He and his wife lived two floors above. They had gone to Hawaii and come home a week early because he wasn't feeling well. According to Eddy, he went to the doctor, the doctor examined him and, as Eddy said enthusiastically, "Pow," inoperable lung and liver cancer. Three weeks later, he was dead. Although they had lived in the same building for more than twenty years, Elizabeth barely knew him or his wife. He always reeked of cigarette smoke. Elizabeth hated when the elevator doors opened to reveal him. Often she would feign having forgotten something in order to avoid riding with him. As for Mrs. Heinz, in the early years of their moving into the co-op, she would invite Elizabeth to political functions for older women. Elizabeth always refused with more than a degree of disdain. Now Mr. Heinz was dead. "Pow." He was, according to Eddy, only sixty-one. The rapidity of his death stunned her, or more accurately, the possible rapidity of her own death frightened her.

Suddenly the co-op felt cold and empty. Walter, she sighed with exasperation as she turned up the heat, is spending too much time away. Good God, I see less of him now than before he retired. He's simply got to slow down. In her mind's eye she saw Walter, corduroy pants, turtleneck, flannel shirt, cardigan, reading glasses sliding down the bridge of his nose, in a shadowy corner of the library, hunched over some obscure journal. Studying, studying, studying. Had he worked as hard to pass his medical exams as he was now working to gain and maintain the respect of his children? Again the memory of last summer at the beach intruded. Why, they think he's little more than a mechanic! Walter, a highly dedicated, respected and skilled surgeon! As if he was no more than a man in grease-caked coveralls giving you bad news about your radiator or brakes. Sometimes children can be so loathsome, she thought, oblivious to her own sympathies.

I must ask Steven to talk with him, take him to lunch or meet him at the club. He really needs to slow down. From across the room her computer said, "You have mail." Mead, she thought immediately, this must be from Mead. Returning to her desk, she went to her mailbox and saw the new e-mail. From Chad. Dejected, she opened it warily.

To: EBennett
Fr: Chad
Did I get the wrong woman? The universe is rarely wrong. I sense fire. Older is fine.
   Breasts ripe with living, hips steeled with years of heat, lips full of the telling, the map of love's many journeys sketched upon the skin. One who has accumulated passion and knows how to use it wisely. Tell me about yourself.

Exasperated, she dropped into her club chair. Dear God, this is preposterous, she thought, at seventy, to be pursued by an electronic amour. Anonymous at that! What an age. The nerve of this impertinent young whippersnapper.

Still, something stirred within her. Agitated, she rose and went again to the wall in search of a certain photo. There, in fading shades of gray and white, stood Walter and Elizabeth on a pier almost forty-four years ago. They – or rather, she – had asked a passing stranger to take the photo. It was after she had made the decision to return to Walter, to make him and their children her life. She had found a freedom in that decision, initially at least. She had surrendered and although she later capitulated, in her own mind, in her own heart, that reunion weekend was the most passionate she had ever had with Walter. Now, for the first time, she wondered if it had been memorable for him. Looking at the photo was like looking at a pair of strangers, the young woman buoyant and obviously in love in the arms of a tall, handsome and determined man. He stood behind her, wrapping his muscular arms around her waist, resting his large, intertwined hands upon her stomach. Her arms resting on his, she looked over her shoulder at him, from the corner of her eyes, laughing with a joy of life that had surprised her, that would not be contained. He looked directly into the eye of the camera. A sea breeze tossed their hair in all directions. Their clothes rippled in a light-hearted way. Elizabeth was sure she had conceived Rand, their second child, on that brief trip.

Walking backwards she now surrendered to her chair. How quickly the passion had faded. She hadn't minded at first, had barely had time to notice. Walter was so busy getting his career started. Luce was a baby. Rand soon arrived, then Avery, then Mead. Over those years, the passion of their reunion relaxed to include a full and busy life. Of course they continued a sexual relationship after Mead was born. And as small and infrequent as it was, it seemed all they could fit into their brimming lives. There was so much else they shared together, much of which was genuinely fatiguing. But now, both of them free, technically at least, of so many prior commitments, Elizabeth had expected more.

As if to validate all those years, she went to the computer and typed:

To: Chad
Fr: EBennett
You are an impertinent and presumptuous young man. You should
be working harder on your studies or for your employer. Obviously,
you have too much idle time on your hands. GOOD-BYE AND GET
LOST.

She quickly reread her response, pleased that she knew enough on-line etiquette to know that all caps indicated that she was yelling, and clicked Send Mail.

She looked around her study, across the hall into the empty living room. Some rekindling of the coals, some physical contact, some warm press of flesh against the long winter. A ridiculous idea? An absurd notion at her age? Perhaps, she thought. Perhaps. After so many years of working and planning, this is not the retirement I had imagined.

Through the window a pall fell over the emptying park as the weak sun vanished behind an approaching cloud front and dusk descended. "Pow," Elizabeth thought. "Pow."

* * *

125

Luce sat in her large, open kitchen sipping coffee. Through the wall of windows, the late afternoon day was hot, unusual for both the time of year and the time of day, and a rare veil of green-gray smog cloaked the city, robbing all structures of their subtle pastel hues. Mid-January, and spring had come early to San Francisco. The princess trees unfolded their lavender blossoms, the agapanthas their white and purple pompoms. Those trees that did lose their leaves in fall now had a shimmering green sheen as the branches slowly unfurled small leafy flags. What a contrast to New York, she thought, still buried deep in winter's clasp.

She looked into the corner of her kitchen at the unopened computer boxes. They had arrived some months ago.

"What is this?" she had asked the UPS delivery woman.

"Computer. Sign here."

"But I didn't order a computer."

"Your name Luce Bennett?"

"Yes."

"Well, it's for you, Ma'am."

Luce had started, taken aback as much by being addressed as Ma'am as by the arrival of the computer.

"Where do you want me to put them?" The UPS woman shifted unhappily.

"Well, I don't know. There's got to be some mistake."

The UPS woman scowled impatiently. "Lady . . . "

"Um, here. No. If you don't mind, there's a better space in the kitchen." Upon closer inspection, Luce had seen that the packing label was an envelope taped to the box and addressed in her mother's neat, antiquated hand. Closing the door after the UPS woman, she read:

Dear Luce,

Merry Christmas, a little early this year. You children are all so difficult to buy for that we [Luce read I] decided to get you a computer this year. I know you don't have one and everyone should. Especially with Mead going to Africa next month and communicating with me via e-mail, I thought I could send copies to you."

We [Luce read I] decided to buy her a laptop - more portable and better for the travel she'll be doing. As your brothers both have computer systems at home, we [Luce read I] decided to give them both the cost of the computers in cash for their savings accounts.

I opened an account for you with America OnLine. Your address

126

is LBennett and your password is AFRICA. (You can change these at any time.) This way we'll all be able to communicate efficiently.

Love, Mother

Efficient communication is what her mother wanted. Luce half-snorted, half-shuddered. In the context of her family that was a mystifying and frightening thought. To improve the efficiency of communication would, should, she thought sarcastically, require a base level of communication that did not exist. Not an issue she planned to raise with her mother.

Her mother's own penchant for, and proficiency at, computers had initially amused Luce. Years ago Elizabeth had owned one of the first "luggables." She had been quick to see the value the computer would add to her tasks of managing the family's finances, and she seemed to delight in spending hours constructing computer-based systems to execute simple tasks that would only take a few minutes if done manually. The technical demands had in no way intimidated her. To the contrary, she seemed well suited to them, eager to conquer the challenges, and she loved to flaunt her victories. An image of Luce's mother surfaced: sitting on the porch of the beach cottage, head buried in some thick and turgid operational manual, attention fiercely focused.

Elizabeth also took delight in the arcane, techno-babble that accompanied the computer. In this arena, Rand was the only one who could converse with her. Even he was not as current on a practical applications level as she. Luce suspected that her mother rather savored Walter's reluctance to become "hands-on," that she had found some turf free of Walter, a domain where she, and she alone, could excel.

Staring now at the unopened boxes and thinking of e-mail, Luce sighed empathetically. She felt the exhaustion her mother must experience trying to keep this disparate and distant family in some cohesive orbit when the natural inclination seemed to be for each member to spin off into a vast, unconnected universe on separate, opposing trajectories. She wondered, with a sense of bafflement and admiration, at Elizabeth's efforts to keep familial futility in check. The annual summer beach gathering of the clan, deferentially, reluctantly agreed to by all, was some tribute to her steel.

Still, it has to be utterly exhausting, Luce thought, trying to maintain whatever it was she maintained.

Thinking of the letter sent with the computer, Luce smiled at Elizabeth's continued dedication to parity and equal love. Still letting her children know, via gifts of comparable economic value, that her love was equally distributed.

127

"I love all my children equally," she would say as she exited a room, leaving the squabbling tribe members to figure it out themselves. Which, of course, they never did.

Luce had long ago reconciled herself to the fact that Mead was the beloved child. Luce had taken herself out of the running when she changed from pre-med to art. She also accepted that the content of her paintings had driven what had been a fissure into a full-fledged wedge. Rand was too much of an ingrown, techno-nerd to be the favored one. Avery occasionally showed interest in vying for the position, but Luce sensed he saw too clearly the burdensome weight of the prize. Mead, the baby, won, by intention, by default.

Luce tried to envisage the e-mail that Mead had sent to New York and her mother had sent to San Francisco. Was it now lying dormant in some telephone line just outside her house? Perhaps it had traveled the wire into the house already, following the circuitry of the phone line down a wall, along a floor, and was clustered by the telephone plug waiting to be released. The notion was unappealing, like a wolf baying at her door. Luce lamely wondered what Mead, who – as far as she could tell via the annual tribal commingling – seemed to have had the last vestiges of humanity squeezed out of her by the process of becoming a doctor, was doing in Africa. Was there a suitable place or viable role for her cold impatience, her hard arrogance in such a setting? Luce had objectively, she was sure, watched the process of Mead's transformation from the sidelines. Last summer was clearly the acme. Luce had actually felt sorry for her father, hounded by Mead's imperious, empirically-correct manner.

Luce sighed. In fairness she knew that she had to cut Mead some slack. The week they spent together annually was hardly representative of who they all were, what they did, thought or felt. Some odd distortion of self-imagery reflected in outdated, dim mirrors – too convex or too concave.

What do you really know about your sister?, she wondered. Except for the years with Tommy, and that one dreadful dinner that Grace had insisted upon, there was a dearth of information. Oh God, Luce thought wearily, remembering the tortured evening when Mead came to their apartment in the Village. Luce would have beaten herself up severely even if Grace hadn't been there to help.

"Good God, Luce," Grace had said in an angry, frustrated tone as she closed the door behind Mead. "You are unbelievable. Completely pathetic. That's your sister, for God's sake. Do you think you could have been any colder? Any more terse? Jesus, what's with you?"

128

Luce had tried to explain how she felt – which was badly – but Grace was still angry. "You didn't even tell her that she was coming to *our* home, didn't even prepare her for the fact that she would not be dining alone with you. Unbelievable. The poor kid looked shell-shocked when she figured out that I live here, too."

Luce felt chagrined. "Grace, I've never talked with any of my family about being a lesbian. We can barely choke out 'How are you?' What? Should I have just slipped it into the phone conversation when I asked her over for dinner? You think she would have come?"

Grace continued to shake her head and glare. "Well, I guess we'll never know, huh? And couldn't you have extended yourself a little, I mean, one or two questions about school or her plans?"

"The minute I tried to say anything, well, I don't know, my tongue was tied. I choked. I agree. I did a lousy job. I'm sorry."

"You're right, you should be sorry. And you should apologize to Mead. This is your sister. You're just throwing her away?"

"Grace, that's not fair. We never really talked as a family. Oh, about current events or science or some such. Mostly we listened to Walter's diatribes."

"Luce, that was then. This is now."

"You didn't hear her asking me, or us, any questions, did you?" The juvenile tone embarrassed her immediately.

Grace, hand on her hip, flashed with anger. "Who's ten years older here? Besides," she continued acidly, "I thought, like your hero Franz Marc, you don't let other people's behavior dictate yours."

"But . . . " Luce had tried to defend herself but was cut off by Grace's silencing hand.

"Whatever," Grace said coolly, "I just think you're making a big mistake."

"Look, Grace, the truth is *you* want a sister. Not me. You're the one with the romantic notion of what having a sister is or should be like."

"Fine. Let's not talk about this anymore, okay?" she had said, steaming off into the kitchen where the dishes and pots and pans were bandied about loudly.

"Fine," Luce had responded facilely to the empty living room.

As Luce stared at the unopened computer boxes, now a resting place for unread newspapers and mail order catalogs, the thought of e-mail, on-line shopping, chat rooms, endless impersonal contact sent a shiver of disgust down her spine. She prided herself on retaining complete computer illiteracy and resented how difficult maintaining that state had become of late. A wired world, she sighed, envisioning a ball of yarn, but with loose, multi-colored wires flying off in all directions.

Through her kitchen window the pale lights of San Francisco came on as day ascended and dusk descended. Like an Escher, she thought, neither white nor gray, neither coming nor going. Pouring herself another cup of coffee she stared blankly at the computer boxes, acutely disconnected.

* * *

"So," Birati Singh sang, her voice a spicy breeze wafting over the Indian Ocean, "you have been to the mountain top? Our returning conqueror?" Her lips curled faintly with jest. "Bravo."

Mead returned the slight smile. "It wasn't quite what you might think."

"It never is, is it?" Her smiled stretched to reveal pearl white teeth under full, well-formed lips. "We are off then." They drove in Birati's Mercedes through town and out to the wealthier suburb, King's Park. The sun was setting. It was a relief to Mead to be getting out of town, leaving the hospital, the crowded streets, the memory of Sofia Town. Francesca Piavani was hosting a cocktail party. Having heard of Mead through her son, Gil, she had issued an invitation. Mead had accepted the invitation readily. Gil's portrayal of his mother had incited Mead's curiosity. Moreover, she was, at last, anxious to see Luce's paintings. Birati, an old family acquaintance, was invited as well and offered to give Mead a lift.

"So, Mead, you are a woman of secrets."

"What do you mean by that?"

"You didn't tell me you know Ghilberti."

"If you mean Gil, I didn't know I was going to know him until after he showed up in tow with my friend Peter."

"Yes, this I have heard." Birati eyed the rear view mirror, shot Mead a surreptitious glance and asked, with great concern, "Are you all right?"

"Of course I'm all right. That tumble on the mountain was nothing." She looked at Birati and saw an unasked question formed on her lips. "What exactly are you after, Birati?"

"Well, the climb was difficult to be sure, but especially given the circumstances."

"What circumstances do you mean?" Mead was full of dread. Did Gil know as well as Linda about Peter's mountain tryst? Did the entire medical community of Nairobi know? God, how humiliating.

"I am referring to the fact that your long-standing engagement was broken by Dr. Peter McDonough. This must have been difficult to be sure. It is hard for the mind and body to function when the heart hurts so."

Mead's head pivoted so violently her neck cracked. "Is that what you heard? From whom?"

"Why, this is what Dr. McDonough told Gil, that he had decided to break off your engagement. Is there some distortion in these facts?"

Mead buried her face in her hands then rubbed vigorously, as though to erase the entire episode from her visual memory, then over her ears to deaden the noise of the zipper ripping the night. Sitting upright she said with pointed emphasis, "Yes, Birati. There is a good deal of distortion in those facts. I ended our engagement. Several years ago."

Birati nodded her head with great understanding. "Ah, I see."

"Dr. McDonough," Mead added unnecessarily, "is, well, delusional."

"Mead, I did not mean to upset you. Or to pry into your private affairs. We – the Europeans and Asians – are a small community here. News, accurate or not, travels quickly. I apologize sincerely."

"It's okay. I'd just as soon know the distortions, as you say. I guess." Birati turned onto Harry Thuku Road. Soon the city gave way to King's Park, a spacious, well-manicured suburb with stately homes on rolling green lawns.

"May I change the subject, please?" Mead loved Birati's ornate sense of manners.

"Please do."

"Jane told me of your visit to Sofia Town."

"Oh, my God, I still can't get over it. To tell you the truth, Birati, I couldn't sleep at all that night." She looked out the window as they passed the Nairobi Bowling Green and Cricket Club, peppered with players clad in traditional whites. An English springer spaniel sat obediently at the sidelines awaiting its master. The long rays of the setting sun imbued the afternoon with a golden, tawny color, the color of the tall dry grasses on the open plains or a lion's haunch.

"It's not as though I haven't seen abject poverty. There's the south side of Chicago, there's Bedford Sty in New York and Roxbury in Boston. But," she shook her head, "there's really no comparison."

"It is most unfortunate that we humans seem to be endlessly attracted to the stimulation of large cities. With inflation at 40% and unemployment nearly as high, well, little wonder that these disease-breeding grounds appear."

They rode in silence until Mead asked, "Are you Jane's doctor?" Birati hesitated. "C'mon, Birati, tell me."

"Yes."

"How is she? Look, she told me she's HIV-positive. You're not breaking confidences," Mead assured, seeing Birati hesitate. "How's her health?"

131

"She works too hard. I worry for her. But, as you might imagine to be so, I cannot get her to slow down. 'Slow down?' she says to me, 'Why? Will the disease slow down? Slow down? How, when there is so much to be done?' I have tried, Mead."

"How are her numbers?"

"There has been a slight shift recently, which troubles me. But her counts are still in an acceptable range. Of course, my greater worry is everything she is exposed to. But I must respect her wishes."

Passing through a large gate, they turned onto a private road lined with pepper trees. Extensive flower beds and rose gardens filled the large, well-groomed grounds. In the distance a low white house, simply designed with elegant lines, dominated the landscape. The road became a circular driveway. Birati stopped the car before the house. Mead had become sullen. She thought of Jane's vibrancy being overtaken by an escalating and nefarious virus, by the power it wielded over all of them.

Birati's hand on Mead's arm was soft but assured. "You must not be too concerned for Jane. We are all defined by our deaths, Mead. Here the definitions are boldly drawn. Fewer distractions. Jane lives her life as we all should, seeing death's shadow cast on her path every day. That is very good, I think. Less waste. And she has the great fortune to be doing with her life that which she wants. And to be of service, well, this is not inconsiderable, is it?"

"That may be so, Birati, but," Mead looked through the car window and across the green thick lawn, "it's still unacceptable."

Sensing that a personal connection with someone who had AIDS was a new experience for Mead, Birati gently squeezed her hand. "Shall we go in?"

Gil stood in the foyer greeting the various guests as they arrived. He gave Birati a kiss on the cheek.

"Hello again," he said to Mead, offering a smile that was more trepidation than pleasure at seeing her again. "I'm glad you could come."

"Thanks, Gil. I see you made it back in one piece. Everything go okay?"

"Yes. Even with Roz on a gurney, going down is definitely easier. When we got to Nairobi, Peter took her over to Jubilee and the doctor on duty fixed her up. Bad break, it would seem. But no long-term damage. Harry and Lydia!" he greeted, looking past them to an older couple who were entering the foyer, "How lovely to see you. Mother will be delighted that you could make it." To Mead and Birati he said, "Please make yourselves at home. I'll catch up with you both later."

From the foyer, Mead peered into the humming crowd Gil's mother, Francesca, had assembled. Birati, with a soft hand on Mead's back, guided her into the large living room. From the far side of the room someone called out to Birati. "Will you be okay by yourself for a moment, Mead?" she asked.

"Sure, go ahead." A white jacketed waiter came by and Mead accepted a Pimms' Cup. Taking a long sip that was cool and fortifying, she gazed around the room. She recognized some of the people, permanent staff from the hospital and a few of the exchange doctors. She nodded a few hellos as she wandered through the crowd, surreptitiously examining the walls.

The interior of the house, like the exterior, was simple and elegant, with Italian touches. Floor-to-ceiling windows and several sets of French doors created a light spaciousness. The sand colored furniture and blond woods emphasized the lightness. Only the art, African ebony sculptures and weavings, offered contrast. Francesca had a cosmopolitan and assured sense of design. In the far corner Mead saw Linda standing next to Jane and a tall, elegant African man. Linda, smiling, gestured for Mead to join them.

"Mead," Linda said after hellos were exchanged, giving her a loaded glance, "Dr. Swareggo is from Jubilee Hospital. He was just telling us of an American doctor who went AWOL."

Dr. Swareggo assumed a quizzical expression. "What is AWOL?"

"Absent without leave. An Army expression, " Mead replied. Tilting her head toward Linda she asked, "Our friend?"

"The same." Linda offered a cautious smirk.

"This is a friend of yours?" Dr. Swareggo was shocked.

"An acquaintance would be more accurate," Linda explained.

Turning to Linda, Mead asked, "Do we have any idea what's happened with our dear colleague?"

Linda was smug. "While her resignation letter was cryptic, I bet we could venture an educated guess."

"Hmm, I see. Required constant attention, did she?" Mead, aware that both Jane and Dr. Swareggo were completely baffled by their exchange, asked Dr. Swareggo, "Are you a pediatrician also?"

"No. My field is internal medicine."

"Good evening to you all," Birati said, joining them and bowing graciously to Jane and Swareggo.

"Birati, this is Linda,' Mead said, "She's a nurse at Misericordia. And a good friend." Linda beamed.

"A pleasure. I have, however, heard of you from Jane. So, Jane, have you asked Mead and Linda yet?"

The two Americans exchanged curious glances then Mead lifted her face in question to Jane. "Well," Jane began, "I was wondering if you would like to take a field trip with me. I am soon to travel to Rwanda to visit some of the regional clinics. You, no doubt, would find this most interesting."

"Jane," Dr. Swareggo's voice was thick with concern, "you really should not go."

Mead's brow arched in question. "Why not? I've heard that country is more stable these days. Less volatile."

Swareggo shook his head sadly, "It is too dangerous. Much too dangerous a trip to make, especially with Americans. I implore you, Jane, reconsider."

Birati placed a comforting hand on his arm. "Ogata, it must be done. You know that. We must provide help. We must provide some medicines." Turning to Linda and Mead she said, "Ogata is correct, going there is most dangerous. There are still rebel insurgents fighting the civil war. It is not clear that the war is over. It is true that it is especially dangerous for Americans. Whether you travel solo or in convoy, even if you travel on official business or for humanitarian reasons, you are apt to be a target." Birati sighed deeply. Mead gave Linda a warning glance. Birati continued, "You must think about this carefully. You must realize the danger you would be undertaking."

"Well, what exactly is the danger?" Linda asked.

"They are now offering a price for dead Americans," Ogata said giving Jane a stern look of reproof.

"First," Jane began calmly, "the roads are very poor. Like everything else in the country, war torn." Her impassive expression was a stark contrast to the danger she described, "Travel is difficult. The military close the roads from 5 p.m. until 10 a.m. in an attempt to prevent the rebels from planting land mines. Even with a medical designation on our vehicle, we are apt to be a target of carjacking and robbery."

"*Especially* with a medical designation," Swareggo added. "Random arrests are not uncommon. And the authorities do not feel compelled to follow international procedures. In short, they may not report your arrest to the U.S. Consulate. You could be the target of aggression or, more likely, find yourself caught in something terrible."

Mead looked concerned. "Is there any particular reason I should go?"

Birati noticed Jane's expression darken at Mead's question. In neutral tones, Jane responded, "We need help. We need doctors and nurses to help us. Most of the regional clinics are staffed by medical assistants and midwives, who care very much and do the best they can. There are limitations, understandably."

"Dr. Bennett is a researcher. She should not, she need not, take a field trip. And both of you," he gestured to Linda and Mead, "are guests of our nation. It is our responsibility to ensure your safety. Jane, I must repeat how strongly I oppose your trip. And if you yourself must go, well, there are others better suited to accompany you." Swareggo was adamant.

Birati looked directly at Mead. "It would be a most interesting opportunity for you, to be certain. However, it is highly dangerous. Do not make a decision now. Think about it before you decide."

"I'd like to go," Linda said eagerly. "Sounds as if they could really use some help."

Mead was slightly appalled by Linda. Having climbed Kilimanjaro, she now seemed ready to dive headlong into all manner of risky situations.

"Linda, why don't we talk about it later? Maybe over dinner one night this week," Mead said, hoping to slow her down.

"Why?" Linda was genuinely curious.

Mead felt a shade of embarrassment that she herself was reluctant to commit to this trip. Birati, observing Mead, squinted almost imperceptibly. "Linda, your willingness is most appreciated. But Mead is correct to ask you to more thoroughly consider this trip and all its possible ramifications." Then, glancing over Linda's shoulder, she said, pointing toward the foyer, "Oh, look, there is Francesca. This is someone you both must meet."

Mead and Linda looked through the doorway where a woman, vivacious, tall and elegant, in her late fifties, entered the living room. Gil stood behind her. Heads turned, captivated by her attractive, alluring presence. For a moment she held court from the foyer, offering a small hand in greeting here, a smile there. Scanning the room she caught sight of Mead and approached directly in long fluid movements before she was lost, engulfed by an eager crowd.

* * *

The waiter at the Arcadia checked Elizabeth's coat, then showed her to a booth. Celia was late. Typical, Elizabeth thought. Her black mood darkened. "I'll have a martini please. Very dry. Onion, no olive." What the hell. The gumdrop renderings of autumnal trees on the walls annoyed her more than usual. The decor struck her this day as contrived and trite. Observing the people at the other tables, she was relieved that she knew no one.

Outside, the day matched her spirits – bleak and dreary. The morning snow had turned to a gray drizzle and dirty slush edged the streets. Last evening Walter had arrived home late, completely forgetting their dinner engagement. She had called the Stewarts, feigning a sudden headache but was angry to miss the social opportunity. They had eaten leftovers at the kitchen table. Walter, barely speaking two words, read the *Journal of Acquired Immune Deficiency Syndrome and Human Retrovirology* over dinner, took a bath and was asleep by nine. "Any word from Mead today?" he had managed to drawl as she slipped into bed. "No," she shot back, her frustration with her daughter hitting a different, but nonetheless legitimate target. In truth, Mead had sent a brief e-mail. Something about a visit to the poorer part of town. "I'll spare you the details," she wrote, and Elizabeth had felt a sudden rage. It's precisely the details that I want. She had almost e-mailed something to that end but thought better of it and deleted the message before sending it.

It is true, Elizabeth thought, as she checked her watch to make sure it was noon before she sipped her martini, I was the one who suggested that she compile a diary or letters. Mead had scoffed at the suggestion, but then her first letters indicated that perhaps she had thought otherwise. They were so vivid, so descriptive. Elizabeth fervently believed that her notion of a published book was a good one. "They might make a nice little monograph," Steven had said on the phone the other day. She had thanked him generously while thinking, 'You ass. Can't you see the potential here?' She had gotten a few names of editors and agents but was awaiting the Kilimanjaro section before contacting them. What's wrong with her? Elizabeth wondered.

"Penny for your thoughts." Elizabeth had missed Celia's entrance.

"Come now, with inflation alone I'd expect a better offer."

"Oh, I see we're full of good cheer today. Sorry I'm late by the way. I ran into that dreadful woman, Vera, you know, the one who's forever forgetting that she knows you? What a pain she is. Thankfully, she looked awful today."

"I don't think I remember her."

"Touché. Say, are you going to have the lobster club?" Celia slid into the booth.

"You and I, Celia, are going to split a lobster club. Have you any idea the grams of fat in that sandwich? If you're still hungry, I suggest a salad. Vinegar, no oil."

"I see you're drinking your calories today?" Elizabeth gave her a scowl. "So why are you in such a foul mood?"

"I'm in a fine mood, thank you."

"Positively gleeful. How's Walter?"

Elizabeth shrugged. "I tell you, Celia, I hardly see him. He's driving himself to an early grave."

"Aren't you exaggerating a tad? He looked quite well at that party a few weeks ago. In fact, and it's more than just my opinion, Walter is the most virile of all his contemporaries." Seeing Elizabeth's pronounced displeasure, Celia concurred, "He does work too much. Michael complains that they haven't played chess since God knows when. Just what does he spend his time doing?"

A small sigh escaped Elizabeth's taut lips. Her loyalties were mixed. Should she continue to defend Walter against the realities of time and age, feeble though that defense would be? Or should she just let it rip, share her marital displeasure, entice Celia to be her comrade in arms? It wouldn't require much effort. For years Celia had stood ready to be a confidant. She hesitated. "I understand, I do. In addition to staying current as a surgeon, he feels compelled to be as up-to-date as possible with the children's fields. Artificial Intelligence, psychiatry and AIDS and infectious diseases. It's a lot."

"But why? That's their jobs - not his." Elizabeth offered no response. "From the sound of it, he's awfully preoccupied. It must be hard on you. Aren't you lonely?"

She straightened. "I stay busy."

"But of course you do. You always have." Sensing Elizabeth's reticence, she moved on. "What do you hear from Mead?"

"Not much. To tell you the truth, I'm worried."

"Really? You sound more annoyed than worried. Is she all right?"

"As far as I can tell. But since she came from Kilimanjaro it's almost like there's been a news blackout. I get a quick e-mail from her every day but nothing substantive."

"Well, she is terribly busy. With doctors in such short supply, working hands-on herself, training other doctors and doing research, I can just imagine how overworked she must be."

"Oh, yes, of course, there's that," Elizabeth said dismissively, "But she managed to send lengthy letters when she first got there. It doesn't make sense."

"Well, she'll be home in another six weeks. If I know you, you'll wrangle whatever it is you want out of her."

"I don't 'wrangle' with my children, Celia, and I never have. It's unseemly. Besides, that's simply not the point. You see, I sense something's going on, something's happened."

"Well, why don't you send her an e-mail asking her?"

"Oh, Celia, you just don't understand." Their sandwich arrived already divided onto two plates.

"No, God forbid you should do something so obvious." Celia eagerly raised her half of the sandwich to her mouth.

"So," Elizabeth strategically waited until Celia was taking her first bite, "how was Luce's show?"

Caught off-guard, Celia choked and put the sandwich down. "Elizabeth . . . " she mumbled through a full mouth.

"Spare me the histrionics, Celia. How was it?"

Celia swallowed with difficulty then gulped some water. "Quite successful, I guess. It was all landscapes. Kind of eerie and depressing, if you ask me. Not my cup of tea. Oh, but the price tags. My, my. And I gather she's selling well. You know, Elizabeth," she said contritely, "I wasn't sneaking off behind your back. I was just curious."

"It's a free country, Celia. Don't apologize to me." Then to the waiter, "I'll have another martini, drier."

"How did you know anyway? Are you spying on me?" Celia asked, somewhat reluctant to take another bite.

"God, you're paranoid. No, I simply made an educated guess. Aren't you going to eat that?"

"Elizabeth, what's wrong with you ? You seem so, I don't know, agitated these days. Are you feeling all right?"

For a split second Elizabeth, still carrying the vivid fear of her own death which had visited the previous day, considered asking 'Are you afraid of dying, Celia?', 'Do you feel ready?', but quickly caught herself, quickly saw how weak that would seem, how silly and utterly inappropriate she would appear. And for a moment she felt a sudden urge to cry. She lifted the martini glass to her lips, scanned the restaurant then leaned conspiratorially toward Celia. "I've been getting lewd e-mail," hoping to throw Celia off the real trail.

"You what?" Celia exclaimed.

"Shhsh, not so loud. Please. Someone, Chad seems to be his name, is sending me . . . ," she paused searching for the exact word, "well, maybe not lewd, but suggestive e-mail."

"How exciting!" Celia's eyes brightened. "Are you going to meet him?"

"Celia, what's wrong with you? Don't be ridiculous. No, I'm not going to meet him. Where do you get your ideas? He's probably some sicko-, psycho-killer who gets his jollies stalking women. Like *Sea of Love*. You know. Only he has a perversion for older women."

"What's *Sea of Love*?" Celia asked, tentatively nibbling at her club.

"A movie. Never mind. The point is, I guess he sent me the first one by mistake. I told him to bug off. In no uncertain terms. But now he keeps writing me, wanting to know more about the 'mysterious EBennett.'"

"Well, isn't there some sort of Internet cop you can report him to? What does he say, anyway?"

"Oh, he's just a kid I'm sure. Apparently he met someone at a club frequented by people who live in cyberspace and they had sex."

"What?" Celia was shocked.

"She left him before he woke up. And she gave him a false address, mine as it turns out, probably trying to give him the shake. Now she's gone and he's intrigued with me."

"You mean, they met, had sex and then she left him. Oh dear, how times have changed. She left him, huh? Well, I only hope she was safe, if you know what I mean."

"For God's sake, Celia, don't you understand? They went to an on-line club. They had electronic sex, not real sex."

Celia looked dumfounded. "What's the point?" Then she widened her eyes and asked, "Have you had electronic sex, Elizabeth?"

"Keep your voice down. Of course not. I'm married. Besides, I'm not a cyber punk."

Celia pushed her plate away and drummed her fingers on the table. "I don't get it. And, I don't want to get it. Can't you just change your address, the way you would your phone number if someone was calling you?"

"Yes, but I don't see why I should have to change my address because of some young punk," Elizabeth said indignantly. "I'm hoping he'll get bored and go away. Besides, if he's a techie, he'll be able to trace me, a trail of cookies or some such."

Celia's puzzled look turned to concern. "Elizabeth, why don't you join my bridge club. I think you're spending too much time at home, alone, and on the internet."

"You know I hate bridge. Besides, you cheat."

"Why don't you use those feminine wiles of yours on your husband and join us on St. Kitt's? I think you need a change of scenery." Elizabeth, finding the thought of using feminine wiles on a man like Walter preposterous, just shook her head. "Well, then, do you want to come shopping with me? I need to get a wedding present."

Elizabeth wasn't sure if she effectively hid her disgust or not. "No, thanks, you go on. I need to do some grocery shopping and get dinner ready. I think I'll just sit here for a bit longer, have a cup of coffee."

"I'll stay and keep you company."

"No, go ahead. Don't worry about the bill. It's my turn anyway."

"You're sure?"

"Sure," Elizabeth was nonchalant. "You still have some lobster club." Elizabeth pointed to Celia's mouth.

"Oh, thanks," she said dabbing the napkin to the corners of her mouth. "Well, okay then. I'll see you at the Academy dinner next Saturday?"

"Of course, I'll be there. We'll be there."

"Bye then."

"Bye. Happy shopping."

Through the glass door Elizabeth watched Celia, under a floral-patterned, designer umbrella, flag a cab and drive off. "I'll have another martini, please. Two onions." Elizabeth closed her eyes. Somewhere deep inside she heard and felt the low, mournful notes of a single cello: bow on string, slowly reverberating in a dark and barren hall.

* * *

The foghorn bellowed deeply. Luce put her brush down and wiped her hands on a rag. She stepped over to the window. Outside, the rain was so dense that virtually all of downtown was obscured. The buildings were faint cross-hatchings on silver point. The Golden Gate was completely lost. The gray steel Bay Bridge stood up to its knees in fog.

Leaning against the brick wall, she looked into the unfinished canvas she had been painting. The background was a bright day, with all the gentleness of an early summer dawn. The sky, mottled in the south with billowy white clouds that had since passed, merged with the open sea out by a distant sand bar. Incipient sun teased the horizon with orange hints. A few birds circled overhead and the clean white sail of a boat lazed against the sky. In the middle ground the ebb tide revealed an untouched shore, save for a few scattered shells. An unbroken shore, a fresh dawn, a new day. Promise.

In the foreground, against the white deck railing of a summer cottage, leaned the tanned figure of Grace. The small of her back rested against the railing as her upper torso stretched up as though reaching to see the sun before it hit the horizon. Her berry-brown legs and arms were taut. Her hands clasped the railing as she sloped her face to the sun. Her body was slender and firm, her muscles well defined. Her face that of a woman dying of cancer.

Luce threw the rag across the room in disgust. Why can't I get the face right? Why can't I see her before she was ravaged? Why won't my hands obey me? Picking up an exacto knife she weighed it in her hand, shifted it to the other. Damn. Damn. Damn. Stepping up to the canvas she took the knife and slit the canvas from one corner to the other in a huge ripping X. The smell of hospital filled her nostrils and she suddenly felt queasy.

In the far corner was a work in progress, *Searching for Grace/San Francisco*. This one was painted at night, mid-way across the bridge heading toward the city. Fog enshrouded the rusty red south tower, which was illuminated with large spotlights and by the yellow-orange lamps strung like amber pearls from span to span. The fog was thick and devoured the bridge in ominous clouds. Through the thick foggy gauze, the lights of San Francisco burned dimly. Ahead, just past the south tower the shadow of a figure slipped into the fog, out of view. A shadow on a shadow. A wisp, a hint. Elusive. Gone.

The smell of the hospital room grew stronger, more pungent. Luce picked up her sweater and keys and quickly left her studio. At street level she got into her car, rolled down all the windows despite the cool, wet day and drove north. Crossing the Golden Gate Bridge, she slowed at the south tower, searching. A tourist bus behind her honked loudly, and in a passing car, three laughing teenage boys jeered and flipped her off. In her rear view mirror, she snatched looks into the clustered faces of the tourists walking over the bridge, into the posed faces of those who paused to take photographs. Still the smell of the hospital lingered. From her CD Ella and Louie sang *Under a Blanket of Blue* as the foghorns bellowed from below.

* * *

"Luce," Mead had written, then promptly hit a brick wall. The cursor on the laptop screen blinked incessantly. The blank white screen, save the word Luce, was an insurmountable chasm.

Mead, sitting at her regulation dormitory desk looked out the small rectangular window of her room, down Manlaka Road and followed it out toward Kenyetta Avenue. The lights of Nairobi shimmered in the clear evening air, floated in the lake in Uhuru Park. She watched the last trains pull into the station and the last trucks pull out of Nairobi and head south along the highway.

The blinking cursor might as well have been a flashing billboard in Times Square. Every thought and inclination that arose in Mead's mind was immediately censored, in rhythm to the admonishing cursor, as too inane, too open to misinterpretation, too obscure or too presumptuous. Upon her return from Tanzania she had confidently fired off a brief e-mail to Luce, friendly and innocuous: "Thinking of you. Hope you are well. E-mail is quite efficient here, if ever you're inclined to chat." Now, her resolve flagging and no response from Luce, she hesitated.

She closed her eyes, remembering the cool evening air as she stood on the terrace behind Francesca's house enjoying a moment of solitude. A pleasant hum of the party in full swing emanated from the open French doors behind her. Above, the moon was rising and cast midnight-blue shadows of the thorn trees on the open field behind the house. Africa was shaking her very foundations. She leaned against a slim column on the terrace to brace herself.

141

"You must be Dr. Bennett." The voice behind her had been deep, with a definite Italian accent. Mead turned to face a stunning woman, tall, frosted hair, tasteful black cocktail dress, encompassing smile. "At last. I am so happy to meet you, Dr. Bennett." She extended her hand. "I am Francesca Piavani."

"How do you do. Call me Mead, please." Mead's eyes darted in search of Birati. "You have a lovely home."

"*Grazie*. My daughter, Sonia, is the one who is responsible. She is a designer in Milano. I am merely her laboratory." Her laugh was full of easy pride.

"Well, she has a nice eye," Mead offered uncomfortably.

"*Si,* she is quite a talent. But, I prefer something a little simpler." She smiled warmly at Mead then tilted her head. "You are curious about the paintings, *si?*" Mead nodded, swallowing hard and taken aback by Francesca's directness. "Please then, let me show them to you."

Without hesitating, she led Mead across the lawn, through a long, well-tended garden to a separate house in the rear, all the while casually keeping a comfortable conversation afloat. "This is my private room. I come here to think, to be alone, or sometimes to be with special friends." She opened the glass double doors and pulled back the white damask curtain, motioning Mead to enter. Mead intentionally avoided looking at the walls. Two small love seats faced each other; an over-sized stuffed chair with side table and lamp occupied a separate corner. A wooden desk and leather chair, both with svelte Italian lines, completed the furniture.

"I love art. Had I not come to Africa, I would have opened a gallery in Roma or Firenze. But, life being what it is, it is my role instead to be, how do you say? a patron? *Si?*" Leading Mead by the arm, she headed to the far wall. "Sonia was the first to notice your sister. She was in Roma buying for a villa she was decorating in Umbria. She wrote and said I would love this new artist's work. When I was next in Roma, I went to the gallery. This is the first one I bought. Lovely, *si?*"

Mead stared into the computer. A design of mystifying linear patterns alternated as the automatic screen-saver kicked in, thin multi-lined rectangles and triangles floating across the small laptop screen. She rubbed her eyes and pinched the bridge of her nose as if to coax her reluctant, inhibited thoughts out.

The paintings were startling, and despite her best efforts, she had found herself unprepared. Francesca, after giving her an introduction to each of the four works, as though they were old friends, had graciously left her in solitude, closing the door firmly behind her as she returned to her other guests.

Marriage 5 was a portrait of her mother and father at the beach, sitting on the deck in the white wicker love seat. It must have been four or five summers ago because her mother wore a new white sweatshirt with "Boston" emblazoned on it. Mead remembered buying it for her in the co-op. Her parents sat next to each other in the late summer afternoon. Mead even thought she remembered Luce, ubiquitous camera in hand, taking such a photo. The painting surprised Mead for several reasons. Despite their physical proximity, they were looking in opposite directions. Within the context of the canvas, a gulf existed between them that Mead had always seen but somehow never recognized. The manner in which Luce painted them was not what Mead had expected. She had anticipated a harsh rendering, a subtext of bitterness and resentment. But there was no trace of either. Instead, Mead felt a compassion for them, individually and together. As she continued looking she realized, almost abruptly, that her parents were old. She saw them with fresh eyes, and the totality gave her a great sense of sadness.

The next canvas, *Promise 2,* was another beach scene but not from the area where the family had their summer cottage. It was primarily a beachscape, although Francesca described it as "a thoroughly curvilinear composition with a curvilinear theme." After hearing that, Mead did notice the curve of the rising sun, already half off the top edge of the canvas, the curve of the water lapping on the sandy shore, the curve of the female figure reclining there. Everything echoed a primary curve. Mead noticed a change in style compared to the portrait of her parents. The brush work was more energetic, freer and a deep sense of happiness pervaded. Although Mead had met Grace only twice, once over a tortured dinner one Christmas college break, and once awkwardly when they had run into each other in a store downtown, she thought Grace was the model.

Francesca's most recent acquisition was a painting entitled *#19/Autumn.* "I love this painting," Francesca had explained, "Here is this wonderful man, you can sense his strength, his masculinity. But he is in his autumn, approaching his last season. It is a wonderful metaphor. I love the poignancy, the aura she's created. And look, isn't that maple wonderful? You can almost taste the crispness of the day."

Before Mead had taken in all the details of the work, she recognized her father instantly – the shape of his frame, his upright, resolute carriage. Francesca caught Mead's strong physical reaction to *#19/Autumn*, but kindly made no comment. Walter's face was drawn in profile but he wore an expression she had never seen before. At the extreme right-hand edge of the canvas a taxi was just driving off. Mead did not recognize the building, a handsome, three-story blue gray edifice with a brass plaque. Through the beveled glass door Mead could see an attractive, tasteful foyer. Outside, a lovely Japanese maple was in a coat of crimson leaves. Mead had an odd sense that she was watching something she shouldn't.

The last work, *Searching for Grace/Amsterdam,* disturbed Mead immediately with its dark, lonely feel. There was an overpowering sense of loss and sadness. Across a quaint canal bridge, a sliver of a figure fled down an empty Dutch street and disappeared into the melancholic, wintery dusk. Mead knew instantly, intuitively, that her sister and Grace were no longer living together. So, Mead surmised, Luce had suffered an unhappy affair as well.

Still the cursor blinked incessantly. Mead looked out across the lights of Nairobi, following the line of lamps lighting Kenyetta Avenue, losing herself in the jumble of downtown buildings, apartments, banks, office complexes, night clubs and suddenly surfacing on a bright New York street in the Chelsea district, one cold winter night, heading toward the Village.

It was Christmas break and Mead had flown down from Boston for a few days. To her complete surprise she had gotten a call from Luce and a dinner invitation.

"Want to have dinner?" Luce had asked bluntly.

Mead, taken aback by the invitation, could only answer, "Okay. Shall I meet you somewhere?"

"No, come to the apartment. We'll fix dinner," Luce had replied.

'We'll fix dinner,' Mead later wondered. Hopefully Luce is a better cook than I am, otherwise this will be culinary disaster. Stopping at a liquor store, she had agonized over white or red, deciding that red seemed better suited to the weather. She found Luce's building, corner store and Chinese restaurant as markers, and climbed the four flights of stairs to the top floor. Standing nervously in front of the door, wondering what they would say to each other, the door opened to reveal a woman Mead had never met.

"Sorry, must have the wrong apartment," Mead muttered.

"Nah," the woman smiled warmly and pulled her into the foyer, "You're in the right place. C'mon in. I'm Grace. It's nice to meet you." Turning her head she yelled down the hall, "Luce, your sister's here."

Mead knew she was gaping at this strange woman and that Grace probably hadn't a clue how relieved Mead was to find someone else there. The thought of an entire evening alone with her sister was a terrifying prospect.

144

Grace, catching only the terror in Mead's face, not the relief, shot Luce a dirty look as she appeared from the kitchen and joined them, looking very dour. Mead thrust the bottle of wine out, unsure to whom she should be giving it, her sister or Grace who, wearing a white apron, was clearly in charge.

"How thoughtful," Grace said, studying the bottle, then giving Mead a gracious smile, "I love this label. I'll pour us some wine."

A moment ensued when Mead and Luce looked frantically at each other and then at Grace. "Ay-yai-yai," Grace said, amused, quick to recover her poise, "You two are going to have to do a little better than that or it's going to be Night of the Living Dead. Luce," she instructed slowly, as though talking to a small child, "take your sister's coat. Then show her around, why don't you?" She turned and walked down the long hallway and disappeared into the kitchen.

They stared awkwardly at each other. "I'll, um, take your coat."

"Thanks," Mead had said, handing it to Luce who tossed it through a doorway. Mead followed Luce down the long hall.

Opening various doors, Luce was a monosyllabic docent. "Closet." "Bathroom." Mead noticed how the two toothbrushes shared one cup. "Study." Mead noticed how the bills on the desk spilled over and casually mixed together. "Bedroom." One queen-sized bed. They retraced their steps and turned right into a massive room that was living room and dining room with a pass-through into the kitchen. One entire wall was a series of plate glass windows looking out over the Village. The opposing wall was floor-to-ceiling bookcases filled with books, mostly on art, and framed photos: Luce and Grace at a beach, Luce and Grace and a older woman who looked a little frazzled, Luce and a striking man she suspected was Jacob, Tommy, lots of people whom Mead didn't recognize. Mead was completely surprised that Luce was living with somebody. Up to that point, none of her siblings had seemed interested in or capable of a relationship. Rand, the first to get married, had not yet introduced his equally nerdy fiancée to the family.

Luce paused. "I'll get you a glass of wine."

"Thanks. That'd be good." Mead watched Luce enter the kitchen and waited. Grace shot Luce a look Mead supposed was frustration, then she waved through the pass-through. "Hey, Mead, come on in here. Join us while I finish cooking."

"Oh," Mead had stammered, "Okay." In the kitchen she noticed how the shopping list under the magnet on the refrigerator was written in two hands.

The dinner had progressed in an awkward, staccato way. Luce, while retaining a calm exterior, seemed extremely uncomfortable. Mead sensed that she regretted her invitation. Grace was nice enough, although Mead found her periodic barrage of personal questions disconcerting.

"So, Mead," Grace leaned forward and asked with great pregnancy, "How's your love life?" Luce nearly choked on her pasta and Mead turned a deep shade of red. No one in the Bennett family inquired about one another's love lives, which were generally assumed non-existent and certainly secondary. Any and all personal inquiries were directed towards one's work.

"I'm pretty busy studying," she replied politely.

"Oh, come on," Grace responded, "Too busy? Why, you're at the height of your hormones. Now's the time." She playfully swatted Mead's arm, causing her fork to lurch into her mouth. "Sheesh, come on, a catch like you?" Grace persisted. "Why, they must be beating down your door."

"I live in an apartment building," she feebly offered, through a full mouth, realizing what a ridiculous, non-sequitur that was. Then, swallowing, she shook her head, "I'm really too busy for that."

"For *that*," Grace repeated in a tone that Mead didn't recognize but suspected would lead to another barrage. Mead steeled herself.

"Grace, pass the bread please," Luce coolly diverted, before falling silent again with Mead. "Pasta's great tonight."

"Yes, really good," Mead echoed.

Quiet reigned momentarily before Grace began a new tack. "So," she slowly intoned, and Mead tensed in preparation, "you work on those dead people? Yikes, kind of creepy, huh?" Mead was struck by Grace's expressions which seemed so plastic and exaggerated. "Guess you don't get too many complaints though," she clowned. Mead looked at her blankly. "'Cause, you know, they're stiffs."

"No, no complaints." Mead weakly played along, hearing her own voice leaden in comparison to Grace's lively tones.

Another lull was followed by, "Hey, Mead, tell me what was it like having Luce for a big sister? I know she didn't hog the conversation." Grace smiled at Mead and panned to give Luce a playful look. Luce covered her lower face behind clasped hands and Mead stared uncomfortably between the two.

"Well, ah, you know, Luce is ten years older than I am, so we . . . " Mead watched as Grace hung on every word she stuttered. A terror struck her core. What to say? Grace obviously wanted a warmer picture than a family of cool, polite strangers. Mead racked her brain for a memory, an image, a vignette that might satisfy this animated, effusive woman who clearly adored her sister. She quickly looked out of the corner of her eye toward Luce, trying to gauge her temperature. Luce's face remained neutral. Mead finally found a thread to follow. "Luce set a pretty tough course to follow. She was

146

an excellent student. She always got straight A's, you know, always won the prizes. And she was the first girl ever to win the chemistry prize in high school." Oh, God, Mead panicked, where am I going with this and how do I get out?

"Yeah, she's pretty smart, huh?" Grace beamed.

"Yes," Mead agreed, knowing that Grace's eager expression indicated she wanted more. Blank, why is my mind a total blank?

"More wine?" Luce offered. Mead instantly put her half-full glass beneath the bottle's spout.

"Thanks," she said, drinking deeply.

"C'mon, Mead, give me the dirt. Did she pull your pigtails? Tickle you on the sidewalk until you wet your pants? Squeal on you when you ate the leftover cake?"

Mead stared dully at Grace. What on earth is she talking about? "No," was all Mead said.

Another awkward silence followed. Mead studying her salad plate, heard Grace draw a deep breath.

"Hmm, Mead, did your sister tell you we're going to Maine again this summer?" Grace looked at Mead and then at Luce, whose expression seemed to darken. "Luce, tell your sister."

"We're going to Maine again this summer." Luce's delivery was dead.

Grace cocked her head and scowled at Luce before continuing, "Boston sure is close. Mead, you ought to come visit for a weekend. Bring some friends. We could have a cookout. Play some volleyball on the beach. Have a bonfire." She looked again at the two sisters who were staring into their empty pasta bowls. "It'd be fun," her voice trailed off in frustration as her suggested fantasy fell flat on its face.

"You know," Grace said over coffee and looking directly at Luce, "I'm beginning to see a strong resemblance in you two. Very strong." Mead surreptitiously glanced at Luce who gave Grace a hard, inscrutable stare. Finally, Grace gave up her attempts at conversation, and lapsed into silence. After a requisite, excruciating period of time following dessert, Mead thanked them and excused herself. As the door closed behind her, Mead heard Grace say in low tones, "Good God, Luce," and Mead could just imagine the ensuing conversation and negative assessment of her that followed.

She had run into Grace the following year, in a department store. Grace had urged her to call, saying that Luce would love to hear from her. But Mead didn't believe her and didn't call.

The cursor beat a insistent rhythm. Mead straightened herself in the hard wooden chair and typed:

Luce,
I know this is a little out of the blue, but I was wondering if you'd like to come visit me in Africa. I'd like to see you again.
Mead.

There, she thought, it's done. She saved the brief message to disk. On the same disk was a letter she had written to her mother telling her that she would be away for a few days on a field trip visiting clinics. No need to tell her it was Rwanda, just as there had been no need to tell her Peter had joined them on the climb. Why worry her? Mead thought. Ever since the climb, Mead had found herself inexplicably paring back on detail to her mother. She felt she was being selfish, but she didn't yet have the perspective she wanted on all the events that had transpired over the past month.

Slipping the disk into her sweater pocket, Mead left her room and went to the university staff offices. Visiting medical personnel had access to facilities that included a rare computer with modem line and one of the few reliable phones in Nairobi. Putting the disk in the drive, Mead opened Eudora. Before sending the letters, she checked her incoming mailbox. Seeing she had mail, she opened it, anxiously wondering if Luce was finally responding to her. She read:

To: MBennett
Fr: EBennett
Mead:
Your father has had a stroke. Please come home as soon as possible.
Mother

Doing a double take, she quickly checked the date. It had been sent today, at 2 p.m. New York time. Mead looked at her watch. It was midnight in Nairobi. Her mother had sent this e-mail just two hours ago. Mead slumped heavily into the desk chair.

"Oh my God," she said out loud. "Oh my God."

* * *

Elizabeth looked down into the stupefied face of Walter lying in the hospital bed. She was in an altered state of consciousness, a state she had experienced

148

on only a few occasions in the past when disaster and emergency had struck simultaneously. Shock permeated her system. Her mouth was dry, her palms wet and her breathing shallow.

She had been in her study when the phone rang. Steven was on the other end. She immediately recognized from his tone of voice that something had happened. The slow, controlled pacing, the guarded way he meted out information, that told her something was wrong

"Now, don't get too worried, Elizabeth. I'm sure Walter will be just fine. I've got the best doctors working on him now. We've got to run some tests, of course. Then we'll know better."

"Oh, dear," was all that she could think to say. "When did he come in?"

"He just arrived via ambulance about fifteen minutes ago."

A gasp slipped out through her hand-covered mouth. She stood by the window, staring wide-eyed into the park, seeing nothing as she slumped against the study wall. The thought of Walter dropping to the floor as the stroke came on, poor Walter, his cheek pressed against the dirty and cold linoleum floor of the library, a gaggle of strangers circling him, a pair of strange hands cradling his limp head. Poor, poor Walter.

"Steven, how, I mean, oh God, he seemed fine this morning when he left. I just don't understand. I've known he's been driving himself. Dear God."

"Elizabeth," Steven's tone changed abruptly, "You have to take care of yourself. Shall I come get you?"

"No, I'll be fine. I'll be right there. What floor is he on?"

"Fourteen."

"Thank you, Steven."

"Can I call anyone for you? The children? Maybe Celia could come get you?"

The children, Elizabeth nearly gasped. Of course, I must tell the children. "No, no. I'll take care of letting them know. And no need to bother Celia. I'll just catch a cab."

"Well, if there's any way I can help, now or in the future, don't hesitate to ask me, okay?"

She hung up the phone and sank heavily into her desk chair. She was overcome with the image of Walter, standing at a bookshelf, suddenly and soundlessly sinking to the floor, collapsing with a slow, pained poetry as the library turned dark.

She had quickly dialed Rand, Avery and Luce, moving logically through the time zones, leaving brief but precise messages, keeping the quiver out of her voice. No one was home. For insurance she sent an e-mail to each, including Mead. Gathering her purse, her coat, muffler and gloves, she switched on a lamp in the hallway and turned down the heat. Lifting the house phone she said to the doorman, "Eddy, please get me a cab. I'm coming right down."

Now, four hours later, dusk gathered in the silent hospital room. Motionless, Elizabeth kept her vigil standing by the bed. His stillness, she thought, is almost tangible. Yet so unusual for him. She resisted the urge to touch his sickly flesh and clasped the metal bed rail tightly, gazing into his shadowy face. She briefly thought to turn on the small lamp but quickly decided not to. She knew her life had been turned upside down, inside out. The small, institutional lamp would be of no help. Better, she thought, to look into the shadows. She looked into Walter's vague, expressionless face, unsure of what she really saw.

* * *

Luce drove through the hills of Marin. The first winter rains had begun to turn the golden grasses green. Small shoots of yellow mustard emerged from the earth. Heading east just north of Novato, she drove along the southern perimeter of the Napa Valley, across Route 37. When she had first moved to San Francisco two years before, she read of a tragic car accident that happened at dawn along this very stretch of road. A young mother with a station wagon full of her own two children and her sister's three children were on their way to Marine World/Africa U.S.A. for a day's outing. A truck, driver up all night, crossed the lane and piled into them head-on. In an instant all were killed, an entire family, two generations, wiped out. This accident resonated profoundly for Luce. In the weeks after the accident occurred, she found herself driving that same stretch, turning around when she reached the end and driving it again in the other direction. Now a sizable concrete barrier stood between the lanes, and there was little likelihood of such a tragedy reoccurring.

Wetlands lined both sides of Route 37. In the marshy waters new ducklings swam and egret chicks stood on fragile, thin legs. Poppies, the first talismans of spring, trimmed the road and punctuated the fields with orange patches. Wild radish, white and purple and yellow, seemed to grow out of the asphalt. As she headed north toward Sacramento, the hills opened up like massive green waves against the blue sea of sky. "Love is a landscape the long mountains define but don't shut off from the unseeable distance." The landscape always provoked Levertov's line of poetry.

Driving was a new phenomenon for Luce. She had taken lessons in high school at her mother's insistence. They didn't own a car, but Elizabeth, the queen of practicality, felt it was a vital skill all her children should possess,

150

even if they never used it. When Luce arrived in San Francisco, she had taken a refresher course before taking the driving test. As soon as she knew she had passed, she went to the auto mall and purchased her car.

It was a rare extravagance for her, but she had felt oddly compelled. The process was extremely foreign to her. Nonetheless, she purchased a mid-range Japanese car with a sunroof, CD player, appealing color and comfortable driver's seat. Those were her priorities, and in that order.

Driving in San Francisco was a shocking experience, stressful and akin to anarchy. No one followed the rules of the road. Every intersection was a game of chicken, every passing driver out to test her mettle, everyone ready to ride roughshod over the next. Willfulness and abandon prevailed. Yellow lights only applied to the car behind. Even red didn't seem to be an absolute. Everything was up for grabs.

The open road was a different story. She loved the highways that stretched forever, the vanishing point that seemed a viable destination. She was fascinated with the relationships people had with their cars, the bumper stickers they proudly sported, stating their positions and opinions and by which they tried to define and distinguish themselves. The car was now a conversation pit, it seemed to her, with animated phone conversations being conducted at 70 m.p.h. or, more poignantly, the conversations people had in their cars without phones – finally thinking of that perfect retort, finally finding the courage to speak their minds, finishing the day's unfinished business with their absent conversation partner. All open to anyone's view.

It was a mobile neighborhood. The wires of telephone poles and high-power electric towers seemed to connect the many dots. She liked the way the road and gentle motion of the car lulled her mind into neutral. Calmed, her agitation of having seen "the unseeable distance" fading, she felt a false sense of forward motion in her life, that she could continue, was continuing.

She drove down Highway 99, from Sacramento through the Valley, astonished by the enormity of the agribusiness. Miles and miles of fields and orchards, uninterrupted by the sight of a farm or ranch. Immigrants, welcome only for back-breaking tasks unwanted by others, filled the fields in meandering lines, the curve of their backs dictated by the contents of the planted field: upright if harvesting corn, a complete circle of pain if stooping to pick strawberries.

Then past the little communities with their ugly strip malls, their requisite McDonalds and Shells, Wal-Marts and Denny's, their neon lights, that beckoned in the night. Electric dazzle against the blackened sky; tacky plastic by day.

She drove into the quiet heart of the night, pushing replay on her CD.

151

Under a blanket of blue
Let me be thrilled by all your charms
Darling, I know my heart will dance
Within your arms.

A summer's night magic,
Enthralling me so
The night would be tragic
If you weren't here
To share it, my dear.

Along the road, a blush of early morning pink, the warm blanket of a reddish-gold sunset, the sudden appearance of a shapely live oak on a swelling green hill as she rounded a bend, offered an occasional promise that somewhere up ahead was somewhere she could go. Or stop.

By morning, she headed north again, up through the Salinas Valley. The uniform, monochromatic houses in tawdry subdivisions as she neared San Jose, looked warm and inviting in the early light. An occasional field of sheep with the newborn lambs, a row of trees dotted with black birds, above the solo swooning of a Swainson's hawk still remained as the city sprawled. In the shrinking orchards incipient blooms, along the road poppies unwrapping themselves, everywhere the shades of green, from forest to lime. How does the world keep renewing itself? Luce wondered as she headed up 280, approaching the city – and, more to the point, why?

Finally, exiting the freeway onto Potrero Hill, downtown San Francisco in full view, she clicked her automatic door opener and pulled into the garage. Closing the door, she sat for a few dark moments. Her hands no longer felt angry or disobedient; she smelled only cool, blank concrete. At last, she breathed deeply, sleep.

Entering her small, overpriced house on Potrero Hill, with bridge to bridge views, she automatically hit the message button of her answering machine and continued walking into the open, modern kitchen.

"Hi, Luce, Bill next door. We're going away for the weekend. Do you think you could feed Jinx? Let me know. Bye."

"Luce," Jacob's voice sounded harried. Luce could hear someone in the background, probably Tina, asking him a question. "Not now. Not you, Luce. Listen, I have some questions for you." The intercom interrupted with "London. Line 3." She heard him sigh. "Got to go. Give me call. Are you okay? Love you."

"Mrs. Bennett? John McKay of World Wide Communications. We're offering a special flat rate to customers who switch telephone carriers. I'd

152

love to tell you more about this exciting new program. You can also earn bonus miles. Please call me at your earliest convenience at 1-800-SAVINGS."

"Luce," she heard her mother say, "Your father has had a stroke. Come as soon as you can. I'm leaving now to meet him at Mount Sinai."

Luce put down the juice she was pouring and went to the machine. She hit replay. Her mother's voice was flat with control. She replayed it again. This time she heard the control fraught with a submerged frenzy. She could imagine her mother standing in her study by her desk, phone in hand, looking out toward the park, trying to sound cool and in charge.

Dialing the airlines, she booked the earliest flight available, packed and called a cab.

In the plane, as she watched the earth fall away, she wondered nervously about her father, the circumstances of his stroke and her mother, and wished the plane didn't have to reach its destination. Despite a child's kicking the back of her seat, Luce fell into a dreamless sleep.

PART FOUR

Mead stared dully at her father's medical chart. "Patient picked up at 1:15 p.m. from #19 Minetta Lane." #19 Minetta Lane? She recoiled as she read the report. #19? The image of the handsome Georgian building from Luce's painting flashed into view; #19 she reread, as the sight of the painted figure of her father, his body poised with eagerness as he stood on the street curb, floated before her eyes; #19 with the Japanese maple, on fire with autumn, discarded crimson leaves a carpet at his feet. What did it mean?, she wondered. The building was so sedate, so residential looking. Could it be a therapist's office? That would be shocking, she mused, her father seeking a clear pathway through his id and ego. The thought was simply unimaginable. Could it be a doctor's office, some arcane specialist who could afford the rich block? Were there clues, forewarnings that he was stroke material? Was there a more troubling ailment lingering beneath this stroke? How would Luce have found out? The painting she saw in Francesca Piavani's private room was dated several years ago. But the figure Luce had depicted was cocked with a pleasant anticipation.

Or perhaps #19 was a private residence? Who would her father visit, and why would Luce capture it in oils? The flailing untied ends of these questions whipped against the inside of her brain like a solar storm. She rubbed her forehead as thin bolts of a headache lacerated her cranium.

The medical details on the chart indicated the severity of his stroke. The potential for complete or partial paralysis was high. The M.R.I. indicated some damage on the right side of the brain suggesting he would certainly have speech and language disorders and probable diminishing vision. Mead dug into her memory banks, recollecting data from med school. The immediate need was to ascertain if the stroke had stopped and determine whether it was a cerebral hemorrhage or a cerebral thrombosis, a broken blood vessel or a clot. Thrombosis, the clot, was more damaging, presented the far greater hazard. She remembered that stroke can lead to Multi-Infarction Dementia, with a step-by-step loss of memory, disintegration of the personality, further paralysis. With a more severe stroke there could be a need for a gastrostomy tube hooked directly to his stomach for feeding. With severe infarctions he had a 50% chance of living another five years. The doctors needed to perform an arteriography, although that ran the chance of inciting another stroke. Anticoagulants could help, but they could also increase the possibility of more hemorrhaging. Even with the limited data at hand, Mead knew this was a high risk situation.

Closing his chart, she started to walk toward her father's hospital room when she saw Steven about to enter and called to him.

"Mead, good to see you. Sorry it's under such awful circumstances." His lips lightly brushed her cheek.

"Me, too."

"You must be exhausted. When did you leave?"

"I took the first flight of the day. Fortunately, it was direct. Steven, there's something I want to ask you about."

"Mead, I'm not on the case. I'm only here to help your mother. You need to talk with Meyer and Johnson for the details. Although I heard that the results of the CT Scan were in."

"No, I just read his chart. I wasn't going to ask about that. Look," she lowered her voice and pulled him away from the door to her father's room, "Where was he picked up? I mean, what was he doing there?"

Steven tried to veil his expression, but the struggle was obvious. "Steven, level with me. Tell me what you know."

"All I can say is that it's a private residence. That's all I know, really." He removed her hand from his arm and tried to discard it in gentle, subtle way. "Really, Mead, I know nothing."

Mead exhaled deeply. "Who does know? Anyone here? Anyone you know?" Steven stood silently, shook his head and lightly lifted his shoulders in reply. "Does my mother know he was found at this address?"

Steven bit his lip and shook his head.

Mead clasped her arms over her chest then unclasped them, turning a half circle in the hallway. "What the hell is going on here?"

"I really couldn't say. I'd like to check on your mother now." He turned, opened the door and walked quietly in.

Mead propped her elbow against the cold white wall and leaned her head into her hand. After a moment, realizing she was not going to find an immediate answer, she followed him into the room. Her mother was just setting down the phone.

"That was Rand. He's going to take a shuttle back to Boston, since you're here. He said he can come back tomorrow, if he's needed, but he's giving a lecture tonight. Avery called and is snowed in in Denver and doesn't know when he can get out. No word from Luce yet." Mead heard the cool, matter-of-fact delivery and saw the labor behind it. "Mead, if you don't mind, I think I could use a cup of coffee. Steven, will you join me? I'll be right back."

Mead watched as they left, then sat down in a chair at the far end of the room. The medical accouterments, the drip systems, the clean white mechanical bed, the heart monitor and oxygen tube, made Mead suddenly think of Bila in her small, smoky hut, crowded and primitive. She envisioned the shape of her weak frame limply lying in the bed, her wide-eyed children, painfully quiet, staring at their mother as life leaked out of her system.

* * *

He's at Mount Sinai, Luce thought with a sharp pang of dread, as she waited for her baggage. Mount Sinai, where Grace was before she came home to die. In a room on the fifth floor shared with another cancer patient. Aimlessly she watched the bags float by on the black rubber luggage carousel. Mount Sinai, where Grace was until, Luce remembered cynically, Ruthie, as Grace's legal family, signed the papers permitting Grace to return to her home, their home.

Getting Ruthie to sign hadn't been a problem. That she was required, as opposed to Luce's being able to, was a deep insult within a deep pain. "I'm sorry," the nurse on duty had said to Luce, "But the law requires that a family member authorize her release." Ruthie, trying to make light of a situation that disturbed both Luce and Grace, hot-rodded Grace's wheel chair out to the curb where they got into a cab. It was getting close to the end. Even Grace had lost the energy to keep up a cheery facade. After they had gotten Grace into bed Ruthie said, "Hate to leave the party but there's a big bingo game next week and I need to practise."

"Only you, Ma," Grace had rasped lowly, unable to finish her sentence.

"That's it, Smarty Pants. No sharing my fortune with you if I win."

"Ruthie," Luce had said as they walked to the front door, "You don't have to go."

"Nah, you two kids need to be together for a while. Alone."

"Thanks," Luce had said, fighting back a gratitude that wanted to manifest itself in tears.

"Hey, don't go soft on me now, Luce Bennett. Besides, I'm only going across the river. And," she waved a threatening finger in the oppressed air of the apartment, "I will be back." Luce had closed the door and leaned against it heavily before summoning the energy, the courage to go to Grace.

"Excuse me," someone said, knocking past her to grab an oversized piece of luggage. Luce saw her two pieces, grabbed them and headed for the cab line. Mount Sinai, she thought, as she slowly worked her way to the front of the line and finally got into a cab, the site of my worst nightmare. The sharp winter afternoon was edged with a faint hospital odor.

Leaning into the corner of the cab, she tried to imagine her father struck down. While logically inevitable, it was emotionally inconceivable. Walter, a tower, hit by the lightning bolt of a stroke. He would stand, scorched perhaps, but surely he would stand.

From Interstate 5, the spine of California, to the FDR Highway in less than twenty-four hours, she mused, it's a small world. Outside the cab window the cityscape was a blur of gray and shadowy verticals as the afternoon thickened.

"And why exactly do you want to move to California?" she had asked Grace several years ago.

"It's horizontal. Not vertical."

"I see. Very compelling. Maybe you could just lie down on your side for a few days and it'll pass."

"I suppose you think that's funny. But I'm serious, Luce. Imagine, all our lives we've lived in a world that's up and down. Elevators, escalators, staircases. Up. Down. Down. Up. Don't you think it would be interesting to try a wide open space for a while?"

"No, not particularly."

"You have no sense of adventure."

"To the contrary, I just have no need for a sense of the horizontal."

"Funny," a sly suggestive look came over her face, "I recall there have been some times . . . "

"Well, now, that's a different matter. And, if you're changing the subject, one I'd happily pursue. And one that doesn't require moving across the country." She reached to pull Grace into her arms.

"Later," Grace eluded her reach. "I'm serious, Luce."

"Okay. Why California? Why now?"

"I was reading an article in *Psychology Today* and . . . "

"I see. I thought I'd canceled that subscription as dangerous and subversive."

"I bought a copy. Anyway, there was this article about an experiment with kittens that had been raised in two types of boxes. In one box they painted vertical lines and in the other horizontal lines."

"I'd be happy to buy two cardboard wardrobe boxes and paint them for you. This is, after all, my profession. Then you could have either environment whenever you wanted."

"The kittens," she said, ignoring Luce's remark, "from the box with the horizontal stripes couldn't jump heights and the kittens from the box with the vertical stripes couldn't jump distances. See what I mean?"

"Hmmm."

"Luce, doesn't it bother you to think that you have been curtailed in some way just by virtue of your environment?"

"This is just occurring to you?"

"Don't be snide. I just feel kind of restless. I want to try something new."

"Would that include our relationship?" Luce was suddenly worried.

"I should say yes and torture you. But you know better. I'm going to be forty in two years."

"And what about Ruthie? It'd kill her if you moved away."

"True. But she could visit."

"Yeah – for like ten months of the year?"

"Hey, Lady," the cab driver shouted through the dingy window between the front and back seats, "we're here already."

Luce looked out the window and into the lobby of the hospital. "Thanks. Keep the change."

The smell upon entering filled her with nausea and for a moment she thought she might actually be sick. Beneath the disinfectant was the scent of mortality: pungent and indisputable. Steadying herself, she went to the Admission Desk.

"Can I help you?" the woman said from behind the desk. Luce tried to remember if she had ever seen this woman before. "Can I help you?"

"Sorry. My father, Walter Bennett, what room is he in?"

"Let me check for you. That would be 1420, the fourteenth floor. Elevators are around the . . . "

"I know where the elevators are. Thanks."

"Well, excuse me for trying to be helpful."

"Sorry, it's just. Never mind." She went to the bank of elevators, got in, took a deep breath and pushed the button for the fourteenth floor.

Luce stood before the door marked 1420, a light industrial gray with flat white numbers and a cold straight brushed steel rod for a handle. The door was slightly ajar and she could see the form of her father, a sagging slab beneath crisp white sheets. A sphinx buried deep in sand. Quietly pushing the door open, she padded into the room that was full of twilight and trepidation – hoping to see before being seen. After a few steps she noticed Mead in a chair in the far corner by the radiator, head uncomfortably slumped on her shoulder, asleep.

She looked at the surrounding environment for clues. The life-support equipment, oxygen tube, drip for medications, drip for nutrients, catheter, all indicated severity. Studying the figure in the bed for further information, she saw his sallow pallor indicated that blood was circulating too slowly within his veins. His limp wrist bespoke a tired, uphill pulse. His arduous breathing rasped with congestion. Gazing into the face of her father she gasped. The face, always charged with vigorous intention, was soft with the stupor of stroke. His lips, an iron portal for emphatic prognoses, strenuous opinions, unsolicited advice and casual demands, were pliant, almost lewd, and saliva ran from the corners. She thought of a stone gone slack. His skin had an alarming cast of blue-white. Without touching him she could feel his cold flesh. Even his hair, flatly capping the enormous crown of his head, seemed lifeless. The slits of his eyes revealed two small stony surfaces, opaque and unresponsive. His whole being was without vitality, without luster. The deep tectonic plates of his being had shifted violently, and Luce could tell that his landscape had been severely altered. The sight of him so rearranged, so incapacitated, shocked her and she turned away to steady herself.

"He's in pretty bad shape," Mead's whisper pierced the still, gray room, startling her. "We still don't know if it was hemorrhage or thrombosis. They're doing an arteriography in the morning."

"What's that?" Luce asked in an automatic arched tone, her long-standing hatred of medical terminology welling within. Not even a minute and already they were on bad footing.

Mead stood up and authoritatively jerked her head in the direction of the door. Taking another look at the vacant face of her father, Luce followed Mead outside.

"Where's mother?" Luce asked.

"Good question. I haven't seen her for hours. She went to have coffee with Steven. Do you know him? Steven J. Parkins. Good man," Mead said. Luce found the clubby, professional endorsement, which Mead interjected so automatically, off-putting. "She said she'd be back shortly. That was a little before noon." Luce looked at the clock above the nurse's station. It was 5:15 p.m. "Luce . . . "

"And Rand and Avery? Where are they?" Luce wondered.

Exasperated, Mead rushed the necessary information out. "Rand flew down yesterday and spent the night but had to take a shuttle back this afternoon. Apparently there's a big lecture he has to give. Avery is snowed in in Denver."

"How long have you been here?"

Mead sighed impatiently, "Since about 10 a.m. Look, there's something I need to know."

Her urgency surprised Luce. Puzzled, she asked, "What?"

"Who lives at number #19 Minetta Lane?"

Mead's question hit Luce like a hammer. "Is that where he was when he had his stroke?"

"Yes. Who is it?" Mead interrogated, gathering herself into an imposing posture.

"I don't know." Anger flashed across Mead's face. "Really, I don't. I mean, I don't know her name. I've seen her, but only from a distance."

Mead slowly bobbed her head. "Her? His mistress?"

"I think so." Luce watched apprehensively as numbness, disbelief and fury struggled in Mead face.

"Jesus Christ," she said, then quickly covered her mouth with a doubting hand which dropped to become a clenched fist. "Jesus fucking Christ." She anxiously ran both of her hands through her hair. "Do you think that's where mother went?"

"Then she knows?" Luce's face filled with horror.

"The address is on his chart, for God's sake. That's where the ambulance picked him up."

"Oh my God, how terrible for her."

Mead turned sharply toward Luce. "How long have you known?" Her voice was accusatory.

Luce put up both hands in front of herself to ward off Mead's intense fury. "Hey, hold on, Mead. It's not my fault that he has a mistress."

Mead, surprised by Luce's sharp tone, backed down immediately. "Sorry. This is just so goddamn shocking. I mean, Christ, we all know what a tyrant he is, but Jesus, I always thought he was ethical. Moral. I always believed in that part of him. That somehow redeemed him. Made the other parts acceptable. Now, I just don't know what to think."

Composing herself now that Mead had withdrawn her sword, Luce asked, "And how did you know that I knew?"

Mead took a deep breath. "Saw *#19/Autumn*," she responded plainly.

Now it was Luce's turn to be shocked. "You what? Where?"

"In Nairobi."

"But that was sold to Rome."

"I know. But shipped to Nairobi." Mead brushed off her impending barrage of questions. "It's a long story – another story."

Luce stared at Mead, speechless.

"So," Mead tried to modulate her voice to a neutral range, "how long have you known about this?"

Luce closed her eyes. "About nine years ago, Grace and I were walking down town. We were on our way home from having dinner with some friends up by Columbia." She laughed, "Grace was on a fitness kick and had banned all cabs and subways." She shook her head lightly, remembering. "It was an accident. Complete coincidence. I saw this couple ahead of us, arm in arm. I knew right away it was Walter. Well, you can't miss him, even from the back." She opened her eyes. "I followed him. We followed him. To #19. Then," she hesitantly confessed, "I guess you'd say I had a stakeout for the next few weeks. There's a bistro across the street. I sat there looking out the window. Waiting. Watching."

They looked at each other silently.

"And?" Mead was practically shouting. The nurses at the station looked up.

"After a few weeks, I got a general sense of the pattern. He'd visit about three afternoons a week. After he retired it was more. And for longer stretches of time."

"Why didn't you say something?" Mead was furious.

Luce looked at her, then away in disbelief. "Like what, Mead?" she shot. "Great barbecued chicken tonight, Mother. Oh, by the way, Walter, how's your mistress?" She paused. "Something like that?" she asked sarcastically.

Mead looked down at the floor. "Well," she said to the floor, her accusatory tones muffled by fatigue and shock, "you didn't have to broadcast what was going on in your painting, did you? You could have said something."

"To whom? Mother? That'd be very useful. Very kind. To Walter? Oh yeah, during one of those many intimate father-daughter conversations he's so famous for. Or to you? Get real. Conversation – good, bad or indifferent – is not exactly a Bennett forte. Especially from Bennett to Bennett."

Mead looked up and watched Luce turn red with anger, surprised her usually quiet and withdrawn sister had flared, could flare.

"Look," Luce continued, calming a bit, "I insisted that Jacob not sell that painting anywhere in North America. And," she said defensively, "for your information, since you've only seen the one . . . "

"You mean there's more than the one?" Mead's voice reached a sudden pitch. "Oh, Jesus."

Luce continued, "I never painted the two of them together."

Mead just stared at Luce.

"I was as shocked as you are when I first found out. Grace threatened to lock me in a closet, I was a maniac. Obsessed. It seemed so utterly impossible." Luce was conciliatory. "So I understand your shock, your disappointment that there's no offsetting paragon of virtue and morality to ease his ways." She paused, remembering. "But you know, Mead, it's funny, after a few

161

years I kind of started to see it differently. It's conjecture, admittedly. Over the years I've probably spent no more than a couple of hours watching mostly him, sometimes the two of them. How can I explain? He seemed different with her than he ever was with us. Softer. Kinder. Happy, even."

Mead almost flew into Luce's face. "Great. That's supposed to make me feel better – that he was nicer with someone else? That he gave those parts of himself to someone besides us?" Mead shook her head in disgust.

"I guess I found it encouraging that he could love. Was actually capable of it."

Mead sneered, "That's pretty pathetic, Luce. A desperate post-facto analysis."

"Maybe." She clasped her arms over her chest. "But it made me feel closer to him."

"Oh, please. He's a whoring bastard. That's the simple truth. An impostor who's been exposed."

They stood on opposites sides of a chasm, each wary of the precarious bridge that crossed over. Too many words, not enough words. Nothing else could be said.

* * *

Elizabeth, two fingers fused tightly together over her rigid mouth, stared at Steven across the hospital cafeteria table. He was imprinting the lip of his paper coffee cup with fingernail marks, periodically looking up at her. He had already attempted to encase her shocked hands in his, but she had immediately withdrawn. She began to rub the tips of her two fingers over her thin lips, back and forth. Zip, unzip. Zip, unzip.

"For how long have you known, Steven?" Her voice was the sudden crack of a frozen lake beneath too much weight.

"I never really knew, Elizabeth. Walter has always kept his own counsel. In all matters."

"When did you begin to suspect?"

"A few years ago. I caught him in a lie. He had told me he was attending a lecture one evening. Couldn't get together with me. That lecture was canceled. But Walter, not knowing, kept up the facade next time we spoke. It was such a little thing. But so unlike Walter. He's so meticulous in every detail."

"What else, Steven?" She knew he was holding back.

"Nothing. Nothing, really." He redoubled his decorating efforts.

"Steven. I want to know. Everything."

162

"There had been some rumors. Talk in certain crowds. Years ago. Nothing specific. It seemed to die out."

Elizabeth bit her lip and slowly shook her head. So others knew, suspected. She thought of all the small clusters of people at all the social gatherings over the years. Had they been looking at her, whispering about her, pointing at her turned back as she passed by?

"Who is she, Steven?"

"Don't know. No one in the health field. Not another doctor or nurse. Not that I know of, anyway."

"For how long, Steven?" He quietly blushed. "Quite awhile, I take it." Steven carried what should have been Walter's embarrassment. Elizabeth was touched. "Steven," she began softly, wanting to release him, "you have been extremely kind to me. Over the years. And now. I thank you." She offered him her full face, reassuring him that she would be okay. "If you don't mind, I'd like to be alone for a while." He grimaced with resistance. "Please."

"Okay, but if you need anything, don't – and I mean this, Elizabeth – don't hesitate to call me."

"Thank you, Steven."

"Promise?"

"Yes, I promise." He got up and she watched him reluctantly make his way to the exit. She cast her gaze around the cold fluorescent cafeteria. A man and woman in white lab coats sat at one table, their heads bent together, murmuring quietly and laughing. That's guilty laughter, she thought and wondered if they were having an affair. Who is left at home, not knowing? At another table a woman struggled with two small children, to feed them, to keep them quiet and well-behaved. Don't bother, she thought. Don't waste your time.

From the basement cafeteria she looked up through a small window and watched a tenacious leaf drop slowly off a low, otherwise bare branch. Funny, she thought, how one's senses are heightened during times of emergency, disaster. She felt the dry brown leaf's slow, balletic journey through the cold, gray air, the tumble of its pattern as it wafted down, heard the soft brush of its landing as it hit the sidewalk, the sharp crackle as a pair of rushing, oblivious shoes crushed over it, the soft scrape as the wind blew it away.

Above her Walter lay in a stupor, well attended. For a moment she toyed with taking the elevator to the fourteenth floor, marching into his room, ripping all the tubes from his body, turning off all the machines, shaking him wildly and throwing him back upon his bed in a hideous pile of rejection.

Instead, she folded her paper napkin precisely, dabbed her mouth and placed it under her full coffee cup.

Emerging into the bleak early afternoon, she hailed a cab.

"Where to, Lady?" The cabbie smelled of stale cigarettes and soiled clothes.

"#19 Minetta Lane," she said as she slipped into the torn and tattered back seat. The cab slowly wove through the afternoon traffic.

At #19 Minetta Lane Elizabeth slammed the door of the cab shut and pulled her coat tighter to her chin. She gazed at the tastefully illuminated brass plaque that said *#19*. With her eyes she scaled the edifice of the building. As though she had arrived in a completely foreign land, she turned a full circle and took in all the detail of the quaint and expensive block. Halfway through her rotation she noticed the bistro across the street and down a few doors and made a beeline for it. Finding a table removed from the window but with a view of the street, she ordered a martini.

The first martini gave her a warm feeling, the first sensation of well-being that she had had in nearly twenty-four hours. She could feel it spreading through her otherwise numb system.

The second martini began to loosen her brain, which had frozen the moment she got the call from Steven and then sunk to sub-zero temperatures with the knowledge of where Walter had had his stroke.

The third martini released her morbid curiosity. Like one inexplicably drawn to see the gore at a fatal accident, Elizabeth wanted to see the gore of Walter's infidelity. She wanted to see the myriad detail of what had delivered a fatal blow to her marriage, although she knew even then that what was a sudden death for her had, in actuality, been an indolent cancer. What did this woman look like, act like? Had there been money involved, their money? Had she ever visited the co-op, most egregious of all possible offenses? Had the two of them taken trips? What did she cook for him? What perfume did she wear? Did she buy him sweaters, ties, books? Had he rested his head in her lap, cozily reading on winter afternoons while Elizabeth envisioned him toiling at the library? Had she ever taken a sultry Caribbean trip with him? The quest for specificity hit like furious sparks firing through her system.

The fourth martini loosened her rage. And her tongue. 'When the liquor goes in, the truth comes out,' her own mother had been fond of saying. Elizabeth stood, having hit her boiling point, paid her bill and marched ruthlessly toward *#19*, relentlessly toward the truth. She went up the short set of steps to the front door and stood gazing at the brass plaque. #19. Below there were three buzzers.

She hadn't thought of that. For a moment she considered leaving, lest she disturb someone from important business or a nap. Oh, what the hell, she thought, let them be disturbed. God knows, I have been disturbed. Mightily disturbed. She pressed the first. No answer. She pressed the second.

"Hello? Who's there?" asked an older male voice.

Probably not the one, she thought, asking, "Do you know Dr. Walter Bennett?"

"No. Should I? Is something wrong? Has someone fallen ill?"

"Never mind," she said curtly. "Sorry to disturb you." Is something wrong? she thought. You damned well better believe something is wrong. Terribly wrong. Now she quickly, aggressively pushed the third buzzer, keeping her finger depressed.

"Yes?" a woman's voice crackled through the speaker.

"Do you know Walter Bennett?" she asked, hearing her own liquor-slowed voice.

A small gasp preceded, "Why?"

Bingo. Elizabeth exploded. "This is Elizabeth Bennett, and I want to know." Elizabeth had moved in closer on the speaker and was nearly shouting. She clutched the handle to the gate tightly, and began to tremble. In the long ensuing silence, she willed the woman to relent, willed her to release the gate, willed her to let Elizabeth Bennett in.

"Come up. Third floor." The woman's resigned voice was shaky.

The door buzzed. For a moment Elizabeth was sure the buzzing sound was of her own kinetic energy flashing from her own furious hand.

* * *

Mead opened her eyes. For a moment she was lost in time, disoriented. Here she was back in her old bedroom. She stared at her bureau, the bookcase with all her high school and college texts neatly shelved, her desk by the window. What was she supposed to do now? Get ready for high school? Fly back to Boston? Back to Chicago? And just yesterday she had been in Nairobi, a few days before seeing Luce's paintings at the Piavanis, a few days before that in Sofia Town. Mead was seized by a sudden realization: there is no going back. Not in time. Everything was altered, different.

The smell of coffee filled her room. She slowly got out of her twin bed, stood by her desk and looked down into the street and into the park. Everything seemed so unreal compared to what she had been seeing on a daily basis in Nairobi. The frozen park seemed so gray, so lifeless, so hemmed in compared to the open tawny plains of Africa. A child pushed an empty swing while the au pair read a magazine.

Mead turned away from the window and examined her room, running a hand over the surface of the desk. This is where she studied so hard, read so copiously to . . . to what? To please your father. To get to where you are today. And, she asked in a quiet, unsure voice, Where the hell is that? She fell back into bed trying to remember, much less sort out the events of the past two months. First there was, is, she corrected, Africa – beyond description in so many ways, on so many levels. The climb with Peter, the sight of him slipping into Roz's tent, the viewing of Luce's paintings, the people, the hospital, her budding friendships with Linda and Birati, and now this. A stroke and a betrayal. Somehow they seem to go together, she contentedly thought, surprised at her own evil thinking.

And for the first time, she wished she were back in her clean, orderly antiseptic lab in Chicago having to deal with a virus that, while overpowering and challenging, didn't threaten her directly the way the events of the past two months had. Did. She longed for the even, climate-controlled environment, the solitude of her research, the clean, simple relationship with her adversarial virus. To put it all under a scope and amp the magnification, to see the detail, to label what she saw and file it away. Approaching the window again, she leaned her forehead against the cold glass. Virus, she thought, the notion of disaster just held in check by intention or by chance. Impending disaster, with just a wafer thin line of defense.

"Luce," her mother's voice called from the kitchen, "Mead, coffee's ready."

Luce, hearing her mother's disembodied voice from down the hall, was reluctant to leave the warmth of the pull-out sofa, the safety of her mother's study. She let her eyes fall sleepily upon the wall of photographs. Someone viewing these for the first time, Luce thought, might think the Bennetts were a close family. Here were the most carefully selected moments of the years. These photos, chosen for their optimum portrayal of the family, were the few that passed the test, the few that, due to circumstance, angle, coincidence or coercion, reflected a bond that didn't exist. Luce wondered what Elizabeth, the master editor, did with the thousands of rejects it had taken to fill this patch of wall. Did Elizabeth find comfort in this false evidence? Could she so easily discard those photos that depicted the family, jangled, fragmented and morose when assembled, in favor of these paltry few?

"Mead, Luce," Elizabeth called again, "coffee."

They stumbled into each other at the kitchen doorway.

"You should know," Elizabeth said matter-of-factly, handing each of her daughters a mug of coffee, "I'm leaving."

"What?" Mead demanded. "You leave the hospital yesterday at noon, disappear for the entire day, aren't awake when we get here at midnight, then tell us you're leaving?" Mead was livid. Luce took her coffee and sat down. She thought her mother's eyes were bloodshot. Tears, she wondered, although a faint odor of alcohol clung to her.

"Let's be direct. You know that your father had a stroke at a woman's house. She, it would appear, has been his," she paused to find a suitable word, "companion for some time. That being the case, I'm taking a leave of absence."

Mead, mouth gaping, stared at her mother. Luce calmly asked, "Where will you go?"

"Immediately, I'm going to the beach house. After that, who knows?"

"Who's going to look after him?" Mead was baffled.

Elizabeth turned toward her sharply. "Someone else."

"But wait, how . . . ?" Mead tried to continue her line of questioning but was cut short by Elizabeth.

"I don't know how he will be taken care of. Or by whom. All I can say is that it is not going to be by me."

Watching her mother, Luce thought that these new, boldly drawn lines were actually deep cracks. She appeared to Luce like a delicate piece of china that had splintered into a thousand sharp pieces and was freshly glued together. There was a wobbling delicacy beneath her emphatic way. And hurt.

"Will you be all right?" she asked her mother.

Elizabeth stared at Luce a long time before responding, "I don't know." Then, with bitterness, "Probably." Changing gears, her voice reached for past efficiency, "I will be back for some things. Or send someone. I'm taking the computer. It has all my files and records. You can trust that I will not plunder any of our accounts."

"Oh, please, Mother," Mead said. "No one would ever even think such a thing."

She's considered it, Luce thought, watching impassively. And I for one wouldn't blame her. Small compensation.

"I've called Con-Ed and they're turning on the electric and gas. The phone should be working by tomorrow. But," she said emphatically, "I'd prefer not to be contacted for a while. If something serious happens, well, then you can call."

"A stroke isn't serious?" Mead challenged sarcastically. "What do you consider serious?"

"Death." Her tone was acid. "I just want to be by myself." In an instant Elizabeth traveled from fury to hurt, shock to betrayal, vengeance to despair. Her usual steadfast and stoic figure trembled with the violent journey, and she touched the counter lightly to brace herself.

Luce, deeply moved, stood up and put a comforting arm around her. Elizabeth stiffened and walked away.

"I have spent my entire married life, even that year after you were born, Luce, when I left home for a while, being faithful to you father, to our vows. Now, I come to discover that he's being seeking . . . comfort else where. And for some time. He's been seeing that woman, you know, for close to fifteen years. That would make her a common-law wife – twice, for God' sake."

"How do you know that?" Mead demanded. "Did you go to see her?"

"I certainly did." Elizabeth was not brooking any of Mead's bullying.

"Oh, my God." Mead whispered.

"And why shouldn't I have? Tell me – don't I have a right? This woman has been a third participant in my relationship with your father for fifteen years. Fifteen years! Unbeknownst to me. While I sat by thinking I had a marriage. Don't I get to know, finally, the truth? Or at least some of it? Don't I get to see with my own eyes?" She gave Mead a disparaging look. "Of course I went to see her. What sort of woman wouldn't?"

Luce, feeling her mother's quaking, stepped back and looked at her, amazed. "Mother," she began and noticed Mead shifting uncomfortably, "I have to tell you something."

Elizabeth focused on her eldest daughter.

"I've known that he was having this affair. I've known for years." Elizabeth stared silently, intently watching Luce's mouth as though she had been speaking Greek. "I guess," Luce continued, breaking the silence, "I guess I should have said something. But I didn't know what to say."

She and Mead exchanged glances, waiting for Elizabeth to erupt. Or collapse. Elizabeth stood stock still for a moment, then, with a brush of her hand, said, "It's hardly your fault, Luce. Don't apologize." She began to leave the kitchen, but turned, and as if as an afterthought, said, "I'm sorry you had to find out first." Luce, completely surprised by her mother's reaction, knew in an instant how drastically she had been transformed by the events of the past two days. The sisters exchanged glances. Luce recognized in Mead's face her own fear at seeing their mother so close to emotion. Elizabeth, always rock solid and contained, teetered on the edge of hysteria and fury. The two daughters were terrified by their mother's new-found precariousness. They remained in the kitchen, stunned and listening as Elizabeth walked down the hallway, opened the door and closed it firmly behind her. Her sudden, irrevocable absence rang in their ears.

* * *

168

Luce clasped her arms around her shoulders and rubbed to eradicate the deep chill she felt being back in Mount Sinai. Looking into the face of her father, pallid flesh starved of oxygen and blood, she saw the life-tired face of Grace. "I want to go home, Luce," she had whispered from her hospital bed two years ago. "I don't want to die here."

Luce watched as the nurse adjusted Walter's tubes, recalling how the hospice nurse had come to their apartment and set Grace up with a morphine drip.

"Listen, honey," the nurse had said as she placed the injection device in Grace's hand, "I've got this set up for a basal rate. If the pain gets too bad, just give a squeeze. If it gets unbearable, keep squeezing and it'll soon be just fine." Luce winced hearing those instructions, knowing they were the directions to death. But they had talked about it with each other, in their respective support groups, with Ruthie. There was no need to endure the unendurable.

Still, Luce, holding Grace's limp hand, had bridled hearing the words, bit her lip and looked out the window. The nurse stepped directly into Luce's line of vision. "Do you understand?" Luce, not trusting herself to say even a single word, nodded yes.

Later, each of them holding one of Grace's hands, Ruthie had said, "Come into the kitchen with me, Luce. Be right back, sweetheart," she whispered to a semi-conscious Grace.

"Luce," Ruthie said, taking her by the shoulders, "You, *you,*" she said softly, pausing to let the word sink in, "have got to let her go."

She looked dumbly into Ruthie's face. Ruthie shook her, trying to arouse her spirit. "For God's sake, Luce, she won't go unless you tell her it's okay. Would ya, please? She's ready, Luce. She's ready to go. Release her."

Luce took one look at Ruthie and fell into her arms sobbing. Ruthie pulled Luce's wet face out of the crook of her neck, and holding it before her whispered, "Please. It's killing me to watch her like this."

Searching for an unknown reserve of strength and after six fatiguing months finding none, Luce took a deep breath. With arms around each other's waists, they walked down the hall and into the bedroom.

"Grace," Luce's voice broke momentarily, as she sat gingerly on the edge of the bed, "if you're in too much pain it's okay. You don't have to stay any longer." She wrapped one hand around Grace's, which was wrapped around the injection device, and stroked Grace's brow, which was damp with pain. "It's okay, hon. Just take a long squeeze." From beneath heavy lids, Grace strained to look into Luce's face for confirmation.

169

Ruthie moved in closer, placing her hand against her daughter's cheek. "It's okay, Grace. I'm here. Ruthie's here. We love you."

Luce felt Grace's hand move within hers, plunging the stopper several times slowly. She let the device fall away and, holding Luce's hand, she took a breath, then stretched her head back as pain and life left her body. In a second she was gone.

The slight but discernible motion of Walter's eyes widening brought Luce back from her reverie. She waited. His eyes blinked again then slowly came into focus.

"Hello," she said slowly. "Can you hear me?" Walter blinked his eyes. Luce took a deep breath, "Good. That's good. Welcome back."

* * *

"Your father's showing some promising signs, Mead," Dr. Meyer said the next morning. With a pen against the illuminated X ray he circled the area of thrombosis. "Not that there hasn't been some severe damage. But he's got a chance at least. With some rest, therapy, good care. Well," he turned to face Mead, whose empty stare was lost in the X rays, all shades of gray, "he'll never be who he was but . . . "

Mead turned sharply. Never be who he was? She snorted bitterly, thank God for small favors. Now that's good news. She could barely stand still in the small office. She was furious. So angry she could hardly see straight, much less think straight.

"Are you all right, Mead?" Meyer asked. "I know this has been a lot to deal with, a real shock. Would you like some tranquilizers? A little something to help you sleep?"

She faced him. She wanted to slap him. A little something to make you feel better? Make it all go away. A little something to help you ignore the fact that your father's an adulterer, a liar, a fraud – of long standing. Instead, she closed her eyes and said, "No, thanks."

Dr. Meyer, dismayed by her behavior, continued cautiously, "These next few days will be key. How he responds will tell us a lot about his future capabilities. And, of course, we don't want him to suffer another stroke."

We don't? Mead asked herself. Why not? Why the hell not? She rubbed the base of her head. "Thanks again. I'll tell my sister."

She walked through the cold labyrinthine hallways back to room 1420. Taking a deep breath, she slowly opened the door and entered. Making brief eye contact with Luce, who stood by Walter's bedside, Mead positioned

170

herself at the foot of his bed, in clear view, given his limited mobility. She looked into his groggy face, saw him strain to focus on her.

"I spoke with the people at the CDC earlier this morning," she announced. "They've offered to extend my fellowship another six months."
Luce watched Mead with a sense of foreboding. She saw in Walter's eyes an exertion to shake his mental lethargy, to surface. The corner of his mouth twitched and his lower lip moved almost imperceptibly.

"I've accepted." Mead leveled her hard gaze directly into Walter's filmy eyes. "I called the Admin in Chicago and told him."

Luce saw Walter's eye's blink slowly, fill with water. Mead stood tall, a venomous snake charmed to full height by anger, ready to strike. Slowly she slid closer to the foot of the bed. Walter's head sank heavier into the pillow.

"You know, I believed in you," she hissed. Luce saw in his eyes his struggle to give shape to his loose mouth, to move the mechanism of his tongue, to mobilize his thoughts from his brain into words and to push those words into the air. Nothing. "What you've done," Mead lashed, "is despicable. Despicable and unconscionable. There are no words to describe how awfully you've behaved. So selfish. So low. So unforgivable. You," she paused for a moment, "you might as well be dead."

"Mead," Luce admonished, "that's over the line."

"You're telling me in the presence of this," her hand flipped disgust at the figure of her father, "that *I've* crossed over the line? In front of this bastard? This infidel?"

Luce saw her father's face begin to quiver more markedly. She shot Mead a silencing glance. Mead took several steps forward. Hate intensified on her face. "That's enough, Mead." Sensing Mead was incapable of prying herself away, she spoke sharply, "Please, Mead, just leave." Mead stood firm. Approaching her, Luce grabbed Mead's upper arm tightly. Mead pivoted, abruptly depositing her hate into Luce's eyes. Attempting to sound authoritative, Luce said, "Mead, leave." Mead's expression went blank. She stared at Luce dumbly. "Please, just leave." Luce slowly guided her to the door, opened it and watched for a few moments as Mead shuffled down the hall. Closing the door firmly behind her, Luce collapsed against it.

"Well, Walter," Luce said looking across at her father after she had allowed a few moments for him to recoup, "Looks like it's going to be you and me for a while."

He slowly slid his eyes toward her, held her gaze for an exhausting moment, then disappeared behind his heavy, veined lids.

* * *

Luce sipped her tea while surreptitiously studying her sister's face. They were both too tired to sleep.

Mead, head propped against the fist of her hand, looked intently into the steaming mug Luce had placed before her. Luce, piercing the wall that existed between them, asked, "What time's your flight?"

"Early afternoon. I don't know exactly. I'd have to check. I'm not going back to the hospital." She checked her sister's expression.

"I know." The co-op was painfully quiet. The sense of absence and change overwhelming. The clock, which in what seemed like an hour ago had read 1 a.m., now read 1:15 a.m.

"How's Africa?"

Mead raised her head heavily and answered, "Unbelievable." An awkward moment ensued. Luce could tell Mead was struggling. Finally, keeping her gaze on the tea, Mead said more than asked, "So you and Grace broke up?"

Luce cocked her head in question. "Broke up? What on Earth makes you say that?"

"Saw *Searching for Grace/Amsterdam*. I don't know much about art but looking at it sure felt like the two of you aren't together."

Luce smiled a tired smile. "In Nairobi, I guess?"

"Yes. I met a woman who's a collector of your work. Nice woman," Mead rushed to say. "Has good taste."

Luce took a deep breath. "Mead, I did that painting about a year after Grace died."

Mead's head jerked up. "God, Luce, I'm sorry. I hadn't any idea. I mean, it never occurred to me. Gosh. Sorry." Her voice fell with embarrassment.

"Don't be sorry, Mead. How would you have known? I never told you. If anyone should apologize it should be me."

A thousand questions flickered silently across Mead's face.

"She died of breast cancer. A little over two years ago." Then, surprising herself, she disclosed, "I miss her terribly."

Mead couldn't speak. Suddenly she was reminded of the torturous moments in Bila's hut in Sofia Town when Bila had asked, "Who will take care of my children?" Looking at her sister, she felt as empty and as void as she had felt looking at Bila, hopelessly wasting away, begging for help.

"Grace told me, after you had had dinner with us that once, that I owed you an apology. I know you felt pretty uncomfortable. I guess we Bennetts are not very . . . " She searched for an appropriate word.

"Warm?" Mead offered, and Luce nodded. "Outgoing, might also work. Communicative? Socially adept?"

172

"That last one's particularly good," Luce said with a slight smile. "But if this is multiple choice I'd have to go with D. All of the Above."

Mead sighed. "Yeah, we're a pathetic lot. Thank you, Walter." Mead saw Luce retreat. "Don't worry, I wasn't going to start a tirade." She sipped her tea slowly, keeping her hands around the mug of warmth. "I could tell from *Marriage 5* you're not into parent bashing."

Luce was curious. "What other paintings did you see?"

"Only the four: *#19/Autumn; Marriage; Searching for Grace/A msterdam;* and *Promise 4.*"

"Oh," was all that Luce said, a small wave crashing sadly on a lonely shore.

"You're good." Mead was sheepish. "Obviously you're good. I mean, what do I know, right? But I liked them."

Luce smiled, pleased. "Good. I'm glad."

"When I was hiking Kilimanjaro, Gil, the collector's son – which is how I got introduced to them, to you, I guess I should say – told me about a series you painted on Tommy, *Neon Plague*. He described what he saw so vividly that I feel as though I've seen them as well."

"You hiked Kilimanjaro?" Luce was surprised and impressed.

"Mother didn't e-mail you that I was going to?" Mead queried.

Luce looked chagrined. "I never set up the computer. The boxes are sitting in my kitchen as we speak, an expensive doorstop and a magazine rack."

"Oh, well, that explains why I haven't heard from you."

"What do you mean?"

"I sent you an e-mail right after I got back to Nairobi after the climb. I," she hemmed and hawed, "I just wanted to talk with you."

"About?" Luce's tone was defensive.

"Nothing in particular." She paused. "Well, it was weird, climbing this mountain with Gil, a complete stranger, and having him be so impressed with you. His knowing about your works and career. And there I was, your sister, and I knew nothing. And then hearing about the *Neon Plague* paintings reminded me of when Tommy was alive and how the three of us would do things and you didn't seem to mind having me around." She took a deep breath. "And then, the fact that Peter was there compounded everything."

"Peter? You're still seeing Peter? I thought you dumped him."

"I did. But he has a charm, a way. I was weak. He managed to reinsert himself in my life." Luce looked concerned. "Don't worry, " she continued, "He's gone now. For good. You never liked him, did you?"

"No, he seemed far too charming to be trusted."

"Smart woman. He's, well, let's just say, he's untrustworthy."

"Like Walter?"

"Yes," Mead squirmed, "a lot like Walter."

"And," Luce asked, "might that explain why you used a battering ram on him today?"

Mead didn't flinch. "I'm not going to apologize for what I said, Luce. I meant every word." She was adamant. "I'm not confusing Peter and Walter. They just both happen to be guilty of the same crime." Then with a tinge of anger, "Just because you've had a decade to deal with this, Luce, to invent some ridiculously absurd excuse for it, to see the sweetness and light in it all, don't go getting righteous on me. Or analyze me. It's bad enough that Avery is always questioning me and my subconscious. You can butt out."

"Fair enough." Luce was neutral. "But I still want to know," Luce asked, "Are you taking the extension to punish Walter, or do you really want to stay in Africa longer?"

Mead slid down in the kitchen chair and looked up. Talking to the ceiling she began, "Truth is, I'm not sure. Another truth is that there's something that really moves me about Africa. It's horribly wonderful." She looked at Luce.

"You're sure it's not wonderfully horrible?" Luce joked softly.

Mead smiled. "Could be that as well. Luce," her shoulders dropped, "I feel alive there. I know it's only been, what? not even three months, but there's something inexplicable about it. When we drove to Tanzania and I got to see the countryside, I was floored. So gorgeous. The natural beauty of the land, the animals. There's a game park just eight miles outside of Nairobi. You can see elephants and lions and cheetahs – all against the backdrop of the Nairobi skyline. And the people are beautiful. The Africans, the Europeans, the Asians. You'd love it – a visual feast. Probably. I've met some great people, a couple of women doctors who I think could be friends. Oh, and how they need medical help. I simply can't describe how awful it is. A 25% increase last year in new HIV infections. What they have to deal with is staggering."

"You say staggering, yet you sound excited. I don't recall this tone of voice when talking about your research work. Doesn't sound like you miss your lab much," Luce observed.

"I don't," Mead confessed, more to herself than to her sister. "I don't miss it at all. There's nothing removed, remote or abstract about my work in Africa."

"Sounds like you've found something," Luce offered. "So what's the problem?" Mead shrugged. "Wouldn't be that little matter of your extremely promising, fast-track career in the U.S. of A., would it?" Mead smirked acquiescence. "Mead, I know nothing about managing a medical career. But I can't imagine that your staying for another six months is going to ruin it. Take the time, you don't have to decide now, you know."

Mead looked at Luce appreciatively. "Yeah, guess I don't."

"You know, it seems to me that you've been on a treadmill for years: pre-med, med, residency, the clinical fellowship, the lab. I think it's good for you to step off. It's hardly as though you're finding a desert isle and dropping out."

"No, not hardly. For what it's worth, I am sorry to be abandoning you with Walter. You can always get a live-in nurse. Or place him in a convalescent facility. At least until Mother comes round."

"You think she will?"

"You think she won't?"

"Don't know for sure. Not yet, of course. But I suspect she's going to need some major time to get over this, if that's possible. And don't worry about me," Luce explained, "I actually think spending some time with Walter might not be the worst thing in the world for me right now."

Mead was curious. "How's that?"

"I've been all loose ends since Grace died. Not able to stay put anywhere for too long. Jacob's been hounding me to move back here. And, if the truth be known, I've felt some pulls. But I haven't known if I'd be able to live here without her. Deal with the fact that she's everywhere. But gone." Luce paused. "This might buy me some time."

"Are you suggesting that you could live with Walter? I mean, he's been somewhat aloof, shall we say, to you. And for a long time."

"True. But you know, that was then. This is now. Besides, I think he'll be a lot quieter."

Mead laughed, surprised by her sister's dark humor.

"Another cup?" Luce asked, getting up.

"Sure. Don't think I'll be sleeping too much tonight." Mead watched her sister heat the kettle at the stove. "It must have been pretty rough," she said quietly to Luce's back, "having Grace die."

Luce turned, then leaned against the sink. "Like having a double amputation. I just don't feel whole."

Mead saw the pain flash across Luce's face. She searched for something to say. "Don't feel bad, Mead, there's nothing you can say." Mead flushed thinking of Jane's ability to sweep Bila up in a reassuring embrace. Mead had been unable to move that day, hearing so acutely Bila wail into the dry and unfair universe. Unable to move now, she stared into the fresh cup of tea

Luce set before her.

"My life was settled. I was settled, to my own surprise. Happily settled. Then it all changed."

"Luce," Mead was finally able to choke out, "I'm really sorry."

A silence ensued, then Luce began weakly, "It was rough. Is rough. I'll be walking along and hear a whisper. Suddenly there's the hint of her presence. I might hear a few muffled words. The tone's so familiar. I strain to hear more. I look around. No one. Or there's a scent, her scent, and it floats under my nose. She must be near. Must be here. Or I see her. I'll be walking along a street and up ahead I see her from the back, as I've seen her a thousand times. I'm sure of it. Suddenly I'm in another time, not in the present. All my senses go on alert, stand at full attention. But, just as quickly as all these teasing fragments come, they vanish. Evaporate. And in between two small seconds, what had possessed promise, reactivated my hope, lies at my feet. Memory's junkyard – strewn with rusty, indecipherable bits and pieces of my former life." She flushed with the embarrassment of self-revelation while Mead stared at her intently. "Death isn't a one-time event. I didn't know that before." She looked at Mead, dazed and uncomprehending. "Ah," she sighed, trying to strike a lighter tone, "I probably should be on heavy meds for, say a decade or two. Care to write me a script?"

* * *

Elizabeth, sitting at the kitchen table, looked out the window. Beyond the scrolling screen of the chat room she was in, the dunes curved then slackened into the sea, and an evening wind whipped the waves into a light froth. The blue-gray of dusk had descended. Reeling from recent events and revelations, she felt that she was in a nether world. Aimlessly she read the inane banter of the chat room and its participants. The window said there were twenty-seven people in the room, but for the last ten minutes only a handful had been joining in a mindless conversation.

RANGER   But the President's a dolt. And a liar.
RAZDAZ   What's the word tonite, friends?
SKINHEAD They all are. President, speaker, senator. What's the diff?
KWAYLUDE Hey, where were you last night, gorgeous?
MADMAN   It's his wife that's more the problem than him, if you ask me.
RAZDAZ   I had a date, a dud. What a creep!
RANGER   What policy, what decision hasn't he backed off of?

176

KWAYLUDE	That's what you get for leaving the virtual fold of friends. Never, ever leave home without us.
RAZDAZ	Get this slime ball off of me.
BLONDIE	Hello room. Greetings from Chicago. Que passa?
MADMAN	Back off, creep. No one but a virtual person would put up with you.
RANGER	Is this room for politics or not?
KWAYLUDE	Hey, Blondie, what sign are you?
RAZDAZ	How's the weather in the Windy city?
MADMAN	I think it's time for true blue Americans to take matters into their own hands.
KWAYLUDE	Does anyone want to cyber me?
BLONDIE	Sagittarius. You? What's everyone's age/sex?
EBENNETT	WALTER BENNETT CAN BURN IN HELL - THE GODDAMN BASTARD.
RAZDAZ	KWAYLUDE, how did you get to be such a pig?
RANGER	What are you suggesting, MADMAN, that we all

Silence. The screen, after the usual delayed reaction, went blank. Elizabeth sat, fingers poised on the keyboard, cocked, ready to shout into cyberspace again.

EBENNETT	You spend your whole life, and I'm 70 so I mean whole life, believing in someone, supporting them, making their existence possible, comfortable and then, POW

Elizabeth thought of Eddy recounting Mr. Heinz's sudden death.

	POW it all blows up. Everything. The false hopes and beliefs, the vows that turned out were only shams, everything. Gone. In a flash, a husband's gone and only a bastard remains in his place.
SKINHEAD	Hey, who's the old lady who's blowing steam?
JESTER	Back off, jerk, let her talk.
EBENNETT	Don't address me indirectly, young man. At least have the courage of your convictions to say them directly to me. I'm fed up with lies and deceit. I'm tired of maintaining what is little more than a facade. If you have something to say to me, SAY IT.
RAZDAZ	Go girl.
JESTER	Right on, sister. Let's get down to it. All you sniveling little

	punks can do is talk about astrology and your self-indulgent piddling concerns. I'm ready to hear more from EB and some real life.
RANGER	Doesn't anyone want to talk about politics?
RAZDAZ	So, EB, what's the scoop?
EBENNETT	I married Walter Bennett at age 20. I bore him four children. I raise those children, managed the business end of his career – quite successfully, I might add. I always made sure that life was comfortable for him, went smoothly for him. I cleaned, I cooked, I changed the diapers, made smart investments. For fifty years I worked damn hard figuring, well, that simply goes with the territory. We've got a partnership here, right? One day, we'll have time to ourselves, time for our marriage. No, that's not accurate. I thought, one day Elizabeth will rise back to the top of the list as a priority.
JESTER	A familiar story, hon. Hope springs eternal.
EBENNETT	But what do I come to find out? What happens instead? I find out that Walter Bennett, pretender to great ethics and morals, has been having an affair, no scratch that, a relationship with another woman for fifteen years.
RAZDAZ	And I thought my date last night was a creep.
KWAYLUDE	Hey, EB, sounds like you need to make up for some lost time. Let's go private and you can cyber me.
JESTER	It's an old, old story, darling. I had a guy, not a husband, but a boyfriend, did the same thing - just over a shorter period of time.
MADMAN	Look, EB, I'm sorry for you, but let's cool the bashing. How do we know that Walter didn't have good reason to try and get something going on the side?
EBENNETT	Don't vows count for anything? Isn't there something that one can trust these days? Believe in?
RAZDAZ	KWAYLUDE YOU'RE A TOTAL PIG. GO TO ANOTHER ROOM OR I'LL REPORT YOU TO THE CYPERCOPS.
BLONDIE	You know, Jester, I had a boyfriend like that just last year. He was a Capricorn, of course.
JESTER	Typical, MADMAN, blame it on the poor victim.
SKINHEAD	And I suppose you ladies out there figure that this only happens to you, right? No female ever two-times a guy, right?
SONICBOOM	Hello room? What's the topic?
KWAYLUDE	Hey, Blondie, go easy on Capricorns. Yours truly is a Capricorn.

You obviously haven't met the right one yet.

RANGER   Doesn't anyone want to talk about politics? ANYONE?

I could have just sat in my study for the rest of life, Elizabeth thought as she looked over the computer screen and out the darkened window. I could have just faded away. Would he have even noticed? Elizabeth rose from the kitchen table and opened the window to breathe the dark sea. I thought I was betrothed. Instead I was betrayed.

* * *

In the darkened hut, Jane and Mead exchanged glances over Bila's thin body that lay painfully in the small bed.

"She's dying," Mead said, panicked. "Shouldn't we send the children out to play?" she asked, knowing immediately how ridiculous her suggestion was. Where would they play? In the doomed alleys of Sofia Town? How would they play, these wide-eyed, woeful children who were doomed themselves?

Jane took the rag which served as a compress from Bila's forehead and wet it in the nearby pan, wrung it and replaced it on her forehead. "You Westerners always act so surprised by death. Maybe embarrassed? It is inevitable, it is implicit. What did you think was going to happen, Mead? These children should not go away from it. They should see their mother through it." She reached for the eldest, a girl, and scooped her onto her lap, stroking her head. She gave Mead a hard, dire look. "You should, too." She then spoke quietly to all the children in Swahili. Most of it was lost on Mead, except for the soothing tones.

Mead wanted to do something. Her mind raced, her hands trembled. There was nothing to be done. They would, Jane had told her before they entered the hut this morning, summon a neighbor man who would wrap Bila's body in a woven mat, tie her to the handles of his bicycle and take her to what served as a mortuary. While Mead was in New York, Jane had tracked down the husband, who had not been around for several days now. If he did not show up before they left, they would take the children to an overcrowded orphanage full of children in similar positions. For now, there was nothing to be done.

"Do not be so afraid of darkness, Mead," Jane said not looking at her. "It is the other side of day." She rhythmically stroked the littlest child's head.

Mead hesitated, then reached for the youngest daughter, and pulling her in her lap, wrapped her arms about her. The child, scared and shivering, let her full weight fall against Mead's body in a quiet plea for help. Her bones were so thin, so frail. Mead shut her eyes and silently screamed, Why must they all die, damn it? Why? Together they all waited and watched as Bila's breathing became slower and more shallow, as her eyes fell further and further away, until, after several hours, she surrendered, and like a burnt candle, sputtered lowly and was gone.

* * *

"How's your father doing?" Jacob's voice on the phone sounded cautious.

"About the same as when you asked yesterday, Jacob. And the day before. Why are we padding about so? What's up?" Luce stood at her mother's desk looking into the park. A March snow had dusted the Earth's surface and everything had a peaceful, quiet freshness. Across the hallway she saw Walter, sitting in his wheelchair facing the window, shawl draped over his legs. Egyptian sculpture, Luce thought, solid, inert, occupying space, unable to move through it. Again she thought of the great Sphinx, no longer protector of the monumental. Abandoned to the desert, defaced by weather and time, sentenced to a vast and sandy silence.

"Well, you probably don't remember but there was a PR Director of a high tech firm at your show in January. You were late and he couldn't wait. He called me the next week. Apparently the chief honcho there is pretty keen on your work. Anyway, he called again a few days after your Dad's stroke. They're still interested in buying something. Perhaps several pieces. I didn't want to bother you before, but . . . "

"But what, Jacob?"

"Well, I'd like you to go with me to meet them."

"Ahhhrrgg, Jacob, you know how I . . . "

" . . . how you hate those things but, it could be multiple paintings. You're in town. And they have several corporate offices. Sounds like whoever this guy is, he'd love to meet the *'artiste.'*"

"And that would be me?"

"'Fraid so."

"Do I have to, Jacob?" Luce whined.

Jacob paused. "You know, when we're old and gray . . . "

"Some already are."

" . . . and I get a million buck advance for my memoirs . . . "

"Highly overpaid, given your memory."

" . . . of my illustrious associations with great artists of my time, the

180

public will no doubt find it fascinating to learn that a certain, quote unquote, painter did nothing but whine."

"Great, Jacob. It's not enough that you threaten me in present tense. You now have to threaten me in the future, too?"

"Okay, don't go. We'll just lose the sale. Better that than you should be inconvenienced by the dirty world of commerce for a couple of hours."

"All right. All right. Let me get a calendar. I'm sure I can do it next week."

"Tomorrow would be better."

Luce let out an audible sigh of exasperation. "Okay, Jacob, I can see there will be no peace until I acquiesce. Let's see," she thumbed through her blank calendar, "I can do it at 3 or 4."

"10 a.m. would be perfect."

"You've already set this up, haven't you? Why didn't you just hire a terrorist to hijack me and save your time on the phone?"

"Now don't get snippy. Besides, I couldn't find one with a reasonable rate. Hey, it's an interesting company, very high tech, very cutting edge, very cash rich – coaxial modems. You might just find it interesting."

"I don't even want to know what a coaxial modem is, Jacob. Doesn't sound like something you should talk about in public, though."

"And after, maybe a little lunch? Just the two of us?"

"Where are they located?"

"Must you sound like I'm torturing you?"

"The address?"

"On Leonard. The heart of Silicon Alley. Meet me there?"

"Sounds awful already," Luce let out a full stream of reluctance.

"Hmm, better yet, swing by the gallery and we'll go together."

"All right," Luce said half-heartedly.

"And Luce, a coaxial modem gives you extra bandwidth."

There was silence on the line for a few moments. "Really, Jacob? God, knowing that, I'm not sure I can wait until 10 a.m. I'm going to build my entire outfit around this really cute pocket protector I just happen to own. Hope it doesn't drive the Prez wild with digital desire."

"Luce?"

"What, Jacob."

"Glad you're feeling better."

"Nothing this meeting can't ruin."

"See ya."

* * *

181

Mead sat on the verandah of the Norfolk Hotel, drinking a sundowner, although the moon was already on the rise. The death of Bila had profoundly disturbed her. To stand by helplessly and watch. She had never felt helpless in her life. Watching Bila over the past few weeks, a woman in her twenties, watching her three young children, all sentenced to death, gave Mead a desperate feeling of impotence. And there are thousands of Bilas, she thought, thousands of thousands.

On her flight from New York to Paris she had surprised herself by thinking, I could throw it all away. In a second. Throw away the narrowness of life that medicine demanded, the years of preparation and training, the promising future. For the first time she entertained thoughts as preposterous as hitchhiking around the world, sitting in a Parisian cafe and drinking coffee, visiting Bali and never leaving. Maybe she, like Luce, was a painter. How would she know? She had never been seriously exposed to anything but medicine. Maybe she could become a mogul, a global mogul, she mused. She had read about captains of industry who built their powerful financial empires on rug cleaning businesses or hot dogs or futures. There were options. She could exercise these options. This surprised her.

On the flight from Paris to Nairobi she thought, "And if I throw it all away, where would I throw it?"

At Walter's frozen alabaster feet, she answered. Her father, who had exhorted her, urged her, pushed her, raised the bar after every successful jump. He had always been demanding, always difficult and always on a pedestal. That he had put himself there was inconsequential to the fact that she had accepted his position. Since his retirement she knew that she had distanced herself from him, from the force he exerted, perhaps even commented on the slight mold growing on the cracking ionic column of his pedestal. Still she accepted it. Never challenged it. Never walked around it. Never saw the dark side. Until now.

Somewhere over the Indian Ocean she thought, Whose life is it, anyway? He's had his, and he's lived it fully. Willfully. He only gets one.

Now, sipping her second gin and tonic, waiting for Linda to arrive, she thought, I've never really walked around much of anything. My life has been a straight shot, a rigid chute. From point to point, goal to goal, achievement to achievement, smoothly and without disturbances or interruptions.

On her way to JFK airport she had impetuously asked the cabby to stop by the Malowitz Gallery. Jacob graciously extricated himself from a meeting to show her a few of Luce's hanging works and then set her up in a small room with a projector. If he was surprised, had any judgments, bad feelings or negative assessments about her, accumulated by virtue of being Luce's friend, he didn't show it. Sitting in a darkened room, in a comfortable leather chair, remotely clicking through slides of her sister's works had fascinated her. She glossed over the landscapes and portraits of people she didn't know in favor of the more revealing, intimate works, clicked angrily through #19/ *Spring, Summer* and *Autumn*. Slowly making her way through the *Searching for Grace* series, Paris, Amsterdam, Rome, Mexico City, Maine, New York, she couldn't believe that she hadn't seen it – Grace's death. It was there, in plain view. Luce clearly showed the viewer the ever elusive figure slipping out of reach. And the pain and loss were obvious. "How could I have missed it?" she kicked herself.

The series of Tommy in the *Neon Plague* had caused her to gasp audibly and cover her mouth in horror. Her good friend, her bridge to Luce, so young and vibrant, full of life and generosity, tried, in each painful canvas, to defy and dignify death.

Two small paintings, *Doctor 1* and *Doctor 2*, painted during Mead's years in med school, had surprised her. Looking at them objectively, she saw the painter's compassion for subject. Behind the sense of triumph and accomplishment was a hue of sorrow, a weight that came from an unseen source. Mead had never suspected that Luce was empathetic or even paying attention to her. More attention than I was paying myself, Mead thought cynically.

And if I threw it all away, she thought, surfacing into the present, sipping her sundowner, who would that benefit?

Linda, seeing Mead on her second gin and tonic said, "Hey, don't get too far ahead of me."

"Don't worry. They're having no effect." Her tone was morose.

"One of those nights, huh? What's up?"

"Really want to know?"

"Of course."

"I've had no problems in my life."

Linda's face molded into a question. "Sorry, I'm not following."

"I retract that statement. Peter was a problem. My first problem. A bit of a persistent problem. Things didn't precisely follow plan or schedule with Peter. An aberration admittedly, but a disruption nonetheless. You see?"

"No. Not really. What's eating you, Mead?"

"Bila died."

"Oh. I'm sorry."

"And it occurred to me," her voice was full of irony, "as I stood by, years of the best training money and connections can buy under my belt, hours of research in the finest labs, incredible specialist that I am – doing nothing, fucking nothing – as I watched her three kids, scared to death and oblivious to the orphanage that was looming in their paltry, truncated futures, now *they've* got problems. Real problems. Even my father, arrogant lying infidel son-of-a-bitch that he is, pales by comparison."

"Whoa, slow down a bit, will you? I thought your father just had a stroke. That's a problem."

"That's just good fortune. A happy coincidence," she said caustically. Linda was appalled. "He was found at the home of his mistress – of long-standing. Unknown to all of us, except Luce."

"God, Mead, I don't know what to say."

"Oh, hell, I don't want to talk about him. I really don't. It's Bila."

"Sounds like Africa's getting to you." Linda was sympathetic.

"Yes it is," she snapped, "How could it not?" Linda, hurt, looked at her. "Sorry. Don't mean to take it out on you." She drew an obscure design on the side of her frosty glass. "You know what? I can't believe I let the bastard off so easily."

"Your father?"

"No. Peter." She stared into her glass.

Linda paused, then said, "Me, either." She lifted her shoulders. "Who can explain it?"

"Jesus." Mead was disgusted anew. "Right before my eyes." She buried her head in her hands and pulled at her hair. "Do you know that my mother, a complete and utter stalwart for fifty years, confronted his mistress in less than twenty-four hours? Checked out of their lives in less than forty-eight?" She sighed, "I did nothing."

Linda leaned her head back against the tall rattan chair, closed her eyes and took a deep breath. "Your mother didn't see. Didn't have to watch. I think that makes a difference."

"Bila," she heard Mead say softly, "she was younger than me."

"I don't know, Mead." She opened her eyes to see Mead, an expectant child, staring at her. " I really don't. All I can say is, had the situation been reversed, had Roz been involved with Peter and the two of you bedded, I think we would have heard about it." She stopped to savor the image. "Instantly."

"Yeah, the scream heard round the world."

"But you're not Roz, and for this we give thanks."

"I don't really understand how anyone can behave like that."

"Peter has his coming. With any luck, karma will be on the scene in the near future."

"I don't mean Peter. I mean my father."

"Oh. Maybe I'll just listen for awhile."

"It makes it hard to know who you're really dealing with. One day you wake up and someone you've known for years, maybe all your life, is suddenly a completely different person. And not one you like. Poor woman."

"Your mother must be devastated."

Mead looked at Linda. "Yes, probably so. But I was talking about Bila."

"Got it."

"Even that night, on the mountain, watching Peter, I didn't feel helpless. Stunned, yes. Furious, eventually. But not helpless."

They were quiet for some time then Linda gently spoke, "You know, Mead, if you're going to stay here, you're going to lose lots of patients."

Mead nodded, then shut her eyes tight. "I know. Bila's just the first in an endless line. She's not even the first – just where I happened to come in. There's got to be something I can do. I hate not being able to do anything."

"Research is a pretty significant contribution."

"Yes, yes, I know. But to stand idly by . . . " She looked up.

"You're going to be fine, Mead. In fact better. An incredibly talented doctor – with a heart."

Mead gave a low snort. "I know I'll be fine. It's just the getting there that's the problem."

"See, you do have problems. Feel better now?"

"Much. Thanks a lot." She sipped her drink and set the glass down sadly. "I'm really sorry you're leaving, Linda. I'm going to miss you."

"Yeah, me too. Well," she said, raising her glass and tilting it in Mead's direction, "to Uhuru."

"To freedom." Mead's smile was bittersweet. "Safe journey home."

"Likewise, my friend."

The soft clink was barely audible beneath the African moon.

* * *

Riding up the elevator to the penthouse office in the trendy, renovated loft, Jacob asked, "So, first time out in weeks, hey? Did you feel okay leaving Walter with the nurse?"

"Sure, especially since I brought in Ruthie for backup." She gave Jacob a devilish grin.

"Oh, God, to be fly on the wall. Ruthie and Walter – now there's a combination."

Luce chuckled. "She brought several weeks' worth of *Weekly Suns* to read to him. Picked out all the stories relating to science and doctors. She's taken his continuing professional education as her personal mission."

"You sure he's going to be alive when you return?"

"He did roll his eyes rather frantically when she told him what she planned to read." Jacob laughed. "If he wasn't already not speaking to me, I'm sure he'd start now."

"There's no revenge on your part with this scheme, of course. No evening the score?"

"Jacob," Luce admonished mockingly, "how could you even suggest that? Not at all."

The elevator opened into an exquisitely decorated high tech lobby. Jacob went to the receptionist, and soon the Director of PR was standing before them.

"Hey, Jacob. Good morning." The PR Director was a tall, thirtyish man with a pony-tail and over-designed glasses. Great pains had been taken to assemble his casual, nonchalant style.

"Hello, Robert." Jacob was instantly in full convivial sales swing. "This is Luce Bennett." Luce quietly nodded a greeting.

"Gosh, great to meet you," Robert said sincerely. "Thanks for coming. We're really looking forward to having your paintings in our offices. Let's go straight to the president's office."

Robert led the way through a maze of cubicles, exposed brick walls and structural reinforcements, along blonde hardwood floors. "There's a real commitment to creating the right work environment. You know, one that's classy and artistic, that says something about who we are, what we're all about. Expression, creativity – that's what we're really about. That's what underlies coaxial modems. Just because we've been wildly successful, we know it's not all about money. And this comes from the very top." Robert was obviously impressed.

Luce turned surreptitiously to Jacob and mimicked vomiting. He poked her so hard she choked. "Sorry," she said quickly as Robert turned around, all concern. "Silly of me. I swallowed the wrong way."

He gave a sympathetic look then continued down the hall that led to a huge glassed-in office.

At the other end of the office, nestled in the corner where two walls of architectural glass met, was a long, sleek black desk. The high-backed black desk chair was turned away from them, and the cord from the phone disappeared into the chair. Everything was orderly and uncluttered. Robert quietly brought them into the office and indicated that they should sit on a black leather sofa.

"Well, sorry I can't stay. I've got work to do," he whispered. Nodding his head toward the turned chair, he said, "Terry shouldn't be too long. Just finishing up a call to our Tokyo office. I'll stop back in a little while, okay?"

"Hey, Robert, no problem. Thanks. We'll see you before we leave."

Luce nodded her head and smiled broadly and let her smile fall as soon as Robert was out of view. Rolling her eyes in disgust toward Jacob, she drummed her fingers on her clasped arms and sighed obviously.

Through a clenched smile, Jacob hissed, "Just cut it out, Luce. Get your attitude together."

The sound of the executive chair swiveling brought both Luce's and Jacob's attention to the desk. Luce, mouth slightly open, watched as Terry placed the phone in the receiver, stood and walked toward the sofa. She was, Luce thought, in her late thirties, tall, with thick black hair and a dark Mediterranean look. She wore a simple black tunic and slacks. In a glance she exuded style, poise and control.

"Thank you so much for coming to my office. I hope it wasn't too much of an imposition," she said, giving both of them warm, firm handshakes. From behind her shoulder as she faced Luce, Jacob raised a brow.

"No imposition at all," Jacob said calmly, "Luce always loves to meet the people who might buy her paintings and see where they'll hang." Terry looked at Luce as Jacob prompted, "Don't you, Luce?"

"Yes."

Terry smiled. Then, with a trained managerial directness and complete assuredness, said, "I appreciate your leaving your father, Luce, to come this morning. I hope he'll be better." Luce just stared. "Well, let's look at some slides then, shall we?"

Jacob set up his small light table on a conference table to the right of Terry's desk. They spent about twenty minutes going through the slides.

"I definitely want one of the highway series. I like this one the best." She pointed to a nighttime scene. Through the windshield of a car the gray concrete highway split in three directions and looped around the canvas. It was foggy, the Tulle fog found in the Sacramento Valley, and the string of lamps that lined the three curving roads created triangular pools of soft, filtered light descending from arched lamp poles. The red taillights looped along the road.

Luce remembered the precise moment of creation. Actually, she mused, inspiration would be more appropriate. She had been driving the highway one night, rounded a curve and saw the scene. Pulling onto the shoulder that night she quickly sketched it. It was a complete composition; all she had to do was paint it in shades of gray and black with accents of amber and red, one of those rare gifts out of nowhere when she suddenly saw something and it was complete just as it was. Chance, good fortune, divine inspiration. It didn't happen often, but when it did it was thrilling.

Terry continued, "I think that would be perfect for the lobby, don't you?" she asked Luce. Luce mutely nodded. "You live in California now, don't you?" Luce nodded again. Terry's gaze didn't waver despite Luce's silence. "We have an office there in Redwood Shores."

Luce felt uncomfortable and muttered, "I actually don't know the area too well."

Terry laughed softly. "I wouldn't have expected you to be exploring that neck of the woods. Somehow, chips, software, ISDN lines, coaxial modems don't strike me as being your pastime." Turning to Jacob, she said, "Did you bring any canvases?"

"Yes. Got a few here," he said unzipping a large black leather portfolio. Luce moved the light table to a chair and watched as Jacob put a canvas on the table.

"This is one of the few remaining works in a series Luce has been painting for two years," Jacob explained, looking tenderly at Luce as he spoke. "As you, know, it's been well received."

It was *Searching for Grace/Brooklyn Bridge*, the painting Luce had done on her last visit to New York. Looking at it now, Luce felt a sudden pang, remembering all the times she and Grace had walked the bridge, stood mid-bridge and stared out to sea, the times they had met Ruthie on summer evenings and sat with her while she regaled them both with the latest family feud or tidbits from the *Weekly Sun*.

A short buzz intruded, followed by a voice over the speaker phone. "Mr. Malowitz, Tina from your gallery is on line five."

Jacob, slightly perturbed and apologetic, walked to the desk and took the call.

Terry looked directly at Luce who was lost in the canvas spread on the table. "It's an incredible painting. Very moving." Luce looked at her, provoked by the consoling tone of her voice. "I've always thought that Grace is a beautiful name," Terry continued, "as well as wonderful word." Flustered, Luce said nothing. "You must miss her terribly," she said. Luce felt her cheeks burn with a sudden crimson of exposure and fixed her eyes on Jacob, praying for his quick return to the table.

"Sorry about that," he gave Luce a knowing look. Seeing her expression, he asked, "You okay?"

"Fine." Luce was curt, emphatic.

"Where were we, then?" Jacob lost his stride.

"*Searching for Grace/Brooklyn Bridge*," Terry replied, "I'd like to buy it. Not for the office, though."

"I'm afraid this one is not for sale," Luce blurted. She picked it up and put it back in the portfolio behind the others. "Sorry, Jacob," she kept her eyes on his, which were caught in a zone between surprise and annoyance "Looking at it now, I see it's really not ready."

Perplexed, Jacob gave her a questioning look, then, seeing her decision while surprising was firm, turned to Terry. "Sorry for the misunderstanding."

"No problem," she said, her level voice and gaze directed at Luce. "Perhaps when it's done. There's no rush."

Later, as the elevator door closed Jacob asked, "What was that all about?"

"I'm sorry, Jacob. Really."

"Don't be sorry. She bought two paintings. I'd consider that a successful hour's work. But why didn't you want to sell her *Brooklyn Bridge*? I know and you know it's finished."

"I'm not sure. It just hit me. A feeling came over me. I just didn't want to sell it."

"I got the distinct feeling," Jacob drawled, "that she likes you." Luce, baffled, looked at him. "You know, *likes* you."

"Jacob, please."

"Luce, I'm serious. You know, you have no natural talent for sensing these things." Luce gave him a weary look. "Seriously, I mean it's kind of sad when my "gaydar" works better than yours. Isn't there a way to fix that?"

"Yeah, I've been meaning to take it into the shop. Keeps dropping to the bottom of my 'to do' list."

The elevator doors opened and they walked through the lobby to the sidewalk. Distracted, Luce said, "I think I'd better pass on lunch. I should really go home and check on Walter."

"Oh, no you don't, Luce. No way." He took her arm firmly. "It's true, you know, that I have a better gaydar than you. Except for Grace, if you'll recall, I've introduced you to a number of women who have crossed my screen."

"I'm glad you remember so well, Jacob, because, except for Grace, they were all losers, bores or maniacs."

"C'mon, Luce, I think I have a better record than that. What about that Swedish woman?"

"Ilsa?" Luce shook her head with disbelief. "Total maniac. Her refrigerator contained wine, beer, Coke, Kraft individually wrapped cheese slices – you know the orange cheese squares that are completely carcinogenic – with a bottle of vodka in the freezer."

189

"So, you didn't like her?" Luce shook her head again. "Hmm, I don't think I ever knew that. Well, how 'bout Marilyn? She was nice."

"Talk-me-to-death Marilyn? Never-leave-me-alone Marilyn? We've-known-each-other-for-two-days- can-we-be-fused-at-the-hips Marilyn?"

"Perhaps a little too friendly?"

"Merger maniac is more like it."

"I thought there were one or two that were okay."

"No. There were none. Zero. Nada. No offense, Jacob, but I don't see a dating service as your forte. Don't give up the gallery yet."

"Well, at least I knew they were all gay," he said smugly. "And I'm telling you, Luce, Terry is interested in more than your paintings." He smiled down at her with great satisfaction.

"Oh, honestly. Are we done with this topic? Let's get a cab and have some lunch, okay?"

"Absolutely."

He walked toward the curb to hail a cab. His smirk turned to frustration as two empty cabs flew by. Luce stepped in front of him.

"Please, if we actually want to get a cab this lifetime, let me."

"She's attractive, don't you think?" he asked, nonplussed.

A cab screeched to a halt. Luce opened the back door. "Jacob," she said threateningly, "one more peep and you're walking."

He walked toward the cab, bent to kiss her cheek while smiling widely and slipped into the backseat. "And no smirking either, okay?"

* * *

Mead stared bleary-eyed at the Nairobi street scene. They were returning from a short field trip to a rural health clinic several hours outside of Nairobi. It was a small and squalid cinder block hut, still pockmarked with bullet holes from some past war. The medical assistant who was on duty had shown them around the facility. In the patient ward every bed was taken. Beds had been disassembled. Bare, soiled mattresses lay on the dirty floor. In the bed frames, on top of the metal springs, patients reclined vacantly, sometimes two to a bed. The assistant was especially proud to show them their "pathology lab" – an empty room with an outdated microscope. In the hallway a child who looked about one, but was actually three, was bloated with malnutrition. Her mother, thin as a rail and in the last stages of AIDS, grabbed Mead's hand. "I am unacceptable. I am scared. Help me." A shroud of listless conversations and groaning enveloped the small building. Mead felt as though she had been swallowed by a whale and was headed to the bottom of the sea. Jane had been very kind and encouraging to the assistant and all the patients, but it had depressed Mead sorely.

On the way back to Nairobi they had made a brief visit to Sofia Town, Jane wanting to drop off a meager bag of food. They had visited Bila's hut, already occupied by a new family, new refugees to the city. The husband, a young man in his late-twenties, was HIV-positive. The wife, miraculously, was not. They were able to leave some condoms.

Jane sat silently at the wheel of the small car. Despite the hot day, all windows were rolled shut to ward off any car-jackers. She touched Mead with a finger on her arm then pointed to the sidewalk.

"That is one of the shops where they sell Pearl Omega." Mead's head swiveled as she quickly saw a crowd spilling out the door of a second story shop, down the stairs and stretching most of the block.

"Pull over," she ordered

"Why?"

"Just pull over," Mead shouted. Jane, taken aback, acquiesced. Mead jumped out of the car and ran back toward the shop. Jane, worried by the impetuous behavior and flash of anger Mead displayed, locked the car and ran after her.

Mead had been hearing for weeks now about the magical herbal potion that was supposed to cure AIDS. She had heard that every day dozens, sometimes hundreds, of people waited in line to buy a bottle of the brew. The milky brown concoction was supposed to contain the necessary ingredients to inhibit an enzyme, protease, which the virus needs to reproduce. It was rumored that very high government officials, perhaps the highest, supported the liquid cure, despite its efficacy and safety never having been tested or established. Word among many of the health professionals was that the government had taken over the sales of Pearl Omega and the money, vast sums, was being funneled back to key individuals. The government repeatedly issued "no comment" when queried.

Mead stopped dead in her tracks when she reached the line of people. A handful looked at her with bewilderment. Most simply ignored her, focusing on their own disease and imminent demise, overflowing with a deep lassitude. In varying stages of decimation, they stood quietly, patiently in line. A dirty, trampled price list was on the sidewalk. Mead stooped to pick it up.

The cost for the recommended 30-day program ranged between $545 and $5,000, depending upon whether the buyer was a Kenyan or a foreigner. The directions required that the person drink 250 milliliters a day for thirty days in order to stop the AIDS virus from replicating itself. The arrival of the syrup had begun to wreak havoc. Many people, especially the poor and

191

uneducated, sold all of their belongings for the treatment. Others abandoned their safe-sex practices on the mistaken belief that a cure had been found.

Jane, catching up with Mead, pulled at her sleeve and breathlessly asked, "What are you intending to do here?" Her tone was high.

"Jane," Mead was emphatic, "we can't let this go on. Look at all these poor people – they've cashed in everything. For what? Lies. Complete, spurious lies."

Mead dashed up the stairs and Jane yelled, "Mead, stop. You must stop." Mead looked over her shoulder as she brushed by the people waiting.

Jane caught her at the door to the reception room and demanded, "What exactly are you planning to do here?"

"Tell them to go home. Tell them to not waste their money. That it's snake oil. Try to shut the quack down."

"Mead." Jane shook her head and pulled her down the stairs. "No, Mead I will not allow you."

"But . . . "

"But what?" Jane was firm, offended. "You have nothing to offer instead. You have no right to take away their hope." Mead gave her a look of total incomprehension. "Mead, how can you know so little about the will to live? Every day we Africans walk closer to death than most. But accepting death does not mean one does not want to live. These people, each and every one of them, want only to live another day, to see another sunrise – not set. Do not take away what you cannot replace." She looked into Mead's baffled, shattered face. Quietly she said, "Come, please. Come away from here." Mead was stuck to the sidewalk. Jane reached down, grabbed both of Mead's hands and turned them face up. "You are empty-handed, Dr. Bennett. You have no business here. Come."

* * *

The two dark clouds symmetrically dotted a perfect pearl moon. The slanting sky was light blue, luminescent at the horizon. The small wooden boat, sail torn and barely clinging to the mast, had fused with the ocean's turbulent surface. The waves, while still fierce, had subsided and the two figures in the boat, a speck upon the vast face of the sea, could pause, take a breath, and fortify themselves against the next inevitable storm. The moon threw down a beam of light that floated in a thick, painterly patch upon the dark, dark water.

"Ryder," Luce bent and spoke into her father's ear, "loved seascapes. They were powerful metaphors for him. He was a recluse in his later life, a bit eccentric. He loved poetry and painting these brooding scenes." She watched Walter absorb *Moonlight,* painted by Ryder in 1887. They were in the back section of the Met. Behind them, through huge plate glass windows, was the park. Melting snow retreated as spring approached. The ground softened. Outside the air smelled of mud and hope. She had wheeled him through her favorite sections of the Met, Vermeer excepted, and now they stood before a small collection of Ryders.

Never a big fan of his, since Grace's death she had come to love his brooding, romantic seascapes. They moved her, encapsulated the terrible loneliness she felt. Alive, tossed about by the unrestrained, uncontrollable forces of nature, alone on the open, dark, cold sea. She saw Walter's lips quiver and stooped so her ear was close to his mouth, the only way she could possibly understand his garbled, slurred speech.

"Wonley," he said, after considerable struggle.

She looked at him directly. "Yes, they are lonely. Some speculate that he grieved a lost or unrequited love. We don't know for sure." Walter blinked his eyes to demonstrate his agreement. "He was a colorist. Experimented with color, textures. Used varnishes heavily. And organic materials, like wax or dirt or tobacco juice from a spittoon. It made his canvasses organic as well. They changed over time.

"Some deteriorated to dark, cracked surfaces beyond repair or restoration. More than a few original buyers were a little put off. But I don't think it's such a bad thing," Luce mused, lost now in the canvas before her, "It makes the work truly living. And the price of that admission is deterioration and death." She suddenly surfaced, hearing her thoughts voiced in such an unfiltered way. Walter, his wheelchair positioned at a right angle to the canvas, strained his eyes to his right to see her. "He painted this, by the way, on a headboard." She wheeled her father over to the next work, *With Sloping Mast and Dipping Prow.*

"He liked dramatic contrasts. His use of light and dark creates incredible mystery. An ominous, sometimes hopeless sense." In the scene before them, two figures sat in the bow of a small boat on a moonlit sea. The moon was lower, the sky white with opacity. The mast, a dark looming triangle in the dimming sky was more intact than in the preceding work.

Luce walked closer and read the small paragraph posted next to the painting, laughed slightly, then turned to face Walter. "Lest we think that these two characters are doing better than the others, you should know they're rudderless."

Walter looked at the painting, then at Luce. "Ou. Me."

Luce studied the painting then glanced back at Walter. "You and me?"

she repeated, incredulous at first, then nodded her head. "I guess so." She wasn't sure if her father's observation made her feel better or worse. You and me, she thought. Now there's a bit of irony.

* * *

The sea, so constant, Elizabeth thought as she approached the cottage door. The faithful rhythm so reliable and soothing. She entered the kitchen and watched the sun rise as the microwave heating her cup of coffee hummed in the background.

Her computer was set up, still, at the kitchen table. She found she spent most of her time, and had during the previous two months, in the kitchen or the bedroom. Her bedroom, she thought, correcting herself. She had taken one of the spare bedrooms. Despite her efforts to desanitize the master suite of any trace of Walter, she was unable to sleep there and now just kept the door shut.

Blowing on her coffee she waited as the computer booted up. Clicking on the main screen of America Online, entering her password, she noticed the kitchen fill with sun. She clutched her mug as though grabbing the sun's warmth.

Once at the main screen, her computer remained silent. She had no mail. Sitting for some time she wondered from whom she'd like to be receiving e-mail. Halfway through her coffee, she opened Compose Mail and keyed in:

To: MBennett
Fr: EBennett
Re:

Her thoughts ground to a halt. Re: what? She hadn't heard much from her youngest daughter since Walter's stroke. Luce had called to inform Elizabeth that Mead had accepted a six-month extension on her fellowship. Somehow, the news did not surprise Elizabeth. Mead had sent her mother a few polite, innocuous e-mail messages. Elizabeth knew that she was terribly upset, the myth of her Walter having been so debunked. Despite the professional tone Mead had assumed over the past few years, despite the chilly aloofness she often displayed, Elizabeth sensed that Mead somehow had remained both the baby and daddy's girl.

Re: What? Elizabeth pondered. Suddenly she found herself keying in:

Re: Apology.

What? she wondered. From where on earth did that come? Of course Elizabeth

194

was sorry, sorry for all her children that Walter, always so difficult, was now a source of disappointment. And embarrassment. But, do I feel responsible? No, she didn't hesitate. Clearly no.

What then? She sipped her coffee. Suddenly she was in her study at the co-op, sitting at her desk, on the phone with Mead. When was it? Three years ago? Four? Exasperated with her cloudy memory, Elizabeth recalled listening to Mead's strained and troubled voice over the phone.

"So it's off. The whole thing. I'm sorry, Mother but you're going to have to cancel . . . "

"But . . . ," Elizabeth had tried to interrupt. Mead was a nonstop train barreling through town.

"The hall, the guests, the registry, the band. Oh, and the caterers, too. Well, everything and everyone, I guess. I know it's an imposition. And awkward."

"But . . . ," Elizabeth tried again.

"Look, I'm terribly busy finishing up here. I called Chicago and they're only too happy to have me come early. So I've got a lot to do to get ready."

"But, Mead," Elizabeth insisted, "are you sure?"

"Am I sure of what?" Mead had angrily fired back. "Sure of what?"

"Sure that . . . I don't know," Elizabeth had started to crumble slightly, "Sure that this is what you want to do? He's so wonderful in so many ways." Her voice trailed off and, in the solitude of her study, she flushed with remorse.

"Just what are you suggesting?" Mead had fiercely demanded and Elizabeth envisaged her daughter's outraged and insulted countenance.

"Well, nothing. I wasn't suggesting anything," she had mumbled lamely. "Just wondering out loud, I guess."

Elizabeth shook herself. Oh dear, she thought, feeling the pain of remorse on an entirely new level. Oh dear. How awful for Mead.

To: MBennett
Fr: EBennett
Re: Apology
Mead, I really don't know how to say this but I know I need to say it. I am sorry, so sorry, I didn't understand what you were going through with Peter. Recalling that time for you, and how I acted, well, I just cringe. Please accept my apology.
Mother

Elizabeth didn't even reread her message to check for spelling, spacing, grammar or punctuation. She quickly clicked Send Mail and turned off her computer.

Mead, later that night in Nairobi, read her mother's message. She stared into the computer, remembering that chapter in her life, remembering specifically the phone call she had made to her mother and how her hand had clenched the receiver until her fingers were white and how she had pulled the wire taut to the breaking point as she stood in a dim, hermetic hospital phone booth. She remembered how she had strained to control her voice, how she had pushed to bury a swelling in her chest, how she had just wanted to get out of town.

Her mother had never mentioned the "situation" again. Upon her arrival in Chicago Mead had received a handwritten note from her mother on monogrammed stationary. "Everything has been taken care of," was all it said.

Now she reread her mother's e-mail, then calmly clicked Delete. The message was saved elsewhere.

* * *

Luce waited until the day nurse had finished feeding and dressing Walter.

"Mary," she said from the living room doorway, "why don't you take the rest of the day off?"

"Really? That would be grand. Are you sure you'll be okay?"

"Just fine. Besides, Olga will be here at 4."

"Why thank you." Mary, exuding delight, patted Walter's knee. "Be a good boy, Dr. Bennett. And I'll see you tomorrow morning." Luce watched Walter wince as Mary left the room and closed the door. A quizzical expression gathered in the corner of his eyes, and he strained to see Luce standing some distance from him.

"Bad news, Walter. Mother's coming for a visit." He shut his eyes immediately and through the grotesque aperture of his contorted mouth moaned. "She wants to pick up some clothes. She also wants to speak with you." Walter looked up, panicked. "Yeah, I'd be scared, too. Can't blame her though. She wants her day in court."

Luce crossed the hall and went to her room, her mother's study, leaving Walter to ruminate without distractions. She flipped through several magazines, paced quietly, and stared out the window. She was relieved when the doorbell rang and she heard her mother letting herself in. Luce met her in the foyer and they stood together for several wordless moments before Elizabeth asked,

"How is he?"

"Not bad, I guess, all things considered. I have a nurse come in the morning and feed him and get him ready. Then one in the evening. A physical therapist has started coming twice a week and . . . "

"Excuse me, Luce," Elizabeth cut her off, "I just want the prognosis, not the regimen." Affronted, Luce curled her shoulders and hugged her chest. "Sorry, Luce. I don't mean to take it out on you."

Luce nodded and proceeded cautiously. "He will regain more speech capability. Still limited. His right hand shows strength. Possibly, who knows when, if he works really hard, he might be able to walk around the co-op with a walker. He's a prime candidate for another stroke." Elizabeth's face revealed her impatience. "He is going to live."

Luce tried to interpret Elizabeth's impassive reaction. Glee? To have him so disabled, to be so imprisoned? Disappointment? That life continued to flow in his veins? Sorrow? Anger? Whatever Elizabeth felt lay buried deep below her marble exterior, strong and as cold as stone.

"Thank you, Luce." Her voice was different. "Is he in the living room?"

"Yes." Luce watched her mother walk down the hall. She then slipped quietly into the kitchen, closing the door but standing next to it with her ear pressed against it.

Elizabeth found Walter in his wheelchair, facing the living room entrance, waiting. She still wasn't used to looking down at him, and quickly adjusted her eye level upon sighting him. She leisurely took the time to examine him, his vast inertia, his complete immobility. His head hung forward a little, his shoulders, once a solid lintel, bent, sagging beneath the weight of his stroke. So much of his height had been in his long legs. Now he sat on that sense of tallness. He seemed a straight line, broken in three spots: head to tail, tail to knees, knees to feet. His color had returned and his cheeks were flush. Was it her presence, she wondered, or the nearby radiator? She noticed his large hands dangling over the arm rest of the wheelchair, the left hand entirely still while the fingers on the right hand trembled slightly. She had saved the details of his face for last and now zeroed in. The chin hung, extending his already long face but adding a hint of misshapen form. His cheeks were hollow and the eyes sunken. Only a very dim light burned behind them. The clarity, the presence they once held had diminished, and he seemed removed several times from himself. His mouth, a portal to dictates, diatribes, commands and wishes, had been crushed. Altogether he looked as if he had been taken apart and reassembled by a rank amateur.

She continued to stand silently, hoping her powers of observation made

197

him uncomfortable. She didn't bank on that, knowing that she didn't know this person who sat before her, perhaps never had. His mouth twitched and labored to find form, to obey some cerebral command but was defeated by a body that had mutinied and was now held by rebel forces. Looking at him, she thought nature has done for me what I would have wanted to do myself. She did not feel overly bitter, just justified.

"I won't be sitting down," she said at last, "I don't have that much to say." And you are unworthy of too many of my words, she added to herself. "You have behaved badly." Her mouth was the barrel of a rifle. Walter was hopelessly trapped in the cross hairs. Her aim was dead accurate, her hand dead steady. "You have made a complete sham of our marriage. You have broken our vows." She paused. "You have broken my heart.

"Of all the selfish things you have done over the course of your long, self-indulgent life, Walter Bennett, this is categorically the worst. I can't – I won't – forgive you."

She walked to the window and looked out. The street below was buzzing with mid-morning activities, the comings and goings of a million people who constantly crossed her path but never intersected. From this vantage point she had held her post for years, had kept track of the family, the finances, the needs, large and small, of all of them but especially Walter. For what? she wondered. Not this. She had never, ever expected this. Feeling his eyes upon her, almost hearing his imprisoned words bang on the bars of his locked cell, she turned to face him. Standing erect, she felt a sudden surge of power from within. With every particle of her being she commanded him to watch her, to pay fullest attention to her, to feel the depth of her anger and the weight of her judgment.

Condemned, she shouted with every molecule in her body while her lips remained lightly shut, condemned forever, Walter Bennett. She was righteous, she was vindicated. She knew the universe agreed and that nature had executed the sentence.

"If we have been wrong, Walter, and if there is a hell, beyond this one, it gives me endless delight to know you will burn there." She watched him. His circuitry went dead. He folded in upon himself. Perhaps, at last, she thought with irony, I have reached you. She slowly left the room.

Luce listened to her walk down the hall into their bedroom and rummage through closets and drawers. Luce sat at the kitchen table and waited. Her mother's footsteps approached the kitchen, paused and then continued. Soon the front door opened and closed. Luce took a deep breath, then crossed into the living room. Walter's head drooped on the stem of his weak neck, a heavy dying sunflower at the end of its season. Hearing Luce's steps, he looked up. She wanted to say, "You deserved that," but held her words and walked away, leaving Walter in the enormous silence and oppressive loneliness of the living room.

* * *

"Jacob, how dare you?" Luce sounded furious. Jacob took the phone from the crook of his neck and transferred it to his other ear.

"What are you talking about, Luce?" He was genuinely mystified. He listened to an irate Luce as he looked across his desk at Jenny, who sat patiently waiting for him to finish his day so they could have dinner.

"Don't pretend you don't know what I'm talking about. You had no right. This time you've really crossed the line."

Jacob was genuinely confused. "Luce, honest to God, I have no idea what you're talking about. I'm in the dark."

"You gave her my phone number, didn't you?"

Jacob, completely bollixed, looked across at Jenny to share his bafflement. "Who? Who are we talking about?"

"Terry," Luce fired across the line.

"Terry?" Jacob dropped his chin heavily into the palm of his hand and shook his head at Jenny. "What," he asked emphatically, "are you talking about?" Jenny shifted her position and leaned back.

"You gave Terry my number here."

Jacob pulled the phone away and stared at it in disbelief. "Luce," he said indignantly, "I did no such thing."

"Well, she just called. How did she get my number? My parents are unlisted."

"Damn it, Luce. I would never do such a thing. And I can't believe you're accusing me. That's insulting."

Luce fell silent for a moment. "Well," she continued in humbler, subdued tones, "how did she get my number? Somebody had to give it to her."

Jacob took a deep breath. "I don't know how she got your number." He continued to look at Jenny who suddenly seemed entranced with her hands in her lap; she crossed her legs and shifted nervously while her right foot kicked the air. He tilted his head and gave her a "What gives? Come clean" look. She looked up at him, canary feathers of guilt protruding from her terse smile, as she widened her eyes to feign innocence.

"Well, did you talk with her?" He gave Jenny a stern look of disapproval. "What did she want?"

"Of course I talked with her. I answered the phone."

"And?"

"She wants to go out."

"I knew it!" He gloated gleefully. "I knew it!" Luce just gave a long despondent sigh into the phone. "Must you sound as if you've been run over by a truck? That's great. You need to get out."

"I'm not ready."

"Luce, you're ready. You're ready. Look, you don't have to marry her. Just go out. If nothing else, just to get a break from Walter." Silence. "So?" His single word was full of expectancy.

"So," she mocked, "so what?"

"Are you going to go out?"

"I don't know. I told her scheduling with Walter is pretty difficult."

"Luce," Jacob raised his eyes to the ceiling in frustration. "Luce, that's so pathetic."

"Jacob," Luce began defensively, "I haven't been on a date in almost a decade. Thanks for the support."

"It's just like riding a bike. You never forget how."

"It's more like falling off a bike."

"Well, you never forget that either."

Jenny, sensing the drift of the conversation, started frantically to mime something to Jacob. She pointed to him, to herself, made a big circle, waved her hands. Jacob shrugged his shoulder in ignorance. Jenny slowly mouthed, "Double." Jacob shook his head. Frustrated, she reached for a pen on his desk and scrawled "Double date."

"Hey, Luce, how about if the four of us have dinner – you, Terry, Jenny and me?" Jenny sat back in her chair in relief.

"Now *that* would be pathetic, Jacob. No way."

"Just trying to help." He was burned by her sarcasm.

"I know. Thanks. Sorry," she took a deep breath, "I'll take care of it. I just don't understand how she got the phone number."

"Me neither. I'll ask around, but you know we never," he gave Jenny a dirty look and repeated, "*never* give out personal numbers. Completely against policy. Even though I might have been tempted myself, well, never."

"Yeah, I know that, Jacob. Sorry if I offended you."

"Hey, Luce, just go out with her. Chalk it up to practice. Kick up your heels." She offered a disbelieving sigh. "You might actually have a good time."

"Good night, Jacob."

Jacob slowly hung up the phone. He clasped his hands together and rested them on top of his desk. Looking directly at Jenny, he asked, "Is there something you'd like to tell me?" Behind a smile she tried unsuccessfully to bury she shook her head no.

"Are you sure?" He gave her a long, hard stare.

"Positively sure. Absolutely sure. Aren't you hungry? Can we go for dinner now?" she asked, standing up, smoothing her suit, putting the strap of her brief case on her shoulder. "I'm starving."

"Jenny?" he arced his voice as she sauntered toward the door.

"Sorry, Jacob, anything I say would be a breach of attorney-client privilege. Totally inappropriate. Put me in a terribly uncomfortable position. Coming?" she called over her shoulder.

"Well, Snow White, far be it from me to jeopardize your professional ethics – untarnished as they are. No, no, I'd never want to put you in a compromising position. And you know, the more I think about the advice you gave on the night of Luce's show – you remember, to give her some space, let her alone – the more I'm convinced you're really onto something."

"Coming?"

He stood at his desk for a moment shaking his head, then turned off the lamp and followed her laugh out the door.

* * *

A canopy of incipient stars stretched overhead. Twilight sifted down through the leafy branches of the sprawling acacia tree. Mead turned over on her belly to gaze down. The wooden planks were still warm with the sun's incessant pounding. It felt good against her bare legs and arms, through her shorts and top. She inched her way to the very edge of the treetop platform and watched the animal world below. Elephants waded knee-deep in water, drinking and hosing themselves down for the night. Elands and a few stray zebras sipped from the shores, while long-legged waders cooled their heels and then flew off.

Gil, lying next to her, said, "My mother insisted that my father build this reservoir when they first moved here. The elephants were ruining her gardens. The property had been abandoned for some time when they bought it and the animals had eaten everything to a nub. You can imagine how delighted they were to have a dedicated gardener take up residence. The bulbs she had shipped from Europe were devoured in a single sitting." He smiled recollecting the past. "Her hibiscus were there one evening and gone by morning. They seemed to love all of her flowers. And her vegetables. My sister Sonia says they would lie awake at night hearing the animals forage, undoing my Mother's hard day's work. The worst evening was when she had had the driveway planted with a pepper tree border. There was quite a feast that night.

"But the pool was the crowning blow. She had it built primarily for the children. The first night it was full of water, all the creatures stepped up to the bar. Quite a party. My mother, who had been trying to co-exist peacefully, decided it was time for serious measures. That's when the electric fence went in around the lawned area and my father built this dam.

"When I was ten I got some of the men to help me build this observation platform. I love watching the animals."

Mead looked at him, then below. "Somehow the word *animal* doesn't seem quite right." Gil twisted his head in her direction. "When I think of growing up with animals I think of hamsters and goldfish, cats and dogs. My brother Rand had a collection of reptiles, nothing larger than a king snake. That's what I think of. Or those poor, dejected animals in the Central Park Zoo. But these," she said looking at the massive back of an elephant who plodded below, seeing the mud-crusted cracks of skin, smelling its raw essence, hearing its steady, deep breathing, "these are too magnificent, too alive to be called *animals*."

Mead was unprepared for the thrill, surprised by the sense of reverence which filled her. She and Gil lay quietly on their stomachs watching until the creatures became silver point shadows outlined by a rising moon.

Mead had been entranced since her arrival. Taking a tour of the property with Francesca, which included driving in the Land Rover to a neighboring Pokot bombas, and hiking for long stretches to get the best view of the Rift Valley, she was impressed by Francesca's deep connection to the land.

"When I moved here, Mead," Francesca said in her hypnotic, Italian accent, as she propped her leg on a boulder and gazed into the rift that began in Russia and stretched far to the south of Kenya, "I was ignorant." She shook her head remembering a younger woman. "I had no idea of my role. I had always dreamed of coming to Africa, of living here. From afar, with very little real understanding, I was intrigued. You could even say called. I read about adventurers. With jealousy. I studied every *National Geographic* I could. Pasted my walls with photos I cut from those pages. But I didn't know," she said dreamily as she looked deep into the landscape, "not until I had lived here for many years, that my role was to preserve and protect this land, these animals. I have been fortunate."

She paused and Mead tried to imagine how a woman whose husband had been mauled to death by those animals, whose entire young life had been thrown into chaos in a foreign and distant land, could honestly feel that she had been fortunate.

"And being fortunate carries a responsibility." Francesca paused. "We must help those who are not as fortunate as we." She looked at Mead. "But I don't have to tell you this." She offered Mead a warm smile which Mead weakly acknowledged, feeling immensely uncomfortable. "Shall we continue?"

They had driven next to the Pokot village, which technically resided on the preserve's land. It was largely because of the Pokots that Francesca had invited Mead to visit after her return from New York. The Pokot tribe had two main branches. One was dedicated to cattle and cattle grazing. The other comprised farmers who led a more traditional, agrarian and stationary life. As Francesca's consciousness grew, and as she came to know her neighbors, she realized, that as in so many other tribes, the young were flocking to the cities. For the old people, the old ways remained, slowly dying off. Meeting the medicine woman, she recognized the wealth of information that was vested in her. So many of the tropical diseases had cures and treatments that lay in the ground, the bark, the leaves. Francesca had started to record these treatments and thought Mead might be interested.

For her part Mead was anxious to understand the shamanistic role, hoping it might help her. She still wanted to shut down the distribution of Pearl Omega. The evening at Birati's when Francesca had extended the invitation, Mead thought that perhaps she might learn something that would help her efforts, provide direction. But in truth, she would have visited without the draw of shamanistic tropical medicine. She was taken by this mother-son combo: Francesca with her exuberant charisma; Gil with his quiet kindness. She liked them both enormously.

Looking down on the scene below, surrounded by the enormous quietude of night along the rift, Mead realized that this was the first time in months when she felt even a touch of perspective, of peace. Since her arrival in Nairobi, she had been trapped in a whirlpool of events, caught by a huge wave that had her spinning down into the dark sea, scraping along the rough bottom of churned-up sand and shells. Now, on this platform, no more than fifteen feet above the ground, she felt a lifting of her spirit and an inchoate calm returning. Rolling onto her back and propping her hands behind her head, she gazed into the endless African sky. She felt Gil's hand gently rest on her arm, saw the shadow of his head move closer to her own.

"Would you mind?" he whispered, inches from her lips. She shook her head, placed her fingers against his cheeks, and pulled him near. For a moment, the vast darkness was not an enemy. For a moment, the darkness was a comfort.

* * *

"What do you think you're going to do?" The cold ocean across Luce's bare feet was bracing and her teeth chattered.

"Well, for starters," her mother replied, "I'm going to live my life for me." They were walking along the shore by their beach cottage. It was a clear, late May day. The sun was strong and a few brave souls ventured into the still icy surf.

"Are you going to divorce him?" Luce was tentative. She was intrigued by her mother, who had rapidly transformed herself into a new woman, yet unsure of how to conduct herself with her.

"Don't you think I should? Wouldn't you?"

"Probably," Luce answered. The prospect of infidelity was never something she had to deal with.

"I'm having a lawyer advise me on the financial implications. That's the only thing I want to be careful about. You know, I could never forgive him. Frankly, I don't think I want to forgive him. If it had been a brief fling – a mid-life crisis or convention type of thing – that might have been different. But fifteen years? No," she said firmly. "Absolutely not."

They walked in silence for a while. Luce finally found the question she wanted to ask, then waited an additional moment to summon the courage. "How is it that you have done this so easily?"

Elizabeth turned fiercely, then softened when she saw her daughter's tone was not pejorative. They walked for quite a while before Elizabeth stopped and looked directly at Luce.

"You think I have done this easily, do you?" Luce nodded her head, and Elizabeth held her daughter's gaze for a few uncomfortable moments before she looked beyond her into the sea. "It's not been easy, Luce. Not at all. I've lost a great chunk of my life," she suddenly seemed captivated by the sea. "When I realized there was nothing there, when I realized there hadn't been anything there for a long time, if ever, there was nothing to hold onto. It was simple, but it was not easy." Luce was mystified. "I don't intend to lose any more of my life, Luce. None." They resumed their walking. "Did I tell you I was going to Arizona?" A breeze carried Elizabeth's voice.

"No. Why?"

"Well, I've met some fascinating people lately. Women, really. Older women who've lost their husbands to death or divorce."

"On the Internet?" Luce was dubious.

"It's an amazing place, Luce. You really should give it a try. Stop being a techno-phobe. And don't look so disapproving. Anyway, we started out as a newsgroup. But that gets frustrating – not being able to talk in real time. And you're so vulnerable to these silly spam attacks." Luce lifted her head in

204

question but decided she didn't really want to know. "So we became a chat group. But that also has its difficulties. All these idiots, punks and teenagers interrupting, flaming you. It disrupts intelligent conversation." Luce looked out to sea. "Anyway, there are about ten of us and we've decided to go to one of those resorts in Arizona – golf, tennis, gorgeous pools – so we can really talk."

"Sounds like fun," Luce said, finding the prospect of a misery congregation completely abhorrent.

"I've always been a loner, Luce. I figure seventy's a good time to change that. You might try it, too. Save yourself a quarter of a century."

Luce chuckled, amused to be getting advice from her mother at this stage of the game.

"How's your painting?"

"I'm just getting back to it. Finished moving into my old studio last weekend. You should come visit."

"I will. After I get back from Arizona. You can paint me. Now that'd be different – painting me while I know about it. And approve. Might ruin your creative process."

"Not likely." Luce was confident.

Elizabeth smiled. "Say, I like that Terry."

"What you like is your new coaxial modem setup." Luce was amused.

"True. As they say, I have a need for speed. But it's also true that I like Terry. She seems nice." Her statement was more of a question but Luce remained noncommittal. "Oh, okay, be mysterious. Next time you see her tell her I'm the envy of all my cyber friends."

"Will do."

Elizabeth looked at her daughter with concern. "I read a quote the other day, made me think of you."

"Oh?"

"Remind me before you leave to give it to you. I saved it. I knew I'd botch it if I tried to paraphrase it."

Luce stared blankly at her mother. "I just wish you wouldn't resist life so much, Luce. I don't want you ending up with a pile of regrets. That's all. " She looped her arm in Luce's and propelled her down the beach. "I'm glad you're home, now."

"Me, too."

On the train home Luce remembered her mother's face, amazed by its clarity, admiring of its strength. Elizabeth was no longer the fragile piece of china that Luce had seen the morning she left the co-op. She was, Luce had thought as they walked the open stretch of beach, and as she watched the long rays of the sinking sun brush her mother's face, more like a Giotto fresco. Beneath the faded colors, through the cracked tempera, Luce saw, with the same amazement, what Giotto's audience had seen at the beginning of the Renaissance – real humanity. After the Dark Ages, after highly stylized flat works, Giotto had brought an expressiveness and naturalism to his paintings. His figures were full, in volume and in humanity, tangible and infused with emotion, infused with life.

As the train bumped along Luce reread the quote her mother had given her, pulled off her desk calendar the day of her father's stroke:

Life, we learn too late, is in the living, the tissue of every day and hour.
Steven Leacock

She folded it carefully and slipped it into her pocket, holding it delicately between two fingers. All day she had fought the impulse to invite her mother home to meet Grace, struggling to remember the tense of her life.

* * *

The descending gorge filled with the distilled pinks and lavenders of early evening. The misty cavernous beauty, which now shimmered in pastel hues, belied the geological battle that was being waged deep below the surface. The Great Rift Valley stretched before Mead and Gil, as it had for millions of years, slowly ripping apart the continent. The conflict of the Somali plate tearing away from the African plate caught East Africa in a fierce struggle. The basin thinned and stretched, as one plate submerged violently beneath the other, creating the high elevations of western Kenya.

Sitting on a blanket, Mead hugged her knees. Her eyes followed the subterranean fault that traveled through the gorge and resulted in the spectacular scene that lay before her. The story of the Earth is one of change, she thought. The land is fractured, the society rifts as well.

This was her third visit to the Piavani Preserve. Francesca generously kept issuing invitations, and Mead had come to treasure the visits. The company, the long walks, the animals, the land all fed her, all restored and recharged her after intense eighty-hour workweeks in Nairobi. Now, at the end of a day's hike with Gil, her body tired and relaxed, the Rift cleansing her visual palette of the myriad scenes from the previous week, she breathed deeply the hot, dry air and listened to a breeze shake through the trees.

"I heard some news that may interest you," Gil's voice was a bird's wing stroking the air. She turned as he let a teasing silence follow. Shades of purple and russet settled in the tall grasses. Above them the sky seemed limitless. Below them the stones were still warm from the day's sunning.

"What's that?" Mead took the bait.

"Peter and Roz got married."

"Oh?"

"Yes. Apparently, some amazing blow-out bash at her parents'. Newport something or other. Rhode Island?"

"And the interesting part is . . . ?"

"Now, Mead, you can't pretend that you don't have a reaction to your former fiancé getting married."

"You're right. I do. I'd call it . . . relief." He plucked a stalk of grass and smiled. "You know, the near-miss type of relief? The car that almost hits you and doesn't? The fall down a long flight of steps you retrieve yourself from?" She imagined a lavish wedding on a sweeping lush green lawn, tables laden with expensive wedding presents, champagne flowing freely from an army of attentive waiters, Roz in a gorgeous, designer dress looking for Peter who was tucked away in the pool house with one of the bridesmaids.

She shivered and smiled, "That is interesting news." She looked deep into the gorge where the two tectonic plates collided and shifted. "I should let Linda know. She'd probably like to send the happy couple a gift – an engraved vial of Marburg or Ebola might be nice." Gil chuckled, and they settled back into the pervasive quietude that cloaked the land.

Along the Rift, at Oldavi Gorge to the south and Lake Turkana to the north, the Leakeys had unearthed the cradle of mankind. From cradle to grave, Mead thought bitterly, as she vainly tried to comprehend with her eyes what her heart held. "I have some news for you, too," she said at last.

"Oh?" he mirrored.

"I'm going back to the states." She watched his expression fall. "Birati and I have applied for a grant. Several actually. We need money. We need pharmaceutical donations. It's a waste of my time to be holding people's hands while they die. Especially when there are viral load detection tests and protease inhibitors out there."

She looked deep into the gorge and then continued, as though talking softly to herself. "These protease inhibitors - so goddamn expensive. And so hard to take. Some require an empty stomach, some a full stomach. All taken on different time schedules. Completely impractical. It's virtually a twenty-four hour regimen. Plus, we still don't know the best drug combinations. And stopping at anytime, which would be an understandable reaction to the extreme nausea many experience, can render any and all of the drugs completely useless. They'll be better in their next generation. But that's then. And this is now." She turned toward him. "I have do something, Gil. I can't just stand by. It's not in me. I'm good at the politics. And . . . " She looked off into the distance again in frustration. Gil sat up from his reclining position and leaned forward in question. "It's all political." She took a deep breath. "The truth is I can be of more help, real help, if I go back and try and sell our case. Use my reputation as leverage." She looked back at him briefly before further explaining, "We applied about a month ago. Beginner's luck, I guess, that one of the funding committees actually wants to meet with me so soon. I need to make a formal presentation. I'm going to try to land a few more appointments as long as I'm there."

Gil was silent for a long time, watching Mead's internal war.

"I don't want to go," she said out loud to herself.

"And do you think," Gil coaxed gently, "that there will be enough time for Jane if you get the protease inhibitors?"

Mead continued to look into the Rift. "Don't know for sure. Almost a third of the people tested are completely immune to any positive effect from them. It's a potent little cocktail. Not everyone can handle it. And, we still don't have any data that extends much beyond thirty-six months. Some recent tests suggest diabetes as a possible side effect." She winced, then sighed. "And the biggest fear is that the virus will develop a resistance to the drugs and mutate into an even more virulent strain." She clenched her jaw and swallowed hard. A hot tear escaped. "But I hope so. I hope there will be time for Jane."

He moved to her side and draped an arm lightly around her shoulder. "You'll be back, Mead," he assured her. "You'll be back."

The lavender gorge darkened several shades before being completely filled by purple night. Above, the sky sent down some starlight. Below, the earth rifted a little more.

* * *

The small grassy fingers shooting through the soft, thawing park gave the mid-morning city a tender freshness. The trees, gnarled ancient warriors, brushed the overhead blue canvas of sky with green blocks of leafy color. Cezanne, Luce thought, as she walked beside Walter, pushed by Ruthie. The air was clean, light, pleated with promise. Luce, half listening to the continual, comforting stream of Ruthie's conversation, took a deep and satisfying breath. Spring, she thought, my second this year.

They stopped by their usual bench, beneath a large tree whose dark brown branches reached far into the sky, beside the open meadow with a clear view of the rolling hillocks and the boat house. Ruthie sat down while Luce, bending over Walter, inspected him carefully, as she had before they left the co-op. He gave her a questioning look. His brow twitched slightly and, through a mouth of marbles, asked, "Whaa?" She pulled his shirt collar to a neat position, straightened the muffler beneath his spring jacket. She ran the tips of her fingers over the large crown of his head, smoothing the soft cap of white. Sitting down on the bench, she smiled and said, "You know, Walter, you look very handsome today. Very handsome indeed."

"Yeah," Ruthie joined in, "Not bad for an old geezer. Just kidding, kiddo." She punched him lightly in the arm and Luce's smile broadened knowing that inside Walter winced at Ruthie's manner.

Luce always positioned Walter's wheelchair so that he had the best and broadest view. From his location, at a slight angle to the bench, he could look down the hill toward the boat house or over Luce's shoulder into the open green meadow. Today he looked at Luce, puzzled by her attentive behavior.

"Hello, Walter." Startled by the familiar voice calling his name, he shifted his focus immediately to its source. A petite woman in her early sixties stood by his side, shivering slightly. She hesitated, then bent to kiss him softly on the cheek. Straightening, she said, "Good morning, Luce."

"Hello, Eleanor." Walter's eyes, fixed on Luce, narrowed to a slit, as he struggled to understand. Red from beneath his muffler spilled across his flaccid flesh.

"Eleanor, this is Ruthie." She paused. "My mother-in-law. Ruthie, Eleanor is a friend of Walter's. She's going to take him for a little walk."

"Great to meet you, Ellie. Good idea, take Waltie for a spin while we lazy broads sit here and soak up the sun."

Walter's eyes hadn't left Luce's face. Now she looked back at him, his trembling lower lip.

"I'm going to sit here with Ruthie for a while. You go ahead with Eleanor. Have a good time."

Walter shifted his eyes toward Eleanor. Luce sensed eagerness tinged with reluctance. For her part, Eleanor struck a demeanor of poise and dignity while offering Walter an encouraging smile. She's got class, Luce thought, something Luce suspected during the phone call she had made to Eleanor. Now her behavior confirmed it.

"Hey, Ellie," Ruthie interjected, pointing to a lever behind the right wheel, "These here are your brakes. No turn signals with this model, so watch yourself. No crashes with our boy."

Eleanor thanked Ruthie, released the brake and the two of them slowly made their way down the path toward the boat house.

"My, my, my, Miss Smarty Pants. Aren't we full of secrets? Is that dame who I think she is?"

"Yep," said Luce as she watched Eleanor and Walter in the distance find a table on the patio and settle in for a visit. "His mistress."

Luce looked at Ruthie then back to the distance where she watched the silent film of Walter and Eleanor's reunion.

"Aren't you something? I don't know, Luce. Setting your father up with his mistress? It's a little weird, don't you think? You been watching those afternoon talk shows? What if your mother finds out?"

"Don't think she will – unless you tell her."

"Me? No, darling, this is going with me to my grave." She marked an X across her chest to seal the pact.

"No time soon, I hope." Luce leaned affectionately into Ruthie and rested her head on Ruthie's shoulder.

"As for my mother, I think she's headed in a different direction altogether."

"It is a little weird, though. You gotta admit. Whatever possessed you?"

Luce thought for a long moment then shrugged her shoulders. "Just seemed right, I guess."

"Oy," Ruthie started, checking her watch. "Meshuga, I'm late. Pearl will kill me. I'm supposed to meet her for an early lunch. It's two-for-one day at Eppies. Everyone else refuses to go with her, the food's so terrible, but Pearl says 'A deal's a deal.' And my sister, the soul of generosity says, 'My treat.' Whoop-te-do. At this rate her generosity's gonna break her - in another century or two." She rummaged through her bag and pulled out a subway token, gave Luce a kiss and hoisted herself off the bench. "I guess that's what sisters are for. Well, I'm off. Sorry to have to miss our little soap opera here."

"I'll keep you posted."

"Guess I won't stop by and say good-bye."

Luce smiled. "Good decision."

"Ay-yai-yai. What a world. We still on for Friday night?"

"You bet."

"Love you."

"Love you, too." Luce watched Ruthie head down the path and veer off to the left until she vanished behind the stone wall and into the crowded street. Looking to the left, she saw Eleanor talking to Walter as she stroked his face with her small hand.

Luce leaned her head back and looked up, observing the leafy green units of color against the solid blue of sky . Cezanne had spent the last years of his life painting the world around him in blocks of color. Discrete units that ultimately resulted in a cohesive whole. He had spent those last years, a recluse, painting Mount St. Victoire. Over and over again, trying to conquer the mountain. She thought of her father, the remainder of his life destined to limited speech and immobility. She thought of her mother at the beach, chatting with distant strangers in the silence of her cottage while the computer keyboard clicked beneath her talking fingers. Not a bad way to spend one's last years, Cezanne, she thought. I should be so lucky.

The late spring sun was a warm breath on her neck and cheeks, a pair of warm hands plying her shoulders. She realized she felt supple. Clear. Clean. Renewal, she thought, it happens despite our efforts to the contrary. Perhaps sometimes it takes two springs.

Around her the park filled with activity. A circle of college students tossed a Frisbee. In the meadow a young Asian boy merrily chased a pigeon. Starlings and sparrows pecked at the ground, while birds squabbled for territory overhead. A robin coasted to a landing near her. As the sun continued to beat, the grass gave off a luscious odor of dirt and humidity, richness and warmth. Uncommon beauty, she thought, from such common sources.

A spring had released within her, somehow, sometime over the past few months. She couldn't ascertain the precise second, the defining event. Like most of life, she thought, it wasn't specific, more the culmination of days and hours and minutes. Like Cezanne's units of color. Or maybe, she mused, I just don't have the endurance for endless grief.

"You like jazz?" Terry had asked when Luce called her back.

"I do."

"There's a little supper club I know. One of my favorite locals is going to be singing on Saturday."

Terry paused, and Luce struggled to think of something to say. "Saturday?" Terry prompted. "Would you like to go?"

"Sure." Luce pushed the single word out through a long, dark tunnel.

"It's not too far from your place. We could walk." Luce was blank. "Shall I come by?"

"Yes."

"Eight o'clock?"

"Okay."

"Luce, I know I don't know you very well, but are you sure you want to do this?"

"Oh," she stumbled, "sure," and hung up the phone, dulled to the bone.

Terry had been punctual, which hadn't surprised Luce. Luce introduced her to Walter, whose limited expressions Luce could read, and did read, as a kaleidoscope of confusion and anger. Luce couldn't tell if it was because she was going out and leaving him, because of Terry or because she was leaving him with Ruthie. Ruthie, who had agreed to sit with Walter for the evening, was overly enthusiastic. "Waltie's a little behind in his scientific reading," she explained to Terry as she patted a stack of newspapers on the coffee table. "Got some great articles here."

"You'll be fine?" Luce had asked, hoping Ruthie might crack or Walter collapse and she wouldn't have to go.

"Fine. Fine," Ruthie had said, shooing them out of the living room. "Go. Go have fun. Now, here's one about how doctors are relying on astrology more and more in their work. Shall I read you that one?

"'. . . Doctors across America are looking to the stars, says Dr. Donald Wharton, a radiologist.'" (Ruthie waved her hand in the air to signal she was impressed.)

"'Dr. Wharton, along with hundreds of other doctors are using astrology . . .'

"Now, I'm quoting here, Waltie. This is all a direct quote.

"' . . . to treat asthma, colitis, ulcers, angina, and allergies.'

"The medical field is really changing, huh, Waltie? What sign are you? Ah, don't tell me. I'll ask Luce later, although just between you and me, I'm not sure she buys astrology. Oh, here's an interesting piece, not about medicine but important all the same. A religious group has found the door to hell. What do ya wanna bet, it's through the storage rooms in my apartment building? Ha. Ha. Say, this paper is chock full of great science. There's a whole article on how you can cure illness with the power of prayer. Did you know, Waltie, that peddlers make more money than doctors in Poland? I know what you're thinking. Let's not even say it, eh? Whoa, Walter," she lowered her voice, "here's a doozy. A bingo accident has given a grandmother non-stop orgasms." She made a clown face and swatted his knee. "Where do we sign up? Okay, let's get serious," she said perusing the article. "This is a good one. Infertility, chronic pain, insomnia, migraines. Yeah, this is good. I'll read ya the entire thing."

"Your parents are quite a couple," Terry had observed as they waited for the elevator.

"They certainly are. You should meet my mother, though, she's the techie of the family."

"Oh, who's Ruthie then?"

"Grace's mother."

Terry squinted. "Oh."

The supper club was small and intimate. Luce had been relieved that she had never been there before. Dinner was too rich, the wine too heavy, the crowd too hip. She longed for a simple meal in her old dining room. She found herself angry to be on a date, to have to be on a date.

"So, you live part-time in San Francisco?"

"I did. I've decided to move back, though."

"Didn't like it?"

"It was an obsolete idea. I'm beginning to realize I can't live without the reference points of my past."

Luce stared into her wine glass thinking, not first-date conversation. You can do better than that. Terry politely looked away. "It's a beautiful city, though," Luce said, trying to recoup.

Terry turned. "Too beautiful a city to live in alone, I think."

The singer was good, a deep throaty voice and terrific phrasing. She sang the standards, including *Under a Blanket of Blue*. Luce, feigning something in her eye, blotted the tear that hung in the corner.

After the song was finished Terry looked at her sympathetically. Feeling cornered, Luce had said, "You don't get to be forty-five and not have certain songs taken."

"Fortunately," Terry had said calmly, "there's no shortage of songs in this world." She looked back to where the singer had started *Fascinating Rhythm*.

A half hour passed. Then another. Eleanor no longer spoke to Walter. They sat holding hands. Eleanor slowly pulled her hand away, stood and began to push Walter up the gentle slope toward the bench. Luce rose to help her at the small crest and stopped by the bench, returning his chair to its original position. Feeling intrusive, she stepped back. Eleanor kissed Walter lightly, caressed his cheek and smiled. Straightening herself up, she said, "Thank you, Luce. It's been wonderful to see him."

Luce defensively waved off her thanks. Eleanor turned and walked away.

Sitting down on the bench, Luce discreetly watched Walter's eyes water. He looked in Eleanor's direction for a long time, long after she was out of view. He shifted his gaze toward Luce. She watched him labor to make his mouth and voice obey. After considerable effort he said, "Ank ou."

"I don't want to be thanked," she said, hearing her shrillness. Intentionally lowering her voice she continued, "I don't approve of what you've done. Not in any way. Don't misunderstand me. You've caused a lot of pain and hurt. You've broken a lot of trust." She paused, looking into the trees above.

"But I do approve of love, Walter, even in you. Especially in you." She brought her eyes down to street level but averted her face from his gaze.

They sat in silence while the city buzzed around them. After a while she asked, "Do you want to go home?" He moved his eyes from right to left several times. No. "Sit here, then?" His eyes touched the sky then the ground. "Okay." His arms, dead weight, lay heavily upon the arm rests. He gazed at Luce directly, catching her attention, then down to his right hand where two fingers raised slightly. Luce stared at him and his hand for some time before understanding. She reached her hand toward his and felt a small pressure as his two finger intertwined with hers. "Ank ou."

"You're welcome," she said softly, withdrawing her hand.

She felt a quiet, reverent spot open within and from it the voice of Levertov:

I know this happiness
is provisional:

> *The looming presences –*
> *Great suffering, great fear –*
> *Withdraw only*
> *into peripheral distance:*

but, ineluctable, this shimmering
of wind in the blue leaves:

this flood of stillness
widening the lake of sky:

this need to dance,
this need to kneel:
> *this mystery:*

Above her birds busied themselves in the trees; the hard frozen ground turned to pliant, wet mud; the sun arced a little higher; the earth gave another spin. In the continuance she had found her footing.

Renewal, she thought, we just can't help ourselves.

EPILOGUE

The autumnal light tumbled into Luce's studio mingling with a sultry breeze. Shadows shimmied like quaking Aspens on the wooden floor, on the brick wall. She stood at a canvas painting. Her palms were warm. She could feel the blood moving through her veins. Her nimble fingers fused with the brushes. Working at a languorous but steady pace, she felt each sure stroke across the face of the canvas. On a stool beside her rested an array of colorful tubes of paint. Their smell hung lusciously in the hot afternoon. From the jazz station came a cascade of standards, swirling the air with a sweet syncopation.

The canvas she was working on was a deviation from her body of work. Terry, having mentioned that she thought grace was a beautiful word, prompted Luce to visit the dictionary. She had never separated the word from the name and the person of Grace. Grace was who and what Luce conjured whenever she heard the word.

In her mother's study one night, as Walter sat in his wheelchair staring plaintively into the darkened park, she read the Oxford English Dictionary. Grace was defined as a beneficence and generosity shown by God, a divine favor unmerited by humans, an act of kindness or goodwill, a free gift for regeneration. Grace.

Now she stepped back from the canvas. It was a painting of her studio bathed in the long rays of a late summer afternoon. In the background the city shimmered in the tawny-rose light and the skyscrapers pulsed with soft angular halos. Mid-ground was dominated by one of the huge floor-to-ceiling architectural glass windows that formed one entire wall. The sun cast itself through each pane, creating rectangles of gold on the blonde floor. Gold on gold. In the foreground was Luce. She sat on the floor and leaned against the window frame. Her knees were bent and her extended arms, ending in painstained fingers, rested on her knees. With eyes closed she tilted her face to receive the sun. The sun shone in and poured over the planes of her face, boldly highlighting the line of her jaw, softly caressing the scoop of her neck and collar, spilling off her shoulders and down the surface of her relaxed body. A deep sense of peace and serenity pervaded the canvas.

From the far corner she heard, "You have mail." Putting down her brush and wiping her hands, she walked to the computer her mother had bought her. Opening her mailbox she read the letter.

To: LBennett/MBennett
Fr: EBennett
Re: Our First Annual Climb
Am sending this to you both as a proposal. Since we did not gather
for our annual meeting at the beach this summer, I was thinking
that maybe the three of us might take a little hike. New times call
for new rituals.

No point in attempting Kilimanjaro since it's already been done
by a Bennett woman.

A Bennett woman? That would make the three of them Bennett Women.
Luce paused to chuckle at her mother's phrasing and at this new-found
association.

There's Mount Abraham in Vermont, which should be lovely later
this Fall. Only 4,000'.

We'd probably be bored, Mead. But it might be the best place
to start for you, Luce.

Luce raised her brow in insult, which quickly turned to amusement. The fact
was that Elizabeth had started power-walking at the beach and recently
entered a senior's master class swimming program. She's probably right,
Luce mused.

I'm glad you can make a living painting, Luce, but it's terribly
sedentary.

We could always go West. Colorado has a few at 14,000' (are
we still boycotting them, Luce?)

Luce shook her head. Was this her mother?

If Mead is still coming back in mid-October to report on the first
phase of her grant, that would be a perfect time. Personally, I opt
for Vermont - less travel time and some great B&Bs. Let me know.
Love to you both.
Mother

The scraping growl of the elevator foretold Jacob's arrival.

"Hey."

"Hey yourself."

"Ready? Jenny's going to meet us at the restaurant."

"Almost. Let me just put a few things away. Did you decide on a movie yet?"

"I'll let you and Jenny duke it out over the movie."

"Coward. What are you going to do if you ever have kids? I can't decide everything for you, you know."

"Probably have to hire an au pair who's also a licensed mediator."

"Perfect solution. I understand it's a real buyer's market."

"Smart ass. So how are things going with Terry?"

"Slowly – which is still too fast for me."

"How is it I missed your ninetieth birthday, Luce? I feel awful."

She swatted him with the towel. "The good news is that she travels a lot."

"This is good news?"

"Yes, this is good news. No time to crowd, or push."

"You must be a relationship riot. Not to mention the queen of romance. So, if this isn't too difficult for you," he slowly enunciated each word, "how-do-you-feel-about-her?"

"I-don't-know," she slowly mocked.

"You must have some idea. I know, here's an easier version – what-do-you-think-of-her?"

"All right, Jacob," she relented. "She's very nice." He rolled his eyes. "Smart. Sensible."

"Sounds like a pair of shoes, for God's sake."

"Thoughtful."

"Better."

"Accommodating."

"Yikes – a naugahide Lazy Boy. Dad's ugly recliner."

"Just what would you like me to say, Jacob?"

Both of his hands shot up and he raised his shoulders. "Okay, don't tell me. Fine."

"I like her, but I've got to go slowly. I'm surfacing."

"No. God forbid you should incur the dreaded relationship bends."

She threw the towel at him. "I pity Jenny. I really do."

"Say," Jacob approached the canvas, "what's this?"

"A painting."

"Ever helpful. Don't overwhelm me with detail, though." He gave her a long glance.

"Jacob, if that's a penetrating stare you're trying to give me, I feel compelled to tell you, you suddenly look 50 IQ points short."

"A self-portrait, eh? I see we're breaking new ground." He slowly paced from angle to angle, studying the work. He was moving into full art dealer mode. "It elicits a very nice mood – contemplative and full. I like the composition with its geometrical themes, the squares of the window, repeated on the floor, the triangle of your seated form. And the colors – warm and evocative – create a . . . "

"You can stop right there, Jacob." He offered a perplexed expression. "It's not for sale."

"Really? I mean, are you absolutely set on that?"

"Absolutely," she was firm.

"Well, it's quite wonderful. In a quiet, contented way. Does it have a name?" He saw her hesitate. "Oh, come on, tell me."

"I'm thinking of calling it Self-Portrait/ State of Grace."

He raised a brow. "This is a new series?" He was hopeful.

"No."

"Not a series, huh?"

"No. Well," she relented, "not that I know of."

"And not for sale?" he persisted.

"No. That's a definite. For my private collection."

He sidled up to her. They both stood looking at the canvas for a few moments. He draped his arm around her shoulders and she leaned into him, resting her head against his chest.

"That seems right," he said at last. "Ready to go?"

"Yes."

* * *

Mead drove the Land Rover down the dirt road and through the preserve. As soon as she passed through the gates of the main compound, her shoulders fell a few inches and her neck softened with relief. She waved at a few of the men – Ken the lead poacher patrol, Mgawe his second-in-command.

The land was open, undisturbed this day. She felt its inherent beauty and dignity as she slowly drove through the open plains toward the house. Gil and Francesca would be expecting her. Dinner would be ready soon. They would settle down to a weekend of catching up with each other. After dinner she and Gil would walk to the small reservoir and treetop outlook.

The Land Rover pulled into the driveway and came to a stop. Gil and Francesca, having heard her approaching vehicle, stood, as she had come to expect, on the verandah, to greet her. Francesca stayed behind as Gil approached the Land Rover and gathered Mead into his arms, giving her a long, welcoming kiss. She mussed his hair affectionately and, from the inside of their embrace, waved to Francesca.

"We have a surprise for you, Mead," Francesca said, hugging her as she reached the verandah. Mead looked from one to the other in question. "Come, we'll show you." They entered the cool, open house and went into the living room.

Propped on the sofa was a landscape rendering of the preserve. In the foreground were the arched property gates with the sign 'Piavani Preserve' dominating the center. Through those the landscape unfolded to reveal the magical, spectacular countryside. "It arrived earlier this week," Gil said.

"It's marvelous, really," Francesca said. "Too generous. I have been admiring it all week. You must help me decide where best to hang it, Mead."

"It's wonderful," Mead admired.

"There's more," Francesca said, indicating a large square cardboard crate leaning against a wooden chair.

"This came with it," Gil said, handing Mead an envelope. Mead opened the letter gingerly and read:

"Dear Mead

"When I got off the plane after visiting you, I went directly to my studio and painted this.

"In all that I saw during my two weeks, all the incredibly horrible, incredibly beautiful imagery, this was my most prominent image.

"Seeing you in Africa, on your rounds in Sofia Town, on our visit to the Piavani's, everywhere actually, against the tapestry of Africa, I knew both visually, and emotionally, that you were home. And a glorious home it is.

"I've done a lot of thinking since my trip, mostly about home, about family. What you said about my creating a family in the form of Grace and Jacob, Ruthie and now Jenny, is true. They are my family and I have been, and am, lucky. But, after all these years, to have found you as a key member is a great surprise – and a great gift. To have someone else who knows to the bone what it was like, who comes from the same fabric, well, it somehow abrades the sense of loneliness that I've frequently found overwhelming.

"I loved meeting Francesca and Gil and visiting the preserve. They're wonderful, as are you.

"With love,

"Luce"

Mead knitted her brows together and approached the package addressed to Dr. Mead Bennett c/o the Piavani Preserve. Gil helped cut open the cardboard crating and Mead tore off the white packing paper to reveal a canvas, full of the blue-gold colors and space of the rift valley. In the distance the land dipped into a large glorious gorge. The mid-ground of the painting was full of the undulating, variegated walls, sculpted by time and nature, that encased the rift. In the foreground Mead, propped against a boulder, surveyed the surrounding countryside. She was dressed in a white blouse, khaki shorts, hiking boots. One leg was firmly planted on the ground, the other, bent at the knee, she held in her clasped hands. On the rock rested her khaki hat. The sun poured down on her face and the breeze softly tangled her hair. Everywhere was the limitless blue sky.

Mead, quickly taking it all in, recognized the exact spot, the exact moment her sister had painted. They had spent the better part of the day hiking the preserve and had paused momentarily to savor the view. Mead could almost feel the reassuring heat of that day, the dry tall grasses brushing against her leg. Looking at the canvas she could not dispute the unfettered sense of happiness her sister had captured in oil. Moving closer to the work she gazed at the words in the lower right hand corner.

Mead Found/Africa.

Our motto – *In order that a good story may be told* – reflects our belief that tomorrow's literary heritage depends on investment in today's writers.

Echo Valley
Chris Westphal

After years of thankless toil as a freelance writer, Tom Huttle finally has a contract in the offing – *Garbage* is to be a scathing exposé of the trash business, and should propel him to celebrity. Unfortunately, moving to a new home in Echo Valley soon puts paid to any feelings of euphoria. The community is dominated by Bagnoosianism, a crackpot religion presided over by the enigmatic Swami Bagnoose; and it is not long before his wife and son have succumbed to its lure. Soon convinced that his own life comprises only failure and betrayal, Tom decides it's time to take a stand.

Echo Valley is a wonderful satire of the commercialisation of religion, the allure of power and the perils of revenge.

Chris Westphal
A former journalist and TV comedy writer whose credits include *Murphy Brown* and *Baby Talk*, Chris Westphal lives in Southern California.

'. . . *a fine, funny, well-paced and well-written book.*'

T. Coraghessan Boyle, author of The Tortilla Curtain

ANOTHER GREAT AMERICAN FIRST NOVEL

Our motto – *In order that a good story may be told* – reflects our belief that tomorrow's literary heritage depends on investment in today's writers.

Over Under Sideways Down
Gordon Skene

Nelson Rivers has just been hit by a bus. One moment he was poised to give his first serious recital as a session musician; the next he is lying in a hospital bed reliving episodes of his life with his childhood friends, Burgie, Buzz, Leslie and Stoika. In a coma and on a life support machine, Nelson may or may not survive; but what follows is a poignant journey of self discovery, one that warmly evokes a young boy's loss of innocence against the background of Los Angeles and San Francisco in the 1960s and '70s.

Born in Detroit in 1951, **Gordon Skene** moved to Los Angeles in 1958 where he currently resides with his wife. He is a freelance journalist, screenwriter and sound recordist.

ANOTHER GREAT AMERICAN FIRST NOVEL